PRAISE FOR
PATRICIA RAYBON

"This story grabs you right at the beginning and takes you on a ride full of plot twists and turns, keeping Annalee Spain—and readers—constantly wading through waist-high trouble that's 'determined,' 'insistent,' and 'insidious.' Yet Raybon makes it clear that all the answers can be found by seeking Jesus, a search that mirrors our own need for ultimate Truth and a deeper relationship with the One who knows and loves us best."

ROBIN W. PEARSON, Christy Award–winning author of *Walking in Tall Weeds*, on *Double the Lies*

"In Annalee Spain, Patricia Raybon has given us not only an unflinching perspective of reality for many African Americans in the 1920s but also a self-determined heroine intent on fulfilling the role to which God has called her— regardless of the social landscape. This richly layered mystery set against the backdrop of Klan-run Colorado will leave readers breathless, guessing, and desperately awaiting the next installment. A truly magnificent read."

JENNIFER L. WRIGHT, author of *Come Down Somewhere*, on *Double the Lies*

"Patricia Raybon's second adventure for her intrepid sleuth, Annalee Spain, is historical mystery at its finest. Annalee's unique voice propels us through her Sherlockian detective work, the mysteries of her past, and her place in a hostile world of racial injustice. *Double the Lies* is double the action, double the intrigue, and double the ~~insight into her~~ heart. A must-read!"

STEPHANIE LANDSEM, author of *In a ...*

D1056539

"An engrossing, thrilling 1920s murder mystery. Patricia Raybon's novel races across its Denver landscape at an exhilarating pace with an unforgettable protagonist, Professor Annalee Spain, at the wheel. The story of Annalee's murder mystery is captivating, the history of the western city's racial divide enlightening. This intrepid sleuth would certainly give Sherlock Holmes a run for his money."

SOPHFRONIA SCOTT, author of *Unforgivable Love*, on *All That Is Secret*

"In Professor Annalee Spain, Patricia Raybon has created a real, rounded, and very human character. . . . Not only a good mystery, but a realistic insight into the African American experience in the 1920s."

RHYS BOWEN, *New York Times* bestselling author of the Molly Murphy and Royal Spyness mysteries, on *All That Is Secret*

"Readers will be hooked from the first line of Patricia Raybon's captivating debut novel, *All That Is Secret*. This well-respected nonfiction author proves her worth with fiction as she delivers rich characters and a page-turning mystery set in the beautiful wilds of Colorado."

JULIE CANTRELL, *New York Times* and *USA Today* bestselling author of *Perennials*

"A winner. Patricia Raybon's *All That Is Secret* is a fast-paced, intriguing mystery that grabs and holds the reader from the opening."

MANUEL RAMOS, author of *Angels in the Wind*

"It's the rare journalist who can succeed at also crafting compelling fiction. But that's what Raybon has done here with *All That Is Secret*, an engaging, evocative period piece as timely as tomorrow's news. Brava, Patricia, for weaving a tale as instructive as it is captivating."

JERRY B. JENKINS, *New York Times* bestselling author

"Patricia Raybon is a masterful storyteller. She is a standard-bearer for honesty as she takes her readers on a journey with an amateur sleuth who has the potential to change our perspectives and help us solve the mystery of how to come together and heal. I highly recommend it!"

DR. BRENDA SALTER McNEIL, author of *Becoming Brave: Finding the Courage to Pursue Racial Justice Now*, on *All That Is Secret*

DOUBLE THE LIES

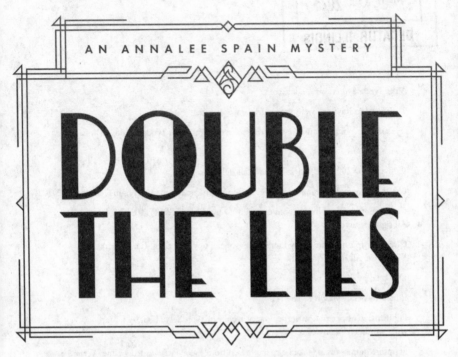

AN ANNALEE SPAIN MYSTERY

DOUBLE THE LIES

PATRICIA RAYBON

Tyndale House Publishers
Carol Stream, Illinois

Visit Tyndale online at tyndale.com.

Visit Patricia Raybon's website at patriciaraybon.com.

Tyndale and Tyndale's quill logo are registered trademarks of Tyndale House Ministries.

Double the Lies

Copyright © 2023 by Patricia Raybon. All rights reserved.

Cover photograph of woman copyright © by Stephanie Hulthen. All rights reserved.

Cover photograph of living room copyright © by VISUALSPECTRUM/Stocksy.com. All rights reserved.

Cover illustration of frame by Lindsey Bergsma. Copyright © by Tyndale House Ministries. All rights reserved.

Designed by Lindsey Bergsma

Edited by Sarah Mason Rische

Published in association with the literary agency of WordServe Literary Group, www.wordserveliterary.com.

Scripture quotations are taken or paraphrased from the *Holy Bible*, King James Version.

Double the Lies is a work of fiction. Where real people, events, establishments, organizations, or locales appear, they are used fictitiously. All other elements of the novel are drawn from the author's imagination.

For information about special discounts for bulk purchases, please contact Tyndale House Publishers at csresponse@tyndale.com, or call 1-855-277-9400.

Library of Congress Cataloging-in-Publication Data

A catalog record for this book is available from the Library of Congress.

ISBN 978-1-4964-5842-1 (HC)
ISBN 978-1-4964-5843-8 (SC)

Printed in the United States of America

29   28   27   26   25   24   23
7   6   5   4   3   2   1

To my beautiful sister, Lauretta.

For every wonderful thing you do for me, I thank you.

"And God spake all these words, saying . . .
Thou shalt not kill.
Thou shalt not commit adultery.
Thou shalt not steal.
Thou shalt not bear false witness
against thy neighbour."

EXODUS 20:1, 13-16

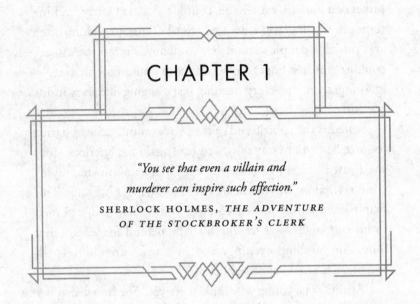

CHAPTER 1

*"You see that even a villain and
murderer can inspire such affection."*

SHERLOCK HOLMES, *THE ADVENTURE
OF THE STOCKBROKER'S CLERK*

MARCH 1924

The husband was handsome. A good liar, too. Maybe too good. Annalee Spain could tell that right off, see it in the man's arresting green eyes, his never-quiet hands, hear it in his blatant, bold lie for leaving his wife alone yet again.

"Meeting with the boss." The busied young man shrugged into his cheap spring raincoat. "I just remembered the meeting . . ." He worked at buttoning the worn, shiny coat, his hands too shaky for calm—making him miss some frayed openings. "Sorry, honey. I've got to run." His voice caught. "Can I drop you off somewhere for dinner?"

Shifting in her seat at a reading table in the glittery Warren Branch of the Denver Public Library, detective Annalee Spain pretended not to watch the couple's strained early evening standoff. On its face, it looked trivial. Tensions, oddly, often are. But this couple's strain felt somehow ominous. Annalee couldn't put her finger on it. She also couldn't look away—ignoring, therefore, every warning bell clanging like crazy inside her curly-haired head.

Seated at the cubicle end of the plank walnut table, she tried to force her eyes to stay down, to read again the Sherlock story she'd just finished, to close her ears to an unknown couple's curious friction. But her heart could feel danger brewing. This man named Jeffrey M.—according to the name badge pinned to his suit lapel—was leaving his wife behind for yet another long, confounding evening, and in a town trembling with trouble. This had happened before.

"Again?" The young wife looked grieved. She frowned at her husband. Her name, according to the badge on her worn but pretty spring dress, was Rebecca M.

She gave her husband a tense-looking smile, her red lipstick faded, gone to smudge in the waning day. "Well, if you must." She sighed. "Gracious, he works you too hard." She stiffened. "Not to mention too late."

She had a childlike voice—some holdover, perhaps, from an unresolved past. Or worse, Annalee thought, from an unkind present. Jeffrey, preoccupied, didn't reply. He ran a hand through his tight, dark curls, took a glance at the important-looking book he'd been half reading, shut it, and tossed it down.

"In fact," the wife went on, "I'll just read a while longer and then walk myself home."

Annalee glanced up, watched the young woman give her Jeffrey another conflicted smile. But it was clear to Annalee, and probably to anyone else looking, that Jeffrey wasn't listening. He, in turn, leaned over to peck a middling kiss atop Rebecca's light-blonde hair. Then in an awkward rush he was gone. His footsteps echoed across the library's glossy marble floor, then down the foyer steps. With a whoosh of the massive front doors, Jeffrey M. was off for another away-from-the-wife evening—and Rebecca M. was alone.

The young wife watched him go, her eyes making her look lost.

Then she started to weep silently—or as silently as she could. Her sobs made an obvious echo under the cavernous marble ceiling looming above.

Annalee could've ignored the weeping, willing to give Rebecca her privacy. They were in a public library, after all.

But other people's trouble had become Annalee's life. Small trouble for now—like tracking down a neighbor's stolen calico cat. Or convincing two squabbling sisters-in-law to start talking to each other again.

As the newest detective in her corrupt "Mile High City," Annalee had prayed to God she could help confused people unravel their dramas and hurts—giving them her brave help. *Even if I don't always feel brave—or helpful.* But as she had learned, help isn't about feelings. Nor is being brave. Help is offering people what they need when they need it.

Thus, at a public library on a cold spring night, young Annalee Spain decided to help a crying wife. Just a small gesture. A little kindness. Or might it become something more? Even a fine puzzle for her to solve?

Setting her jaw, Annalee opened her small, worn, second-hand pocketbook, looking inside for what she could offer. The humble contents weren't promising. Her crumpled-up business card. A half-eaten peppermint sweet. Her run-down purse seemed half-useless. Only one thing of true value peeked out at her: a gorgeous new white-lace handkerchief, her initial *A* embroidered on one corner in fancy red script. Its silk thread lay smooth and perfectly stitched just for her. So in truth, she hesitated to lend it. Sure, it would seem a little bit of nothing—just a handkerchief. But she'd received it only the night before, the most beautiful gift she'd ever known.

Accepting it with trembling hands, she'd lifted it from its white tissue paper, offering her thank-you to the young man who'd presented it to her with one shy but longing kiss. He'd held her a bit too close, which she allowed. But he was her "one and only," as she saw him. So she snuggled closer, showing her thanks—certain she'd treasure his handkerchief, if not him, surely forever.

"I'll never let it out of my sight," she'd promised him.

But now, here she was one night later, and a woman named Rebecca M. was sobbing.

Annalee could've decided not to get involved. No crime was afoot. No dangerous hurt unfolding here. But she felt a delicious tension between the young wife and her husband—and in a city of secrets and hurts like Denver—it appeared to Annalee like a daring new case.

She wanted it.

I'll solve it, she told herself—whatever it turned out to be.

Besides, she'd felt an odd alliance with this young woman. With her husband, Jeffrey, too? He even looked familiar. Where in the world had she seen him? Or was that too flimsy a reason to offer help?

"Pardon me . . . Rebecca?" Annalee's voice was a whisper. She reached into her purse. "Here's a fresh handkerchief."

The woman shook her head, trying between sobs to say no, but her cries—getting louder—wouldn't stop.

Other people were looking their way now, shifting in their seats, cutting their eyes. An annoyed balding man, one table over, glared. A frowning mother wrangling two restless toddlers, her eyebrow hiked, showed not just contempt but, mercy, full-out hatred? In a public library?

Annalee didn't react to any of them. She knew she wasn't welcome in the library by many in town. As a young Black woman, she'd be seen as out of place. At this sparkling branch, however—named for one Henry White Warren, a Methodist bishop famed for doing good works for freed slaves—the clear-eyed librarian had told Annalee to patronize her place "whenever you want, as long as I work here." She'd slammed a fist on her library counter to show she meant business. "I dare *anybody* to object."

Thus, Annalee slipped to the end of her reading table, acting as if she belonged because she'd come to believe that she did, and offered the sobbing woman her help. In her plain black dress and starched white collar, Annalee herself could've been a young do-gooder, maybe a college teacher offering kindness and sympathy—which just a few months ago, as a poorly paid professor at a Chicago Bible college, she had been.

Now she was offering a crying stranger in Denver her gorgeous lace handkerchief.

The young wife Rebecca grabbed for it, ready perhaps to say thank you. But looking up at Annalee, she froze. Annalee, reacting, froze, too.

"It's clean," Annalee assured her, still in a whisper, seeing Rebecca had noticed she was colored and maybe poor—meaning she'd assume the worst?

But Rebecca didn't look put off. Instead, she looked stunned. She stared at Annalee.

"You're the detective." Her whisper sounded surprised. "The colored detective. The one in the newspapers." She searched Annalee's face, circled as usual by its mass of wild black curls. Her bounce of coils and ringlets gave her away almost every time.

"Annalee *what . . . ?*"

"Annalee Spain." She swallowed. "But I'm just starting to be a detective." *Because it's demanding and scary. Some days I feel plumb crazy to even try.*

"Still, the papers said you caught that rich woman for murder, got her sent to jail." The young wife made a face, raised her voice. "And good riddance. She got just what she deserved." She straightened in her chair. "And now, here I am, bothering you with my trouble." She started to weep again. "Oh, this hateful town!"

"Well . . . let's not disturb everyone," Annalee whispered, trying to quiet her.

"Corrupt judges, cops, even your neighbors." This woman Rebecca hissed her words, provoking louder weeping. "Oh, Jeffrey! I hate this town!"

Annalee took a deep breath. *Gracious, what is going on?* She scooted into the chair next to the young woman. "Here, wipe your face."

Rebecca's nose was running heavily now, her face looking gloppy and unbecoming, her cheeks streaking with tears. But the young wife didn't seem to care, refusing the handkerchief with a shake of her head. "I can't. It looks brand-new. A gift for your Christmas? Your birthday?"

"Well, not for my birthday." *Even if I knew my real birthday.* Annalee loosened her grip on the handkerchief, not wanting to show her uncertainty—or was it eagerness?—to let it go. Detectives use what's in their hands . . . *right, Sherlock?* "It's just—"

"From your nice young man probably." Rebecca swiped her nose with the sleeve of her pretty purple dress, its cheap fabric frayed at the cuff. "A *nice* young man. That's so lovely." Then suddenly she was sobbing again.

"That's enough," Annalee whispered. "You're upset." She pushed her handkerchief into Rebecca's trembling hands. "Yes, it's a gift from a young man. But he'd want you to use it. I'm sure of it." Of course, she wasn't sure at all. What would Jack say about her lending his hard-earned gift—created special for her—to a crying stranger?

But too late. Rebecca was grabbing at it, pressing the lacy handkerchief against her mouth, crumpling it to stifle her sobs, her fading red lipstick smearing the spotless white square.

"Oh, what a day. I'm so sorry—"

Annalee waved off the apology. "Do you need help?" She heard herself speak those words, knowing she could choose to stay out of it—whatever "it" was. But in her short and humble experience of working as a detective—only a few months—people's trouble still found her anyway. She found her voice.

"I can help you." She spoke her offer, thinking, *This is how it starts.* A new detective sometimes has to insist on helping, especially people who don't go looking for it—indeed, those who seem to need help the most—even if that detective doesn't know what she's doing. Not always anyway.

"But I can't pay you much." Rebecca looked weary. "Not much of anything—even if I knew what to ask you to do. Or how I'd pay."

"I'm not worried." Annalee cocked her head, knowing she was more worried than she wanted to be. "The Lord provides." *Please, Lord.*

Rebecca swiped at her eyes with Annalee's beautiful, soiled, no-longer-new handkerchief. She cocked her head, too. "Then why won't he provide for *me?*"

That's what Annalee let Rebecca wrestle over after the library closed. She'd tried to nail down the reason for her crying but didn't get far. So she returned to her reading, left Rebecca to hers. But now it was just after 8 p.m., the long day over, the library dark, the streets churning with nighttime traffic. The moon was barely waxing, hardly a thin crescent. But glaring lights from Model T cars and trucks, fancy sedans and other vehicles brightened the dark streets.

Annalee buttoned her coat, hurried toward the intersection in front of the library, turned toward Five Points, the humble but busy neighborhood where she lived.

"May I walk with you?"

Rebecca again?

The young wife tried to match Annalee's pace. "Here's your handkerchief." Rebecca held out the damp hankie but still looked distressed, tears still trying to fall.

"Keep it for now." Annalee slowed. "You might need it later."

Rebecca didn't argue. Instead, she added: "Thank you." She pulled her light spring cardigan tighter around her shoulders, stuffed Annalee's handkerchief in her sweater's pocket, watched the passing cars. "Goodness, where in the world are so many people going at this time of night?"

"Searching for answers." Annalee allowed herself a laugh. "Just like us."

"That's what we're doing?" Rebecca frowned. "If only I knew where to look."

Annalee weighed that more deeply. The young woman seemed to speak in riddles. She'd try a direct question. "Is that the reason you were at the library? For answers?"

"No, my husband's job. Something for his boss." Rebecca sounded unsure. "At least . . . that's what he said."

"Where does he work?"

"Out at the airfield."

Annalee frowned. "A barnstormer?" Trick pilots were rule breakers, living on the edge. That made them hot tickets. "I've seen his picture on a poster, out east past Colorado Boulevard— on every other lamppost."

"No, that's his brother, Buddy—Buddy Mann. That's our last name. Those two look almost alike. But Buddy's the rising star." Rebecca went on. "'Handsome young daredevil!' That's what all the posters say."

"Then what does Jeffrey say?" Annalee had seen the tension on his face.

"Not enough. But something's on his mind. Sure, he's finally a stunt pilot. He got approved at the airfield last month. They both fly there. But Jeffrey's scheming for something more. I can feel it . . ." She frowned.

"Feel it in your bones?" Annalee understood.

Rebecca tossed her hair. "Maybe deeper. But I've said enough about those two." She scrunched her face. "Why were you at the library? For your next case?"

Annalee pressed her mouth. Rebecca's question hit close to home. She'd longed for a fresh, tough case. But there was more.

"I went to the library to find my mother." Annalee blinked in the dark. *Why am I telling a near stranger this?* But she went on. "I grew up . . . without her. So I'm hunting for her in a census record. I figured the library might have something. Then I got distracted by a detective story." She tried to laugh. "But I was there for my mother. She lived in a mining town in the mountains—a little place called Annalee."

"Like your name? The ghost town?"

Annalee peered at the sliver of moon. "It's abandoned now. And so was I." She stiffened her back. "Up near Telluride."

"Telluride?" Rebecca pulled at her woolen scarf. "My dad owns an old cabin near there."

"Your dad? Small world."

Rebecca slowed her pace to a stop. "May I tell you something?"

Annalee gave her a look, showing she was listening.

"Jeffrey steals. That's one reason I was crying. He stole my late mother's jasper necklace."

Annalee took that in. "Steals jasper?"

"It's not even worth much. I know."

"You want me to find it?"

"I know where it is. It's in the window at the big pawnshop in Five Points. I saw it there."

"So what's going on?"

"Gambling, probably. Jeffrey has a job, but we're always short. He's always in debt. Something's always missing. Even my wedding earrings." Pain crossed her face. "They're small pearls—small but real." She glanced away. "He lies, too. He's not going to meet his boss. That's just some excuse. I checked once. He goes somewhere else, but I don't know where or what he's doing, staying out all hours."

"Have you talked to him about it—the stealing and lying, the debts?"

Rebecca half laughed, sounding bitter. "A talk?" She looked at Annalee. "How about now? Can you come in? I'll make us tea." She blinked hard. "For a real talk."

They were at Franklin Street, not quite to Five Points—the city's colored neighborhood. Rebecca pointed to a small house. "This is me. Jeffrey won't be home for hours. Please come in and warm up."

Annalee licked at her lips but hesitated. Something didn't feel right. Barnstormers were high-profile trouble. Some were, anyway. If one was having money woes or marital worries too, she should steer clear. That wasn't her kind of case.

But the airfield angle stirred her like a bad itch. Half the folks in town were fighting to get in early on airport deals. High rollers battled to put up the cash for Denver's new municipal airport, just being planned. Others fought to be the builder, some already testing fleets of planes. But why? To appear modern and smart? Catch the excitement of flight? Annalee didn't know enough about it yet, but she could confess to being intrigued. Flying around in fancy machines? It offered thrills. Maybe a crazy freedom, too. Rebecca might have an inside scoop.

Still, Annalee pushed back.

"The colored detective visiting your house? Having a cup of tea? Now that's a sure way to start trouble."

"I've already got trouble." Rebecca gave the bitter laugh again. "So please come in. Just one cup. It's the least I can do for someone today. I won't cause us trouble."

But of course there was trouble.

Trouble is a determined thing. Insistent but also insidious. Her steadfast old Bible confirmed that. Trouble and anguish find us out, its psalmists said. In this world, Jesus himself declared, you'll have trouble as sure as you live, even though he offered a remedy. Annalee knew that more than most.

Thus, as she stepped onto the porch of the Manns' darkened house, trouble met them with full force.

"Rebecca!" Annalee tensed. "A break-in!" She froze. What was this young wife getting her into? "Watch out! There's glass."

"What break-in?" Rebecca gaped at the smashed window on her front door. It stood ajar, glass jagged.

Annalee pushed back the door.

"Wait." Rebecca reached for Annalee's arm. "Should we go in?"

But Annalee was stepping inside, her eyes checking every corner, hands grabbing at the wall for a light switch, which didn't work. The electricity turned off? Light bulb burned out? Bill not paid? Finally she reached for a small lamp, its shade missing, and yanked its fraying cord, groaning at what met her.

The front room of Rebecca's small house was a smashed, glass-splattered, vandalized, frenzied mess. Furniture upturned. Curtains ripped. Mirrors broken.

Rebecca gasped, stepped into the chaos. A small, pretty desk lay overturned, one leg broken, its contents—papers, mail, bills, advertisements—strewn across the floor. Annalee pointed the lamp's bare bulb at the trouble. A mantel over the fireplace was swiped clean, its glass whatnots thrown to the floor. Shattered vases, cracked statuettes, chipped glass candleholders, broken picture frames of family photos.

"Papa." Rebecca grabbed up a photo of a harsh-looking man, his picture now encased in shards of glass. Even a small painted picture was ripped from the wall, its pastoral scene slashed with a sharp object, the frame jagged. This was sheer violation, and Annalee hated the cold meanness of it. Rebecca's place looked modest. Now it was in shambles.

"My house!" Rebecca whispered at the mess, stumbling from room to room, moaning at the sight of her two upturned bedrooms, the smashed bathroom, the upended dining room—finding the same sickening mess at every turn.

"Who did this?" Annalee stepped over debris, suspecting Rebecca must know—or at least have a decent guess—who'd broken in and trashed her earnest-looking home. An angry neighbor? Some riled "other woman"?

Annalee tried to think like a detective. "Is anything missing?"

"I don't know!" Rebecca looked lost. "Please no, Jeffrey! Why aren't you here!"

Annalee pushed through the dining area into the kitchen, Rebecca following. They both froze. Stopped cold. Because unlike the others, this room was neat as pie. No dishes smashed and broken. No pictures or calendars or whatnots ripped from the walls.

Two breakfast bowls still sat in the sink, the faucet not dripping. A clock still hung on the wall, still ticking proper time. A table and chairs also didn't appear moved. Clean plates and glasses sat unbothered on a wooden shelf. The small icebox stood closed and upright. The stove, too, still stood in its corner, awaiting its next meal.

But in a narrow hallway off the kitchen, leading to the back door—standing ajar—lay the night's worst trouble. Annalee saw him first. Shaking her head, sad and with a knowing she hated to feel.

Rebecca screamed.

It was Jeffrey. Sprawled faceup, still wearing his shiny raincoat, the buttons half-done, name badge pinned on his lapel, he lay silent and unmoving—no sound or breathing—void of evidence of the precious essence of treasured life.

"Oh, Rebecca, I'm so sorry." Annalee's pained words might've sounded empty, but she knew this hurt. That's why she'd pushed past the broken glass—to discover what was wrong and maybe try to stop it.

The young wife screamed again. *"Jeffrey! God, no! Jeffrey!"* She sank to the floor, falling across her husband's still body, death leaving him crumpled and silent, a final and harsh insult. Rebecca's sobs were moans, then shrieks, then repeated screams piercing the jumble of her wronged house, breaching far beyond the walls, out into the night.

Annalee felt every shriek and sound, her heart pounding, her mind racing. What was she seeing? A murder? But what else? Indeed, she could've avoided this, headed straight home, curled herself in a chair to read another Sherlock story. Or she could've tracked down Jack, letting him tease her about being his upstart detective "lady friend" who solved little crimes. Instead, a real murder had happened. Here she stood, in fact, right smack in the middle of it.

Annalee fought to stay calm, to think of the dead man's

wife instead. Kneeling beside Rebecca, she cradled the woman's shoulders, letting her cry, watching Rebecca reach blindly in her frayed sweater pocket for Annalee's thoroughly crinkled lace handkerchief, the embroidered letter *A* soggy with Rebecca's tears.

Consoling her as best she could, Annalee watched the young wife cry, forgetting about herself. She then understood her new case—to figure what had befallen this Jeffrey. Who did this awful thing? In their crazy town, what kind of messy, stupid anger had left a young, barnstorming husband dead on his kitchen floor?

In death, Jeffrey gave nary an answer. His handsome face looked oddly peaceful, its tension wiped fully away, his deep-green eyes staring up in a soft emptiness, unable to see his distraught wife nor hear her anguished sobbing. Then Annalee saw the trouble: blood oozing from behind Jeffrey's head onto the linoleum floor. A mortal wound for certain, although no weapon was apparent. But it had been wielded to its effect. Annalee felt her stomach squeeze, but her spirit ignited. This killing needed answers. This wife did, too.

"I'm so sorry, Jeffrey. It's all my fault." Rebecca was sobbing.

"You've done nothing wrong, Rebecca." Annalee tried to console this stranger.

"But *I have*."

Annalee felt confusion, but as well, she felt strangely alert. Something wild and horrible had happened here. But what exactly, and what was Rebecca saying? *"It's all my fault?"* Annalee helped her to stand, setting her in a kitchen chair, trying to focus herself.

"Is your telephone working? You have to call the police."

"No, please. Not the police—"

But it was too late.

Annalee heard sirens screaming toward Franklin Street, then a screeching stop—car doors flinging open and slamming. Neighbors must have heard Rebecca's awful screams and called the Denver Police Department. Annalee stood quickly, knowing she needed to leave now. A young colored woman at a murder scene would have no defense.

"Police! We're coming in!"

Annalee gripped Rebecca's shoulders, jerked her around hard, making the young wife face her—and hear her. "I'm leaving *now*."

Rebecca panicked, grabbed Annalee's hands. "What shall I say to them?"

"Tell them what happened. What you found." Annalee pulled as kindly as possible from Rebecca's grasp, moved toward the open back door, slipping past Jeffrey's sad body. "Show them your ransacked house! Your husband—*dead*. Rebecca, he was murdered!"

"But I can't!"

"What do you mean?" Annalee searched Rebecca's eyes, now strained clearly by fear. Rebecca had oddly stopped crying, but she still clenched Annalee's handkerchief in her hands.

"I invited you in," she told Annalee, "because of what happened!"

"Tell me! *Hurry, Rebecca.*" Annalee breathed hard. The police were shouting from the front room. Annalee, at the back door, couldn't wait. "Rebecca, I can't let the police find me here."

"We're coming through! Denver police! Detectives!"

"Rebecca. *Tell me.*"

But detective work, no matter what people believed about it, was never about hurrying people who can't be rushed. Or demanding answers that can't seem to be spoken. The detective story in the library had told her exactly that, reminded her that crime fighting could be tough and complicated—so she'd have to be alert and shrewd.

She flung the back door wider, knowing she couldn't wait another second to hear Rebecca's remorseful words.

"Please, Annalee. You have to help me—"

"Tell me, Rebecca. *Now!*"

Rebecca shook her head.

"Tell me!"

"I think I killed somebody."

CHAPTER 2

"There is some deep intrigue going on round that little woman."

SHERLOCK HOLMES, *THE ADVENTURE OF THE SOLITARY CYCLIST*

"She *thinks?*"

Her young pastor Jack Blake had been waiting in Annalee's river cabin, her late father's place—and now her rustic home—when she finally arrived just after 10 p.m. She'd walked there by a roundabout way, hiding herself in the shadows, determined to appear fearless and confident but feeling her heart in her throat and hating the feeling. She'd be in jail right now if the Denver police—whose chief was a dues-paying Klan member—had found her at the scene of a white man's murder.

Thus, she'd taken her good, sweet time walking home, ignoring the chill, demanding her heart stop its pounding, moving from the blare of police sirens—and the questioning stares, hiked brows, and upturned noses of alarmed people near

Rebecca's neighborhood. Tightness in Annalee's chest finally eased at the sight and quiet of her own narrow, humble, run-down but beloved street. Home at last.

She saw Jack's dark-blue touring car parked in her tiny yard, so she crossed her corner and took the rocky path to her cabin. Jack Blake stood in the door, his height filling it. Brooding, he watched her approach, his black eyes smoldering in the night-time dark.

"You like me to worry, don't you?"

"I'd do the same for you."

She looked up at him, tried to smile, and climbed her two wooden steps, which he'd recently repaired, so the approach for her was steady and stable, so unlike what her evening had just delivered. Jack looked steady, too. But he was frowning, so maybe he was peeved—even at her. She couldn't tell, but she let her heart swell anyway at the sight of him—her mind still not prepared to fully understand how a complicated young someone like Jack—a war hero and now, at twenty-seven, her pastor—could seem to care so much for her. Even if they spent far too much time arguing. About what? Life and love and solving crime and how to be good and holy and right for each other—and even disagreeing about that last point too much for their own good.

Why couldn't they figure it all out? Although Jack himself had preached to his church how hard it was for a people who are hated in the world to find a way to love without complication. "We're wounded," he'd told his colored congregation. "So some of us might make mistakes in life. Especially when it comes to looking for love."

He'd winked at his congregation, easing the tension, and they laughed.

"Preach, Pastor!" many teased, still laughing.

For now, however, on this night, there was no laughing. Well, not yet. Annalee let him help her out of her coat, borrowed from a Five Points rooming house lady who saw she'd needed one. Then Annalee turned, letting herself go ahead and fall into his open arms, sighing as she let him hold her for a moment, hearing his own sigh, enjoying the feel and closeness and gorgeous scent of him. If there was any man in the world who smelled better and, well, more exhilarating than her clean-shaven, aftershave-wearing Jack Blake, she'd rather not know. She leaned into his embrace a moment longer, taking in a deep breath, finally pushing herself away.

"You okay?" His eyes took in her tension.

"Long walk home."

"I drove by the library half a dozen times, looking for you. They were closing. The librarian—can't think of her name—"

"Mrs. Quinlan—the librarian."

"Mrs. Quinlan. She said you'd left just before a young woman who was crying?"

"Crying? That's the least of it." Her neck tightened.

Jack looked just as stressed. "Here, let's eat first." He pointed her to two wrapped plates of food on her small eating table. "From Mrs. Stallworth."

Annalee's former landlady, now living a half block from Jack's Denver church, could cook like nobody's business—often making hot meals for Annalee but also for Jack. The arrangement wasn't formal, just what they'd devised a few hard months ago after Jack's church was burned to the ground, along with the parsonage where he'd lived—both structures scorched to ashes in one fiery, awful night. Nobody was ever blamed or charged. The fire chief ruled it arson. Church members suspected the Klan. Jack had urged his church members to look on more hopeful things. Then, for lodging, he'd moved to a rooming house, sometimes bringing to Annalee—his lady friend, as church members now called her—hot meals to share.

"Even though it's probably too late," Jack said tonight, "and you're not hungry because you've been out in the world solving mystery and crime." He allowed a smile, pulled an envelope from a pocket. "And look, here's another message for you. Found it in your doorframe. Probably a new case for you to solve, Detective Sherlock."

She tried again to smile back, telling him no. She hadn't been solving crime. Not this time. Not at all, in fact. Instead, on this night, as she simply put it: "Somebody's dead." She shut her eyes, wanting to erase the picture in her mind.

"Again?" Jack frowned. "Folks aren't satisfied unless they're killing each other."

"What, another killing?"

"One of my church members. Well, he's not dead—but he might as well be. He's a taxi driver. Neighbors found him mugged, barely alive, this morning in his cab. The doctor tending him doesn't think he'll make it."

"When did this happen? Do I know him?"

"Yesterday. He's new in town. Didn't know the 'rules' about who to pick up and drive."

"He picked up a white fare?"

"A woman. Last time for him."

Annalee twisted her mouth. Trouble in Denver. Could it get any worse? She sat down at her table to describe her own confusing evening—meeting Rebecca, walking home with her. Rebecca's suspicions about Jeffrey, their ransacked house, Jeffrey's dead body, and the young wife's odd confession.

"She *thinks* she killed somebody?"

"She's confused about things. Terrified actually. But of what? Some family mix-up? A bad business deal? Some Klan double cross? Scandal at the new airport?"

"The fancy new airport? Half the folks in town have their fingers in it. Trying to get in early on the deal. Maybe you'd better stay out of it."

"I don't know yet."

Jack frowned again, sat across from Annalee, unwrapped one of the plates, and grabbed a plump piece of roasted chicken. He handed it to Annalee, then closed his eyes.

"Lord, we thank you for this food. And bless us now, the living and—"

"The dead, Lord. Amen." Annalee considered a nibble but put down the food, excused herself, and went into the tiny bathroom that Jack had helped a plumber install for her. She thoroughly washed her hands, face, the back of her neck—trapping the bad stress of the evening in soapy lather, then letting it rinse down the drain.

Back at the table, she told Jack her plan.

"I saw a horrible thing tonight—at this woman Rebecca's house. For her and her dead husband and, well, for our mess of a city, I'm going to find out what happened. Get it all sorted out. She needs good help." Annalee cocked her head. "I think I can solve it."

Jack listened. His look held her gaze. "Can I talk you out of this one?"

"She's scared, Jack."

"And you should be, too. Denver streets are humming with killers. This woman's husband was murdered. In cold blood."

"But not by her. She was with me all evening—at a public library. I don't know what happened, but I know she's not a murderer."

"Actually you *don't* know that." Jack pointed Annalee to her chicken. She chewed a sober bite, searching his dark eyes, letting him question her. "Take a minute, will you? What if that turns out wrong?"

"Murder always does—turn out wrong. Because it is wrong." She swallowed. "Besides, I gave her my new handkerchief."

Jack twisted his mouth, but he didn't reply.

"To borrow," Annalee tried to explain.

Jack unwrapped the second plate of food. Started eating with his fingers, avoiding her eyes, still staying silent but suddenly peeved a bit? At her?

"She was crying, Jack. Sobbing."

He licked away sauce, looked for a dishcloth. Finally he pulled out his own handkerchief and wiped his hands well.

"I understand that," he finally said. "But goodness, Annalee, is there any gift I can give you that you won't give away?"

She searched his face, trying to read his words. "Any gift?" She tried to give him a smile. "Don't make me answer that."

He wrapped up the plate again and put on his light jacket, turned to the door. "It's late. I'd better go. Sleep well."

These were kind enough words, but by turning his stiffened back, Jack was telling her almost everything. He wanted her safe. He'd told her that from their beginning. He also wanted her to know something more—that he'd spent weeks deciding on her gift, many more weeks saving for it. A custom-made, embroidered lace handkerchief, sewn by hand by an Italian immigrant seamstress on the west side of town, purchased with purpose. He wanted her to know one thing above all: she mattered to him, maybe more than anything. The hand-stitched *A* was meant to affirm it. But his patience wasn't endless. *Drop this case,* he was pleading. But how could she?

"I'm getting your handkerchief back. I made her promise. I'll go see her again. Maybe tomorrow. I'll get it back for certain."

Jack nodded but didn't answer. He reached for the door handle. Annalee stood, not wanting him to leave like that. But she knew her handkerchief wasn't the issue, even if it would never be brand-new again.

She pursed her lips, wishing life wasn't so complicated, especially between the two of them—regretting she'd lent his gift.

Finally she spoke. "There's something else, too. Can I tell you?"

Jack turned to look at her.

She moved closer, looking up at him. "Have you ever been to Telluride? Well, near Telluride. Up by the mines?"

"Once." He turned up his jacket collar. "But never again. It's too far, Annalee. Too rocky, too cold, too dangerous. Snow's too deep. Avalanches kill people up there. Even in the spring. Worse, the ore is too high."

"But I'm not going for ore."

Jack narrowed his eyes. "Your mother's not there anymore."

"I know, but—"

"Nobody's there. It's a ghost town."

"But if you won't go, I'll have to go by myself."

He gave her that look again. "Lord, that stubborn streak. Where'd you get it?"

"You don't think I should go. I see that. I'm starting to feel the same way. Just—"

"Just heartbreak up there, Dr. Watson."

"Probably, but I can't shake the feeling there's more. If I don't go, how will I let it rest?"

"Right here." He reached inside his coat, pointed to his heart.

"Of course. I know, but—"

"It's dangerous. A dangerous secret. People have already killed to keep you from knowing it. Your own daddy was murdered."

"That's exactly why I want to find out."

Shaking his head, Jack opened her cabin door, but he turned back with a question. "Would it matter if I'd made plans for us on Friday? Nothing dangerous. A picture show. Then dancing at the Rossonian. *If* you can ever allow yourself to take a break." He gave her a look. "I need one, too. I love my church. You know that. We'll be out in Dearfield tomorrow and Friday—preaching, praying, lifting spirits, as best we can, as God is our helper, *please, Jesus.*"

"They'll be so grateful."

"Well, most of them." He sighed. "But I need quiet time—with you. Just you and me. At the pictures."

"Dancing and a picture show." Her eyes widened. "We'd enjoy that so much."

"Let me treat you this Friday. *The Hunchback of Notre Dame.*" He pronounced the French part of the name with flair, using the accent he'd heard on the battlefields in France during the awful big war. Still, he laughed. "It's a horror picture. It'll be fun. They're showing it at the Rialto. Nine o'clock show."

"The Rialto? We'd sit up in the crow's nest. We don't need the insult. Isn't the Five Points Y showing a picture we could see?"

"Probably. But not for my best girl—"

"How many girls you got?"

"Don't you start counting."

They both laughed.

"Besides, I know the Rialto's ticket taker. From the war. A good kid. He'll take care of us."

"You're not angry at me?"

"I just invited you to a movie. *And* dancing. Which means a fancy meal at some point between all of that."

She smiled again. "Big spender. What time should I be ready?"

"Pick you up at eight. You'll be my first stop coming back from Dearfield."

"It sounds like a date."

"I'd call it that."

"Guess I'll fix my hair pretty."

"Guess I'll do the same." He ran a hand over the crown of his dark hair.

She laughed. "I love your fresh cut."

"Thank you, detective."

He moved a curl off her forehead, sighing, not kissing her even though she wanted him to do precisely that, and she could tell he would've been willing to do that, precisely indeed. Instead, he shook his head at her again, adding, "Good night, Miss Holmes. Off I go to my cold, lonely rooming house to get some sleep."

"Happy dreams."

He winked at her, slipped out of the cabin, and closed the door behind him. From outside, she heard him lock her dead bolt. He had the second of two keys.

Standing at the door, she could still hear his voice.

"And tell that woman to give back your handkerchief! We might need it in Telluride."

She leaned on the door, allowing a shy smile, grateful he'd relented a bit. Then she sat for a while again at her small table, in her small cabin, beside a small candle, on a dark night in the small of the moon.

Shadows danced on the wall, inviting her to reflect on all she'd seen, heard, and contemplated during the hard, odd evening. She'd met a young woman who knew of the town of Annalee. But offering her kindness, Annalee had fallen headfirst into the matter of a murder. Over gambling?

Every instinct told her no. Jeffrey Mann wasn't gambling—except with his life. And he'd lost it. So what was really at stake?

She let the question rattle around her for a moment, changed into her nightclothes, curled into her small bed, pulled up her quilt covers, and with a sleepy sigh, closed her eyes.

Jack had lit a fire in her stove, so the cabin exuded a snug warmth. But she knew the cabin wasn't totally safe and secure. Especially these days. People rendered the world complicated and often harsh, throbbing with danger and bad will. Rebecca Mann's nice kitchen, with her husband cooling dead on the floor, was proof enough of that.

Still, she watched the flicker in her stove give off a hopeful heat—this fire lit for her by her nice young man. He meant the world to her. She believed she meant the same to him, despite the complications of their relationship.

But so did the one person she'd pleaded with God to help her find—the one who'd abandoned her at birth, just tossed her in the mud of a broken-down mine shaft near Telluride and walked away. Her doggone mother. Why on earth had her mother done her wrong like that?

She gazed in the dark, feeling the depth of her question. Thus, she allowed herself two more:

Who did Rebecca Mann maybe kill? And mercy alive, who killed Jeffrey?

More than that, one more question demanded an answer, especially for her bustling, modern, too-corrupt-for-its-own-good Denver city:

Lord in heaven, why?

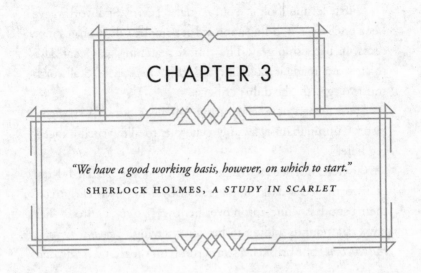

CHAPTER 3

"We have a good working basis, however, on which to start."
SHERLOCK HOLMES, *A STUDY IN SCARLET*

SNOWFALL AWOKE HER. Annalee could hear it spitting on her cabin roof, against the one window in her tiny but beloved place. Hurrying to get dressed in the morning chill, she paused to read again the note left on her door, asking her for a morning meeting. *If you agree, I would like to meet you at the Cunningham Rooming House on Welton Street. Eight thirty on this Thursday morning, please.* But no signature.

Another stranger?

That's what she asked Mrs. Edna Stallworth, who cooked at the Cunningham place and was setting up coffee and rolls when Annalee arrived. Her walk there left her chilled to the bone and Annalee was glad now to be standing in the warmth of the cozy Cunningham kitchen, greeted with a smile by her former landlady, a no-nonsense friend.

"First, let me look at you, Annalee." Mrs. Stallworth gave her a once-over, nodding approval at Annalee's thrift store crepe dress, in battleship gray. The almost-matching gray coat, also thrift store, made it look like an outfit. *I hope.* Mrs. Stallworth must've agreed. She didn't criticize.

She'd turned now to perusing Annalee's note. "A stranger? Sister Cunningham is awfully generous to allow such a meeting here."

Giving Annalee's curls a smoothing, the grizzled Mrs. Stallworth tied a dark-blue kerchief over her own curly hair, then a spotless white apron over her oversize cook's dress—her few extra pounds adding to her look, saying, *"I'm in charge of this kitchen."* She brushed a stray crumb off the round hardwood eating table.

"At least I can keep my eye on this person for you. Whoever it is."

"Well, they use sturdy stationery." Annalee examined the handwritten note. "That could mean something."

"A paying client—I hope."

Mrs. Stallworth poured their coffee, pulled out chairs for them in the bright, cozy room, and gave Annalee an affirming hug. They weren't mother and daughter, but they both were poor and colored, both knowing all that had meant in each of their lives and worlds.

"You're thin as a rail, baby. Eat two rolls. Slap on extra butter, too."

Annalee didn't argue. But she wasn't thin. Whatever that even meant.

In truth, however, she'd run herself ragged in recent weeks, answering requests for her help as Denver's newest detective.

With the police chief a Klan member and his department teeming with Klan cronies, trust for the department had hit a hard low. But so had morale. Even a rookie cop had sought Annalee's help, suspecting his sister-in-law of stealing from elderly people when she cleaned their homes. Except her victims wouldn't talk to police.

Yet when Annalee rang a doorbell and chatted with a graying widow, listening to her reminiscing, then finally asking if she suspected the house cleaner had sticky fingers, the woman smiled and said, "Of course. Every time she comes, she takes something. But she keeps coming back, and I'm grateful. If she didn't stop by, I'd never have company."

And thus ended that "case." The aging woman refused to file a complaint. Instead, to "pay" for Annalee's time, the woman gave Annalee two slices of stale but earnest mincemeat pie, wrapped in reused wax paper, and a stack of yellowing Methodist newspapers. Then she made Annalee promise to visit her again soon.

Reflecting on the aging woman, Annalee slipped out of her used coat and blew on her scalding coffee. "Who knew detective work would be so heavy on listening?" She thought of Jeffrey Mann and her odd conversation with his wife, Rebecca.

"But you keep doing it. Letting people bend your ear. Don't you want a real job?" Mrs. Stallworth frowned, stirring cream in her cup.

"Every job is real." Annalee pondered that. "Well, real in its own way." She chuckled. "Remind me to write a paper about that."

Mrs. Stallworth rolled her eyes. She knew Annalee was still writing and selling theological monographs, but the pay was miserable. Annalee was barely getting by. She had bills and land taxes. She sneaked to help out a white orphan boy, just twelve years old now, who'd once saved her life, but her finances stayed slim. *But if my morning visitor can pay?* She weighed that. The Lord provided, without a doubt, but she could use a paying client.

"Any other mail come for me?" She tried to sound casual. But she hungered for a breakthrough. Maybe someone else had written, asking for her help. Maybe even someone from Telluride?

"Did you check the front hall? On the table? The mailman just delivered." Mrs. Stallworth turned back to her kitchen worries and work.

Annalee made her way to a small hall table and, in fact, found a disheveled stack of circulars, bills, and messages, including a slim envelope with her name on the front, typed in neat letters. No return address.

She picked it up carefully, gratefully.

Something about it made her smile. Had Jack left her a sweet letter again? He'd done that before, knowing how much she enjoyed the surprise. She held the envelope tenderly, hoping it contained something pleasant. *And not too scandalous, Jack.*

"It's like the post office here," she called out to Mrs. Stallworth, thinking as she peeled open her letter that the Cunninghams must be grateful for a full house of paying lodgers—most of them already gone off to their jobs, including Mr. Cunningham, a taxi driver. Thus, so much correspondence sat in bundles on the table, awaiting their return.

"Piles of mail," Annalee added to herself.

"What'd you say?" Mrs. Stallworth called to her.

But Annalee suddenly could barely speak.

"I—" she stammered. She was reading the letter, held in her own hands, trying not to be shocked at what she was seeing.

Hate mail?

Of all the awful things. Or to make it sound better, a "poison-pen" letter. *Call it that, detective,* she told herself.

But Annalee felt her hands shaking. She'd received hate mail before. Every time her name made the papers—for getting a monograph published or about causing her father's killer to be jailed—hate mail followed. The letters called her awful names. Some threatened harm. Nothing bad had come of the threats, but she despised being a target. Hateful words were cruel. They stung.

"What is it now?" Mrs. Stallworth called again from the kitchen, sounding preoccupied. She was washing up the breakfast dishes.

"Well, I—" Annalee considered trying to explain, to put words to the annoying business-looking, fine-papered correspondence she was holding. Despite her best wisdom, she'd started reading it.

Take that Jeffrey Mann case, Miss "Sherlock"?

Her heart skipped. Who knew about Jeffrey Mann? Or knew she'd been at his murder scene? Annalee swung around, looking down Mrs. Cunningham's hallway, feeling as if she'd been followed. Who'd had time to sit down and type a letter—addressed to her—and post it in time to arrive with the Cunninghams' early morning mail?

"Everything okay?" Mrs. Stallworth called again, still sounding busy. Annalee didn't answer. Breathing deep, she tried to calm herself.

Because something uncommonly nasty and mean wafted off this letter—in its mocking of her, calling her "Sherlock." Making it sound ugly, not like Jack's cozy teasing.

She crumpled the page. What kind of person wrote that? She could guess, but she'd feel rattled. So to spite fear, she unfolded the crumpled page and kept reading.

Take that Jeffrey Mann case, Miss "Sherlock"? Or whatever you call yourself . . .

Annalee pursed her lips.

And it will be your last.

She cocked her head. A poison-pen letter? What a silly attempt to terrify her. Except this was no trifle. The author was dead serious. No misspellings. No cutout letters pasted on helter-skelter to look dramatic. So no cheap attempt by a learned person to look poorly educated.

Instead, someone who could read, write, spell, afford high-quality stationery, and knew exactly where to reach her had sat himself (or herself?) down at a typewriter—which wouldn't be cheap—and composed this nasty threat. To her.

She tightened her jaw but kept reading, ready to dismiss the whole thing. But with every typed word, her stomach tightened.

Make no mistake, we've got our eye on you but also on that colored pastor of yours. Take the Mann case and he dies first. Dead and gone.

"Your coffee's getting cold!" Mrs. Stallworth called from the kitchen.

"I'm coming." Annalee tried to sound like herself, refusing to show nerves and anger, acting calm about what she was reading. But her eyes were on fire. A threat against Jack? *Who sent this?* She was furious. The next few lines stoked her anger higher.

We won't stop there. We'll take out your Chicago friend, the Cunninghams' cook.

At that, Annalee crushed the letter, then crumpled it even more. Who on earth knew Mrs. Stallworth had moved recently to the Cunninghams' place? Or had relocated to Denver from Chicago and was working here as a cook?

She yanked open the crumpled letter to keep reading.

Then that white boy you call yourself helping. What's his name? Eddie? How tragic. All of them. Dead and gone. Then finally you. End of the line.

Annalee stepped back from the table, looked across the front stairwell into a small parlor. Mrs. Cunningham was occupied dusting her furniture, picking up magazines, straightening the room. She looked up and saw Annalee, smiled at her—her smooth brown face breaking into a grin. Annalee smiled back, but her stomach had squeezed to knots.

She half folded the crumpled letter, stuffed it in the waist pocket of her prim crepe dress, and turned toward the kitchen.

She'd get to the bottom of this. She didn't even feel afraid or worried—well, yes, for her friends. But she wasn't worried yet for herself. Instead, she felt furious. Because somebody had known, even before she knew, that the Mann case was a hot one. But more importantly, as Annalee could see, it would be doggone deadly.

The doorbell rang.

Annalee froze, stood stock-still in the hallway, heard Mrs. Cunningham walk through her parlor, step into her small foyer, and open her front door.

Some pleasantries commenced.

Annalee struggled to parse the voices, expecting that a woman, for some reason, would be her client. One singular or self-important person, lowering herself in Five Points to seek help with a mystery. Annalee would help her anyway. Everybody needs release.

Instead, when Mrs. Cunningham called to her and Annalee slipped into the foyer—the annoying hate mail crumpled in her pocket—she saw *two* people, neither expected nor desired nor female.

A Denver policeman in full uniform glared at her, frowning. Her heart thumped. *Lord, no.* Next to him, standing taller, loomed the federal government's bureau man, the one from her first case whom she'd called Lemonade Hank. Plain brown suit, dark overcoat, menacing face.

She chewed her lip, breathed hard, felt for the hate letter and pushed it deeper in her pocket, waiting, not trusting herself to speak.

"We need to talk." The tall man spoke. Flat voice.

The bureau man, Robert Ames, had surprised her before, almost like this. He'd shown up when she'd least expected him. Not drunk, as he was the first time she'd encountered him on a train—overpaying a Pullman waiter to bring him booze despite the strict Prohibition laws. *Just a* tiny *lemonade!* He'd winked at the waiter, his words slurred.

But it was all an act. His undercover disguise.

Now here he stood in Mrs. Cunningham's front foyer, stone-cold sober. With a Denver policeman.

Mrs. Cunningham turned, straightened her back, gave Annalee a look—"*Don't start no mess in my house*"—and marched up the stairs.

Annalee understood her, loud and clear. She turned to the two men. "What's this about?" She didn't sound cordial or feel it.

"Is there somewhere to talk?" Ames asked the question.

"Why should I say yes?"

Ames didn't answer, but the policeman did.

"Because you were at Jeffrey Mann's house last night and he's dead." The policeman was square and bulky. He spoke from the side of his mouth, his words sounding harsh, nothing friendly about him at all.

Annalee stepped back, feeling pressured. Jeffrey Mann was an up-and-coming barnstormer—young and also white—trying to make his way. So his death meant trouble for her, with bad people paying attention, hungering for someone like her to blame.

She acted indifferent. "Me at his house? That means nothing. I was with his wife—at the public library. Ask the librarian."

"We did." Ames looked beyond the foyer. "We'll also need a few minutes with you."

Annalee knew she didn't have a choice. She'd been at the Manns' and they both knew it—probably from a nervous Rebecca. They'd use that fact as leverage, exactly what she'd hoped to avoid.

But she didn't head to the kitchen. She refused to pester Mrs. Stallworth with these two. Or maybe they'd wither under her former landlady. Annalee could just imagine what Mrs. Stallworth would make of the two hulking men: Mincemeat. Not stale.

Mrs. Cunningham's front parlor was two short steps away. Annalee turned on her heel and headed there. The two men followed on heavy feet.

Annalee didn't sit or offer seats. Mrs. Cunningham had spent good time dusting and cleaning the bright, welcoming room, a display of her hospitality. It was her knitting room, yes, but also where she greeted visitors but not troublemakers—such as Ames, who now was growling at Annalee.

"You're in hot water."

She cocked her head, but she couldn't deny it—and these two knew it. She'd walked home with Rebecca Mann. She'd been at the scene of the husband's murder. Annalee's soggy handkerchief proved that. She longed to solve the murder—to prove that she could. But instead, she seemed to be on the hot seat herself.

"Sit yourself down." Ames pointed to a small sofa, but she stood her ground, standing taller.

Ames yanked over Mrs. Cunningham's knitting chair, however, perched himself on its edge. The policeman still stood.

Ames looked at Annalee evenly. "You're in the frame. For *murder*. But I need you for a job. Tomorrow night. This Friday—"

"*No,*" Annalee nearly shouted.

Ames looked surprised. "*Yes.* This Friday evening. I need you for a case. No option. Seven thirty."

"I can't. Find somebody else. I'll be occupied."

At that, the policeman reached into his pocket. He pulled out a wrinkled white-lace handkerchief—her initial *A* still looking damp in one of the corners. With one of his huge hands, he balled it up, squeezing hard.

"That's mine—" she started to protest. But they knew the handkerchief was hers. It was their bargaining chip. Hard leverage. She couldn't beat it.

"This Friday night," Ames started in again.

Annalee glared at him, wanting to grab Mrs. Cunningham's knitting needles and jab them someplace not the least unpleasant.

"Colorado Ladies' Club—"

"The *what?*"

"Seven thirty sharp at First Denver National Bank. Second-floor boardroom. A fella named Wallace is president. He lets the women meet there. Civic gesture. It's good for his business. You're on at eight."

She shook her head. "I'm not working as a maid for you."

"No, you're the guest speaker."

This was all wrong. Everything about it. She'd never heard of anything more ridiculous.

"Me? The speaker?" She'd spoken before to groups, not to mention to college students as a young professor, and Ames knew that. She'd attended countless lectures, too—including a packed house just a few weeks ago at a Five Points church to hear a big-ticket "race" speaker. The man was fearless, inspiring, dangerously charming, and even funny, despite his topic. The audience ate up his talk, gave him a standing ovation. Annalee couldn't compare and she knew it.

"Why me?" She bristled. "At this ladies' club?"

"You want to find out who killed Jeffrey Mann." Ames sounded matter-of-fact. "We do, too. Police report it was just a break-in with Mann as the random victim. But I don't believe that one bit. The Klan don't either. So they've got their eyes on you."

She squinted. "Yep, you," the policeman added, taking a seat. "So let's work together." He gestured to the three of them.

Annalee looked at the officer, then at Ames—unsure what to think. *Work together?* "Give me one reason to trust you. The two of you." She pointed to the brawny policeman. "I don't even know who you are. Don't know your name. And you . . ." She gestured at Ames. "When I needed you the most, to help solve my father's murder, you turned me down. He wasn't important enough—"

"I was wrong. If you say no, I can't blame you. But . . ."

"But what?"

"You were at the Manns', Miss Spain, and that's enough to

make you the lead suspect unless we, Officer Luther and I—that's his name, Officer Philip Luther—forget we found your soiled fancy handkerchief on their kitchen floor, a few feet from a dead body, and you agree to help us." He crossed his arms. "On Friday night."

She frowned, took in an angry breath. "But why are you two working together?" She pointed to the police officer again. "And who is he exactly?"

"A street cop." Luther's side-talking mouth answered her question. No flourish.

"And?"

"Klan people run his department," Ames said.

"Of course. They run almost everything."

"But his family's a target. He's Catholic. Klan hate Catholics. His dad owns a moving and storage company. Nobody will hire him anymore—not even old customers—by order of the Klan. All over Colorado. 'Don't hire Catholics.' Or Jews, of course."

"Or colored." Luther added that.

Annalee twisted her mouth.

"Or Mexican," Ames said. "Or white folks who have the gall to love all their neighbors."

"They've gone too far—this so-called Klan." Luther spat out his words.

"His dad's a good man." Ames nodded toward Luther. "He's worked hard his whole life. Honest guy. Been fair to people. Now he's losing business left and right. Same with their church friends, neighbors, relatives—anybody Catholic."

"I hate what's happening here as much as anybody. Maybe more. But I don't see what this has to do with Jeffrey Mann. And with me." Annalee frowned. "And Friday night."

"We're not sure either. But Klan women are recruiting new members like crazy, dictating who can be in civic clubs, vowing to keep their associations 'pure.' They've got their eye on the Colorado Ladies' Club, urging them to purge members who are Catholics or Jews."

"But what does that have to do with Jeffrey Mann's death?"

"I don't know yet. But Mann's wife was just installed in the Colorado Ladies' Club, so she might've heard something, even if she hasn't connected all the little pieces." He set his jaw. "Somebody in that club knows something. I can smell it."

"And you think that somebody will tell *me*?"

"I don't know what I think. I just need a female agent at that meeting, so I'm sending you—with your ear to the ground."

"As the guest speaker." She still couldn't believe it. She'd decided to find Jeffrey's killer, but in her own way and from behind the scenes—not standing at a microphone before a bunch of society women, giving a speech.

But Ames wasn't backing down. "A friend of mine who's in the group set it up. They'll want to hear about your detective work." Ames cocked his head. "It's a hot, fresh topic. You'll get a great turnout."

Annalee pursed her lips. "But why me?"

"Putting you front and center makes it harder for Klan types to sabotage you—to drag you off the street with nobody knowing. Now the most prominent women in town will be asking about you, looking for your next event. Besides, a clue might come your way. You're a detective."

Annalee sighed, looked for a place to sit down, pushed aside Mrs. Cunningham's knitting from the small couch, and took a seat. "But I'm new at it. As for Rebecca and Jeffrey Mann,

I don't know one thing about either one of them. I don't know what I'm looking for." She frowned. "Or maybe I should start at the airfield."

"You know something?" Ames narrowed his eyes.

"I know nothing. Not one thing." She pursed her lips.

"But what?" Ames asked.

"But clues don't stay hidden. I learned that the hard way, on my first case. So I'll go to your crazy meeting, 'ear to the ground,' and see what comes sallying forth."

"You better pray it's a solid clue."

"Praying's not my strong suit. Not usually." *Please, Lord.*

"It's not mine either. But you're in hot water, Miss Spain, even if you're denying the heat."

"I haven't murdered anybody—"

"But almost every judge in the state is tucked inside the Klan's back pocket. Framing a young colored woman for murder is nothing for them. Same with getting a real murderer out of jail."

"What murderer out of jail?"

"That's not your worry. I can divert the police with other things for a few days—enough time for you to unravel what happened to Jeffrey. Because I'm crazy enough to believe you can do it."

"And save my own neck?"

"You think I'm joking?"

"In fact, I do. Silly men marching around in pointy hats. They're just—"

"A menace! Be glad that Luther here was first on the scene or you'd be in jail right now. When Rebecca told him the soppy handkerchief was yours, he held on to it and brought it to me.

The other cops know you walked home with Rebecca, but they don't have any evidence on you."

"But why lie about me?" She rolled her eyes, exasperated.

"*Because they can.* They'd as soon kill you as step over you. Or kill one of your friends. Just for spite."

Annalee pressed her mouth, hating to hear Ames's warning. She pushed the hate mail deeper in her pocket—not telling Ames about it for fear he'd put the kibosh on her case, switching gears, leaving her friends in even worse danger. Crazy logic, maybe. Or was it as confounding as his odd faith in her?

"You've got a good head on your shoulders," he was saying, "so you'd better put it to work. Go find Mann's killer. Or you get the frame. Simple as that."

"What about you? Why not just help me?"

"I can't afford to be involved. If they know I'm helping, I go down, too."

Annalee bit her lip.

"The bureau will pay you," Ames said.

"I'm not worried about that." Well, not totally true. So she added, "For the night?"

"No, for the case." He stood, pulled a business-size envelope from inside his suit pocket, her name typed on front, and handed it to her. "Here's your first payment."

The envelope held cash, not a check. She could tell by the slight thickness. Ames working under the table? She looked down at the envelope, realized she wasn't worrying how much—or how little—was inside. Instead, she'd noticed the typeface from the typewriter used was different from the one on her hate mail. This was larger, typed with a heavier hand than the nasty letter.

Feeling the hate letter still in her pocket and thinking of its awful threats, she grimaced.

"What's wrong now?" Officer Luther looked confused. He stood, too.

"It's nothing, Officer. Just thinking of Friday night." She turned to Ames. "Seven thirty, right?"

"Arrive a little early. A guard will admit you. They know you're coming. Take the lift to the second floor."

"They'll let me ride it?"

Ames would know what she meant. Most downtown business elevators were for whites only. An unwritten rule, she despised the insult.

"They're expecting you."

"I can stay one hour." That was a demand, but she had to make it. Staying later would mean scratching her evening with Jack. *Not an option.* No matter how much the Klan wanted to lock her up, keep her off elevators—or worse. She'd call Jack's rooming house before he left today for the little colored settlement of Dearfield. Well, he might get angry. But he'd come around.

Let him understand, Lord.

"One hour." She repeated her limit.

"Make it a good hour, detective." Ames turned to leave.

"Count on it. I'm wrapping this up fast." *I hope.*

"The bureau wants that, too."

"How can I reach you? For updates."

"Here's my card. Keep it close." He looked at Luther. "Anything else, Officer?"

Luther looked down at Annalee's handkerchief. "My uncle runs a laundry. We'll get this cleaned up."

"Thank you." She didn't feel sure. *Will I ever see my beautiful handkerchief again?* But she couldn't protest. It remained their leverage.

"Goodbye, Mr. Ames." She pointed to the Cunninghams' front door. "Officer Luther."

But Ames turned back, took a deep breath, showed he wasn't quite finished.

"This doesn't feel good to you, I know. But as you're aware, these cases are bigger than any one of us. They always are. Well, murder especially."

"Always. That's why it's so awful."

He reached out to shake her hand. She wanted not to take it. But doing the right thing matters. She moved her arm, deciding to extend her hand. Too late. Ames pulled his back. An awkward moment. *But at least we tried.*

"Well, goodbye." She pointed again to the door. *Why doesn't he leave?* She needed to think over everything, plan her next steps, not to mention make her call to Jack. But Ames wouldn't go.

"I'm glad I could hire you," he said from the porch.

"Agent Ames—sir." It was time to make her point. "I haven't forgotten how you failed my father."

He gave her a sober look, showing he understood. "I'm trying to make it right, Miss Spain—by warning you about these goons. Convincing you to help solve a murder for your own sake." He sighed. "Because regarding your father, I was wrong—and the same bad people are still out there, adding more people to their ranks every day." He winced. "They've wormed their way into my family."

Annalee understood. Ames's niece Elizabeth Castle was a Klan member.

Ames stepped back. "I'll leave you now. I hope to hear from you soon."

She gave him a curt nod, showing she meant it. "I'll pray it's sooner than you think."

CHAPTER 4

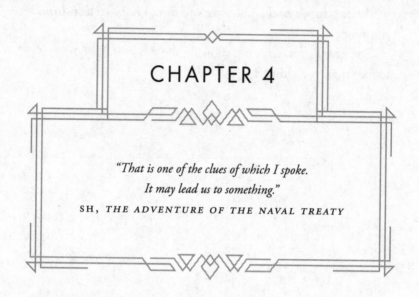

*"That is one of the clues of which I spoke.
It may lead us to something."*

SH, *THE ADVENTURE OF THE NAVAL TREATY*

AT LEAST SHE HAD MONEY. Ames's envelope held an astonishing three hundred dollars. Three bills, folded in half. A hundred dollars each. Annalee spread them out on Mrs. Cunningham's kitchen table, letting Mrs. Stallworth see for herself. It was more money than either of them had ever seen at one time. Both frowned hard, Mrs. Stallworth especially. "What in the world are you going to do with that?" Mrs. Stallworth pointed to the cash. "Good Lord. What was he thinking?"

"What was he thinking? He wasn't. Not about everything."

Annalee had told her about her meeting, hard-nosed Ames and his demands—also about her handkerchief at a murder scene—and the danger hanging over her head if she didn't solve the killing herself, and soon.

Mrs. Stallworth turned up her nose. "But you can't take that much money to the bank. Big bills like that. They'll call the police and arrest you for sure. I can hear it now. 'Where'd a gal like you get that kind of money?'"

"People like him—they don't understand, not everything." Annalee reached for the bills, slipped them back in the envelope, pushed it into her pocket with the infernal crumpled hate mail. "I'll figure out what to do."

But Mrs. Stallworth wouldn't drop the matter. "Just give it back. You don't need this trouble."

"I can't. I was at the murder scene. A young pilot's dead. I don't have a choice. Besides—"

"What now?"

"I believe I can solve it. Sure, I'm just one person. Just me— a nobody ex-teacher who hardly matters. But with every case I take—big or small—this broken, bad city gets a correction. And God knows it needs it."

"Goodness, you're feeling it today, honey. Can I help you?"

"Not with this case." Annalee searched her eyes. "For now, I just need you to stay safe."

"And what's that supposed to mean?" Mrs. Stallworth made a face. "I'm not in danger. Well, not anymore. Not after Chicago." She'd been swindled there, losing her house. She pulled at her apron. "I dare anybody to try."

"They'd better not." Annalee reached for her former landlady, gave her a steadying hug, feeling her stout warmth, grateful for it. Mrs. Stallworth returned the embrace but stepped back with a look, raising a brow. "You must know something. Have any clues?"

"To tell the truth, not yet." Annalee pecked a light kiss on

Mrs. Stallworth's forehead, then pushed away a curl from her own face. "But for now, I need to call Jack!"

"About what?"

"About Ames. Jack's going to—"

Annalee interrupted herself, ran to the hallway, grabbed Mrs. Cunningham's telephone receiver, but slammed it down and ran back to the kitchen. "Is it okay to make a call?"

"Go ahead, baby. I'll explain."

Annalee ran to grab the phone receiver again, clicked the lever, tapping her foot while waiting, waiting, waiting. Then finally:

"Operator. May I help—?"

"Main 4172." Annalee's breath pushed out the exchange. "Thank you."

After what seemed like forever, a woman's cheerless voice broke through.

"Mason Rooming House. This is Mildred Mason—"

"Calling for Pastor Blake." Annalee tried not to sound rushed. "Please."

"He's not here." Mildred Mason seemed ready to hang up.

"Did he say when he'll return?"

The phone was silent for a moment. "I'm sorry. Who's calling?"

"Excuse my rush, Mrs. Mason. Let me start over. This is Professor Spain and—"

"Oh. Annalee. I didn't catch your voice." Mrs. Mason rarely sounded polite, always irritated, just like now. "I'm starting my laundry. You're calling for Pastor Blake?"

"Yes, please, ma'am, thank you." Annalee pulled on all her manners but knew that wouldn't appease Mrs. Mason, knew she surely sounded desperate. "It's . . . important. Has he already left? Do you know when?"

She tapped her foot again. This was awkward. As a member of Jack's church, Annalee had asked him to keep their courtship quiet, out of respect for him, but also for her, as best they could. But with church gossip, more people figured rightly they were now "an item," and many enjoyed knowing that, giving Annalee coy Sunday winks. Not every church member approved, though. Least of all Mildred Mason.

Annalee tried to get on her good side.

"Thank you for your help. He was going—"

"Out to Dearfield. He left early." Mrs. Mason was tight-lipped.

"Early?"

She heard Mrs. Mason sigh deeply.

"Couple of hours ago. He's due back tomorrow—on this Friday." She sighed again. "Friday *night*."

"I understand, thank you." Annalee tried to accommodate, but she kept asking the wrong things. "Did he leave a telephone number?"

Mrs. Mason grunted. She'd heard enough apparently. "Like I said, he's in Dearfield. There's no telephone lines out there yet. Everybody knows that. He won't be back until—"

"This Friday."

"Friday *night*."

"Well, yes, thank you—"

"Is there anything else you need?"

Anything else? What a question. At this moment, Annalee had more needs, as she saw it, than Mrs. Mason of Mason Rooming House Ltd. could ever imagine. *Starting with my need to solve a murder. And my need to figure out a hate threat. And my need to contact the Reverend Jack Robert Blake.* She pursed her lips. *Also, my need to figure out what to say in a speech to a bunch of rich Denver women who meet at a bank—but might know something about a murder?* Annalee rubbed her neck, knowing Mrs. Mason didn't have one clue about any of it, not even about Jack—who was on his way to Dearfield, seventy miles away.

She wished she were with him now—riding along leisurely, in her nice gray outfit, to such a brave, beautiful place. Dearfield was the mostly Negro settlement southeast of Greeley—started by a shrewd ex-caterer and a handful of followers who just wanted to breathe free. Grow their crops. Live their lives. Get left alone. *Please, Jesus.*

Jack would preach out there. He'd counsel, listen, laugh, break bread, plow fields, pound nails, slap backs, lift spirits, encourage hearts.

She could see him now. Standing in the pulpits at Dearfield's two little churches, preaching two Thursday night prayer services. Next day, he'd sit in sunny little kitchens and newly built small shops, stand in hayfields, barns, pastures, and fruit orchards, and exhort the hardworking folks to keep going, trying, believing.

Her Jack, yes. He was the gorgeous, complicated, amazing man somebody had threatened to kill if she took on Jeffrey Mann's murder case. Mrs. Mason wouldn't begin to understand that. But why not? What did she have to be angry about?

"How can you put up with her?" she'd asked Jack about his caustic landlady.

Jack had laughed at that question. "Put up with her? But you already know why, Miss Professor."

She'd searched his handsome face, finally sighing, feeling annoyed. "Because God puts up with each of us."

"End of discussion."

"Why do you know all these things?" But she'd laughed at her answer, too.

Thus, she resolved now to act kinder to the landlady.

"Thank you, Mrs. Mason. That's all."

But nothing was solved, especially not Ames or this Friday night—which had, at first, seemed so glorious and hopeful. She'd already imagined it: Jack arriving from Dearfield, driving up to her little cabin, expecting her to swing open the door—greeting him freshly bathed and wearing not gray, but her flattering only new dress, a sleek blue sheath, a joint Christmas gift from Mrs. Cunningham and Mrs. Stallworth, her hair done up pretty in one of the ways that Jack liked it. Then Jack would pull her into his arms and kiss her as no man in the world ever kissed his young woman, pulling her closer, his breath feeling warm and sounding eager.

They would laugh at his passion and her shy reception of his passion. Then they'd scurry to his Buick touring car, Jack asking Annalee to scoot over close to him as he drove her to his favorite Five Points eating place before going downtown to the late picture show.

Annalee wanted all of this more than she could find words to express.

But now, because of Ames, when Jack arrived at her cabin, he'd knock, but she wouldn't answer—because she wouldn't be there. *I'll be in the ridiculous boardroom of a ridiculous bank giving a ridiculous speech about being a detective to a bunch of dubious women—many who won't approve of me—while keeping my ridiculous ear to the ground to find a murderer.*

Annalee gave it one more try.

"If he happens to come early on Friday, would you ask him to contact me right away? Tell him my plans changed?"

"If I'm here." Mrs. Mason sounded annoyed and didn't hide it. "My women's club meets Friday evening at Mrs. Westbrook's house, so I'll be over there. You need anything else?"

"That's all." Annalee held her sigh. "Thank you, Mrs. Mason. Goodbye—"

Mrs. Mason said nothing more. In fact, she'd already hung up.

Annalee hung up, too. Miffed but not defeated. If anything, Mrs. Mason's hard edges stoked her determination to confront all she now faced—solving a murder and finding who sent that nasty letter, but also finding Jack on Friday night to explain why she'd missed their date. He'd just have to listen and understand.

Back in the kitchen, she gulped down her cold coffee and pulled on her coat. She had a lot to do and the morning was more than half-over.

Mrs. Stallworth eyed her. "Mercy, you've got that look."

"Good." Annalee tried to laugh but took in a hard breath. She buttoned her thrift store coat. "I don't have one solid clue. But I know one safe place to start."

"Where in the world is that? An airfield?"

Annalee picked up a newspaper sitting on Mrs. Cunningham's kitchen counter. Pointing to a list of advertisements on the back page, she saw precisely where she'd go to start finding answers. She wrinkled a brow at Mrs. Stallworth, felt the typed hate letter in her pocket.

"My first stop? The typewriter store."

It wasn't a fancy place, however, and the typewriter man? A sour grouch. He turned his back as Annalee reached for the handle on the front door of his place—the Rocky Mountain Typewriter Exchange. Fancy name. Sad store. Located north of town on a worn-down street, it couldn't hold a candle to the big downtown typewriter outfits or even the campus shops for the college set.

Cost of a machine at a high-roller store? Sixty bucks, type-writer with case. A small fortune for all but the well-off. But a "rebuilt" at this place? Three dollars a month to rent. Sometimes less.

Its tiny storefront, meantime, was closest to Five Points. So Annalee could walk there in a scant fifteen minutes, which she did.

Opening the store's squeaky front door, she wasn't surprised that the cheerless man at the counter didn't look her way. That gave her time, as she walked between two open-faced cases of used, dusty typewriters, to laugh a little at herself. She'd read the Sherlock Holmes story where he solved the case by figuring that a particular typewriter—with "some little slurring over of the *e*, and a slight defect in the tail of the *r*"—had been used to forge a series of suspicious letters, pointing to the culprit.

Now here she stood, in a run-down typewriter shop, deter-mined to learn what? Who'd typed her poison-pen letter? By studying the "slight defect" of the *e* or the *r*?

She moved past the dusty machines built by Corona, Remington, Royal, Underwood, Smith—once new and cov-eted, now sad-looking and overworked—stepping over pile after pile on the grimy linoleum flooring. The place was a type-writer graveyard.

"What d'ya want?" The man at the counter was Mildred Mason's emotional cousin. He couldn't bother to look up. His bald head gleamed, sweating, under the naked bulb of a work light. A dismantled typewriter, displayed before him on a cluttered worktable, held his attention. His other concern was an unlit cigar, which he chomped and chewed—its sour smell fouling every layer of air in the store's dank atmosphere.

Annalee ignored the odor and his grumpy tone. "I want a brilliant man who knows everything possible about typewriters."

The man huffed. "I'm busy. And you can't loiter in here." He glanced up. "I'll call the cops."

Annalee rolled her eyes. "You're smarter than all of them put together. But you already know that—"

She stopped. She wasn't going to play games with this man. He *was* smart and busy. *And so am I.*

She snapped open her pocketbook, stepped to the man's work-table, and pulled out the envelope *not* from the poison-pen letter but from Lemonade Hank—that is, from Agent Robert Ames.

The grumpy man gave it a glance. "So?"

"What can you tell me?"

"Underwood number 5. Government issue."

"Are you sure?"

He ignored that. With the back of a hand, he shifted his work lamp, moved his head closer to the broken machine, aimed his metal tool deeper into its innards.

Annalee dug into her pocket now, pulled out the enve-lope from her poison-pen letter. She placed it on the cluttered worktable.

The grumpy man glanced hard at it. He set down his tool. "Where'd you get this?"

"What are you saying?"

"Who typed this envelope?" His voice was low and gruff.

"*Who* typed it? That's what I'm asking you. What's wrong with it?"

He grabbed up the envelope, peering at her typed name, threw the envelope down on his table, pushed it toward her. Then he finally looked at her. "Who are you?"

"Me? This isn't about me. I received this letter in the mail this morning and I'd like to know what you can tell me about the typewriter used—"

"Ridiculous. Ask whoever sent you the letter!"

"It was unsigned."

"Look, it's an Olivetti. M1 model. European typeface."

"So it's got the accent marks? The *tilde*? The *cedilla*? All the diacritics?"

The man narrowed his eyes at Annalee. "Whoever you are—"

"I'm just a person with a question."

"Look, I don't know your game. But the Olivetti typed your envelope. The typeface tells me. It's European. You can type Italian, French, and Spanish on it." He set down his cigar. "If you ever find the machine, I'll buy it. Fifty bucks. Fifty-five with the case. No questions asked. Now I'm busy—and you need to leave."

He was unpleasant, but she wasn't done. Especially since he was willing to pay, what, fifty dollars for the Olivetti, five bucks more with case.

"Do you have a picture of it? A brochure or something?"

The man growled a sigh. He threw down his repair tool, yanked open a drawer in a nearby cabinet, rifled through a crush of papers and brochures, finally pulling out a crumpled one-page photo with a red-faced man in a vivid red robe, pointing to the M1.

"Who is—?"

"That's Dante. The Italian poet. Olivetti sports his picture in their fancy ads. But you probably already know about him, too, right?"

Annalee ignored that. "Who around here would have one of these Olivetti M1s?"

"Hard to say. But not your average secretary." He cocked his head. "Or your average colored gal asking about Dante and diacritics."

"You're trying to be funny?"

"You see me laughing?"

She grabbed her envelope and shoved it in her pocketbook, snapping the hook. "If I find it, and I can sell it, I'll let you know."

She pushed her way to the front of the store, stepping over the piles of discarded typewriters on her way out. She'd had her fill of the Rocky Mountain Typewriter Exchange. But the exchange had had its fill of her, too. Well, almost.

The grumpy man had one more thing to say. As Annalee pulled open the shop door, ready to step onto the sidewalk outside and take her leave, he growled again.

"Hey!"

She looked back, expecting a final insult. Instead, the man's face suddenly showed almost concern. Then he spoke.

"Watch your back, sister."

She listened but held her tongue. He went on. "Your acting so high-class and highfalutin could get a gal like you in trouble in this town."

"It's not an act. I'm just doing my job."

"So watch your back."

She gave him a look. "God knows I'm trying."

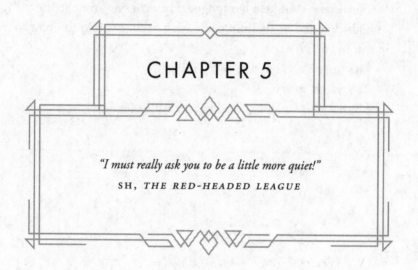

CHAPTER 5

"I must really ask you to be a little more quiet!"
SH, *THE RED-HEADED LEAGUE*

ANNALEE'S WALK FROM THE TYPEWRITER STORE, however, was more than trying. As soon as she stepped out to the sidewalk, a peculiar thing occurred. Strangers started pointing to her, whispering, calling to her.

"You're that detective!" Then laughter, scoffing, even eye-rolling. "We're coming to your speech!" More laughter. "See you at the Ladies' Club!"

They knew about her speech?

Annalee turned off the main drag, escaping the looks and catcalls—but still noticing lampposts plastered with airport posters, advertising barnstormers. *"Handsome daredevils!"* But what was this? A poster about her speech? Plastered on every other pole. For her private talk?

Something crooked was unfolding with this case. *What is it, Sherlock?* But he'd start investigating from its beginning.

So turning on her heel, she marched smartly from downtown, and a few blocks later, pushed through the big front door at Denver's Warren Branch Library, her footsteps echoing on the marble floor.

Flora Quinlan, head librarian, was on duty but looked annoyed. Busy, too. Her neat bob haircut—usually her crowning glory—lay mussed and dull. Her auburn waves, dyed to hide a thatch of gray roots, hung lackluster and flat. Her flashing green eyes lacked their usual sparkle, too—her laugh lines looking today more like wrinkles, deep and pained, showing the mournful truth of her widow's life. She was alone in her world and a horrible thing had happened in it.

"Let me help you." Annalee spoke clearly. She stood at the main desk, waiting for Mrs. Quinlan to put down her pile of paperwork, but the librarian didn't look up. She kept working, but she spoke.

"You want something from me, Annalee, and I can't give it to you."

Annalee understood. Police would've awakened the librarian seconds after learning a murder victim had spent the evening in her branch. *Sitting at a reading table with me.*

"Did you sleep?"

The librarian rolled her eyes, still fussing with her paperwork. "You're trying to sweet-talk me. Please don't—"

A young woman walked up to ask Mrs. Quinlan a question. The two spoke for a minute; then the young woman returned to the shelves, searching, apparently, for her desired book.

Annalee moved closer to the long wooden counter, lowered

her voice. "Mrs. Quinlan, I owe you . . . more than I can measure." Annalee deeply meant this. While she was just a schoolgirl, this librarian had swung wide the door of the world to her by opening up the library's new branch—allowing her to come inside and plow through the shelves, not just in the children's section, and letting her sit for hours during long Saturday afternoons with a book in her hand, ignoring complaints from people who didn't believe people like Annalee should be allowed inside.

"Go to the colored library!" a man had hissed at her one afternoon, not hiding his anger. But a colored library? None existed. Not in Denver. Besides, the city's two libraries—built with piles of Andrew Carnegie's generous cash—were supported by local taxes and Annalee's daddy had been a taxpayer, even if he hadn't paid as much as most. Still, he'd paid what he owed. Mrs. Quinlan understood that, so she opened her branch to all and refused to budge on it.

"Your help changed my life, Mrs. Quinlan. And not just mine."

Mrs. Quinlan set her paper down, looked up at Annalee. "I've faced a thousand problems as a librarian—half of them this morning. But you know the biggest problem I'm facing?"

"I can only guess."

"Privacy."

Annalee winced. "People asking—"

"People *demanding* I tell them what books or maps or reports other people—yes, library patrons—are reading."

"Patrons such as Jeffrey Mann."

Mrs. Quinlan searched Annalee's face. "I can't tell you about him."

"Did he come here often? Was he researching airports?"

"I can't tell you that." She glanced away. "Please don't ask me again."

"What if it's a life-and-death matter?"

"Well, that's obvious." Mrs. Quinlan looked down. "He's dead. Poor kid. Probably not much older than you. Dead before his life got started."

"And I'm trying to stay alive, too."

Mrs. Quinlan frowned. "I know you're working now as a detective. Giving lectures, too. I saw it in today's paper—"

"What paper?"

"Afternoon edition. They just delivered it. You're giving a speech?"

"But it's a private meeting. That shouldn't be in there." She grimaced. "Because I've been threatened. Not just me—other people, too. People I care about. You can't open a murdered man's records to me. I understand that. But maybe you could drop a hint. Just a nugget?" Annalee cocked her head. "Unless you're scared."

"I am scared, if I think about it hard enough." A pained look crossed Mrs. Quinlan's face. "In all my years, I've never had a library visitor murdered." She picked up a clipboard, started to turn away. "I'm doing inventory now. Even if I wanted to help, Annalee, I don't have time. Besides, I told the police *no*—no information from me. Not without a warrant. Now if you'll excuse me."

She turned her back, strode to the periodicals section, started counting issues of magazines, starting with the *As*—*America*, *American Builder, American Journal of Science, American Legion, Atlantic Monthly*. Dozens and dozens more, all through the alphabet. The branch was well-stocked.

Annalee considered following her, to ask about *Aircraft Journal*—she could see a stack of them—and if Jeffrey Mann ever asked about that periodical. But she could see the distressed look on Mrs. Quinlan's face. So she let the librarian get on with her work.

Taking in a deep breath, Annalee walked instead to the farthest back table, where she'd been reading the night before. Pulling out a chair, she sat in the seat where Jeffrey Mann had disappointed Rebecca. Peering straight ahead, she let her eyes peruse the nearby shelves, seeing what Jeffrey had seen. Mining books, reports, archived articles. None of it remarkable. But critical to Jeffrey Mann?

Annalee, last night, had pulled out books of Sherlock stories. Then before leaving, she'd pulled down books on Telluride, looking over town records and history, finding ordinary information. Rebecca, meantime, with her mouth poked out, had spent much of the evening flipping through ladies' magazines, some still sprawled on the table.

And Jeffrey? Annalee closed her eyes, squinted, trying to recall what Jeffrey Mann had been reading all evening. A certain book, magazine, newspaper? All of those things? A map?

She turned her gaze to the maps wall. A tall, thin man was lifting a holder from the wall. Spreading a map on a library table, he pulled a magnifying glass from a briefcase and scanned the page, totally preoccupied with his work.

So he looked up with surprise—as startled as Annalee felt—when Mrs. Quinlan started yelling at someone, her voice tense.

"Put that down!"

Annalee had never once heard Mrs. Quinlan raise her voice in this way to anyone, not that she could remember. But right now, she could feel the librarian's anger, understanding the sound of it, wanting to know who was causing it—and why so many in the world were filled to their gills, it seemed, with so much contentious resentment.

Annalee grabbed a miner's report off a library shelf, held it up to hide her face, and turned halfway, looking to see to whom Mrs. Quinlan was giving the business.

Holding forth in the magazine section, midway in the spacious library, Mrs. Quinlan had her finger waving in the face of a man Annalee had recently seen. But where?

Past his prime and looking worn, the man had a tight mouth and hooded eyes, his face bitter as all get-out as he tussled with Mrs. Quinlan over what? A wooden tray of book cards? The man had walked behind the main desk, apparently, and picked up the catalog of library patrons and their loaned books.

"That's library property!" Mrs. Quinlan grabbed for the wooden tray.

"Then *you* don't even own it!" The man held on to the tray, his mouth twisted, spewing defiance in a heavy-sounding accent—not quite Spanish-sounding, but maybe Portuguese? Annalee wasn't sure. But in any accent, he poured forth a torrent of anger.

"Leave me alone!" the man shouted at Mrs. Quinlan.

Looking at him, Annalee suddenly thought of Mildred Mason. Surely, like this man, Mrs. Mason wasn't born to be embittered. But as with countless others in the world, Mildred Mason had felt the cold rake of life's unfairness—and her spirit didn't rebound. Thus now, this man, like Mrs. Mason, gave life his brittle worst. That's how angry people must wake up in the morning—their necks rigid, hearts closed, souls hurting. The angry man had this pattern stamped on his grizzled, hard—

Face.

Annalee went cold. Rebecca's father. She'd seen his hard-looking visage last night, a portrait of discontent, under a shattered glass picture frame splattered on the floor of Rebecca Mann's living room floor. *"Papa!"*

This man? Rebecca's father. Well, if so, he was one angry piece of work.

Cursing now at Mrs. Quinlan, he threw the card tray to the floor. Her eyes went wide. She opened her mouth to upbraid him, but the man shouted at her, defying her, cursing even louder.

At that, Annalee had heard enough. Others had, too. The tall man near the maps wall tossed down his magnifying glass and stormed over.

"What's going on?"

Annalee marched up at the same time. She moved in toward the angry man. "You need to leave!" Her voice was steady, sober. "For *Rebecca.*"

The man's eyes flashed, his arm rising as if to strike her. "Get out of my way—"

"That's enough!" The tall man yanked at the angry man. "Take your leave! Or we'll—"

"Sure, call the cops! Want me to wait for 'em?" Rebecca's father pushed past the man, past Annalee, past a knot of library patrons, past Mrs. Quinlan, walking with worn, muddy boots across the catalog cards, grinding his foot on a pile of them. The librarian bristled, gasping as he first stopped to hock in her face and then spat, hurling his ugly spittle in a metal Denver Public Library trash can.

"That's it!" The tall man pointed toward the front doors, scowling. "Get out! *Now!*"

Rebecca's father responded with a sneer, grabbed up a handful of muddied catalog cards, balled them up, and threw them back on the floor, stomping over them. Cursing, he stormed out of the library.

Mrs. Quinlan dropped to her knees, reaching toward her cards, struggling to collect them all. "Mercy, I *never!*"

"Can you believe?" Annalee dropped close to her. "I'll wipe these off."

Others gathered to help, but Mrs. Quinlan shooed them away. "Please, I'm fine. We're perfectly fine. Thank you anyway! Go back to your reading!"

She stood to thank the tall man, who still was offering help.

"Let me call the police." He pointed to a telephone on the counter.

"Oh, no need." Mrs. Quinlan gave him a half smile. "You already helped."

The tall man nodded humbly, evoking more thanks from Mrs. Quinlan, both of them talking on about the ruckus.

"I guess I should introduce myself . . . ," the man told Mrs. Quinlan. "Hugh Smith."

Mrs. Quinlan returned the courtesy, both looking suddenly bonded by standing up to a disturbance.

Annalee let them talk, kept picking up library checkout cards, trying to sort them by date, wiping off the muddy ones, hoping she was helping Mrs. Quinlan. *Even though I know nothing whatsoever about organizing library materials.* She pulled over the wooden catalog tray, started stacking in the book cards. Then she saw it.

Jeffrey Mann's name. It was written on the last line of a card, as recorded by Mrs. Quinlan in her precise but quite lovely handwriting. The date due was already past. The card peeked out from a pile of muddied cards on top of it.

Annalee stared at the name, then closed her eyes—wrestling over whether to break the sacred library rule, open her eyes, pull out the card, and simply look. To read, yes, what Jeffrey Mann was researching. She glanced up at Mrs. Quinlan. The librarian was finishing her thanks to the tall man, him now blushing at the woman's attention—as she was blushing at his assistance. They both managed to break away from each other, Mr. Smith walking back to the maps, Mrs. Quinlan brushing back her hair, her eyes suddenly looking brighter.

Annalee stood and took a deep sigh. With another wary breath, she moved toward Mrs. Quinlan.

"What's wrong?" Mrs. Quinlan dropped her voice.

Annalee held her look, handed over the wooden tray of cards, with Jeffrey Mann's notice and name sitting near those stacked on top. In that moment, Mrs. Quinlan looked down at the card tray, noticing the Mann name, too.

"Oh, Annalee."

"I didn't look," Annalee rushed to assure her, if not to assure herself. "I heard you. Privacy's your first rule."

Mrs. Quinlan avoided her eyes, shook her head, casting her eyes upward. "Oh, what a world."

"What do you mean?" Annalee searched her face. "Is something wrong?" They were speaking in whispers now but both intense. "I don't understand. Please look at me."

"I don't understand either." Mrs. Quinlan lowered her gaze, gripped the card tray. "Oh, goodness."

"What are you saying?"

"In my line of work, I don't question what people read or research. I make wrong assumptions if I do. The police do, too." She hiked a brow. "Denver police especially."

She gave Annalee a pained glance—a look Annalee tried now to read, but she only saw uncertainty.

Mrs. Quinlan then walked behind her checkout counter, motioned for Annalee to follow her. Annalee complied, standing close, both of them still talking low.

"Was Jeffrey Mann breaking the law?" Annalee asked.

"I have no idea. I didn't know him. Like I said, I never assume—even if police come with a warrant. And this time, even if they do, I'm leery of showing them every piece of a patron's reading history. But . . ."

"But you want me to know." Annalee could hear that now, but she didn't understand. "Why?"

"I don't want you to get hurt. Especially after what just happened—after a man I've never seen in my life tried to assault me for the same information you came in here to find."

"So now you're going to show me?"

Mrs. Quinlan pressed her mouth, spoke even softer. "Only if you remember that, in the library world, assumptions are *always* wrong—assumptions, that is, about what people are reading. And *why*. Will you promise me to remember that?"

"May I see it now?" Annalee swallowed.

"If you agree that you didn't get it from me." She gave

Annalee an odd half smile, still whispering. "Oh, look! It's just sitting here on the counter—while I have to walk away to my office for a moment."

With that, Mrs. Quinlan plucked the card from the tray without reading it, dropped it faceup on the mahogany countertop, and walked to her office—a small room a few feet away. The librarian closed the door, locked it, then shut the venetian blind on the door's glass window.

Annalee took in a breath, looked up to see if anyone in the library was still watching her. Seeing no eyes glancing her way, she allowed herself to break a rule that librarians all over the country had begun debating: a rule of confidentiality—yes, to hold in confidence their patrons' reading habits, book requests, and checkout details.

But Jeffrey Mann was no ordinary patron. He was murdered. Then his wife's angry father crashed his way through the library. Thus, Mrs. Quinlan now wanted Annalee to know what the murdered man was reading.

So Annalee complied. She looked down at the card, not believing what she was seeing. Because it didn't make sense.

Listed under the first book that Jeffrey Mann had checked out—*Building the Profitable Airport*—was one that said more about her than it said about him. His overdue library book, in fact, was one she didn't know existed, not until this minute. She stared at the title.

Colorado's Most Beautiful Forgotten Ghost Towns: Beginning with Annalee.

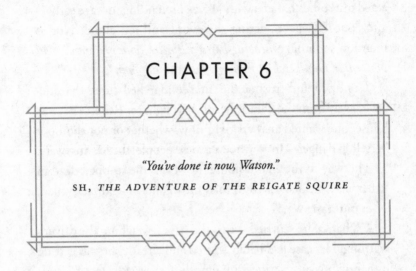

CHAPTER 6

"You've done it now, Watson."

SH, *THE ADVENTURE OF THE REIGATE SQUIRE*

ANNALEE WALKED TO THE BACK TABLE of the library, grabbed her coat and stupid secondhand pocketbook, and left the library immediately, feeling peeved as all get-out.

But what else was she feeling?

Confusion? Fear? Anger, indeed? Sure, let me feel that. Except she wasn't sure why she should be angry because she wasn't sure what she'd just discovered. Some scam? To dupe her? Or take advantage of her? Jeffrey Mann reading a book about her namesake—a ghost town near the mine shaft where she'd been abandoned at birth—felt like more than a coincidence. Thus, it felt both wrong and suspicious.

So had Jeffrey and Rebecca staked her out, sitting at her regular table at the library? Put on a little show just for her, acted out some charade, with Jeffrey pretending to leave early—and "poor" Rebecca acting sorrowful and left alone? Not to mention sobbing. *Smearing her red lipstick onto my brand-new, white-lace handkerchief from my "nice young man."*

Confused and frustrated, Annalee marched along the sidewalk, away from the library, heading straight for Rebecca Mann's house. She wanted answers right now, whether or not she'd put herself in danger—from whoever these people, the Manns, were.

Halfway to the Mann house, however, she stopped dead in her tracks. A car swerved to miss hitting her. The driver yelled, "Get outta the way!"

"What?" She scurried across the street, weighing the driver's warning. Her case had barely started and already she was getting in her own way, reacting with emotions, not clear facts.

Get on track, detective.

She switched directions, walking *away* from Rebecca's—heading, instead, two blocks south, then west. Right away, she felt more focused, even when a different driver beeped his horn at her and waved.

Mr. Cunningham.

"Hey, Miss Annalee!" he yelled out of his open window. "I'm heading your way. Want a ride?"

"Best thing I've heard all day."

He reached across his big car's front seat and hit the handle on the door.

Swinging it open, she climbed in, grateful for the lift. His large sedan shone clean as a whistle, inside and out. Dashboard spotless. Chrome shining. The soft leather seats smelled lemony and aromatic from scented saddle soap. Mr. Cunningham looked spiffy, too—his tweed driving suit brushed and creased, his driver's cap set at a jaunty angle. But his face showed concern, especially for her.

"Something's bothering you. What's going on?"

"I've been given a case, but—"

"Dead ends?"

"How'd you know?"

"I know a thing or two about wrong turns."

Annalee understood. Denver's taxi union didn't accept colored members, so Mr. Cunningham drove for a scrappy Five Points outfit, promoted in colored newspaper ads for its "quick, reliable, and confidential service."

But now?

"Driving a taxi is getting dangerous."

"I heard about the mugging."

"One of the young drivers, too. A fella new in town. But you know something?"

"You'll keep driving your cab?"

"You better believe it. I worked too hard to give it up now."

Annalee listened, taking in his confidence. "Do you pick up every customer—even white fares?"

"If I did, I couldn't tell you." He looked over at her and pretended to wink.

"Anybody at a little airfield outside of town? Or one of the airstrips—?"

"You ask a lot of questions!"

"But I'm Joe Spain's daughter. You two were good friends."

"Great friends, in fact. But I still can't tell where I drive or who I pick up—not even to you. I keep it private."

"I keep hearing that today." She leaned back on the leather seat, frowning, hoping he might change his mind.

Instead, Mr. Cunningham had a question. "What's wrong? The colored detective can't crack a case?"

"I can barely crack an egg."

"You must be trying too hard." He laughed.

"Nope, I'm trying the wrong way."

"No problem. You want information? Act like you couldn't care less."

"Where'd you learn that?"

"Driving this here cab." He pointed at the windshield. "Eyes front! Mind my own business. Just swinging down the lane." He whistled a melody, "Swingin' Down the Lane," popular now on the radio.

"No matter what's going on in the back seat?"

"Especially in the back seat. Tell myself, 'Don't listen, don't even guess.' Then next thing you know, you're hearing it all anyway. Besides, if you know about people, you can figure most things out before you hear it."

"Business deals? Family secrets?"

"Not for me to say. But truth is, I've heard it all."

"I can't even imagine."

"Actually you don't want to imagine. End of every shift, I shake that stuff out my head like loose change."

"Eyes front!"

"Now you're talkin'!"

They were on her little road, so Mr. Cunningham steered the taxi to her cutoff and let the engine idle.

"Goodness! Look at your little cabin. Who fixed it up?"

"Pastor Blake. He's been helping me."

He gave a low whistle. "Eyes front!"

She grinned. "No, nothing like that." She grew serious. "But can I ask you about something else? Something . . . private?"

"Shoot away, little bit. Confidence is my middle name."

She smiled at him, grateful for him—her father's longtime friend—calling her "little bit" as her daddy once did. She leaned closer to Mr. Cunningham.

"If somebody had a one-hundred-dollar bill—"

"Hundred? Somebody like who?"

"Well, like me, actually."

"Good gravy. That's a lot of money, honey. You need to make change?" He pushed back his cap.

"Could I do that privately? Nothing illegal. Just private. Do you know how I'd manage that?"

"Got the cash with you?"

"Actually I do." She pulled out Agent Ames's envelope from her worn pocketbook, retrieved one crisp hundred-dollar bill, letting Mr. Cunningham see it.

"Well now . . ." Leaning down, he nudged a small cashbox from under his driver's seat, looked around to see if anyone was walking nearby, but all clear. Her little road was rarely traveled.

"Here you go." In a flash, he made the change—giving her three twenties, some fives and tens, and the remainder in singles. He shoved the large bill in his cashbox, pushed it under his seat, looked over at her. "You didn't get this from me."

"Not on your life. Just swinging down the lane." *And not worrying about the other two hundred-dollar bills I didn't mention.* Or worrying if she'd solve her case or ever get hired to solve another one.

Mr. Cunningham was still whistling as she gathered up her things to exit the taxi and head into her cabin.

"I miss your daddy." Mr. Cunningham reset his cap, still rakish.

Annalee didn't reply. No need to start with that. This wasn't a time for her tears. Or regrets.

Instead, from outside of the car, she leaned into the taxi window. "Please tell Mrs. Cunningham thank you. She's always a big help."

"She thinks you're the bee's knees." He winked at her. "Take good care. Oh! And break a leg tomorrow night . . . when you speak."

"You know about that?"

"Sure. You're in all the papers. The afternoon news."

Turning to his back seat, Mr. Cunningham reached for his neat pile of newspapers. He handed her half a dozen or more—the *Colorado Statesman*, *Denver Jewish News*, *Denver Star*. Even last week's Klan paper, the *Rocky Mountain American*. On page one of several of the papers, her photo appeared above a short article, "Negro Detective to Share Her Secrets at Ladies' Club."

"This shouldn't be in here."

"You're not the speaker?"

"It's a private affair. This says, 'Open to the public.'" She read down further. "'Free and open. No tickets required.' They might as well say, 'Come one, come all.'"

She gripped the stack of papers, turning her nose away from the day's fresh ink, wanting to crumple the papers up in a ball and throw them back in the car.

"Somebody set you up, honey."

"Right, and I have a good guess. It's my new case, and it's already grieving me." She tried to smile but felt her stomach go tight. She knew what the feeling meant. *I'm frightened.* But no help there. She needed to feel smart. Smart enough to find a killer. Who wanted to kill her, too? Was that what Ames figured? That if he publicized her talk all over town, the event would draw out the murderer? She reached into the car window to hand Mr. Cunningham the papers.

"No, keep them. Might be something in there that helps."

"Or I can use it for kindling."

"Not a bad idea." He laughed. "Most days."

Holding the newspapers, she stepped back so Mr. Cunningham could back up and make a three-point turn to depart. Jack had shown her how to make a turn like that, teaching her in his car so she could feel confident to take her driver's license test—which she'd passed. He'd teased her when her first efforts stalled his hefty Buick, both of them laughing, then cozying, then cuddling when she finally got it right.

"You're the best teacher ever," she'd told him.

He'd pulled her closer. "What can I teach you next?"

She pulled away. "Nothing I need to know," she said—making them both laugh again.

Thinking of him now, she felt her eyes tingle, missing and needing him more than she perhaps should. *But I wish you were here, Jack, to help me unravel a puzzle I don't understand.* Wiping her eyes quickly with the back of her hand—*since I don't have my handkerchief*—she gave Mr. Cunningham a wave.

"Thank you for the ride."

He tipped his hat and smiled. Then his face turned grave. "You be careful, honey."

"Eyes front."

"I'm serious. Watch your step. If things don't smell right at your talk, get out of there."

"In a flash."

He pulled off and she waved again, smiling at him, looking assured—for his sake, if not more for her own.

Inside her cabin, she set her dead bolt, tossed down her things—coat, newspapers, pocketbook—hiding her extra two hundred dollars in a small first aid kit on her shelf—and took in a breath that started in her gut. That's how deep her fears, worries, anger, and confusion roiled.

She picked up a newspaper, frowned at a page one article about Denver's new proposed airport—"Will It Be Built?"—placed next to a photo of a group of barnstormer pilots. "Handsome Young Daredevils." She looked closer. They were, in fact, all handsome and brave-looking. And standing in the center of the photo was Jeffrey Mann's look-alike brother. Buddy Mann. Most handsome, perhaps, of all.

She could admit that, even though this pilot Buddy was a young white man—so she'd probably dare not dwell on him. What did *handsome daredevil* mean anyway? Something on the inside of a man? That something she'd admired in Jack? Even if she couldn't define it?

She turned from the photo. It just made her think of Jeffrey, lying murdered on his kitchen floor. Who did that awful thing? The question made her wonder what job he'd filled at the airfield, besides his barnstorming. But no answer there either. *Gracious, I'm behind on this case.* Worse, she didn't know where to go next for a decent clue.

She looked at herself in her little mirror, let herself absorb her conflicted feelings about all of it, including Friday night. Why'd she say yes? *Because I don't have a choice.*

But what would she say in a speech, of all the unlikely things? She wasn't sure. She just knew, whatever happened, she couldn't fail. Too much was at stake. She had to appear smart, sniff out clues about Jeffrey, watch her back, *and* finish in time to meet Jack.

So she cocked her head, then gave herself a pep talk.

"Watch my back? I'll knock 'em dead." But the thought chilled her. She swallowed, whispered a little prayer. *Be my help, O Lord. My help cometh from you.*

She didn't feel it, but she knew she had to believe it. Still, she added a word that God would understand. *Please.*

That's what her young friend Eddie Brown Jr. asked her later that evening. *Please.* He'd tapped on her door about 7 p.m., just as she sat down by the warmth of her little stove to read the last of Mr. Cunningham's newspapers and make some final notes. He'd come to beg a favor. But first:

Tap-tap-tap-tap.

She tensed. Living alone was risky. *But I will not fear.* What would that accomplish?

"Who's there?" she called out, trying to sound casual and confident.

"Open up, Professor! It's me." Eddie then sang a bar of their "secret signal," the song they'd used in her first case—"I'm Always Chasing Rainbows." His twelve-year-old voice still rang out high and clear.

Opening the door, Annalee grinned and reached for him. He clung to her, too. He'd saved her life just a few months ago on a Chicago-to-Denver train. Then he'd helped her on her first case. Despite their big difference—him white, her Black—she'd grown to love him like a brother. Or perhaps an orphan son? And now his life, too, had been threatened in that nasty hate mail.

"It's been weeks." Annalee stepped back, determined to smile. "Let me look at you."

"It's still me." Eddie pulled off his hat. "Except for this." A ragged haircut left him nearly bald—well, in patches. "Some barber gave free haircuts at the boys' home."

"Mercy, was he practicing?"

"Felt like it. He nipped my ear, too."

"I've got Mercurochrome." From a shelf, she took down the first aid kit for the disinfectant. "How'd you sneak away this time?" She dabbed on the liquid, set the kit aside.

"Movie night. I sat in the back row. Soon as the lights went down, I made for the door."

"Must've been a bad movie."

"Nope, it's a great one. *The Hunchback of Notre Dame*. But I'd already seen it a couple of times."

"Seen it where?"

"Oh, you know, here and there." He shrugged. He didn't want to say more. Eddie, an orphan, lived in a brand-new orphaned boys' home on Denver's east side, but he hated the place—or that's what he claimed. Either way, he was always finding ways to creep away for a few hours, sometimes ending up at Annalee's place. Or Jack's. Or with Mrs. Stallworth, whose cooking he craved.

"Brought us some sandwiches." He pulled a small package from his coat pocket, started unwrapping it. Half a dozen cookies were in the wrapping, too.

She walked to the sink to wash her hands, poured water in glasses from her tiny icebox, then sat down at the table with him. His eyes were closed.

"Thank you, Lord, for these sandwiches. They sure look good. Amen."

Annalee watched him pick one and take a hefty bite. "Why tonight, Eddie?

"What do you mean?"

"You haven't stopped by in weeks. Why'd you come tonight?"

"Well—"

"Finish swallowing. Then tell me."

"Because I saw your picture in the papers today." He pointed to the newspapers stacked by Annalee's stove.

"That's a mistake. I shouldn't be in there. My speech is for a private ladies' meeting. Not 'free and open to all.'"

"I wondered about that." He swallowed another big bite. "Are you on another case?"

"And what if I am?" She took a bite of her sandwich, searched his eager face.

"I knew it!" He jumped from his seat, grabbed his sandwich, and bit off a hunk. He did a little dance. "Let me help you, Professor!"

"Chew your food!"

"I'm chewing!" He swallowed. "I bet you need help! What do you want me to do? Go with you to that meeting tomorrow night? *Please.*"

"Not the meeting. Don't even think about it." She ate more

of her sandwich. It was roast beef with a spicy mayonnaise on toasted bread. Delicious. Chewing it, she considered Eddie's request. "Besides, this case is a bad one. Another murder. So it's not straightforward. Something about it isn't adding up."

"That's why you need my help." He chomped on a cookie.

She watched Eddie eat, knowing he was right about one thing. She needed help—all the help she could get—and Eddie was doggone good at sleuthing, as long as he didn't get himself hurt. That she couldn't stand.

"Well, there's a guy."

"Okay, Professor. I hear you. A guy."

"The dead guy, I mean."

"Who is he?"

"That's the thing. I don't know a single bit about him. Not really." She told Eddie about meeting Rebecca in the library and walking home with her—only to find Jeffrey murdered in their kitchen.

"The same guy in the papers? The barnstormer? The break-in and robbery?"

"Not a robbery."

"Then what was it?"

"Until I know who Jeffrey Mann was—where he was from, who he worked for, what he did in his spare time, who he hung out with, whatever else there is to know about him—I'm flying blind."

Eddie whistled. "Gee, I better get some paper, start taking notes. Right?" His eyes brightened.

"Not this time, Eddie. This case is . . . well, it's dangerous. I want you to stay clear on this one."

"But you need help!"

"True, but what I need most is for you to stay safe." *In fact, to stay alive.*

He sank in his chair. "But—"

"Promise me, Eddie."

"Geez, okay. But nothing's going my way anymore."

"Nothing? Like what?"

"Like you and Reverend Blake."

Annalee sat back in her chair, crossed her arms. "Don't start that again, thank you very much."

"I thought you two'd be married by now."

"Eddie, that's enough—"

"Then I could come and live with the two of you. And leave that stupid boys' home." Eddie stood and shoved his chair back. "Guess I'm leaving now. Back to the *orphanage*." He slumped toward the door, swung it open, looking dramatic.

"You know the score, Eddie. The reverend and I are citizens, but we're also colored people. So we can't take you in. I'm sorry—"

"But if you get married—"

"Pastor Blake hasn't asked me. Not officially. And I'm working a case!" She sighed, wrapped the remaining cookies. "Listen, even if we were married, a white child in Denver cannot move in with a Negro family."

"You two could adopt me! We're already like a family."

"Not possible. It's against the rules—"

"Stupid rules!" He yanked on his hat. "Besides, the reverend *wants* to marry you. He told me so himself. He's just waiting till his church gets rebuilt. And his house next door."

"The parsonage."

"Right. He can't marry you living in that stupid rooming house with mean ol' Mrs. Mason—"

"Hold it, Eddie."

"You'd be his pretty new bride and he couldn't—"

"That's enough! I'm not discussing any of this with you. You're *twelve years old* and you know *nothing* about such things. *And* I'm working a case. Here, take your food."

"Not true, Professor." Eddie grabbed the cookies. "Actually, with all due respect, I know a lot more than you think."

"Well, *with all due respect,* you don't know what I need you to know right now—which is who was Jeffrey Mann. Who was he really?" She wrinkled her brow. "Same with Rebecca. Who is she? I don't have a clue, and that's the information I need first."

"But that's easy. I know who she is."

She gave him a look, feeling suddenly that he *did* know.

"Close that door," she whispered. "Start talking, Eddie."

"She's that rich guy's niece." Eddie sat back down and chomped on another cookie.

"Don't you kid with me." Annalee pulled her chair toward him. "What are you saying?"

"Rebecca Mann. She's related to that rich guy. He's her uncle."

"What rich guy?"

"The guy who owns the bank downtown. First Denver National Bank—"

"On Tremont Street?"

"Right, First Denver. The big one—"

"Who told you this?" Annalee didn't trust coincidence. She'd be speaking at the fancy bank—and now she learned the bank president was Rebecca Mann's uncle? "Who told you?"

Eddie fidgeted. "Well, Mr. Castle."

"Sidney Castle? When did you talk to him?" Annalee shifted

in her chair. Sidney Castle's wife was, in short, a convicted killer. She'd murdered Annalee's father, and Annalee's sleuthing had identified her as the murderer.

In the end, Elizabeth Castle was arrested—hauled off in infamy but not to be scorned by the Klan. As a Klan member herself, she was lauded. They were furious at Annalee that Elizabeth had landed in prison.

But Sidney Castle? He didn't blame Annalee for any of it. He'd told the papers Annalee was a hero for helping unveil the truth, despite it involving his wife, who also was cheating on him. But also involving their only son—killed by his own gun while threatening to shoot Annalee. *Oh, what a tangled web we weave.*

Still, Annalee and Castle hadn't spoken since the shooting and his wife's arrest. Only Eddie had kept in touch with him. Castle admired Eddie's gumption, apparently still showing kindness to him as an orphan—even paying his own dentist to repair Eddie's sadly rotten front teeth. Two new crowns gave him reason to smile, which he did—even though Annalee didn't feel now like smiling back. She was trying to focus instead on what Eddie was saying.

"You saw Mr. Castle today?"

"Sure, on the way down here. I stopped at his house around dinnertime. So I ate supper with him—"

"Supper? And you begged for sandwiches, too?"

"He has a new cook. Miss Bernita's not there anymore, but the new lady's real nice. She just served soup tonight. That's all Mr. Castle wanted. So she gave me some sandwiches and cookies to take with me in case I got hungry later, which I did. Get hungry, that is."

Annalee listened to this, trying to focus her thoughts on what mattered most. "And the rich guy? At the bank?"

"He's a friend of Mr. Castle's. We were talking about him because Mr. Castle had just read about him in the papers, right before I came. He was reading about the murder, too. He said the dead man's wife was the niece of his good friend. The president of the bank."

"And what's this friend's name?"

"Hm . . . let's see."

"Oh, Eddie."

"It's . . . Wallace!"

Agent Ames had said the same. "Yep, that's it, Professor. Simon Wallace."

Annalee let the name roll around in her mind. "I've never really heard of him." *Well, not before this week.*

"He keeps his head low. That's what Mr. Castle said. But he's loaded. Mr. Castle said that, too. Well, you know what I mean."

"And the niece—Rebecca Mann. Did Mr. Castle say anything about her?"

"Nope."

"Or about her father?"

"Nope."

"Because if Rebecca is Wallace's niece, her father must be Simon Wallace's brother. Or brother-in-law. Goodness, I need a chart."

"Nope. He didn't talk about any of that."

"Well, you've told me a bunch, Eddie. Much more than I knew five minutes ago."

"Mr. Castle—I like talking to him. I want to be like him when I grow up. He knows stuff that most people don't know."

"You're right about that."

"Stuff like airport bonds and—"

Annalee grew quiet. "Say that again, Eddie."

"Nothing." He shrugged. "Just saying Mr. Castle knows about lots of stuff—the kind of stuff I never heard about before. So I learn things from him."

Annalee stood. "Lock the door."

"What? Why—?"

"Just do what I say. Lock the door."

Eddie looked confused, but he scooted out of his chair. He set the lock. Turning back, he stepped toward her but froze—seeming to see something troubling in her face. "What's the matter? Did I do something wrong?"

"You're fine. But I'm going to ask you about some things," she said, her breathing fast, "and after you tell them to me, I want you to promise you'll never speak of these things again to anybody else. Do you understand me?

"I think so—"

"I mean it, Eddie. Promise me!"

"Yes, Professor. I promise."

"You mentioned airport bonds. I want you to tell me everything that Mr. Castle told you about that. Whatever you remember. Here, sit down."

She pushed a chair over to Eddie—a chair that Jack had cleaned, sanded, repaired, and varnished for her, even adding a new cushion to the seat. Eddie grabbed the chair, his hands shaking a little now, and sat down.

Annalee sat opposite, their knees almost touching. She nodded at Eddie, telling him to start.

"It wasn't much—"

"That's okay. Tell me."

"It's nothing. We were eating dessert. Chocolate cake. It was really good."

Annalee listened, not interrupting, letting him tell her in his way.

Eddie swallowed. "Then Mr. Castle asked me if I knew what bonds are. When I said no, he started explaining—that bonds are like money, like cash. And there's lots of different kinds of bonds. He told me different names. I don't remember them all. But when you have a city, like Denver, the people who run the city—"

"The government."

"Yeah, the government. When they want to build something big—like an airport—the city will 'issue' bonds and that means selling them. Municipal bonds. I think that's what they're called."

"Okay."

"Anyway, the bonds are like a loan to the city, so the city has to make payments—with interest. That's how people make money on the bonds they buy. That's what Mr. Castle told me. He explained all that because I didn't know what payments are or interest, but he explained that, too."

"Yes, I understand. And then—"

"And then he said that, in a few years or whatever, the whole loan is due." Eddie scratched his head. "I think that's right. Is that what you want me to tell you?"

"That's good, Eddie." She studied his face. "Did he say anything about Mr. Wallace and any bonds for the city of Denver? Like airport bonds?"

"Well, yeah. He told me Mr. Wallace's bank was all set to

sell airport bonds on behalf of the Denver city government—to build a swell airport here and everything. He'd make a nice fee with every sale. But the Klan killed the deal because of Mr. Wallace. He's Jewish. And the Klan doesn't approve of Jewish people. That's why Mr. Wallace keeps his head low. Same with his niece. Not everybody knows their real religion. That's what Mr. Castle said, anyway, because the Klan also don't like—"

"A lot of folks—they don't like." Annalee sat back in her chair. She didn't want to think about a hate group's loathing or discuss it with Eddie. She took a deep breath. "Goodness, Mr. Castle told you a lot. And you remembered it all—although I don't understand why he was telling you these things. You're twelve years old."

"I don't know, Professor. With Mr. Castle, sometimes he tells me things. But other times he seems to be talking to himself. So I just listen."

"Well, you got an earful this time."

"But that's not the best part."

"What do you mean? There's more?"

"The best part is what Mr. Wallace did when his deal got killed because of the Klan." Eddie smiled. "He must be really smart."

"What are you saying?"

"When the Klan killed his deal with the city, Mr. Wallace set up another company and put a different guy, who isn't Jewish, in charge of it. So the city did the deal with the other guy, but guess what?"

"It's still Mr. Wallace's company."

"Right! And the nice fee is even higher!"

"A ghost company," she whispered.

"Right, Professor! And guess what he named it? Phantom Trust. Mr. Castle laughed at that. I did, too. That Mr. Wallace is one smart cookie!"

"Smart, indeed." She thought a moment. Except his plan hinged on a lie. Thus, his scheme might involve more than just outsmarting folks. She narrowed her eyes. "I wonder what the Klan said about his new company and how he tricked them. Do they know?"

"I'm not sure, but when they find out, they'll be hopping mad." He laughed. "I think it's funny. Don't you?"

"Depends on who's laughing." She thought of Jeffrey Mann. "And who's dying."

"You mean the dead guy?"

"Well, not exactly. Listen, you promised me you'll stay quiet about this."

"Who would I even tell?"

"Nobody." She wagged a finger at him. "Tell nobody."

"Gee, if it's so bad, I'm sorry I told you. Will you get in trouble? Are you in danger?"

Danger hardly described it. But she didn't say that to Eddie.

"It's nothing bad. You've helped with my case. So don't worry about me." But her mouth went dry as she said it. Her fear reflected her own concern but also anxiety about Eddie. *Please, Lord, keep him safe—safe from this dangerous information.*

Pursing her lips, she sat back in her chair, then brightened her tone, not wanting him to worry.

"Ever been to an airfield, Eddie?"

His eyes got big. "Can we go?"

"Sure, maybe this weekend. Reverend Blake is in Dearfield, but he's due back tomorrow—on this Friday. I'll ask him to drive us east past Colorado Boulevard, to the little airfield, when he has time. Maybe on Saturday. Or Sunday afternoon."

"We can see the aviators!"

"And their planes. Maybe some will be taking off—"

"And landing! Wow, Professor. Who knows what we'll see out there."

She smiled at him again. "Yes, who knows? I can't wait." But she had a question for herself.

Why are my nerves zinging just thinking about it?

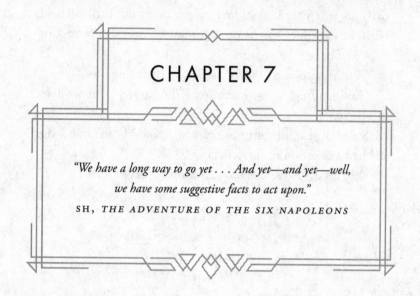

CHAPTER 7

*"We have a long way to go yet . . . And yet—and yet—well,
we have some suggestive facts to act upon."*

SH, *THE ADVENTURE OF THE SIX NAPOLEONS*

BUT FIRST, TO HER ANNOYANCE, Annalee had to write her
blasted speech. That's the task she woke up bemoaning on
Friday morning. The night before, she'd walked Eddie to the
nearest streetcar stop in Five Points, paying his fare so he'd get
back safely to the boys' home.

He'd waved at her from his streetcar window until the road
turned. She kept waving too, still smiling, but knew she felt no
glee. Eddie had told her deadly information. For him. For her.
For Mr. Simon Wallace. Even for Rebecca?

Whatever this Wallace's bond scheme could mean, it gave
Annalee extra incentive to solve Jeffrey Mann's murder without
delay. Not just to save herself from being a suspect—thanks to

her fancy, beautiful, crumpled, *loaned to Rebecca* handkerchief, found lying next to Jeffrey's dead body.

Now she also needed to solve the case to keep Eddie safe. He was walking around town knowing just a little too much insider "dope" about airport bonds and bankers outsmarting the Invisible Empire—all of it putting him in grave danger. Her, too. *Darn it all.*

To face the day, she fixed herself an actually tasty breakfast—the remainder of the delicious sandwich from Eddie's visit last night, plus half a cookie, a leftover apple from Mrs. Stallworth's kitchen table, and a steaming cup of fresh coffee, the strong aroma bracing her spirits. While downing her meal, she studied the last of Mr. Cunningham's newspapers, ignoring the stories about her ridiculous talk but finally grabbing her writing journal and pencil to make speech notes.

She'd made remarks before, off the cuff, in talks and classes. Still, she made her notes for this night—feeling fairly sure, after reading the papers, what she'd say this evening to her audience, whoever in the world they turned out to be.

Her thoughts, however, kept circling to other things—including that typed poison-pen letter she'd received the day before in Mrs. Cunningham's stack of mail. *"Take that Jeffrey Mann case, Miss 'Sherlock'?"* She gritted her teeth, hating every single thing about the infernal letter.

But who'd sent it? Threatening her but also her closest friends?

Looking at the back page of one of the newspapers and searching down a list of advertisements, however, Annalee let herself pause on a smaller detail for tonight—ordering new business cards from the stationer's in Five Points. Next, she'd figure out what to wear. But first to Mr. Robinson's stationery shop.

"Rush order?" Raynard Robinson pounced the moment she hurried into his tiny but orderly store. "For your talk tonight?"

"If I hear another word about that talk!"

"What's wrong?" Mr. Robinson acted surprised. "You'll knock 'em dead."

She groaned.

"Don't complain. It's high time you got new clients. But you'll need fresh cards."

Annalee laughed lightly, shaking her head. She enjoyed bantering with Mr. Robinson—one of the last few white residents in her part of Five Points. "I'm not moving!" he'd often told her. "They'll have to carry me out feetfirst."

"Is fifty cards too many?" she asked him now. "For a rush order?"

"That's hardly worth my time. I'll give you a hundred for five dollars."

"I'll need more than new clients to pay for that."

"That's a deal, young lady! Rush fee included."

She turned to go. "I don't need them that bad."

"Wait. I'll do you fifty for three dollars."

"Two."

"Two and a half. Rush fee on the house."

"You drive a hard bargain."

"Just doing business." He laughed. "Come back in an hour. You'll make me proud."

"I'll try. See you then."

Outside, a sunny sky had dried yesterday's springtime snowfall. The air felt crisp and fresh. Annalee's plan was to rush home, finish her speech notes, make sure her nice blue dress was brushed and ready—that's what she'd decided to wear—then circle back to the stationer's for her printed calling cards.

But she passed the neighborhood pawnshop.

She tried not to look. Her late daddy had warned her against going into pawnshops. *"Nothing but trouble in those places. Grown folks' trouble. Plus, you need cash—which you don't have."*

She didn't plan on buying anything, even though—for one of the few times in her life—she actually had cash in her pocketbook. But she was recalling what Rebecca Mann had said about her dead husband.

"Jeffrey steals . . . He stole my late mother's jasper necklace." Not worth much. But Rebecca knew where it was. *"It's in the window at the big pawnshop in Five Points. I saw it there."*

Now, here it was—a necklace of jasper—staring back at Annalee from the Fletcher's Pawn display window. It hung on a small stand in the corner, not center stage like pricier items. But to Annalee's eye, the jasper piece had a fine look. The stone, a solo pendant of ocean blue—as she imagined an ocean would look, anyway, in wavy shades of azure—hung on a thin, gold-plated chain.

She'd step inside and ask about it.

In fact, as she peered past the glass window into the shop—expecting to see tables cluttered high with merchandise—a pair of female eyes stared back at her. Mrs. Fletcher.

Annalee didn't know the shop owner nor her husband. They weren't members of Jack's church, although she'd seen Mrs. Fletcher at Mount Moriah a couple of times for community programs, always looking primly dressed and dead serious. Annalee gave her a nod.

The woman didn't react. Instead, her look asked Annalee's intentions. *"You coming inside? Or not?"*

Annalee beat her to the punch, pushed through the pawnshop's front door, setting off a bell. It jangled like crazy.

"Mrs. Fletcher." Annalee nodded but no smile. *Just be straight with her.*

"You need a necklace to wear?" Mrs. Fletcher pointed to the window, indicating the jasper pendant. "Tonight?"

Annalee knew what she meant. Mrs. Fletcher had read the papers, too.

"Not to wear," Annalee answered. "But I have a question about the jasper."

"I'm not surprised."

"What can you tell me about the owner?"

"Mr. Jeffrey Mann?"

"Mr. Jeffrey Mann—yes."

Mrs. Fletcher stepped to the window and removed the jasper pendant and its stand. "Don't you want to try it on?"

"Not today."

"I understand—since the man who pawned it has been murdered."

"You saw that in the papers?"

"I recognized his name right away. And now here you are, standing in my shop, asking about that same man."

Annalee swallowed. Mrs. Fletcher was all business. Hair scraped back in a tight black bun. A spotless shopkeeper's apron worn over her no-lace shirtwaist dress. She'd built up her shop with grit, sweat, and her husband's help and elbow grease. Among pawnshops, Fletcher's was one of the city's largest—everybody knew that—although Klan influence was probably chipping away at their business. Annalee decided not to add to any troubles she might be having.

"I wish I could tell you more, Mrs. Fletcher. I happen to know Jeffrey Mann brought in the jasper—and maybe other jewelry items, too. It would help me a lot to know why, although I doubt he disclosed that to you."

"I never ask. Not my place to know. Although I refuse stolen goods." She pointed to a large framed sign on a back wall. Annalee let her eyes settle a moment on the sign. *NO FENCED GOODS.* Impossible to miss it.

"Anything unusual about his dealings with you? Can you tell me—?"

"If he were still alive, I wouldn't tell you a single thing." She hesitated, set the jasper necklace down on a round table crowded with costume jewelry. "Better" jewelry items were locked up inside a glass case. In its entirety, the store looked well stocked, organized, clean, and safe. Grown folks' trouble might have brought customers to Mrs. Fletcher's pawnshop, but the place wasn't tawdry. Not in appearance anyway.

"I don't want a hint of trouble or scandal with my business." Mrs. Fletcher cocked her head. "I've worked too hard and too long to get it going. We're finally doing well. So I was ready to tell Jeffrey Mann to take his business somewhere else."

"Why?" Annalee's question was direct.

"You didn't hear this from me. But I'm telling you because I know you're on your own now, working as a detective—if you call yourself that. You act discreet, and you're trying to make a way for yourself." She set her chin. "Well, I know you're stepping out with Mount Moriah's pastor, Jack Blake—"

Annalee blinked, stifling her emotions. *Just listen. Say nothing.*

"But you're keeping your head down and staying quiet about it. I haven't heard one word of complaint about you from anybody who's worth listening to—"

"Thank you—"

"Don't let it go to your head."

"Never." Annalee meant that.

"So I'm going to share some things with you today. Because sometimes, when you're in business for yourself, things don't smell right and you need to tell somebody."

"I understand."

Mrs. Fletcher pointed to her office. "Can I show you something?" She turned toward the back of the shop, indicated she expected Annalee to follow—which Annalee promptly did. If a moment could be a breakthrough, this might be one. Big? Small? Annalee wasn't sure, but she didn't want to ruin it.

Holding her breath, she watched Mrs. Fletcher grab keys from the pocket of her prim dress and unlock her office door. Stepping, as told, inside the neat, small room, Annalee took a seat on a wooden stool beside Mrs. Fletcher's desk and stayed quiet. She let her eyes move around the room—to the file cabinet, wall calendar, sharpened pencils in a holder, bookshelf holding neatly organized ledgers, everything dusted and well tended.

Mrs. Fletcher opened a desk drawer, removed a thick ledger, and placed it on her desk. Opening to a page, she pointed to the name written in black ink at the top: Jeffrey Mann.

Annalee gazed at it, feeling a certain anger that the young man whose name stared back at her had been stolen from his life in a coldhearted way. *I'll find your killer.* How? No clue. Annalee just felt she would, even if she'd yet to learn how.

"You want to hear this?" Mrs. Fletcher broke into her thoughts.

Annalee leaned closer. "These are his pawns?"

"Starting last July, yes. He came in the second Tuesday of every month near closing time and offered an item in exchange for cash."

Annalee listened. That might've been unusual, but it didn't seem criminal. Or even suspicious. "That raised a red flag?"

"Not at first. But after the third time, I realized he was selling me the same item. The same jasper necklace. He'd bring it in to pawn. I'd pay him for it, put it in the window—at his request. Then I'd mark up the price, charging for window display. Then the next day, the item would sell—"

"To the same person?"

"Different people—at first. Until September. Then on that second Tuesday, Jeffrey Mann brought the necklace back in, again, to sell. A young woman, about your age, purchased it the next morning. Then the same young woman bought it again in October, November, December, January, and February. But in March, I told him I didn't know what he was doing exactly, but I wouldn't accept the necklace for pawn anymore."

"What'd he say?"

"'Just one more time! Just one more time!' So I accepted it, he paid, I put it back in the window. That was on Tuesday night. Next morning, the woman didn't come in. Then that Wednesday night, he was found murdered. I saw it in the first edition of Thursday's paper."

"What did she look like? The young woman who bought it? A blonde?" Annalee was thinking of Rebecca.

"No, she was a colored girl."

Annalee's breath tightened. *Pay attention.* "A colored girl?"

"A young girl. Like you. Kind of your age and size. I'd never seen her before she started coming in."

Annalee pushed a curl off her forehead and glanced out at the shop—thinking about the array of tables, cabinets, shelves, clothing racks, consoles, jewelry stands, all filled with merchandise—trying to understand what Jeffrey's pawn exchange with a Black woman her age could even mean.

"Did he bring in any other items?"

"Just once. According to my records, he brought in a pair of small pearl earrings. Good quality. They sold a few days later—"

"To the young woman?"

"Somebody else did the buy. Jeffrey Mann had seemed reluctant to part with them, but he did."

"Anything else about him that you remember? Did you know he worked at the airfield?"

"Saw it in the papers. A barnstormer."

"Did he ever mention it?"

"I don't snoop in my customers' business." Mrs. Fletcher gestured toward her display floor, looking proud. "I run a clean shop. I don't ask questions. People pawn. I buy and sell. I'm as fair as I can be. Try to be anyway. But I never had a customer murdered like that. With that back-and-forth jasper business, his death rattled me. Puts me on guard."

Mrs. Fletcher's face showed her outright worry over the Jeffrey Mann mystery.

"Do you work in the shop by yourself all the time?"

"Usually. Although Fletcher, my husband, runs the shop every now and then. His record keeping is a mess. But he worries about my safety. So we're getting a dog—"

"Really?" Annalee paused. "What kind of dog?"

"A *big* dog." The shop owner chuckled. "Fletcher's out looking for one today. I know nothing about dogs, but I'll learn."

Annalee smiled, thinking of dogs she'd seen and coveted as a child. Other children's puppies. Her daddy always said no, so that was the end of it. She started to say more, but the shop bell jangled and Mrs. Fletcher stood, called out through her office door, "I hear you. Be right there!"

Annalee thanked her and headed toward the exit, not taking time to stop and look through the pawned merchandise. Grown folks' troubles. You could build a whole business with them. But what exactly was Jeffrey Mann's trouble?

She headed out, intending to cross the street to Mr. Robinson's. But at the last minute, she turned back to look at the jasper necklace.

"Sorry to interrupt you, Mrs. Fletcher. But I've decided to purchase this."

Mrs. Fletcher didn't question her, just wrapped up the necklace in brown paper and pressed it into Annalee's hands.

"On the house," she said.

"I have money—"

"I'm glad to get rid of it. Please take it. I hope it leads you to some answers."

"Or maybe the right questions."

Crossing the street to pick up her calling cards from Mr. Robinson, she only knew this: *No matter what it takes, I'm going to find out what it means.* She set her jaw. *Maybe even tonight.*

CHAPTER 8

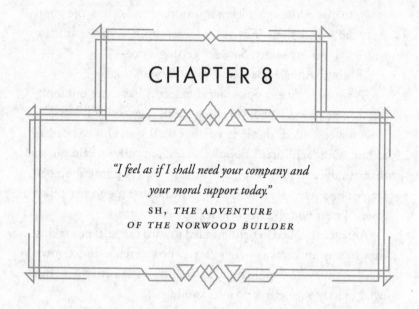

"I feel as if I shall need your company and your moral support today."

SH, *THE ADVENTURE OF THE NORWOOD BUILDER*

ON HER WAY HOME, HOWEVER, she first did an odd thing. Odd for her, anyway. On a weekday, that is. She actually stopped at a church. Not Jack's church, of course. The rebuilding had barely started. But walking along the sidewalk by Five Points' many churches, on her way to her cabin, she passed one of the smallest and felt a call—or a dare—to come inside.

A little sign hanging next to the door said: *Altar Open for Prayer 9 a.m. to 9 p.m. Monday to Saturday.*

She couldn't count the times she'd walked by that door, that sign, this sanctuary, this little building among so many—and never once, on a weekday, thought about stopping inside. Just for prayer? At the altar? Like an actual praying person? A person, that is, who understood more about prayer than her fumbling attempts.

She stood there a moment and took a breath.

"You going in?" The church janitor was pushing a broom down the sidewalk. "It's open, young lady."

He seemed to know who she was and she knew him.

"Nice to see you, Brother Porter." He cleaned churches all over Five Points. At the YMCA, too. "Thank you so much."

Brother Porter touched his cap—out of habit and to show respect—then pulled the simple wooden door open and held it while she entered. Thanking him, she let the door close behind her and stood in the tiny narthex, looking around—for what? *Lord, why am I here?*

Of all the times, over all the years that she'd stood in church buildings—on her way to Sunday school as a child, young people's church as a youth, chapel services at her Bible college, worship services as an adult since returning to Colorado last December, and for community meetings, speeches by famous visitors, concerts by renowned singers, and even meeting Jack at different churches a few times on their way to an impromptu dinner together—she'd never once stood in a church building alone.

To her surprise, it felt, well, holy. Sure, no angels singing. No lights a-glowing. This was just a quiet old building, shut off from the noises and traffic and bustling and janitor-sweeping-the-sidewalk whisking outside. But the atmosphere felt . . . kind. She'd have to ask Jack about that. Why did the church, on an ordinary weekday, feel not fancy but like a good ol' home? All it really offered was the worn but polished hardwood floors; the prayer table with the prayer cards, box, and stubs of pencils; the

Sunday school roster showing last week's attendance. A pretty good showing actually, for this little place. Still, was it just a building?

She smiled to herself at her question, thinking first and candidly here about Jack but also knowing already how he'd answer such a question. *"A church isn't the building—it's all the people who struggle in it. Good, bad, and otherwise."*

I'll have to write about that one day, too, she told herself.

For now, she let the altar, just a wooden table, call to her—because she had a speech to give tonight. *And mercy, Lord, I need help. Also a clear mind.* That was the truth and she liked telling it. Maybe those were the prayers God answered first. Honest ones.

Standing in the back of the modest sanctuary, she took a sturdy breath and walked the few steps to the front. The simple kneeling rail sat just below the step-up pulpit. Looking at it, she thought again of Jack and all the preaching he'd done in his own beloved sanctuary. Reflecting on the work that good preaching demands, she promised herself that when she got through tonight's speech and found a way to connect with him afterward, she'd do all she could to help them enjoy a relaxing, honest evening together. No tiffs, arguments, and keeping score.

Please, Jesus, please.

She started to kneel at the altar but instead stepped back and just sat in the first of four narrow pews. Picking up a worn Bible lying on the wooden seat, she thumbed through it, not sure what she was looking for, landing in the Psalms. *"Whom have I in heaven but thee . . . ?"* She whispered a couple such verses, letting the words settle her. Finally she let the Bible just sit in her lap, folding her hands on it, feeling the weight of it—not a heaviness but a certain comfort and assurance—letting it simply calm her. She needed that.

Then she tried to imagine the people who would come to hear her tonight. She moved the Bible aside and stood, facing the empty pews. Jack faced pews every single Sunday, almost every seat filled with somebody staring back at him, longing to hear a word of help.

So they weren't scary—not like the crowd she was imagining tonight. That crowd would be judgmental. That's what she'd feared. Or they'd be rude? Or question her every point? Or make fun of her?

So they'd be like some of the students she'd had at the Bible college in Chicago where she'd taught for two hard years—until she realized something. They were more afraid than she was. Fearful of life and how they weren't mastering it. Frightened they'd show their ignorance if they didn't ask a twisty question that put her on the spot.

Help me, Lord, she suddenly thought, *to see the people tonight as I see myself. A little confused sometimes. A bit uncertain too many times. Struggling to put my best self forward even when others prefer to see me as my worst.*

No, she wouldn't "speak" tonight as much as try to teach. That's what she'd tried in the classrooms at the college. But to teach tonight about being a detective? She wasn't an actual expert on solving crime. Her audience wouldn't be either. But together, what could they learn? That would be her approach. *Is that right?* She stayed for the waning afternoon, sorting through answers, kneeling part of the time at the worn and humble altar, praying that would be the case, letting any fears or worries get quieted. *Indeed, don't let me be a scaredy-cat.*

Then before departing, she added her deepest prayer. *Keep me alert. To any clues, to vital information. Especially about Jeffrey Mann.* But when a prayer like that reached God's ear, would he answer it?

She even thought then about Sherlock Holmes, who never once prayed his way to clever solutions. Few detectives in mystery stories did. Prayer was considered a verboten tactic for fictional detectives. Did Sherlock even believe in prayer? Or in God? Many experts said no. They'd apparently forgotten Holmes's gratitude for "the goodness of Providence." His sidekick Dr. Watson, sometimes a doubter, might have disagreed.

But Sherlock believed that God is real.

So yep, I'm praying, Annalee told herself. Because unlike the renowned Holmes, who could unravel the densest mystery, *I'm a colored girl trying to solve a crime so that I don't end up in the slammer for a murder I didn't commit.*

She pursed her lips, thinking of what she'd learned so far about her case. The dead man was a stealing husband who also flew stunt planes. His wife, Rebecca, was a rich man's niece—with nary a penny herself. That rich man was financing the city's new airport but with a clever ghost company. His angry brother (or brother-in-law?) disrupted the peace at the library. Meantime, the dead man had been pawning his late mother-in-law's stolen jasper necklace—and then a young colored woman had been buying it and returning it to him. And Annalee? She'd received a poison-pen letter typed on an Olivetti.

But one more thing: the dead man's wife thinks she killed somebody.

Annalee pressed the Bible closed. What a swell kettle of fish. Or worms? Or whatever because none of it made a lick of sense.

It was as confusing as discovering that a rich woman, Elizabeth Castle, had murdered her poor father. At least that woman was in jail. One problem solved.

Annalee looked around. The tiny sanctuary was growing dark, the afternoon sun fading in the west, so the one stained-glass window on the opposite side of the building had grown dim, its few simple colors darkening to gray, no longer glowing.

For a moment, she thought she heard footsteps in the narthex. A rustling? Or just a tree branch scraping against the sagging roof? The wind was picking up, whistling and groaning into day's end. Still in the building alone, she needed to leave now. It wouldn't look good for her or Jack if his "lady friend" had to grab an altar candlestick and bonk some sad interloper over the head.

She picked up her pocketbook and scurried out, looking back at the tiny holy building, wondering if an altar candlestick wouldn't be such a bad thing to have on hand for later tonight.

Her bright-blue dress fit her nicely, if she had to say so, gratefully, herself. A soapy sponge bath left her feeling revived, and so did a spritz of lavender water. Yep, Jack's favorite. "I love when you wear it," he'd told her, pulling her to him, breathing in the summery scent. Looking at the small clock on her shelf, her heart sank a little—knowing he'd drive up at eight to pick her up, but she'd already be gone. She wrote a note for him and left it in the doorframe of her cabin. *Please, dear God, let him find it. And please, windy night, don't blow it away.*

Walking at a good clip, she made it to Mrs. Cunningham's

in time to have a light snack with Mrs. Stallworth. Then later with Jack? Their amazing dinner, together and alone.

"You have everything? Your notes? Your thoughts? Your peace of mind? Know what you're going to say to those folks?"

"If I don't know by now, it's too late to figure it out."

"I'm proud of you." Mrs. Stallworth stepped closer and looked Annalee over, moving a curl back from her face. "Although I have a funny feeling about tonight."

"You and your funny feelings."

"Still, if things don't feel right—"

"I know! Mr. C. told me already. Get out of there."

Mrs. Cunningham came into the kitchen then with her boudoir kit—a newly washed comb and brush, hairpins, and lipstick among the items.

"No lipstick!" Mrs. Stallworth wouldn't hear of it.

"Goodness, lipstick won't hurt anything," Mrs. Cunningham said. "Keep it in your purse."

"Maybe just a little," Annalee said, relaxing her lips, letting Mrs. Cunningham dab on a touch. She was aware of being pulled in two ways. She longed to look lovely tonight for Jack . . . *if I can find him.* Mean ol' Mrs. Mason wasn't answering her phone so Annalee could update her message for Jack. But to save her own hide, Annalee had to stay focused on her speaking event to ferret out at least one clue about Jeffrey Mann's awful death.

"How about a little jewelry?" Mrs. Cunningham asked. "My pair of small earrings?"

"Jewelry?" Annalee thought about the jasper necklace, still wrapped in brown paper, jammed in the bottom of her purse. It would go perfectly with her dress, a slim sheath with a sheer illusion bodice, open sleeves, and a rather scandalous low back. Annalee was surprised Mrs. Stallworth had approved, but she was glad for it. She adored the lovely dress and hoped Jack would, too.

"Extra sparkle, too?"

Well, the jasper necklace might draw a suspect to her. But the piece was Rebecca Mann's late mother's. Out of respect, she wouldn't exploit it that way. "No extra sparkle."

"Now then, your hair." Mrs. Cunningham was chatting about hairstyles. Holding a brush, her hands in Annalee's hair, she prepared to dive in.

"Nothing fancy," Annalee said. "And can you make it quick, if you don't mind? I need to get going."

"No rush. Mr. Cunningham will drop you off in the taxi."

"He doesn't have to—"

"Hush! We're not letting you walk all the way downtown in the dark all dressed up."

"You two spoil me."

"Well . . ." Mrs. Cunningham left it at that.

Mrs. Stallworth did the same. Both women were childless and Annalee had become like the daughter they both shared. To her, in turn, they were like the mother she'd never known—all of it too complicated to discuss, especially tonight.

"Well . . . ," Mrs. Stallworth finally said. "As if spoiling is a bad thing—on occasion, from time to time, at least."

"Well . . . right," Mrs. Cunningham added but ended the topic there.

The hairdo didn't take long. Mrs. Cunningham was good with a brush. Smoothing down Annalee's jumble of curls, she added a black velvet headband and hairpins to hold the look in place. She handed Annalee a small mirror.

"Oh, my goodness." Annalee patted her curls. "I love this."
Jack will, too.

"And here's Mr. Cunningham," Mrs. Stallworth said.

"Right on time."

"Is the man ever late?"

"Never." Mrs. Cunningham winked at her husband.

He laughed. "Your carriage awaits."

And Annalee was off.

But to do what? Find a killer? Pick up a clue? *Dear Jesus in heaven, please don't let me make a fool of myself tonight.* She gazed into the dark. *And please let me find Jack. Or let him find me.*

"Here you are." Mr. Cunningham slowed the taxi in heavy traffic and stopped in front of First Denver National Bank. He looked out at the impressive white marble facade. "You pickin' high cotton tonight, little bit. Break a leg."

She thanked him for the ride, reminded him to be careful, too. Then she scooted out of the cab but turned back. "If you see Reverend Blake out tonight, would you please ask him to wait for me at the Rialto?"

"Nine o'clock show?"

"That's right. I'll wait by the ticket counter."

"Got it. Now you be careful tonight!" Mr. Cunningham saluted her and drove off.

Looking up at the bank building, Annalee let her nerves rattle around a bit but finally told her pounding heart to *settle down.*

She had nothing to fear, she told herself. *I'm just a small cog in the wheel of a busy, big world.* No matter her speech, that world would keep turning.

The streets, in fact, were bustling. Not a surprise. Friday

nights in Denver were electric. After a long workweek, people were hot to trot, as Mrs. Stallworth put it—eager to come downtown, hit the streets, let their hair down, enjoy a night on the town.

Street vendors were selling roasted peanuts, buttered popcorn, candy, hot chocolate. Newsboys were hawking papers on every corner. "Extra! Extra!"

"Newspaper, lady?"

"Not tonight, thanks."

Walking across a courtyard to the bank's massive front doors, Annalee felt grateful to see only a few people queuing up in a line outside.

Maybe her audience would be small. *I hope.*

Like earlier today, some whispered behind their hands when she walked up. She just said hello, although not a single person replied in kind. *Tough crowd.* But she told herself not to worry. *I'm here to sniff out information. Not to win speaker of the year.*

At the front door, a gangly police officer in uniform and cap watched her, giving her a stone face, as she approached.

"I'm Annalee Spain," she announced herself.

The officer didn't reply. Ignoring her, he turned to answer a question from a woman in the line. The two chatted a moment before he stepped back to the door.

"Excuse me. Do you have my name?" Annalee knew this drill. The cop wouldn't be satisfied until he made her feel like a nobody. *But I don't even care,* she thought. She had only one thing on her mind—getting through her silly speech, securing a clue or two, and making it to the Rialto by nine o'clock. *To see my man. Thank you very much.*

She turned toward the door and grabbed the handle.

"Hey! You can't go in there."

She ignored him and pulled on the door.

"Hands off!" the cop shouted, grabbing for her arm, pulling hard. "Get back, I said—"

"Beg your pardon!" She yanked her arm away.

"What's the problem here?" A second officer—older, skinny, gruff-looking—rushed up from another end of the courtyard. "What's this, Duncan?"

"Troublemaker, sir. She's trying to—"

The second cop ignored that, glared at Annalee. "You the Spain woman?"

"Annalee Spain."

"She's on the program." He pointed at the door. "In here. Take the lift to the third floor."

"That's wrong. It's the second floor."

He glared. "Got changed. Last minute. Floor three." He pointed at the door again. "In here."

She waited for the second officer to open the door for her, but of course he didn't. So she pushed past the other cop and pulled it open. Heavy and imposing, it was a bank door, after all, so it took some effort.

Still, she stepped bravely into the lobby, straightened her coat, tried to settle her mind, look composed, and not worry about the last-minute change in location—floor three, not two—while stifling her anger at the two ornery cops. *Just walk to the elevator and get in the lift.*

But then she looked up.

Holy cow.

The First Denver bank lobby.

Oh, my goodness.

She smiled to herself with awe, taking it all in—the soaring elegance, the glowing beauty. It was a marble-and-glass show-piece. Three stories high with a catwalk along a second floor, accessed by a double-wide marble staircase—the entire space was lit for the evening by a trio of massive, dimmed, matching glass-crystal chandeliers. The elaborately carved lobby emoted grandeur but gravity, style but security. For anybody with more than a penny to save, this was a place to bring your hard-earned bounty.

Annalee walked toward the staircase and gazed up, longing to scoot behind the red-velvet rope blocking it off and ascend the stairs—like a fairy-tale Cinderella. Instead, with regret, she saw the Elevator sign and followed its arrow to a narrow corridor behind the staircase, leading to another Elevator sign with an arrow, pointing down a poorly lit hallway to the back of the building and finally a two-person lift.

She took in a breath. She'd ridden on a few elevators before, including an empty one marked "whites only"—just to defy the awful rule—but never alone. Where was the operator?

In fact, where was anybody?

It was almost eight, probably, and here she was, debating whether to step inside a dingy, cramped lift, close the caged door, figure out how to work the controls and ride up to floor three. Where were the stairs in this part of the building? But would a narrow, dark staircase feel any safer?

Something doesn't feel right, Mrs. Stallworth.

Steadying her nervous hand, she pushed the Up button and waited for the elevator to descend to the first floor. And she waited. And waited. And *waited.* After what seemed far too long, she could hear the elevator shudder and groan and squeal its way as slow as Grandma's molasses onto the first floor. *Finally.* Annalee found the lever to open the outer door, pulled back the caged gate, and peeked inside. Warm, cramped, stuffy air met her—as if the lift hadn't been used for weeks. One tiny bulb flickered weak light.

Twisting her mouth, she stepped inside. *Well, here goes nothing.*

Turning to face the door, she reached for the big control handle, ready to push it forward, bracing to feel the elevator jump into action. But she stopped. Noticing.

The mind did that, she knew, when something wasn't right because it needed to be seen for wrong. So here was something to see across the hallway—a crumpled paper in a tiny metal waste can pushed into a corner. *Not my business,* she told herself. *I'm running late.* But she couldn't stop looking at it.

Frowning, she exited the narrow elevator and moved to the waste can, picking up the crumpled paper, not surprised to see what it said: *This Elevator OUT OF ORDER.* A handwritten sign, written in red ink.

She could see *right here* what happened. She'd been directed, on purpose, to this wreck of a lift. *Somebody's got my number,* she warned herself, *and wants me out of the way.* But they didn't count on what she knew about herself.

After a tough childhood with a father who too often failed her, and the pain of a world that seemed to often hate who she was—Black and young—she was too stubborn now to back off. She'd find a clue tonight no matter what it took—and she wasn't going to jail for it either. Surely not for killing Jeffrey Mann, whose killer was still on the loose.

She grabbed the waste can and placed it beside the elevator

door, keeping it from closing, then shoved the warning sign inside the caged gate. It could be seen from that angle, warning away others from using the elevator.

Wiping her hands on her borrowed coat, she marched back toward the lobby, hearing people talking and laughing, sounding casual and Friday night happy. The two policemen were letting people inside, directing them up the wide marble staircase—no longer blocked by the red-velvet rope.

The older cop, seeing her, pursed his lips, gave her a sneer, and turned his back.

She ignored him. But looking back, she whispered a sort of prayer for him—*Fix him, Lord*—then joined the crowd ascending the stairs. With each step, she knew she could be walking into another trap. To calm herself, therefore, she hummed— under her breath—some old hymn she'd heard Mount Moriah's choir sing last Sunday. *"Come, we that love the Lord . . . We're marching upward to Zion."*

Good song actually.

At the second-floor landing, she moved with the crowd as folks turned toward double doors off a long marble corridor, opening to an oversize meeting room. But a well-dressed, middle-aged woman wearing a purple feathered cloche hat rushed up.

"Annalee!"

"Annalee Spain. That's me, yes." She was glad to see somebody glad to see her.

"You're here! Thank goodness! Come this way. Let's get out of this mess. So many people. We had no idea!" She linked her arm into Annalee's, moved them through the crush. "Excuse me!" the woman said. "Coming through! Pardon me!"

"Are you with the ladies' club?" Annalee felt she wanted a name, an introduction.

"Oh, my word! I forgot my name badge. I'm Violet. Violet Vaughn. Mr. Ames told me to watch out for you. I'm program chair. But we weren't expecting this." She gestured toward the crowd. "Last-minute change. We'll be in the Mile High Room—"

"Not the boardroom?"

"Nope, in the bank's big meeting room—the auditorium actually. You're a hot ticket." Violet rushed Annalee through the double doors, past row after row of cushioned folding chairs and onto an elevated podium. She pointed to a large settee, showing Annalee where to sit. "I'll introduce you after announcements. Then the floor is yours. Everyone's so excited—although you're probably not. After what happened."

"What happened?" Annalee's stomach tightened.

Violet's eyes got big. She cocked her hat, looked out at the gathering audience. "Oh, my word!"

Annalee followed her eyes. "What's the matter?" She wanted Violet, for all her friendliness, to stop her chattering. But she kept at it.

"You didn't see the evening newspapers? The extras?"

"I didn't have time. Please, ma'am, can you explain—?"

"That woman who killed your father. They let her out of jail a few days ago—"

"Let her out?"

"Early this week. But the judge waited to announce it till today—to give her time to get settled."

"*Settled?*"

"I thought you knew!"

"How would I know?"

"Oh, my goodness!"

"What's the matter now?"

"She's here tonight. Right over there. Sitting in the front row." Violet gripped Annalee's arm, then gave Annalee a shocked look with a hard whisper.

"It's Elizabeth Castle!"

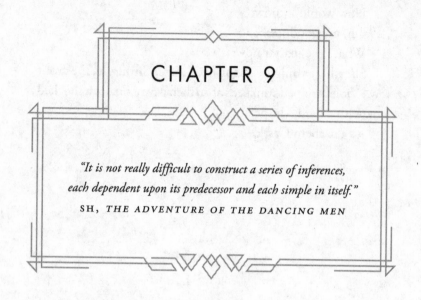

CHAPTER 9

"It is not really difficult to construct a series of inferences,
each dependent upon its predecessor and each simple in itself."
SH, *THE ADVENTURE OF THE DANCING MEN*

THERE, INDEED, SHE WAS. Elizabeth Castle. Front row center.
Annalee could barely breathe at the sight of her. The woman
who murdered her father was seated in the glittering, sprawling room like Klan royalty, wearing her all-white getup—white
mink, white beaded cloche hat, white silky dress with a million long strands of white pearls adorning its front, plus white
silky hose, white T-strap pumps, and white diamonds on wrists
and ears.

She was a sparkly, defiant, triumphant, magnificent, royal-
looking conqueror.

She was bested, however, by her seatmate. On Elizabeth's left
sat the top dog of Denver's Klan, a "Grand Dragon" something

or other—his face familiar from a thousand newspaper articles either boosting or blaming him.

Annalee didn't blink, just let her eyes pass right over him, seeing on Elizabeth's right side her regal mother, garbed head to toe in dark red. Annalee recognized the older woman from her last case, when she'd worked undercover as a maid in the Castle household.

On Elizabeth's right, down two seats sat her uncle, Agent Robert Ames—tonight looking as his family knew him, as the red-faced, often-drunk Lemonade Hank. He looked three sheets to the wind, his eyes half-open and drowsy.

Annalee gave him a questioning glance, but he didn't respond.

Next to Ames sat the burly policeman—Officer Luther—wearing a suit. Not in uniform. He avoided Annalee's glance, too.

Elizabeth didn't deign to look her way either. She was greeting well-wishers, many rushing over to congratulate her, it appeared, on getting let out of prison. Not bothering to shake the dozens of hands thrust her way, Elizabeth put forward a satisfied smile, nodding her acknowledgments as some pointed to the stage at Annalee, some cutting their eyes at her.

And what an evening this is turning out to be.

"Why was she released?" Annalee whispered to a still stunned-looking Violet.

"A judge said insufficient evidence—or something like that. You know these crooked judges. I didn't have time to read all the news. Oh, my word! This is not what we'd planned. Are you going to be all right?"

Annalee heard the question. She thought of everything

wrong that had already happened so far this evening—not to mention so far in her life—and made her choice.

"I'll be just fine," she said, defying how she felt—shocked, furious, but somehow not surprised. Elizabeth had murdered her father and an innocent little baby—left her in the cold to die to protect her son from being connected to the child's colored mother.

Annalee pulled off her thrift store coat and set it down on the settee next to her pocketbook. Nice and easy. She took her seat, grateful to feel neat, groomed, and professional-looking, she hoped, in her pretty blue dress. No jewelry.

She looked out at the crowd as Violet stepped to the podium and delivered a chatty welcome. A couple hundred people in the fancy room trained their eyes on the stage. Annalee ran her eyes across the rows, glancing at faces, looking for Rebecca Mann but not surprised by her absence, ignoring Elizabeth Castle altogether. *I'm here to sniff out another murderer.* Or to hear something that would help find him. Or her.

Poor Jeffrey Mann. She didn't know what game Robert Ames was playing, but she'd make the most of the evening in one way or another.

As she heard Violet introducing her—"a child of Denver, college graduate, making her community proud," blah, blah, blah—Annalee was preparing to stand when she noticed a familiar, friendly face. Mrs. Flora Quinlan from the Denver Public Library sat three rows back, one seat from the aisle.

Annalee nodded at her. Mrs. Quinlan smiled, set her jaw, and winked. Annalee could read her eyes. *"Knock 'em dead, young lady."* Annalee smiled, hiking a brow when she saw Mrs. Quinlan was seated next to her male rescuer—the tall man,

Hugh Smith, who'd left the maps wall to save her from Rebecca Mann's disruptive father. *"Take your leave!"*

Now that tall man was sitting—*a bit close, actually, Mrs. Stallworth*—in the aisle seat next to Mrs. Quinlan. The two of them looked downright cozy, which made Annalee happy for Mrs. Quinlan—when she should be feeling terrified for herself.

"And now, without further ado, Professor Annalee Spain!"

No applause. A lot of whispering, muffled laughing, and shifting in chairs met Annalee instead.

She stood. *Let me get this over with.* She nodded at Violet, who reached out and gave her a quick surprise hug. Violet whispered, "The bank president wants to talk to you afterward."

"Mr. Wallace?"

"Yes, do you know him?"

Annalee shook her head, thanked her for the introduction.

At the podium, she stood tall. Felt a smile growing on her face. "Any detectives in the house tonight?"

The crowd shuffled. Nobody answered.

"That's a serious question for you. Any detectives in the house? Or anyone who'd like to be a detective?"

At that, a few reluctant hands went up, prompting some chuckles.

Annalee gave a grin to those with upraised hands. "C'mon, there have to be more than that. You've all read Sherlock Holmes—at least I have. You've seen detective stories at the pictures. And only three people here have even given a thought to solving a crime? Let me ask again—and let's agree to be honest tonight—how many people have dreamed of being a detective? A real detective?"

Now dozens of people raised their hands.

"Good for you! Honest detectives! Okay, another question. *Why* do you want to be a detective?"

She pointed to a man in the front row. "You, sir. What's your reason for wanting to solve crime? Why'd you like that job?"

And she was off and running. Teaching, not speaking. She felt comfortable and in charge—as if she were in a classroom at the college where she'd prayed like crazy to learn how to teach reluctant people. Just relate to them. Affirm them. Help them understand they were as smart as the instructor—maybe more so, about some things, anyway.

So just like a student, the man stood to answer her question.

"Speak louder!" she reminded him but smiled. "They want to hear you in the back. I do, too."

Given the chance to speak to a roomful of captive people, the man talked on and on, as Annalee expected. Some even applauded him before he sat down. So on she went, giving several more people a chance to speak, including a man with a gift of gab and humor who answered every question with a funny retort.

Before long, folks were laughing, enjoying themselves. Annalee looked over at Mrs. Quinlan, who gave her a thumbs-up. So Annalee took a risk.

"So, my dear Dr. Watsons, why'd you come tonight? What did—?"

"A minstrel! I'm here to see a minstrel!" a man near the back yelled out.

Annalee wasn't surprised. She'd expected precisely that. "You expected minstrel tonight?"

"Yeah! A minstrel detective. Start the show!"

The room grew unsettled, people whispering behind their

hands. She'd never been to a minstrel show—with the black-faced performers and nonstop ridicule of Negro life—but she knew such shows were popular all over the country, including in Colorado. Churches, clubs, drama societies, schools, all manner of groups hosted minstrel troupes, or put on their own minstrel shows, somewhere almost every weekend. Big towns and small.

"Do you laugh at the shows?" she asked the audience.

The room was quiet. Then another man growled, "Yeah. Start the show! Give us your dialect! Talk like a Negro!"

The room erupted. Some people applauding, others groaning—telling the man to shut up.

Violet jumped up from the settee, raised her hands, trying to quiet the crowd, but Annalee gestured for her to sit back down, letting her know she wasn't rattled.

"If you'd like, I can tell you a little something—a brief aside—about minstrel shows. Starting with the word *minstrel*. Does anybody know what that word means?"

She almost laughed to herself, thinking about Mrs. Stallworth, who would've rolled her eyes. But with this crowd, she didn't wait for an answer.

"It comes from the Late Latin *ministeriālis*, which means a household officer or a servant—and that comes from the Latin word *ministerium*, which means ministry."

The room was stone silent.

"Ironic, isn't it, Mrs. Quinlan?" She nodded to the librarian, who nodded back. "A show that makes some people laugh has somehow lost its way. Or perhaps it didn't, because the root of both those words means to reduce—or minimize. But here's the odd thing, my friends—"

"You're not my friend!" The man in the back still stood. Others around him shouted at him to sit down. Annalee ignored his outburst, kept reflecting and sharing—inviting the crowd to reflect with her.

"The root for *minstrel* is the same for the word *mystery*. And that, of course, is what detectives solve."

The crowd seemed almost breathless, not sure how to react. They were in her hands now, and most seemed to know it—but should they be? Because controlling the audience wasn't her concern anyway. She wanted to finish up here, talk to Mr. Wallace, and then go find Jack. But she knew she needed to finish right.

"So, funny thing about mysteries. They always look impossible to solve. But if you keep talking to the right people and asking the right questions and knocking on the right doors, one will open. Then you'll see the light—which is what we're all looking for in life, right? We're looking for our light. For our truth." She shrugged. "So don't stop looking. Like a detective, if you want truth in your life, never stop searching for it. Truth *wants* to be found."

She glanced a moment at Elizabeth Castle. "Some try to hide truth, to dress up lies as what's real."

Elizabeth gave her a look that at first seemed vicious, but finally she looked away, almost sad.

Annalee shifted her gaze, focusing again on the audience and on what she was saying. "But your truth can't be hidden, not forever." She shrugged again. "In life, in fact, we're all truth detectives. I am. You are. The person sitting next to you is. Say, 'Hello, detective!'" Many in the audience chuckled, glancing at their seatmates, mumbling hello.

"Keep hunting for your truth. That's what real detectives do. They get up every morning and take on another new mystery. As you solve it, you're serving others, ministering to them." She let her eyes scour the room. "Someone here tonight may even know something that solves a crime. Maybe even a murder. If so, maybe you'll tell me. Share the motive—or reveal a lie." The room grew quiet again.

"But first? Start looking for your own truth. And I promise you this, Dr. Watson: You'll find it."

She looked at Mrs. Quinlan, who was . . . crying?

She looked at Agent Ames, whose face was a blank slate.

She glanced again at Elizabeth Castle, whom she expected to be seething—her jaw set rigid, her eyes flashing. Instead, Elizabeth's face looked pained and confused. Annalee didn't know what that meant, but she couldn't worry over the woman. Not now. Instead, she looked back at the crowd. They knew, as she did, that she hadn't spoken that long, but she'd said enough. Of that, she felt certain. She spoke one last thing.

"You've been a great audience. You're good people. Most of us are. Thank you and good night."

Annalee walked to the settee, thanked Violet, and sat down.

The man who'd made everyone laugh stood up first—clapping. Others around him stood and started clapping, too. Soon others in the room were on their feet. Against all odds then, it seemed the entire room, except for a few, was applauding her. Everyone standing.

Annalee stood in return and made a modest bow of thanks before the crowd.

Violet rushed to the podium, hands outreached to the audience. "Thank you! Thank you!" She looked relieved. Grateful, too. "Thank you for coming! Good night, everyone! Good night!"

She'd turned to thank Annalee, who was picking up her secondhand coat, when the stage was suddenly swarming with people. In the same moment, Annalee noticed Elizabeth Castle grab her mink and gesture angrily at her mother and the Klan dragon for them to exit. Agent Ames followed them. But a crowd of folks now blocked Annalee's view.

"Professor Spain! Professor Spain! Miss Spain!"

People were extending their hands, shaking Annalee's, waving notes at her, thanking her for her talk, asking her more questions—making her look, see, and hear them. In that way, her eyes locked suddenly on a face she hadn't expected in this crowd. A young Black woman—a tiny little thing, whose big brown eyes showed desperation, or maybe it was fear—pushed a note into Annalee's hand. She turned just as quickly to leave.

"Wait!" Annalee called after her.

But without a word, the young woman melted into the crowd.

A knot of other folks, meantime, were requesting Annalee's calling card. She managed to smile at them all, thinking of kind Mr. Robinson as she passed out her fresh card with its simple message. *Annalee Spain—Main 4124.* That was the Cunninghams' phone number. She hoped Mrs. Cunningham wouldn't mind any extra calls.

Mr. Simon Wallace, president of First Denver National, didn't look the part. Dressed in an ordinary brown suit, plain white shirt, and lackluster tie, he could've been one of his clerks or tellers. Maybe that was the point. With his sad suit and sadder eyes, nobody would've ever mistaken him for the president of one of the largest banks in the Rocky Mountain West.

He introduced himself, thanked her for coming to his bank. Then he had a question:

"Do you have a minute, Miss Spain?" His slightly accented voice—excellent English and lightly Spanish-sounding, or maybe Portuguese?—sounded as sincere and humble as his face appeared.

She returned his smile, curious to know what he wanted, even if she couldn't help looking past his shoulder at a clock on the Mile High Room wall. It was 8:40.

Wallace saw her checking the time. "This won't take long. Do you have an appointment?"

"It's okay, but I'm meeting someone at the Rialto at nine."

"My driver can take you."

She hiked a brow.

"He won't object. But first, may I have a minute with you in my office? My private secretary, Miss Gray, is there now."

Annalee followed him across the marble hall, their footsteps echoing, as she still accepted thanks from a few stragglers leaving the event.

Violet pressed an envelope in her hand. "Just a small thank-you."

Annalee thanked her, feeling relieved, indeed, that the speech was over. *But stay alert.* She was still on the job. Mr. Wallace was Rebecca Mann's uncle. *Pay attention.*

"I'll cut to the chase, as they say," Wallace told her. He'd brought her to a massive corner office overlooking Denver's busy downtown streets, but thick windows muffled the sound. Artwork probably costing a pretty penny covered the walls. An impressive, angular sculpture adorned a credenza. His secretary—a slim, preoccupied woman with hair determined to go gray—sat at a much smaller desk across the room, bent over paperwork, her back to both of them.

Wallace offered Annalee a seat opposite his gigantic desk and then sat down in his imposing leather chair. He apologized for the fancy digs. "Big customers expect me to have an office like this. Big, fancy desk and all. In the daytime, I can show them the mountains, brag about the view, show off the paintings. It's a beautiful space. Same with the marble lobby. But it's all a show."

Annalee listened, agreeing, but he didn't bring her in here to talk about his big desk, marble lobby, fancy artwork, and mountain view. "Can I help you with something, Mr. Wallace?"

"I have a niece—"

"Rebecca Mann."

Wallace showed surprise. "You already know?"

"Well, I've met her."

"Then you know her husband, sadly, was killed this week."

"Yes, Jeffrey Mann. Police are blaming a break-in."

"Nobody believes that. Least of all me. That's why I wanted to talk to you. About investigating. What would you say to looking into it?"

"I . . ."

"I would pay you well."

"Can I ask first about Rebecca's father?"

Wallace leaned back in his kingly chair, looking totally

dwarfed by it. He made a face, sighed deeply. His secretary coughed discreetly.

"My only brother. You know him, too?"

"Well, I've seen him."

"He's my biggest heartache. I've done well in life. My brother, Uri, hasn't. When we came to this country as young men, we each had a small stake from our late mother. He chased the silver boom, crawling through mines, dreaming of big strikes. I went into mercantile, selling supplies to the miners and mining companies. When the boom crashed, Uri was flat broke, strangling in debt. I'd made enough to go into banking. Uri has just kept struggling, refusing my offers to pay his debts and take him on here. But for some reason, he resents me. He wants nothing to do with me."

"And Rebecca?"

"Rebecca's like a daughter to me—or that's what I'd like. My wife died of illness soon after I moved here. Our only daughter, Marie, died a few years later in . . . in an accident."

"I'm so sorry."

Wallace nodded, looking away for a moment. "Afterward, I asked Uri if I could support Rebecca—pay for her schooling, travel, a wedding, buy her and Jeffrey a nice home. But Uri put his foot down. Poor Rebecca barely has a dime to her name. Now, with Jeffrey gone, I offered again to help. Even to pay for an investigator, not to mention cover Jeffrey's funeral. But Uri refuses. 'I'll find out what happened myself! I'll bury him myself!' Everything he touches seems to fail. All he owns are a few square feet of worthless property up near Telluride."

"Telluride—"

"At this point, I just want to help Rebecca. She's in my will, of course, but I'd have to die for her to inherit. Uri, too. But for now, it would give her peace to learn what happened to her husband. Peace for all of us."

Annalee shifted in her chair. *Lord, our families.* Did any family, rich or poor, not have drama, trials, and troubles?

"I'd like to help you, Mr. Wallace. But you don't have to pay me. I'm already researching Jeffrey's death for a private agency."

Wallace's secretary coughed again softly.

"I'm sorry I can't reveal any more. When I can, I'll let you know."

Annalee was desperate to leave to find Jack, but Wallace's despair stopped her from rushing off cold. Besides, he'd know things.

"Just one question—do you know why anyone would want to kill a barnstormer like Jeffrey? Anyone at the airfield where he was employed?"

"It's a small field. The rather modest one out east. He managed the hangar there. Recently they let him barnstorm. As for a killer? No idea whatsoever." Wallace paused. "He wasn't religious." He shrugged. "Maybe that's something. But who knows these days?"

Wallace didn't mention his ghost company, of course, and Annalee didn't ask. Not the time. Besides, who wanted to debate tonight about the Klan? Or double-crossing schemes. One thing at a time.

She stood, and Wallace stood, too. They exchanged business cards, making Annalee hold her breath humbly. Who would imagine? *Me exchanging cards with the president of First Denver National Bank.* His private phone number was on it, too.

Wallace asked his secretary to call the driver. "I trust him implicitly. But Miss Gray will ride with you to the Rialto, see you safely there."

"Sir, I'm finishing your letters—" the secretary started to object, her voice barely a whisper.

"I'll sign them later." Wallace wasn't moved. "Please get your coat."

The prim secretary stood and took a long black chesterfield off an elaborately carved mahogany coat stand—oversize and weighing probably a ton, but she moved it back in its corner as if it weighed nothing, pursing her lips, not looking eager to ride even half a foot with Annalee, let alone a few blocks to the Rialto, but she appeared obligated to obey.

As the woman donned her coat, Annalee blinked hard, noticing a typewriter sitting on the secretary's desk. An Olivetti? Remington? Underwood? Annalee glanced away, not wanting to appear too interested. Besides, as she could see, the typewriter was a Royal—its brand name sprawled in large gold letters above the machine's carriage, the name visible across the room.

Annalee donned her coat, too.

"You've been kind, Mr. Wallace." She grabbed her purse, eager to go. "If I can help you, I will."

"You already have." Mr. Wallace shook her hand. "You're a good listener."

The Rialto was only six blocks away, but to Annalee, the short ride seemed to take forever. She felt every inch of every block in the depth of her soul. *Please let Jack be there.* She had so much to tell him. Even more, she longed to see him. To watch his eyes light up at her arrival. To make his brow hike at her pretty hairdo, pink lipstick, and lovely blue dress. To feel his arms holding her too close, but not minding.

Mercy, such thoughts. *But I miss him.* She could barely wait for the driver to stop the car. She thanked gloomy Miss Gray—the silent, discreet, see-no-evil, hear-no-evil, speak-no-evil private secretary of Simon Wallace—who barely nodded her a goodbye, never actually speaking to her. No wonder Wallace trusted her. The woman was a closed book. Or seemed to be. *So goodbye and good night, Miss Gray.*

On the street, a thick crowd was pressing up at the Rialto ticket counter. Some made comments as Annalee exited Wallace's enormous black Cadillac limo, helped out by hand by Wallace's uniformed white chauffeur. But she couldn't fret. *Where's Jack?*

The crowd didn't part, and Annalee had to wait her turn at the ticket counter.

"How many?" The ticket taker saw her and stopped.

"I'm not buying. But have you seen Reverend Blake? The colored pastor? We were supposed to meet here tonight. He said you'd know him."

Counting a stack of bills, the ticket taker gave her a look. "Yeah, I know him. Jack Blake. Haven't seen him tonight."

"Are you sure?"

"How many?" He looked around her shoulder. The next people in line were anxious to pay.

Annalee let that couple move ahead, buy their tickets. "Did he come to the earlier show?"

"Nope. Ain't seen him."

"Can I give you my card if he comes through? Tell him I'll meet him at the Rossonian?"

"Ain't running no message center, lady. I'm selling tickets here. Step aside."

And how quickly things changed. One minute Annalee was sitting in the president's corner office at First Denver National, beaming after a standing ovation in the bank's fancy Mile High Room. Now she stood on a sidewalk outside the Rialto picture show, getting ignored by the indifferent ticket taker, begging him to pass along a message to the man who, for all she knew, might be angry at her for breaking their Friday night date.

She moved aside.

It was ten after nine and couples were rushing to buy their tickets and get seated before the main feature rolled. They wore that Friday evening glow, many arm in arm, some sneaking kisses and "hugged up," as Mrs. Stallworth would put it. Their faces gleamed in the bright marquee lights of Theater Row, as that downtown section of Curtis Street was called.

Parked cars lined both sides, the street filled with moving traffic, the electric streetcars in two center lanes all lit up brightly for the evening, jammed with people.

I should be here with Jack, Annalee told herself. But maybe that was just a fantasy, something she'd imagined could happen because she wanted it so bad. Besides, they weren't even allowed inside the main doors of the Theater Row houses like white couples. After buying their tickets, they'd have to walk to the back alley, up rickety, steep wooden stairs to the warped door of the crow's nest, and sit like exiles in the back rows of the balcony.

Annalee waited another fifteen minutes or so, watching the ticket line dwindle. She started to ask the ticket taker one more time for help. But he was preoccupied with counting up bills and change, reckoning receipts, and straightening his workstation. Seeing no more customers, he pulled the money pass-through closed, clicked off a small light over his head, and locked up his cage. With a metal money box under his arm, he headed inside the theater, leaving Annalee standing alone outside.

She had nothing else to do but leave.

But I'm not happy about this, she told herself. Being alone was a kick in the gut. Eddie wasn't even here, although she'd told him to stay away tonight. But now, if she were honest, she wished he'd disobeyed and shown up.

Turning alone, she headed toward Five Points. Gave herself a pep talk. *I'm Annalee Spain, detective.* So the night wouldn't end without her digging up an answer about Jack. He didn't just disappear. *So here I go.* She set off walking.

But with every step, she knew there was more to it. *Something doesn't feel right, Mrs. Stallworth.* Doubt nagged her. Not a good sign. But if it must, she hoped this night's new worry would show her why.

CHAPTER 10

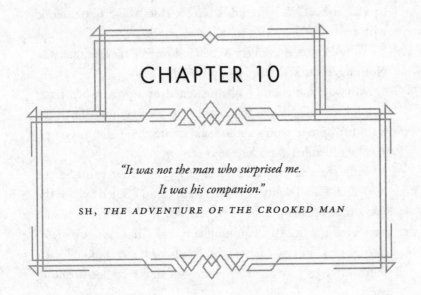

"It was not the man who surprised me.
It was his companion."

SH, *THE ADVENTURE OF THE CROOKED MAN*

IT WAS A COLD, STUPID WALK. Annalee didn't hurry because she wasn't sure at first where to go. Head back to the Cunninghams'? Back to her cabin? Or to the Rossonian Lounge? She'd never been there by herself and didn't relish walking into a nightclub alone. Not even for Jack.

Where in the heck was he? Why wasn't he out and about, searching all over town for her, like he'd done the night she'd arrived in Denver last December on a train from Chicago? Denver's downtown wasn't that big. If he was even half looking, they'd run into each other.

Instead, she was dragging down a nearly dark street alone, knowing—on one hand—she'd made decent progress in starting to find answers about Jeffrey Mann's murder. She knew who he was at least. Yet she didn't have a clue where things stood with *my man.*

Why'd she ever even try to be "in love"? Whatever that was. Nothing in life was more complicated.

Anyway, somebody had threatened in a poison-pen letter to kill them all. Maybe that would solve everything. Then she wouldn't have to worry about Jack, or anything else, anymore.

She rolled her eyes. *Stop your pitying.*

Still, she was bothered by the evening's sour turn. So she turned on East Twenty-Seventh Avenue and headed toward the Welton Street nightclub. Mrs. Stallworth, if she knew, would have a natural fit. Mrs. Cunningham, too. *"You went to a night-club? Alone?"* But no matter what happened, she could tell Jack she'd looked everywhere for him—to make up for breaking their date.

So here I go, she told herself, finally reaching Welton Street and seeing, a block away, the dimmed outside lights of the Rossonian. The place would be filling up, although the action didn't peak apparently, on a weekend night, until almost midnight.

If a famous Negro act was in town, they'd finish up their performance at some fancy downtown hotel. Then they'd head for the Rossonian to unwind, order a late supper from the restaurant, and set up in the lounge to play their music, partying with the locals until all hours. Some weekends, as she knew, the place didn't shut down until almost dawn.

But not for her.

She'd peek inside, look for Jack, and if he wasn't there, head for home. She couldn't ask more of herself. Not tonight. After all, she'd given a speech. *And I'm solving a murder.*

Approaching the nightclub, however, she saw a bigger crowd than she'd expected. Outside the club doors, people dressed in their Friday night best were socializing, calling to each other, some "hugged up" too, enjoying end-of-week fun. It was a noisy crowd, gleeful and exuberant. The entire street was abuzz, in fact. Lots of traffic. Cars honking. Friends hanging out of car windows, waving each other down.

Annalee wasn't comfortable walking into the revelry by herself. But she wouldn't have to now because, as a car pulled off, a navy-blue Buick touring car pulled into an open space on the curb, and her heart leaped. *Jack.*

He swung open his car door and Annalee, from half a block away and across the street, called his name. "Jack!"

Her eyes tingled. He looked that wonderful to her—wearing his pressed dark suit, his preacher collar, his lovely face freshly shaved, hair neatly brushed, shoes shined. Carrying his small Bible—into a nightclub of all places. She couldn't help herself. "Jack!"

But he didn't hear her. He was rushing to his passenger door and opening it and helping out his passenger, and *she* was . . . *No, God.* So beautiful. And lovely. Smiling up at Jack. Pretty brown-skinned girl.

Jack put his arm around the young woman's shoulders, headed into the crowd toward the Rossonian's front door.

"Jack." Annalee barely whispered his name. So he couldn't have heard her voice. But for some reason, he turned back. He looked across the busy street. He saw her. She was standing on the sidewalk, cars whizzing past, looking right at him, her stupid used coat hanging open, new blue dress peeking out. He whispered something to the young woman, who then stood off to the side.

Jack ran across the street, dodging traffic, rushing up to her. "Annalee!" He stuffed his Bible in a pocket, scooped her into his arms. "*Thank God.* I'm so glad to see you!" He pressed her close, sighing into her ear.

She didn't react because . . . *I don't know what to say.*

He settled her on the sidewalk, pulled her to him again. "Goodness, you're freezing."

She blinked a thousand times, trying to speak. But again, *I really don't know what to say.*

"C'mon inside." Jack gestured across the street and then he reached for her hands. He rubbed them between his own for a moment. "I want you to meet someone." He squinted at her. "Why are you so cold?"

"Did you get my message?" Her voice was a whisper, but she needed to know.

"Mrs. Mason left a note. I couldn't make heads or tails of it. Said something about you had to cancel."

"No, my message for you on my door at the cabin. I wrote your name on it."

"I didn't go to your place. Mrs. Mason's note said—"

"I thought you were heading straight to my place—"

"I needed a clean white shirt . . . Listen, let's not argue tonight. I had a great two days in Dearfield. All I could think about was you and now here you are and—" He stepped back. "And look at you." He slipped open her coat. "*Man alive, Annalee.* Is that a new dress?" He looked her over, searched her face. "Wow. I feel like I've waited all week to see you."

He reached for her again, but she stood there stone-still, confused and uncertain and, yes, cold as all get-out. *Mercy, why is everything with Jack, well, so complicated?*

"We've had a mix-up," he was saying. "I don't know what happened. But I don't care! You're here now. And you'll never guess what happened."

"Okay."

"Are you listening to me?"

She nodded.

"Remember I told you about Katherine—the young lady I met in France?"

Annalee nodded again. What was he saying? Katherine was dead. A colored volunteer with the YWCA, she'd met Jack at a Paris nightclub, gone out with him once, both of them enjoying the date. But it was war. He never saw her again. She was killed the next day in a bombing raid.

But Jack had never forgotten her. He'd admitted as much. But he didn't love her, he said. *"I didn't know her—not really."*

"Turns out she has a sister. A *twin* sister. And she's *here*. In Denver!"

Annalee swallowed, listening. Trying to hear this without worry or judgment or, well, jealousy? Except she could barely listen to what Jack was saying for the joy in his voice, the sparkle in his eyes, and the silly grin on his heartbreakingly handsome face. He looked downright giddy.

"Her name's Dora. She's on her way to St. Louis—that's their hometown—and she booked a one-day layover to find me. To say thanks for being kind to her late sister. She met folks from New York who told her I'd moved here. On her way back from seeing family in California, she made plans to stay a night in Denver and—"

Jack went on and on. Talking about Dora this, Dora that. Him stopping off at Mrs. Mason's. Needing to freshen up. Then finding Mrs. Mason's cryptic message saying Annalee had canceled. Even crazier was finding the lovely Dora. "Sitting in Mrs. Mason's parlor. The spitting image of Katherine—they're identical twins actually. I couldn't believe it."

"Listen, Jack—" Annalee tried to focus her thoughts.

"No, you listen. Come across the street and say hello to Dora. I've been bending her ear all night about you. I took her to dinner tonight—"

"To dinner?"

"And all I talked about was—"

"Thanks, Jack."

His voice fell. "I'm just trying to show her a good time." He stepped back. "But it looks like I messed things up."

She shook her head. "It's not you. After you went to Dearfield, so much happened. And Mrs. Mason was wrong. I didn't cancel. I was just going to be late. My note explained everything, but you never got it—"

And I'm solving a blasted murder. Or I'm trying.

"Let me drive you home then. Dora can ride with us. You can meet her and say hello. She's leaving for St. Louis first thing in the morning, early train."

Annalee turned away. "I'll let you make my excuses. Have a good evening." She started walking away.

"Annalee!"

She kept walking.

"You're breaking my heart right now." His voice sounded torn and distraught.

"I'm breaking my own," she murmured under her breath. Because a smarter young woman would know a better way to react now. *Right, Mrs. Stallworth?* Or if she'd only had a mother—she would've taught her of love and life and mix-ups and men. Taught her how to let Dora or a twin sister or a million other things where men are concerned roll off her back—so she could get back in the game. Instead, with Jack, she always seemed to get it wrong. Even with his beautiful stupid handkerchief.

"Go find Dora," she said over her shoulder. "I'll talk to you when you're free." *Because you're not free yet, Jack.* But was she? She'd be in jail, in fact, if she didn't hurry up and figure out who killed Rebecca Mann's husband. *Lord Jesus, Rebecca's broken heart must be weeping tonight,* Annalee thought. She couldn't imagine how awful the poor young woman was feeling.

For herself now, she just kept walking, pressing down Welton and across Five Points back to her place. Jack didn't follow her. She didn't blame him.

Thus, after walking in the cold and dark, afraid of the shadows but acting like she wasn't, she arrived at her cabin, yanked off the note she'd left for Jack, and crumpled it up, tossing it on the ground or wherever it landed.

She let herself in, locked the door tight, and sat on the side of her bed in her pretty blue dress.

It was freezing in the cabin, so she made herself a fire in her small stove. She washed her face in her tiny bathroom. Brushed her hair back, plopped Mrs. Cunningham's velvet headband back on her head. Then she crawled into bed and did what good detectives never do.

She cried.

Then she wiped her face and went to sleep. Her reason was manifest. *I can't solve a murder—or anything else in this life—with a stupid runny nose.*

A rough banging sound awakened her the next morning. Some half-wild person was rattling her cabin door. What in the world? Eddie? Mrs. Stallworth?

She yanked open her door and her jaw dropped.

Mildred Mason.

"Wake up, Pastor Blake!"

"Excuse me?"

"Where is he?"

"I beg your pardon?" Annalee was in no mood for crazy. Jack's landlady—mean ol' Mrs. Mason, as Eddie had called her, and rightly so—stood on Annalee's little porch, her hands on her hips and a snarl across her mouth.

"I know he's in there. And look at you. Still wearing your clothes from last night—"

"What?"

"Or whenever you put those clothes on. All wrinkled and twisted. Who knows what you've been doing in that dress—"

"Excuse me?" Annalee couldn't believe her ears. "You've got your wires crossed, Mrs. Mason. Pastor Blake is not here—and he's *never* stayed in my place all night!"

"Well, where is he, then?" Mrs. Mason tried to push past Annalee.

"Stop that! I haven't the slightest idea where he is! What is wrong with you?"

"I'm not leaving till I see for myself." Mrs. Mason tried to peer around Annalee's shoulder, her breathing fast and angry.

Annalee's breath raced even faster. She put her hands to her chest, trying to calm herself.

"I'll let you inside, Mrs. Mason. But you need to calm yourself. This is my home. I'd never push myself into your place like this. Especially at the crack of dawn."

Mrs. Mason pursed her lips, looking chastised but annoyed. "Well, let me in, then. *Please.*"

Annalee stepped back, giving way for Mrs. Mason to enter. With a huff, the landlady pushed past her and marched into the cabin. She walked in a small circle, eying every corner, even peeked in the tiny bathroom, seeing the place was empty—but clean, Annalee thought gratefully. She'd straightened and wiped down everything last night before leaving for her speech. Only her bed was unmade.

"Well, where is he?" Mrs. Mason said again.

"He didn't come back to your rooming house last night?"

"No, and neighbors said he'd left earlier with a young woman."

"Well, she wasn't me. But why are you asking me about him at, what, seven o'clock in the morning?"

"The police woke me up at *six*. They found Pastor Blake's car at the train station downtown, engine still running, doors wide-open, key in the slot, car jammed halfway into the baggage section near the parking lot, one tire up on a bench, his driver's license on the floor of the car."

"Don't kid me, Mrs. Mason."

"Kidding? They're going to impound it if he doesn't pick it up by eight o'clock this morning, and I'll have to pay because my address is on his new driver's license. Here's the key!"

"Why give it to me?"

"Well, you and him—"

"Me and him nothing! His car isn't my business. Besides, I can barely drive. Ask one of his trustees to drive it home."

"Home? I don't want that car parked in front of my property. You've got room here outside your place. Besides, time is running out. You need to go get that car!"

"Why is the world so crazy?" Annalee didn't roll her eyes but felt like it.

"You're going to insult me now?"

"That's the last thing I want to do, Mrs. Mason."

Jack's landlady took that in. She'd started to calm down, kept looking around the cabin.

"This was your daddy's place?"

Annalee glanced away. *Not that now, Mrs. Mason. Please not that.* She waited.

"Well, you keep it nice in here." Mrs. Mason looked around again.

"I try."

Mrs. Mason huffed again. "Just need to make your bed."

Annalee stifled a groan.

"And it's freezing in here. I'll have Mason bring you over some wood. My husband, Mason."

"No need, ma'am. Jack—" She pressed her mouth. She'd started to say that Jack brought wood over for her, chopped it, gathered kindling for her too, and she had plenty. But after last night, she didn't know what Jack would do for her. Or even where he was. Leaving his car running at the train station? Doors open, key in the slot, with one tire up on a bench?

Was he rushing Dora to her train? Were they running late? Because they'd been together all night?

Lord, have mercy.

Or did he leave on the train with Dora, so excited he forgot his key in the car? And somebody went joyriding in it? And now he was on his way to St. Louis with Katherine's twin sister?

Too many questions.

It was ten after seven.

"I may live to regret it, but I'll pick up Pastor Blake's car. Bring it back here."

"Here's the key. It's parked in the waiting area at the station. You know what it looks like."

Oh, I know, Annalee said to herself. "Me and that car—we have history."

Indeed, there it was. Jack's Buick touring car was parked at Denver's Union Station in the waiting area, last space, tight corner, next to an unmovable wall. Swell. Just getting in the car would take some work.

Annalee was still wearing the same blue dress. For spite? She didn't know or care. Instead, she'd yanked on her borrowed coat—the old sad one—and pulled a scarf over her head and fast-walked to the station. Managing to squeeze along the driver's side, she unlocked the car, opened the door a few inches, and curved herself like a pretzel past the door and onto the driver's seat. She shut the door and closed her eyes—only to smell Jack's bay rum aftershave and a young woman's lavender-scented perfume.

Swell again. The lovely Dora wears lavender. Jack's favorite. Annalee pursed her lips. *Where is he now?* But she'd asked that question too many times already on Friday night. *Enough.*

She looked around, saw Jack's driver's license jammed in

a corner of the back seat. Turning to sprawl over the seat, she also grabbed a train ticket from Los Angeles to Denver, arriving yesterday afternoon. Dora's ticket. A third item, a calling card with Dora's name on it in a pretty typeface, listed the young woman's St. Louis phone number.

Annalee grabbed the items, ready to ball them up to toss later in a trash can. At the last minute, knowing that was too dramatic, she jammed everything in her crowded pocketbook—already filled with papers, notes, Violet Vaughn's thank-you envelope, peppermint sweets, Mr. Wallace's calling card, and half a dozen other whatnots from last night. She'd never even had a chance to tell Jack all that had happened.

Now she had to figure out how to start the car, put it in reverse, and drive home—with only a few times of driving experience under her belt.

She flicked the starter button, hit the steering-wheel lever to retard the spark, mashed down on the starter pedal—just as someone banged on the passenger door.

A Denver policeman.

"You've got five minutes to get this car out—"

She nodded. *I know.*

She flipped the On switch and the engine turned over. Then coughed and died. Good grief. Now what? She started it again. It died again. She looked at the fuel gauge. Empty. Of course.

She tried one more time, praying the car had enough fumes to get it off Union Station property, up Seventeenth Street, and to the nearest gasoline station. On a fourth try, the cold, empty car turned over; she managed to get it in reverse, do a three-point turn, and get the car moving.

The cop stood there the entire time, not helping. But she

ignored him. *You can do this,* she told herself. Although she wasn't sure exactly what she was doing with Jack's car—or if he was okay. What did that hate mail say? *"Take that Jeffrey Mann case . . ."* and Jack would meet his Maker.

She'd been fretting about Jack and lavender-scented Dora, running off together. But what if he'd been mugged, abducted? She swallowed. Even killed? But if not, where the heck was he?

She rolled down her window, gestured to the cop.

He didn't move.

"Was there a disturbance here last night?" He could hear her, she felt sure. But the cop didn't answer. With a hard look, he pointed her off the lot.

The gas station looked closed. She'd wait it out until nine or whenever they opened.

Just then, an attendant came around from out back. "Need a fill?"

She thanked him, grateful for the help, glad for an early-to-work young man who now was wiping down the car's front window and fenders, checking the oil and water, filling the tank, topping it off.

"Nice car," he said, taking her money.

"A friend's," she answered, but that didn't even feel true this morning. She changed the subject. "You open this early every Saturday?"

"Nah, but there's an air show today and—"

"Air show?" She acted nonchalant, but her heart skipped. "Where's that?"

"Out east, way past Colorado Boulevard at the airfield. Some stunt pilots. We're supplying the fuel. Gotta make the delivery, then get back here to open up at nine."

"Air show this morning? It's chilly."

"Nah, at two this afternoon. Should be warmer. Know any kids? They'd love it. I'll be out there, too. Helping out. Should be fun."

"Thanks!"

He pulled the morning's newspaper off a rack. "Want a paper?"

"Sure." Then for the first time in her life, she acted like a big spender. "Keep the change."

That sounded good when driving a fancy car. Even if it was a fancy car she didn't need or want.

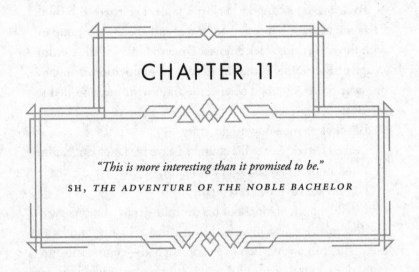

CHAPTER 11

"This is more interesting than it promised to be."

SH, *THE ADVENTURE OF THE NOBLE BACHELOR*

It felt odd driving through Five Points in Jack's pretty Buick. It was still early, so few folks were out to see her cruising—well, missing the clutch and stalling time and again—down Welton Street. A good thing. Especially since she didn't even want the doggone car. She wanted Jack. That was truth.

But she also needed to solve a murder. *Right, Jeffrey Mann?*

Parking Jack's car beside her cabin, she backed in so she wouldn't have to do another three-point turn if she had to leave in a hurry.

For now, she locked the door, found an old tarp among her late daddy's stash behind the cabin, and draped it over the car. When and if Jack returned, at least the car would be in good condition. She'd do her best anyway.

Back inside, sitting at her little table, she tried to rethink what might have happened to him—and she always came up with the same thing. Jack enjoyed Dora so much—"the spitting image of Katherine"—that he gave in to temptation, bought a one-way ticket, climbed aboard the train with her, and fled to St. Louis.

But that seemed downright crazy.

Leave Denver? Leave his church? Leave his fancy car, engine running, in the train station parking lot?

Her breath caught. *Leave me?*

Or did a pack of kids spot his car in the train station's parking lot, take it for a joyride, bring it back in the middle of the night, run away when cops approached—engine still running, doors flung open, hitting the wrong gear, leaving the car jammed into the baggage area with one wheel perched atop a bench?

She couldn't fathom it. Yet worse, maybe Jack was deep in danger, just as the poison-pen letter threatened. But she squelched that thought, too. Instead, *get back to work.*

Grabbing her pocketbook, she dumped out its contents onto her small table, determined to find that note handed to her by the young colored woman who attended her speech. Petite and brown-eyed, the secretive young lady did look something like Annalee, as Mrs. Fletcher said—if she was the same person who traded the jasper necklace with Jeffrey Mann.

So what would her note say?

Annalee dove into her purse jumble, plowing past calling cards given to her last night, including the Simon Wallace stunner—printed on heavy stock with his private number.

Gorgeous card. She couldn't imagine ever picking up Mrs. Cunningham's telephone and calling him.

Same for Dora's pretty card. Would Annalee ever have reason to call her? She hoped not.

But where was that note?

Sighing, Annalee stopped at Violet Vaughn's thank-you letter, assumed it held a kind message and maybe a five-dollar bill at the most.

Instead, Violet had written a check, made out to Annalee Spain, for twenty-five dollars. Annalee held it up close. She'd never opened a bank account, not even in Chicago when she had her teaching job. She'd never had enough money to matter. But she'd have to open one now. And how things changed. She actually had enough money to make a deposit.

That made her think of her daddy and how proud he'd be of her—actually making her way in the world, or trying her best, even if she hadn't solved the murder and she kept messing things up with Jack Blake.

She raked through the final pile of items from her purse. Peppermint sweets. Her new pink lipstick. Notes from people who'd attended her talk. *Call me!... Can you find my brother?... Do you need an assistant?* This thing, that thing, and the other.

The jasper necklace, still wrapped in paper, peeked out of the pile. She pulled it free, opened her first aid kit, and placed the necklace inside, not sure how or when she'd wear or use it.

Back to her purse pile. The note finally? Nope, that poison-pen letter, typed up on somebody's Olivetti. *"Take that Jeffrey Mann case?"*

Annalee unfolded the hateful note, loathing to read it

again. Such nasty threats. Even targeting *"that colored pastor of yours . . . he dies first. Dead and gone."*

Her stomach churned. If Jack left with Dora, at least he was safe from this menace.

Her hands shook as she finally reached the crumpled note at the bottom of the pile. She smoothed it.

May we meet? About Jeffrey Mann.

The handwriting was slight and feminine, the phone number smudged, but Annalee could read it. *York 3885.*

She let out a low whistle.

Looking at the phone number, Annalee knew it was one number she would call without delay. She'd rush over now, in fact, to the Cunninghams'.

Except what was that racket outside? Truck gears grinding? Loud voices jabbering? Pulling open her door, Annalee saw a large Ford truck backing up near her cabin. When the driver got out, he waved at her, swung down the truck's tailgate, and started unloading a load of firewood.

The truck's passenger door swung open and the stern voice of Mildred Mason announced itself.

"We're back, Annalee! Mason, put the lumber *there*!"

Annalee rushed out to stop the operation. "Please, no, Mrs. Mason. I have enough wood."

"It's barely March, and snow's not over yet. This is Mason."

The woman's husband, a rotund, well-fed, smiling man—as kind-looking as Mrs. Mason was harsh—gave Annalee another wave. Dropping an armload of firewood, he stomped onto her porch, asking to see her stove.

Before she could protest, he was peeking into her front door, then standing in the little space.

"Nice cabin, honey. But it's freezing. And that little stove won't heat much."

"Nice to meet you, Mr. Mason."

"Look at that tiny stove. Nice to meet you, honey. Pastor Blake's been chopping your wood like crazy, and now I see why. No regular-size firewood will fit in that itty-bitty thing."

"Pastor Blake?"

"He's paid up till May on your wood. I'll stack it up real pretty in your woodpile and chop a few pieces for you. When he shows up, he'll do the rest of the chopping. That okay?"

Annalee thanked him, appreciating Mr. Mason's confidence that Jack would, in fact, show up. But when?

She needed now to put away her purse, get herself some breakfast, get to the Cunninghams' to make that phone call. She walked to the door to close it, but Mrs. Mason was standing square on her threshold.

"Thought I'd sit and visit while Mason stacks the wood."

Annalee could've pursed her lips, but she knew better. "Of course, ma'am." She stepped aside. "Like some coffee while you wait?"

"Don't want to bother you."

"No bother at all." Which wasn't true. But Annalee understood the elements of hospitality, even if she didn't feel like having guests. Yet as she knew, there are times when folks need to welcome others inside. So she gave Mrs. Mason a smile, put on her kettle, and took down two cups. She put the last of Jack's chopped wood in her stove, added kindling, and blew on the embers, trying to warm up the place—but not sure what in the world she and Mrs. Mason would have to say to each other.

"You're moving up in the world, aren't you?"

Annalee heard the question, but she didn't know how to answer.

Mrs. Mason went on. "Nice article in the paper about your talk last night."

"I haven't seen it."

"Here's your paper." Mrs. Mason picked up the *Denver Express* that Annalee bought at the gas station, pointed to a headline. "'Colored Detective Wows Bank Crowd.'"

"Well, the evening was unusual." Annalee poured their cups. "Coffee's ready. Sorry I don't have cream. Here's some sugar."

Mrs. Mason declined. She grew somber, perhaps misreading Annalee's worries about Jack, the threatening letter, an unsolved murder. "I'm trying to be friendly, Annalee. But that's not why I'm here. I'm worried—about Pastor Blake."

Annalee pulled up her chair. She looked over her cup at Mrs. Mason, seeing a pained frown suddenly crease the woman's forehead, feeling still confused about how to assess Mrs. Mason. Mean ol' woman, as Eddie had concluded? Or was her story more complicated?

"You enjoy him as a boarder?" Annalee tried to sound, well, nice enough.

"Not just enjoy him. He's become like a son to me." Mrs. Mason's voice caught. "Our boy died, you know, in the war."

And here it was. Mean ol' Mrs. Mason wasn't mean for no reason.

"I'm so sorry." Annalee sincerely meant that. "I never knew your son—that he didn't come home. War is . . . it's hell, if you'll pardon the expression. That's what Jack . . . what Pastor Blake always says. No two ways about it."

"We begged Lennie not to go. But he signed up right off. They wouldn't even let him fight. Said colored boys aren't soldiers, can't fight good. He was what they call a stevedore. Never even heard of it."

"He unloaded ships?"

"Hauled guns and office furniture and canned food. What kind of war is that? He could've stayed home and helped Mason deliver coal."

Mrs. Mason stood to pour herself another cup but set it down hard and stood over Annalee's little bed.

"Girl, your bed is hardly big enough for a body to sleep in."

Mrs. Mason bent and started straightening the sheets and blankets, yanking the bedclothes in place, putting the bed to rights.

Annalee knew she couldn't stop her, so she didn't protest. She walked to the bed and picked up the top cover, helped Mrs. Mason to shake it out. Two women, missing their young men, working together. *Maybe this,* Annalee thought, *is hospitality.*

"Lennie is your son's name?"

"Leonard, yes. Leonard Harmond Mason." Mrs. Mason's jaw trembled. She pressed the cover to her face for a moment, holding back tears. "A stupid crate fell on him!"

"Lord, have mercy." Annalee reached for Mrs. Mason. "I'm so sorry," she said again. Then to her surprise, she cradled Mrs. Mason in her arms for a moment. Mrs. Mason wasn't exactly huggable, but at least she could show her genuine concern. *Detective work takes funny turns.* She would just listen.

"They said it was his fault. Not following proper procedure. So they didn't pay the death benefit. I would've donated the money to the church—it was just twenty-five dollars to each of us—Mason and me. But we never got it. Mason finally stopped asking."

Annalee smoothed out the cover on her bed, thinking of Sidney Castle. "What if I know somebody who could help you? He's a retired Army colonel."

"I'm through with it now." Mrs. Mason fluffed Annalee's pillow, placed it just so atop the cover. "Looks like Mason is finished. Hope I didn't bother you." She gave the bed another pat. "If you make your bed first thing, your little place will always look neat and tidy."

Annalee held her tongue, not daring to remind Mrs. Mason that she'd woken her up from a deep sleep in this very bed.

But now Mrs. Mason was pointing to the little piles of trash next to Annalee's purse. "And just look at your pocketbook. Always keep it neat. You never know when you'll have to open it up wide in front of somebody. Like the police."

Annalee cocked a brow. "Yes, ma'am."

"And clean off your table. If you're going to marry Pastor Blake, you need to know how to keep a decent house."

Annalee gritted her teeth, trying to smile but wanting now to throw Mrs. Mason straight out of her house, wondering why half the folks she knew thought she was marrying Jack. But hospitality demanded kindness.

"Would you like to see an air show today, Mrs. Mason? Take our minds off things. Off, well, Pastor Blake—"

"And what happened to Leonard—well, that could be nice."

"It's at the airfield. I'll just drive out in Pastor Blake's car— since I have it. I could pick you up about one o'clock." *Even if I regret this,* Annalee thought, especially when Mrs. Mason sighed and said yes.

"If you insist, I'll go."

"Something different. We'll enjoy it." Annalee gave her another quick hug.

"Well, don't be late. I hate being late for things."

Annalee gritted her teeth again. Why'd she ask "mean ol' Mrs. Mason" to join her? But she knew her answer. *Because something is telling me not to go to that air show alone.*

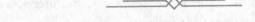

On the way, she stopped first at Mr. Robinson's stationer's shop to use his public phone, set in a private booth.

"York 3885. Please!" Her voice intense. *Answer the phone, please.*

But no answer.

"Dial again?" she asked the operator.

Still no answer.

Sighing, she then called the boys' home, surprised when Eddie answered.

"Boys' Home. Who's calling, please?"

"Eddie?"

"Professor! I knew you'd call. I've been hanging around the phone nook. We still going to the airfield? They're putting on an air show! Can you pick me up?"

"Nope, we'll both get in trouble. Can you take the streetcar, the Colfax line? It'll take you east. Have any change? I'll meet you at the airfield and give you a ride home when it's over. It starts at two."

"Is Reverend Blake coming, too? Wait, somebody wants to use the phone. I'll see you out there!"

Mrs. Mason was waiting on her front porch, pacing, looking at her watch. When she saw Annalee pull up, she stepped through her front door for a moment, quickly returning with a massive picnic basket—followed by Mr. Mason carrying quilts and blankets.

"Open the back door, Annalee. I fixed us a lunch."

"Oh, my word," Annalee whispered to herself. "When did you have time?"

Their drive to the airfield was sunny, dry, and breezy, so Annalee's blue wool dress felt a little warm but comfy.

She drove carefully, letting Mrs. Mason talk on about this complaint or the other about the world, including her anger-worry over Jack. "And when I lay eyes on that young man, he's getting a good piece of my mind, believe you me."

Annalee laughed to herself. She felt pretty much the same.

Her other worry, meantime, was not attracting attention, despite the two of them—both colored women, one young and one old—driving across town in the too-lovely Buick, with her stalling the thing every other block. Then folks would turn, point, stare. When Jack's uncle deeded him the car, why hadn't Jack traded it for a plain-Jane Model T?

Driving toward the airfield, however, her concern shifted. Past Colorado Boulevard, she could see ahead a continuous line of cars snaking in a crawl eastward, apparently toward the airfield about five miles away.

"We're going to be late!" Mrs. Mason scowled at the traffic.

Annalee chuckled. "You're in a rush, Mrs. Mason?"

"Aren't you?"

"I don't mind this slowdown. Gives me time to think."

"About what?"

"My case. I can't make heads or tails of it. I'm trying to figure out where everybody fits."

"At the airfield? Your case is there?"

"In fact, yes. Somebody who worked there was murdered—"

"Mercy alive. Is that why we're going out there?" Mrs. Mason scowled again. "Well, I'm not surprised. All the no-good that goes on at those places."

"Who told you that?" Annalee peered at Mrs. Mason, her curiosity piqued.

"Well, don't tell Mason . . ."

"Tell Mr. Mason what?"

"I shouldn't have mentioned it . . ."

"What are you saying?" She looked over at her. "And I won't tell."

"Well . . ." Mrs. Mason glanced away. "The smuggling."

Annalee felt her hands go cold. "You're not kidding, right? Smuggling?"

"Should've kept my mouth shut."

Annalee wanted to stop the stupid car, pull off on a side road, and let Mrs. Mason spill her beans. Instead, she shifted to first, letting the car creep forward. As she drove, she passed light poles—these bearing posters of "Handsome Daredevils," the barnstormers they were on their way to see. Now Mrs. Mason was saying they were smugglers?

"Guess you better tell me."

"Well, Mason was delivering coal one day—to a nice house over in Lakewood."

"Is this a long story? Can you tell me about the smuggling?"

"I'm telling you! Because the lady asked Mason if he'd clean out the clinkers in the furnace because her husband and son were in a meeting upstairs and too busy. So Mason goes down to the basement to clean out the clinkers, and the basement is loaded with liquor. At least forty or fifty boxes. Said so right there on each box."

Annalee listened, keeping her eye on the car creeping forward ahead of her. It was a little Ford truck, a mom and dad in the front, three little kids in the back, sticking their tongues out at her and Mrs. Mason and then falling all over each other laughing. She stayed silent, ignoring the kids, thinking about illegal booze. She'd seen boxes of illegal liquor in Sidney Castle's basement—his son's stash of sacramental wine, probably stolen, and never mind Prohibition's rules against it.

"So there was liquor down there."

"And helmets. Half a dozen helmets hanging on a wall. Like what air pilots wear."

"The lady's son is a pilot?"

"He flew in the war, yes. The lady started bragging about her son, showing Mason the helmets. Also showing off the son's big model airplanes displayed on a wall. The lady took one down, saying her son flies around the country. Then she tells Mason lots of young war pilots do that now—to earn a living. That barnstorming doesn't pay much. So basically they're using planes to—"

"Smuggle?"

"She didn't use that word—but she didn't have to. Because after the lady went upstairs, Mason could hear the husband and son and other men—their voices through a heating vent— arguing about their next 'runs.' That's what they call them. Flying guns and whatnot down to Mexico, flying perfume and watches and whiskey and *people* back up to the US."

"Lord, have mercy."

"If the barnstormer's in on it, he takes his cut after the air show and flies off to the next place."

"Gracious. Mr. Mason got the whole scoop."

"Enough to understand what they were squabbling about. The son wants to quit, hates the pilfering and cheating and carrying on. He wants out. But the other men put up the money for his plane. So they were coming to fists almost."

"With Mr. Mason hearing it all."

"Once he caught the gist of it, he hightailed it out of there. Didn't want the husband or son or other men to find him down there—a colored man in the basement, listening to their schemes. No telling what they would've done. I'm telling you, Annalee, the things some folks are doing."

"I'm sure glad you told me."

"If you're working your case, best to know as much as you can." Mrs. Mason wrinkled her brow. "But please don't say you heard it from me—or from Mason."

"Not a peep." Annalee glanced at the kids in the Ford truck. They'd grown tired of trying to bait her. Now they were smacking each other atop their heads, laughing like crazy with each tap but hiding their hands, trying to look innocent, making Annalee think about smuggling.

"Curious thing, though, Mrs. Mason."

"What's curious about smuggling?"

Annalee's place in the car line was a mile or so from the airfield, allowing another minute or so to think about what she'd learned from Mrs. Mason.

"It's against the law. But does it have anything to do with my case?"

"Maybe you'll find out today."

Past the next corner, the road turned to dirt, and pulling forward in the line of cars, Annalee saw Eddie Brown Jr. At the same moment, he noticed her and ran over.

"Professor! You're driving!" He yanked open the passenger door, ready to scramble onto the front seat when he saw "mean ol' Mrs. Mason." He reared back.

Mrs. Mason reacted the same way to him, shutting the door clean in his face.

"Geez!" he grumbled.

"Eddie! Climb in the back!" Annalee ignored them both, pointed Eddie to the big back seat.

"But where's Reverend Blake?" Eddie scrambled in, slammed the door.

"And where's your manners?"

"Hello, Mrs. Mason." Eddie looked and sounded sheepish.

"Young man." Mrs. Mason gave him a curt nod. She let it be known she'd seen him before, surely with Jack.

Their greetings over, Eddie unleashed his excitement. "Look at this crowd, Professor!"

"How'd you get here? Streetcar?"

"Thumbed a ride—"

"What? Never again!"

"Too dangerous!" Mrs. Mason gave him a scowl.

"But they were nice folks!"

"You'll end up dead in a ditch!" Mrs. Mason scowled deeper. "Don't you go climbing in strange folks' vehicles."

"But they know the pilot!"

"I don't care—"

"What pilot?" Annalee broke in.

"One of the guys flying today. After the show, if I come to the hangar, he'll give me a free ride! He's their friend. This pilot."

"His name? Did you get the pilot's name?"

"Buddy—Buddy *Mann*." Eddie winked at Annalee. "*Mann*, Professor. As in *Jeffrey* Mann."

"Who is that?" Mrs. Mason gave them a frown.

"He's part of my case." Annalee pushed back a curl. "Don't worry yourself, Mrs. Mason. I'm trying to figure things out myself." She turned to Eddie. "So this Buddy Mann gives airplane rides to people? After the show?"

"Right! So will you ride with me, Professor? After the show? With Buddy Mann?" Eddie grinned at her. "We'll take to the skies! You, too, Mrs. Mason!"

Mrs. Mason huffed. "My feet ain't leaving the ground."

But Annalee wasn't so reluctant. "Take off with Buddy Mann?" The handsome daredevil barnstormer? She craved trying, but it wasn't possible. No pilot in Denver would take a young colored woman up in his airplane. But why squelch Eddie's excitement? She bit her lip, then indulged him.

"If that's all it takes, Eddie—to make a dent in my case—you can bet your life I'll fly."

CHAPTER 12

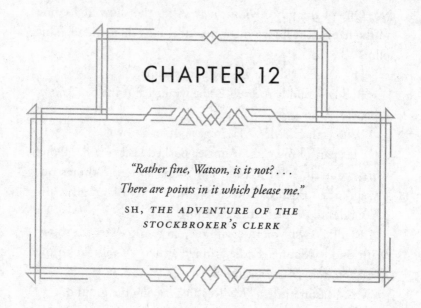

"Rather fine, Watson, is it not? . . .
There are points in it which please me."
SH, *THE ADVENTURE OF THE*
STOCKBROKER'S CLERK

THE AIRFIELD BELONGED TO A FARMER. The runway was an unplowed field. A wind sock, barely flapping, was stuck on a stick near the barnlike hangar. A cloudless sky sparkled blue overhead.

"Great day for flying." Eddie wet his finger and held it to the wind.

"What do you know about flying?" Mrs. Mason wouldn't let Eddie rest.

"Not much. But I'm studying it. Right, Professor?"

"In fact, we all are. Keep your ear to the ground, Eddie."

"You, too, Professor!"

As their car approached the field, a young man in overalls stopped them to collect an entrance fee. A sign propped next to him in the seat of a rickety kitchen chair said *Entrance—25 Cents Per Car.*

"Why so much?" Mrs. Mason asked. "We're not going to a picture show."

"I've got it," Annalee said, grabbing her purse, grateful she had enough to pay.

Cars were getting directed along the south side of the field, lining up like dominoes.

Annalee looked in that direction, trying to identify an open spot. But seeing her, the young man put out his hand.

"Stop, pull your car over that way." He pointed north.

"Why?" Eddie scowled to her. "The best places are the other way."

Annalee pursed her mouth, not looking at Mrs. Mason— not wanting to see what the landlady's wounded eyes were probably saying. *My Lennie died for this? So I'd be treated like this?*

Annalee decided then to tell a lie. "My boss needs his car. This is his boy in the back seat. His people are down that way." She pointed south.

"I don't care—"

"He's waiting for us."

"I don't care."

"What's going on here?"

Walking over was the young man Annalee recognized from the gas station this morning. He looked at the car a second, then at her.

Knowing he recognized her, Annalee made her case. "He's pointing me behind the hangar, but the boy's family are this way and—"

"She's fine." The gas station man said this to the ticket man, then waved Annalee toward the better parking area.

Annalee gave him a nod but let it go at that. The young man had turned away anyway. No need to stir up anything by acknowledging his kindness earlier. He'd have to explain himself to a man who *wasn't* kind to someone like her. So Annalee turned the car—on a hope and a bald-faced lie. *Forgive me, Lord. Oh, these times. They bring out our worst.*

She worried less about her lie, however, than unraveling a pile of disconnected clues, threats, people, and trouble—including her lost or missing Jack. None of it was adding up, at least not yet. But *somebody* killed Jeffrey Mann. Somebody in her town. Maybe even somebody at today's air show.

She parked Jack's car, helped out Eddie and Mrs. Mason—ignoring any people frowning at them, especially when Mrs. Mason shook out a picnic blanket and started arranging her giant basket of food, ordering Eddie to help.

"But the airplanes! Can't I go look? Please, Professor!"

Annalee couldn't tell him no.

Five impressive biplanes sat on the runway with crowds of men, women, and children pressing around them. Pilots sporting their helmets, jumpsuits, and leather boots swaggered amid the crowd, chatting up folks, signing autographs.

"If you come right back," Annalee said. "Before the show starts—when they clear the runways of people. See where we're parked?"

"Thanks, Professor!" And he was off, running toward the planes, whose names—Vickers, Curtiss, de Havilland, Douglas—gleamed in the bright afternoon sunshine.

"Well, he's excited." Mrs. Mason covered up a plate of sandwiches. "I thought he'd want to eat first."

"Don't you worry. You won't have a crumb left when he's finished."

Mrs. Mason huffed at that but still chuckled.

So they were both smiling—a rare moment for both of them, in some ways, on this day—when a man whose car was parked nearby stepped over to scowl.

"Are you in the right area?"

Annalee considered the man, taking in his frowned-up face. She stifled a sigh but also a weary laugh. *What a city.*

"Thanks for asking. We're actually fine."

Turning her back, she knelt on the picnic blanket, reached for a sandwich, complimented Mrs. Mason on her chicken salad, and silently asked the Lord to move aside the scowling man—get him out of her sight, in fact—before she did or said something that would land her for sure in a Denver jail.

In the meantime, as she munched on Mrs. Mason's glorious sandwich, a woman she wasn't expecting to see knelt down next to her.

It was Rebecca Mann.

"Annalee, it's me."

Annalee pressed her mouth, yielded a smile to Rebecca, noticing she was wearing the same frayed but pretty dress she'd worn at the library—and also realizing it wasn't clear what to say to such a fresh widow or if she could even trust her.

Instead, Annalee picked up Mrs. Mason's platter, holding it between them. "Have a sandwich."

Rebecca appeared about to decline. Then she looked at Mrs.

Mason's beautiful food and helped herself, took a small bite and started to munch, but looked mournful.

She'd tried to fix her hair. A yellow barrette held back one side. But her curls hung limp, matching the dull look in her sad eyes. "We buried Jeffrey yesterday." Her lip trembled. "Jeffrey wasn't Jewish, and my family isn't observant. Some ancient reason. So we're not sitting shiva. Poor Jeffrey. He's just dead and gone. Hardly a handful were at the cemetery."

Annalee listened. "Mercy, I'm so sorry." This was what her Sherlock stories often skipped over, the hard work of mourning an actual dead person. She handed Rebecca a small cloth napkin, took one for herself.

"I miss him . . . ," Rebecca was saying.

"I can't imagine. Don't try to explain. Here, let's eat first."

As they did, the scowling man finally left, still grumbling. A bitter, confused man. The world seemed full of them. But Annalee's breath eased, and the bright sun kept shining. Feeling grateful for the warmth, she lifted her face skyward, closing her eyes a moment, soaking in the kind March grace. Rebecca did the same.

The sky was clear blue and cloudless, a watercolor backdrop for the flight of hawks and even eagles riding the updrafts, their wings stretched wide as if calling to the man-made birds below. Annalee and Rebecca watched the display, munching their food—Annalee glad that Rebecca looked grateful, as she was, for the moment of peace.

Mrs. Mason considered them both, half-smiling when Annalee introduced her to Rebecca, looking wary at the young woman, but finally mumbling, "Glad you're enjoying the sandwiches." Rebecca nodded a shy greeting in return and accepted a cup of lemonade.

Annalee sipped from her own cup. "You're not looking at the airplanes?" she asked Rebecca. "To give yourself a break?" She pointed to the field, still crowded with gawkers.

"To tell the truth, I've seen enough planes."

"What else have you seen? Do you feel like chatting a minute?"

Mrs. Mason interrupted. "I'm going to look at the planes, Annalee. Look for Eddie, too."

Watching Jack's landlady disappear into the crowd, Annalee put down her sandwich and drink, took in a deep breath. "I hate to bother you at a time like this, Rebecca. But I'm in hot water. I hardly know anything about you. But I'm going to need your help."

"Because of your handkerchief? That's my fault. A hard-talking policeman forced me to tell him it was yours. But where do you want me to start?"

"With your Jeffrey."

Rebecca bit her lip, wiping her eyes, but she didn't start crying again. Her sorrow, however, was plain as day.

Annalee touched her hand. "You're really hurting. I can see that. I'm sorry to be asking, but maybe Jeffrey stirred up some trouble. Here at the airfield or with your dad or with your uncle Simon." She narrowed her eyes. "Or with the pilot Buddy Mann? He's his brother?"

"Right, his twin—"

"*Twin?*" Annalee's breath caught. She'd come to the air show to forget, for an afternoon, about Jack disappearing—almost certainly, she felt, with the lovely twin of his dead Katherine. "Were they identical? Jeffrey and Buddy?"

"Apparently. But they didn't look exactly alike. Buddy was always taller. More confident. More dashing, to tell the truth. If you like that type." Rebecca lifted a shoulder. "Jeffrey was jealous of him."

"So Buddy didn't kill him."

"Of course not. Why would he?"

No motive? That seemed right. But she'd look for one to be sure.

"Is Buddy married?"

"Can't find the right girl."

Annalee squinted. "Well, did Jeffrey have enemies? Someone willing to kill him?"

Rebecca grimaced. "Uncle Simon asked the same thing. But I can't imagine such a person. Whoever it is, they're horrible."

Annalee perused the sky, feeling as if she were standing at the bottom of a steep hill, looking up into a foggy swirl of thick mist, knowing a clearing awaited behind the smoke but for now unable to see half a foot in front of her.

Suddenly she thought of Mrs. Fletcher at the crowded but orderly pawnshop. *Go one clue at a time,* she thought then. *Clue by clue.*

"Just a couple more questions, and I hate to ask. But did Jeffrey know a young colored woman, maybe about my age?"

"If he did, I didn't know about it." Rebecca looked embarrassed. "I must seem like a hopeless wife. So much of my husband's life seemed like a mystery. But no. I don't know such a woman."

"Your mother's jasper necklace. Any special significance there?"

"Just sentimental. My mother died when I was a child. I don't remember her."

"Where? Here in Colorado?"

"Actually, yes." She looked pained. "I can't talk about that now."

"I understand. I'm sorry." She longed to ask Rebecca so much more, but enough. Not now.

But Rebecca suddenly started to reflect. Ready to confide?

"Jeffrey saw Buddy as his rival," Rebecca was saying. Annalee listened. "Buddy had 'the best life'—the one Jeffrey wanted. Buddy flew in the war. Jeffrey barely passed the tests and never was assigned to fly."

"A rivalry? Did Buddy rub it in? His feats?"

"He's not really like that. He's just barnstorming all over the place, testing prototype airplanes for new companies. The young war hero, drawing crowds around the country—across the world, actually. Poor Jeffrey managed a couple of hangars around the Front Range. Did some mechanical work. Tried to talk farmers into opening their fields for air shows, maybe even sell their land for airports one day."

"But not his dream life?"

"He was looking for his big break. To outdo Buddy—no matter what it took. But isn't that true for everybody? Always looking for more? For better?"

"Your questions sound like mine." Annalee gave her a look. *But most of us don't end up dead on our kitchen floor.* She pushed aside Mrs. Mason's plate of sandwiches, finished the lemonade. "Looks like the air show's ready to start. I'd better find Eddie and Mrs. Mason."

"I'm here with my dad," Rebecca said. "Uncle Simon, too. And of course Lilian, his secretary."

"Right." Annalee thought. The silent Lilian. "Was anything missing at your house?"

"Our pitiful place? Everything was secondhand. Even Jeffrey's pilot whatnots—books and helmets. His silly old typewriter."

Annalee blinked.

"Jeffrey had a typewriter?" *What brand?* "He wrote letters on it?"

"He typed up reports for his boss. Or so he said."

"It's still at your house?"

"I didn't look. I was so upset—neighbors took me to Uncle Simon's house to stay. I haven't been back. I couldn't bear it." Rebecca grabbed her purse. "Now I'd better find Papa before he starts some trouble."

Annalee tried to smile in a knowing way, but that typewriter was on her mind.

"Was it an Olivetti model? The typewriter?"

"Couldn't tell you. I never paid attention. Just some silly thing."

Annalee nodded, but suddenly she grew sober, telling Rebecca about the ruckus at the library—and then discovering Jeffrey's book search on ghost towns named Annalee. Rebecca shrugged, saying she was unsure what any of that meant. Hearing that, Annalee grew reflective herself.

"What if I'm looking in the wrong places?" She thought of smuggling young pilots. "What if the real key to Jeffrey's murder isn't anywhere near here at all but someplace far away?"

"You mean in another state?"

"Or another country? Mexico? Cuba? Or on the other side of the world? Who knows? France? Poland? Germany?"

Rebecca glanced skyward for a moment, squinted at the sun. She leveled her eyes back at Annalee. "Or Spain."

"Spain?"

"My family's from there. Uncle Simon never talks about it. Papa either. I've never even visited. But maybe you're telling me it's time?"

"*Spain.*" Annalee whispered the word, her own last name— saying it in her mind as she gazed out at crowds of people, gathered now in bright sunshine, as they walked back with smiles, holding on to family and friends, arranging themselves along both sides of a farmer's field, waiting for an air show to begin. But right here—in Colorado.

"Actually, no. Not Spain. I can't go there. Passports. Expenses. Too much to arrange." She watched the crowd. "But what if some things of Spain have found their way here?"

"So we just need to find them?"

"That's right. I'm making a start on my sleuthing. Want to go with me the rest of the way?"

Rebecca had stood up, straightened her worn and pretty springtime dress, looked ready to turn and walk away. Then she knelt again. "What if I'm afraid?"

"I'm afraid, too, if I'm honest. But fear keeps a detective sharp." Jack had told her that. *But get out of my mind, Jack,* she thought. Except at that, she was failing. What, indeed, would Jack say were her next best steps?

"Let's meet soon. To talk over everything."

"So I understand exactly what 'things of Spain' we need to look for, but here in Colorado? Is that what you mean?"

"I'm not totally sure myself. But to figure out what happened to Jeffrey, maybe we go back to where everything started—for your family and for Jeffrey, too."

Rebecca nodded, looking determined. "I'm afraid. But it's time to clear up everything."

"Clearing up is good. We'll work together."

"I've never done that before."

"Done what?"

"Work."

"It's not complicated." Annalee cocked a brow. "You just keep telling yourself you can do it."

Now, however, Annalee needed to find Eddie and Mrs. Mason. She already knew what Eddie would say. *"Your new case! Let me at it, Professor!"*

Mrs. Mason would scoff. *"You keep your feet on the ground, young man!"*

But where had Eddie and Mrs. Mason gone?

Annalee stood and smoothed her dress, started walking through the crowd of gawkers waiting for the planes to take off and the show to start.

The pilots and their handlers were pointing people off the runway. "Back away! As far back as you can go!"

No bleachers were set up, so the entire viewing arrangement was makeshift.

As Annalee wrestled against the crowd, wanting to search around the airplanes for Eddie and Mrs. Mason, the press of people—and the airfield workers—kept pushing her back.

Still not seeing her friends, she returned to the long lines of parked cars, deciding to walk the perimeter of the entire airfield if necessary. She wanted them safe, especially because a nagging feeling from that poison-pen threat, mentioning Eddie, grated at her.

The pilots were revving their engines. Soon they'd start their propellers, an obvious danger.

Striding fast, she passed the ticket man, ignored his glares, kept marching to the field's north end, even quickly looking in some car windows. But no Eddie and no Mrs. Mason.

Her blue wool dress felt wrong now. Far too fancy. But she kept searching the crowd, kept eyeing the scruffy field. Finally approaching a marker—where the unplowed ground turned into plowed rows of seedling beets—Annalee started to cross over to the opposite side of the field.

A field-worker rushed over to her. "Stop, señorita! Stop right there!"

She acknowledged him but kept walking. "I'm looking for my friends. Is anybody still in the hangar?" She pointed toward the barnlike building.

"Just the boss. Maybe a pilot, too."

She thanked him, still walking.

"Please, señorita! No crossing here until the show's over." The fieldman looked worried. "It's dangerous! No crossing!"

"Will you get in trouble if I do?"

"Probably not, señorita, but you will. The boss might call the police on you."

She scoffed, still headed toward the barn. "Call the police? On me? They've already got my number."

Annalee strode off, not trying to be rude but determined to

lay eyes on Mrs. Mason and Eddie, especially with the air show starting. The sun beat down on the field, making her squint as she looked upward—following the sound of planes taking off into the air joining the hawks and other big birds.

To Annalee, the flying machines were beautiful—climbing, twisting, looping—looking and sounding close enough to reach up and touch. Their magical sky dance surprised her with its nimble beauty. One day, she told herself, she'd fly in one. Well, if she found the nerve. Then she'd be the flying detective. She smiled to herself. Eddie would be so proud. But where was he? Bending a pilot's ear?

She approached the hangar, feeling jumpy, knowing it was off-limits. The squat building wore a massive hand-painted banner under the roofline: *Mile High Aviation (No Trespassing!)*. Its large wooden doors were pushed wide-open, the hangar empty of all but two planes. One large, one small.

Two men were arguing about that. Annalee could hear them—one an older man, the other younger—as she stepped toward one of the large doors, waiting just behind a stack of boxes.

"Get out there now and fly!" the older man growled. "The Jenny's fueled up and ready."

"Not for the pennies you pay me!" the younger man shot back.

"Pennies? Half the ticket sales go to you—"

"Half? You're a thieving liar! Besides, I need to move the Tri-Motor this afternoon. I'm testing her."

Annalee peered around the boxes, trying to see the men's faces, but jumped back when a third man stormed in from the other side of the hangar, fuming.

"*O'Hara*'s flying today? We warned you! No papists!"

Annalee rolled her eyes. The Klan were here. Stewing against Catholic pilots—at an air show, for pete's sake. But the Klan rep had another gripe.

"And some colored gal's been sitting on a blanket in the white section."

"Not my problem!" the older man said.

"Don't think so? She's going to jail if we find her and you will, too—"

"What colored gal?" the younger man shot. "What's the difference?"

"Help me find her! Cops want her!"

"I'm running an air show!" The older man cursed.

"Not anymore! Scour this field. Both of you. Both sides."

The men stormed off, all grumbling. Annalee swung around, suddenly seeing two things: she couldn't risk getting stopped by police, and here, before her, stood an empty hanger begging to be searched for clues about Jeffrey Mann's killing. But looking across the field, she could see two beefy cops barking at the field-worker—and the worker cowering, pointing toward the hangar.

She groaned. Of all the silliness.

She slipped into the hangar, letting her eyes adjust to indoor light. She despised the insult of hiding from the police—like a blasted thief. But this was her life, detective or not. The world didn't seem to want people like her around, acted as if her very presence was an affront, even at a Saturday air show. Still, she was *not* going to jail for sitting on a blanket—or for anything else.

So hide, detective.

She scanned the hangar, seeing not a single good spot. A small office in a far corner didn't even have a door. The place was just a sprawling holding pen for planes. Well, the one airplane nearest her—the big one—beckoned. But she wasn't sure she could muster the nerve to touch it, let alone climb inside.

Men's voices were getting louder.

The plane still summoned.

In fact, it sat low to the ground, wings stretching out on both sides, the cockpit door at waist height.

She ran to it but hesitated, hating to breach something so modern and daring, not believing that was exactly what she was doing.

The voices drew closer.

She swung open the cockpit door, eyes taking in the sleek interior, climbed into the airplane, suddenly smelling gasoline, motor oil, and the fresh scent of—what? Lavender perfume?

Annalee gently shut the cockpit door, dropped to her knees, and wriggled to the back of the narrow machine, pushing behind stacked boxes in the rear, each one wafting its lavender scent.

The men were just inside the hangar.

"Over here!" one cop yelled to the other. "Check that office! I'll check the planes."

Annalee squelched a moan, breathing hard, heard the policeman stomp around—head toward the small plane first. She sighed, saying a little prayer. But here he came toward her hiding place, rattling the handle on the cockpit door. But she didn't scooch herself farther behind the lavender haul or try to disappear. She didn't have the heart for disappearing, not after last night's confusion with Jack.

Instead, she sat in the back of the plane, in the shadows, breathing in the scent of lavender, counting the seconds until she was discovered.

Or maybe she wouldn't be discovered.

"Hey!" the younger man had returned. He stormed over to the cop. "Get off that airplane!"

"Police!"

"Hands off! Private property!"

"We're searching for—"

"Got a warrant? Then get off that machine!"

Annalee tensed, hearing the young pilot's nerves. He truly had something to hide—his load of illegal perfume. Annalee looked at a different stash of boxes, guessed they held liquor or some other contraband. And here she was, sitting smack in the middle of it.

"Listen." The cop changed his tactic. "Chief's order. We're looking for a colored gal."

"Well, she's not on my airplane!" The young pilot stood his ground. "I'm flying it now. Testing it! And I'm late. Stand back!"

The pilot yelled half in Spanish, speaking apparently to the field-worker, now in the hangar, too. "Hey, José! Help me move *el avión. Gracias!*"

Suddenly the airplane was being pushed outside into the sunshine. Annalee felt the movement, knew exactly what that meant. If she yelled *stop*, revealing her hiding place, the cops would haul her to jail—discover who she was, accuse her of escaping a murder, and blame her for Jeffrey's killing.

But if she kept silent behind the boxes, she'd be choosing to be brave—because she'd be taking to the skies. *And I don't feel ready for that*—no matter what Eddie begged her to do.

"Sir!" she yelled at the pilot, knowing that sounded silly. "Excuse me!" *May I get off?*

But a plane isn't like a streetcar. Besides, the pilot couldn't hear her. The plane was hurtling down the field, bumping her in every direction possible.

So she squatted behind a box of probably smuggled perfume, blinked hard, and told herself to get ready for what she'd wanted, but now she was praying it would—*please, Lord*—stop.

But no stopping now. Annalee Jane Spain was racing to the skies.

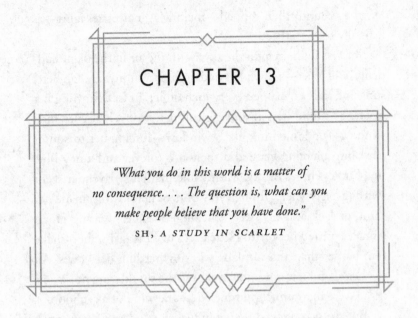

CHAPTER 13

"What you do in this world is a matter of no consequence. . . . The question is, what can you make people believe that you have done."

SH, *A STUDY IN SCARLET*

HER STOMACH WAS IN HER MOUTH. Or that's how she felt. She lay scrunched in the back of an actual airplane—her nerves firing, feeling a crazy thrill, but also more cramped and downright terrified, if she told the truth, than she'd ever felt in her life.

She was in an airplane and it was *taking off*. And she wanted to open her mouth and holler like nobody's business, feeling her heart in her throat, her body tingling head to toe from a vibrating so loud and awful that she only knew for certain one clear thing: this was insane. *So get back to earth.*

But the Tri-Motor airplane—if that's what it was called—was roaring ahead, its three screaming engines and their spinning propellers shaking for all they were worth as the plane left the ground, then dipped—making Annalee feel faint—as it finally took to the air.

She was flying. Up in the sky. With the air in the plane suddenly cold as ice—which felt odd on such a sunny day. Up here, sunshine fully enveloped every inch of her, in fact. Turning her head, she found herself looking through a tiny, half-curtained window—or something like a window—forcing her to squint hard into piercing glare and then at a forever-and-a-day blue sky. Endless miles of sky. Meanwhile that crazy lavender scent swirling everywhere, filling every pore of her nostrils, made her think of Jack and his sweet-smelling, lavender-wearing Dora. Annalee gritted her teeth. If she ever saw him again, she'd shake him harder than this airplane was now rattling her bones. All she heard and felt now, however, was the shuddering noise—as if she were in a tunnel pummeled by the wind of a typhoon.

But she was, indeed, *flying in the air*. Modern and smart. *Is this really me?*

It seemed like a darn good question for her detective work. Nope, she didn't know who killed Jeffrey Mann, but if she was brave enough to fly in an airplane, she sure as heck could figure out his murder. She sat herself up, scooted on her knees closer to the tiny window.

"Dear God in heaven!" She managed a whisper—instead of a scream. "Look at this!"

But God, who she trusted as good, seemed busy with his beautiful golden earth far below and with all that was safe and secure on solid ground—where she should still be standing on this afternoon of a Denver air show. Daring to look down, she could see the tiny squares of green and brown and gold of far-away farms, and a road with farm trucks driving on it, and a thin, meandering ribbon that must be a sparkling, narrow stream. But all of it seemed miles away.

Up front in the plane, however, was an actual pilot—and she was hitching a ride. Illegally. Should she wait to tell him? Bad choice. The fancy flyer, whoever he was, had to be told. Time to announce herself.

"Help me!" she shouted. Or maybe she wasn't shouting. Because her voice got sucked into the noise and sunshine and aroma of lavender and endless blue sky.

"*Help!*" But the pilot couldn't hear a thing. Crammed into his cockpit, he was preoccupied with his dials and gadgets, never guessing she lay scooched next to the riot of stacked boxes in the plane's rear. Neither a stowaway nor a prisoner, she could even stand up, if the ceiling above her wasn't so low. But whatever her situation, she had to get out of it—or half freeze to death in her too-fancy dress in this ridiculous and amazing machine. Just two questions: *Why me, Lord? And why this plane?*

But she knew the precise answer. Back on earth, Jeffrey Mann's killer wanted her cornered and dead, too. He (or she?) probably alerted cops at the air show, sparking their hunt for her. Hiding in an airplane, she had no choice. Time to fly.

She crawled her way toward the front of the plane—angry now about being flown around in one of these appalling, dangerous, beautiful contraptions. Peering forward at the cockpit, she saw the pilot—the back of his dark hair curling out in silky tight waves from under his leather helmet—and suddenly knew exactly who he must be. Buddy Mann. Jeffrey Mann's twin brother.

She pushed toward the cockpit, trying to yell his name. "Buddy!"

He couldn't hear her.

"*Buddy!*"

The plane jostled and shuddered. The air this high was a swirling, bumpy sea of constant movement. But also this: the sky this high was wild and blue and glorious. Poor Jeffrey Mann would never fly in it again. For his sake, but also for hers, if she survived this flight, she'd do everything possible to find out who killed him.

Annalee grabbed at the floor, still crawling forward, finally squeezing her way through the cramped space almost to Buddy Mann's pilot seat. She grabbed his right arm. "*Buddy!*"

Buddy Mann jumped back in surprise, eyeing her with shock. He sputtered and cursed. "*What the . . . ?*" He jerked back to watch his dials, yanked his head her way, glaring at her—or trying not to stare at her? His green eyes flashed. "*Get off my plane!*"

"Buddy, help me." She gripped his arm tighter.

"Get off me!" He shook his arm loose, but as he did, the plane banked left, pressing Annalee harder against him; then it banked right, jerking her against a wall of tiny levers, leaving him pressing against her.

"*Get off me!*" Buddy yelled.

"Get off *me!*" Annalee had enough. The airplane shuddered. "*Buddy!*"

"*Stop saying my name!* I'm . . . I'm throwing you out right now!"

"It's not my fault! *Help me—*"

The plane dipped harder.

But Annalee didn't scream. She needed this pilot's help and shrieking in his ear would hardly gain her that. She could see he was furious, and he had the right. A complete stranger, appearing out of nowhere, begging for help inside his airplane, and while he was flying it?

Buddy Mann gripped his steering device—or whatever it was called—steadying the plane. They were climbing toward the mountains now, his eyes trained fiercely ahead, but *he* was still screaming at her, his voice angry and confused and furious.

"I'm throwing you out."

"But somebody killed Jeffrey!" Annalee tried that tack.

"*What?* Who the devil are you? How'd you get in here?"

"The police were after me!"

"Good!"

"I'm freezing! Will you take us down?"

"Then I'll call the cops. Soon as I land. The cops! You hear that?"

"*But you're smuggling!*" Annalee yelled this without knowing it for sure but feeling it, smelling it—certain a lavender-scented airplane could only mean one thing. "Perfume! Liquor! What else are you hauling?"

"You're questioning me?" Buddy Mann threw her a confounded glance.

"Just take us down! I can help—"

Buddy turned to retort, but—

BAM!

"*What was that?*" Annalee gripped Buddy's arm again.

Stupid question. She could see.

"*Blast it!*" Buddy cursed.

All over the windshield, a massive hawk lay beautiful but broken across the thick glass, flung there by the left propeller, now bent and broken and no longer spinning. The middle propeller had stopped cold, too.

The plane, in response, dipped hard.

"Help me!" Buddy screamed at her.

"What?"

"Grab the stick!"

What was he saying? He was gripping the stick already. But the plane was swaying wildly.

"Grab it!" He lurched forward. *"Help me!"*

Cramped into an impossible position, she squeezed herself forward and aside Buddy and grabbed on to the stick. She could feel it wanting to jerk the plane forward—and *down*.

But Buddy was trying to pull it back, to keep the plane halfway level, preventing it from spiraling downward to their sure deaths below.

She wouldn't be like Sherlock Holmes today. The famous detective "perished" in a fall into a thundering, rocky waterfall—until Conan Doyle brought his detective back to life in a new adventure. Holmes was a literary Lazarus.

But the rocks below promised no such revival for Annalee. Sharp, cutting, and angular, they jutted straight upward, catching the sinking sunlight with a shining, deadly beauty. God's view from this high up was a marvel, a sharp contrast to her fighting struggle to hang on to a steering stick trying to help Buddy Mann keep them aloft.

In contrast, the scene below was a tranquil portrait of harmony and peace. Gentle curls of smoke wafted from chimneys. People in cars moved along on roads. A herd of bighorn sheep followed their narrow trail, oblivious to the battle for life now underway just a few hundred feet above them.

Look up! Annalee wanted to scream. *We're dying up here, fighting our way back to solid ground.*

But people don't often see other folks' desperation. Too far removed? Unseeing and unknowing? Maybe just not caring? No wonder hearts cried out only to God. Nobody else was listening. Or were they busy calling on God themselves? *Write about that,* she chided herself. *If you ever get back to solid ground.*

But now, looking down from Buddy's shuddering plane, she was grateful to see where he was struggling to take the wildly wavering machine. Below to the west lay a half-snowy field and, beyond that, a massive, white-brick lodge resort. *The Stanley Hotel.* The glory of a thousand Colorado postcards, it was the pride of Estes Park, gracing the town just outside of Rocky Mountain National Park, fully living out its reputation as Colorado's fanciest mountain hotel.

But it could've been a shack for all Annalee cared. Buddy was just trying to land his blasted machine—and she was just trying to help him. But the whole contraption was juddering and diving and then flattening out, then suddenly juddering and diving again—she and Buddy gripping the stick for all they were worth.

Because the plane was coming in *fast*, a crazed thing seeking only solid ground—which came up at them like some defiant, unmovable, angry, unyielding, solid-as-concrete wall.

"*Hard . . . land-ing!*" Buddy tried to get his words out. But the ground absorbed all sound, flinging his voice away like some cheap rag doll. And flinging both of them, too.

Annalee knew the word *impact* but never anything like this.

The landing knocked every ounce of breath from her chilled, stiff, cramped body. The same apparently for Buddy. He'd let out a holler as the plane descended wildly but went stone silent when it slammed hard against the ground. Seeming to veer in every possible direction at once, it finally came to an abrupt and ugly stop, windows shattered. They were in the weedy field, about half a mile from the imposing hotel.

"*Out!*" Buddy yelled at her, clambering up and over the cockpit door, which refused to open.

Mimicking him, Annalee did the same but looked back over her shoulder. "My purse!"

"Leave it! Out!"

Scrambling behind him, Annalee pushed up the hem of her blue wool dress—modesty begone—and made her way up, over, and out of the airplane, following Buddy at a crazy run across the half-snowy field.

At nearly eight thousand feet, Estes Park was hardly the highest mountain town in Colorado. But running, she could feel the altitude in her lungs, wished Buddy would stop his galloping already. He kept racing away from the half-crumpled airplane, looking back over his shoulder as if expecting to see the plane and everything around it explode.

Finally, however, he stopped, bending over from the waist, gasping for air. Then he stood, still breathing hard, looking back at his plane. Crumpled in odd, inexplicable places, its three motors smoked like chimneys, too near a gas tank. But no explosion. This was a miracle.

Annalee dragged herself to a stop. She turned back and looked at the plane for a long moment, too.

"That was some landing," she finally whispered.

Buddy Mann looked at her and kicked at snowy dirt. "Who the heck are you?"

She stepped toward him. "Annalee Spain. I'm a detective." She straightened her dress. "Well, sometimes."

"The one in the stupid papers?" He looked her over. "Look at you!" He shook his head. "Where's your coat? How'd you get on *my plane*?"

"Police were after me . . . at the Denver air show. I think I know why."

"Well, you better tell me! Here comes my hotel contact." Across the field, they saw a man running toward them.

"Somebody murdered Jeffrey, your brother, in cold blood," Annalee said. "That same person is trying to frame me. Or kill me. Or scare me away. You're probably in danger, too. Because of your smuggling."

"Stop saying that!" He yanked off his helmet.

"Listen, Buddy—"

"How do you know my name?"

"Names? All I've got is names. Rebecca, Jeffrey, Simon, Uri." Buddy Mann winced.

"Know any of those folks? I bet you do. Or maybe the Fletcher woman at the pawnshop or Mrs. Quinlan. Or hey, Elizabeth Castle . . . I could go on. If you're smuggling with any of these folks, I don't care. But I need to know who's after *me*." She frowned. "Then I'll find the other thing I need to know."

"Which is . . . ?"

"Where is Jack Blake?"

"Never heard of him."

"I'm not sure I believe you."

"Well, we're two for two. But I can't argue now. Here comes Hale from the Stanley. I'll do the talking. Can you let me do that? *Please?*"

"On one condition. Only if you tell me!"

"Tell you what?"

"If you're smuggling. Because if you are, I can help you get free of it."

"You? Help me?"

"I helped you fly your plane!"

"You're like a bad nightmare!"

"If the Feds find your stash, it'll be worse! So yes or no? You're smuggling, right? But you want to get out of it? So you don't end up in a federal jail?"

Buddy Mann groaned, ran both hands through his dark curly hair. The frantic man from the hotel was waving at them, almost within hearing distance now.

"Okay!" Buddy glared at her. "But that's all I'm saying to you." He turned toward the wide-eyed man. "Mr. Hale! Did you see that landing!"

"See it? Holy cow! You okay, Buddy?"

"Sure, I'm fine. A big bird hit her. Broke up the left propeller. But I got her down."

"Cargo okay?"

"All good. Dang thing didn't explode. I must be living right."

"Or somebody was praying!"

The two men laughed, the wide-eyed Mr. Hale asking Buddy what he did to bring in the plane, then asking when hotel guests could start their sightseeing flights again. "I got a long list of folks."

"Just a few days. I'll just need to get parts for this one. Start repairs. Let's go call Denver—"

Buddy slung an arm around Mr. Hale's shoulder, letting him

jabber on as they started walking together across the field, back toward the hotel.

As if Annalee wasn't even there.

She watched the two men—older and younger—while trying to decide how she should feel. Insulted? Overlooked? Grateful to be alive and glad that Hale didn't give her the time of day? She wasn't a guest at the hotel, of course. Only wealthy white families vacationed there. Celebrities, too. She'd never be mistaken for being any of those folks—neither rich nor famous.

Maybe Hale thought she'd flown in with Buddy for work. The Stanley Hotel hired Negro waiters, all males—including some members of Jack's church—who staffed the dining rooms, cafés, banquet halls, outdoor patios, and whatnot. Some Black women might have worked in the kitchens but probably not as hotel maids. Rich folks traveled with their own people—handpicked valets, butlers, maids, sometimes their own cooks, too.

She looked down at her pretty but wrinkled blue dress, hugged herself in the cold—knowing she did need a coat, not to mention her pocketbook, a warm hat, gloves, brush, a lipstick—*if it's not too much to ask*—and a good undercover story, not to mention a place to stay the night and lay her head.

She gasped. Her purse? She'd left it at the airfield on Mrs. Mason's blanket. She had nary a penny.

Instead, she was standing alone in a snowy mountain meadow filled with weeds and the half-crumpled carcass of a fancy airplane stinking of smuggled perfume. Contraband booze was also probably on that plane.

Still, she didn't know who killed Jeffrey Mann. Or who'd set the cops on her at the air show. But also . . .

Where is Jack? She didn't have a clue. And Buddy? What insider scuttlebutt had he stumbled upon because of smuggling? Standing in this field, she didn't know any of it.

But for every one of her questions, she knew this:

I didn't survive a blasted airplane crash not to find out.

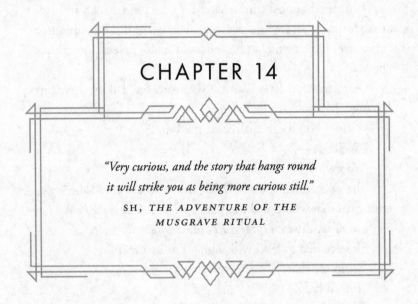

CHAPTER 14

"Very curious, and the story that hangs round it will strike you as being more curious still."

SH, *THE ADVENTURE OF THE MUSGRAVE RITUAL*

THE STANLEY HOTEL WAS A GLORY. Built on a rise before the Lumpy Ridge mountains outside Estes Park, it sprawled out, resort-like, from a center lobby that led guests to 142 richly appointed rooms. Or that's what the blizzard of postcards, brochures, and printed publicity mailed and passed out on street corners since the hotel's 1909 opening all declared.

Annalee only knew one thing: She didn't dare approach the grand porched entrance or step inside the front doors. Standing outside, watching fancy cars come and go, she set her jaw and turned to walk, head held high, beyond the front entryway toward the hotel's back side—as if she had a reason to be in this setting. She made her way past several small side doors, finally seeing one marked Service.

It opened almost immediately, a tall colored man in black tuxedo pants and white waiter's jacket stepping out to light a cigarette. He frowned at her but said hello. "Need something, honey?"

"A telephone. I need to call Denver, but I don't have any change. My pocketbook is gone."

"Gone? You mean stolen? At the hotel?"

"Well, it's—"

"You work here?"

She twisted her mouth. What in the world could she say to this man that would make any sense? *No, I don't work here. I just fell out of the sky in a smuggler's busted-up airplane.*

She decided to level with him. "I'm in a jam."

"I can see that."

"I need help."

The man squinted at her. "Do I know you?"

The door opened again. Two more Negro men in waiter's jackets and tuxedo pants came out, gave a wave to the first waiter, then gave Annalee a curious, quick glance but kept walking. They headed west toward the mountains, talking and smoking.

"The less you know the better," Annalee whispered to the first waiter. "But is there a telephone, out of the way, where I can make a quick call?"

The waiter shook his head. "I need my job. I got a family."

"I understand—"

"You Pastor Blake's lady friend?" He peered at her harder. "That detective?"

"You know Pastor Blake? Have you seen him?"

He shook his head again. "You better leave. You can't go in here."

"I won't get you in trouble, sir. But I need a telephone!"

The man mumbled, *"Lord, have mercy."* He glanced around, opened the service door a few inches, stepped back when two more tuxedoed Black men pushed the door open wider and walked out, both carrying sheet music and trumpet cases.

They greeted him with a friendly salute. "Hey there, Johnny."

"Have a good night," the waiter called after them, watching them walk away, turn a bend, and disappear into the evening twilight.

Then in a flash, the waiter swung wide the door again, gestured Annalee inside, fast-walked down a long, half-lit hallway, turned back, whispering, "Say *nothing*."

She nodded. They were in the bowels of the hotel's kitchen and service area. An army of waiters, cooks, dishwashers, janitors—everybody in some kind of uniform—scurried about in some well-rehearsed, choreographed, secret dance whose steps only these people understood and knew.

Annalee felt out of step, sticking out—she was certain—like a sore thumb. So she kept her head down, averting her eyes, willing herself to be unseen—despite her fancy blue dress—closely following the waiter Johnny until he came to a door marked Manager. He knocked lightly, heard no reply, and pushed her inside.

"Two minutes! Phone's free."

"No charge?"

"It's a Denver line. One minute!"

She rushed to a desk piled high with invoices, receipts,

record books, all manner of hotel private business and whatnot. *Lord, don't let me get caught in here.*

Picking up the receiver, she waited a month of endless Sundays for the Denver operator to answer. "Number please."

"Main 4172!"

Then after a million clicks and buzzes: "Mason Rooming House. This is Mildred Mason—"

"It's Annalee!"

"Where are you?"

"In Estes Park!"

"Are you crazy?"

"At the Stanley!"

"How'd you—?"

"Listen, Mrs. Mason—"

"No, you listen! Why'd you leave me and Eddie? Mason had to come get us and tow Pastor Blake's car—all the white folks watching our every move—and then drive Eddie to that boys' home. I can't drive."

"Have you heard from Jack?"

"Nobody tells me nothing."

"Can Mr. Mason drive Jack's car up here?"

"To Estes? You lost your mind!"

"And bring some clothes for me. And my coat? And some money. I have two brand-new hundred-dollar bills in my first aid box on my shelf."

"You sound like a crazy woman!"

Annalee heard one hard knock on the door.

"I gotta go! Please bring the car tomorrow!"

"*Sunday?* It's the Sabbath! We keep it holy!"

"I *know*! But I need my things. For my case. I'm making

progress. I'll look for you . . . around town on the main drag." Annalee yanked the phone from her ear, then brought it back. "Thank you, Mrs. Mason! I'll explain—"

She slammed down the phone, rushed to the door, opened it a slice to find the waiter Johnny plastered in front of it, chatting idly and casual-like to another waiter—or trying to sound casual-like and idle—until the other person finally walked away.

Slipping out the door, she pulled on the hem of his jacket. He didn't look her way but turned back into the service cacophony, leading her silently through it but not acknowledging she was with him. Keeping her head down, she followed, willing with all her might to disappear into the hotel's basement swirl. That way, to anyone who might be looking, she would appear to be just another Stanley Hotel employee—when, of course, she was the furthest thing from anything like that.

At the main kitchen door, Johnny paused a millisecond at a tray filled with stacks of brown paper bags, picked one up, along with a nearby cup from another tray, and headed toward the outside door. Pushing her through it, he shoved the bag and cup at her. "Here's some dinner!"

"Thank you, Mr. Johnny—"

"Now, *leave*! We're proud of you, Miss Spain. But don't you ever come back!"

When a door slams in her face, a pastor's lady friend can feel dismissed and hurt. But Annalee felt grateful with every fiber of her being. Mr. Johnny the waiter might've risked his job, and who knew what else, by helping her use a hotel telephone.

Some people were gold. He was a brick. Gave her food, too. She was grateful beyond words. She breathed deep, trying to calm herself and suddenly smelling something delicious. Whatever was in the paper bag made her salivate. But where could she sit down to eat? Picnic tables set out on a side lawn sat adjacent to a painted sign: Hotel Guests Only.

Besides it was dark now. Frigid, too. The mountain air in March was cold as ice, especially after sundown. But the night sky was spectacular. Stars lit the heavens like a holy fire, millions twinkling in every direction.

Looking across the landscape, Annalee saw the only place on earth that she knew might be a safe haven.

Buddy's half-crumpled airplane still sat in the weedy field. A small hangar sat beyond it, but she could see work lights coming from an open door. Somebody must be inside.

So she headed for the plane, actually running toward it, hoping to warm herself up.

Raising her dress hem, she did the opposite of her earlier escape, clambering into the plane and squeezing herself into the back with the boxes. They lay everywhere. Some contents had fallen out—bottles of Scotch whisky, Mexican tequila, and oh yes, case after case of expensive French lavender perfume, some broken and seeping their pricey aroma.

She'd always loved the scent—the cheap version she could afford—but now wasn't sure if she'd ever wear it again. The air in the plane was alive with summer lavender, making it almost impossible for her to think about eating anything. Meantime, the plane was an icebox.

In the near dark, across from broken glass, she found a bundle of tarps—thankfully not sopping with any illegal liquids—wrapped herself in a couple of them, and propped against the back of the plane.

Unwrapping the food, she found a small chicken breast sandwich, still warm, dripping with mayonnaise. A narrow slice of chocolate cheesecake, topped with a fresh raspberry, completed the contents.

She popped the raspberry in her mouth, closed her eyes, chewing the perfect little piece of fruit—unable to imagine where, in chilly March, it had come from—so she thanked God for the food.

The sandwich was delicious, too. Chewing on it gave her time to think about her remarkable day. *I survived a ridiculous plane crash.* Well, it was an emergency landing. But that escape didn't quiet the nagging worry she still had about Jack and his well-being. Something was wrong and she wasn't fully convinced now that he'd just run out of town with Dora to start a life with her.

Instead, what if he had been forced to hide like her—or worse, was actually abducted—and now was somewhere cold and alone, huddled in the dark?

A bright light suddenly flashed.

Annalee sat still as a stone. *What now?* She quietly pushed herself deeper into the shadows, holding still her sandwich and its wax paper and brown paper bag. *No rustling,* she told her food, training her ears on a sound outside.

Footsteps crunched in the weedy snow. A bright beam sliced the darkness. A flashlight. A thief? Somebody aware of Buddy's cargo, coming to take their fill? What if they were armed? She feared alarming anybody climbing into the plane to steal and finding her.

But why reveal herself if the person outside decided to leave and walk away?

She took a deep breath, ready to shout out her presence.

Then a flashlight blared in her eyes, followed by a man's voice, and instantly she realized who it was.

"Buddy!"

"I *knew* that was you!" he yelled back.

"Stop shining that flashlight!"

"I can't believe you're saying that to *me*—in *my* plane."

"You just fly it!"

"Listen, Annalee—or whatever your name is . . ."

"No need to be rude. I didn't ask to end up here." She glared at him, taking a defiant bite out of her sandwich.

"Well, you must be living right. Rebecca and all her people are here in Estes tonight. Her dad and her uncle . . . the rich guy."

"Simon Wallace? The banker? He's in Estes?"

"Not only that. He's looking for you."

"He knows I'm here?"

"Why? Why you? When I saw them all at the Stanley—eating dinner there—and explained what happened to the plane and mentioned you'd stowed away—"

"That's not true."

"Truth? Lies? So what? Everybody I know is a liar."

"Oh, is that why a great pilot like you wastes his time and skills smuggling *perfume*?"

Buddy clicked off the flashlight. Annalee took a final bite of her sandwich and wrapped the remains in the paper bag. She swallowed.

"You treat me like your enemy, Buddy." She was speaking in the dark, but she knew Buddy could hear her clear as a bell.

"But I'm not. And this isn't just about smuggling. It's about murder. Your own *twin brother*—"

"You think I don't know that?"

"I'm going to find out who did it—and also who's trying to stop me from finding out."

"Somebody desperate."

"Ruthless, too."

Buddy grunted.

"But your smuggling, Buddy, puts you on the wrong side of everything. Probably keeps you from thinking right. Makes you think I'm your problem."

"I can't work with you. Nobody in the country would let me fly again, and flying's my life."

"But that's the thing. If you don't help me, your life might end up like Jeffrey's anyway. Always looking over your shoulder. Then one day, murdered—just like him."

Buddy remained silent.

"At least help me out of 'your' plane. I can't stay here all night. Does Simon Wallace have a place in Estes? Maybe I can stay there."

Buddy flicked on the flashlight. "He's got a place. Not far. They're still at the Stanley. Hurry up."

Annalee clambered out of the plane, still wearing one of the lavender-smelling tarps over her blue dress for warmth. Buddy actually helped her down, glaring at her as they headed toward the hotel.

"Why aren't you married?"

"What kind of question is that?"

"Jumping into airplanes. Hiding outdoors in the dark. Chasing after murderers. What kind of a life is that?"

"Well, first, if you must know, it's a good life. Important, too. I'm solving crimes, making this crazy world a better place—"

"Sure, you and that Sherlock Holmes." He scoffed.

"If you only knew," she fired back. "Besides, I work for myself. In fact, I'm actually my own boss, making my own money."

"Right. Therefore no husband."

"Nope, not yet." She gave him a look. "But maybe I'm working on that."

"Pity the poor man—" he shook his head—"who ends up with the stubborn likes of a little Miss Try It All like you."

"I'll tell him." She yanked off the tarp and threw it at Buddy. He struggled but caught it. "But for now, lead me to my help."

CHAPTER 15

"On the contrary, Watson, you can see everything.
You fail, however, to reason from what you see."

SH, *THE ADVENTURE*
OF THE BLUE CARBUNCLE

SIMON WALLACE LOOKED DELIGHTED—and even relieved—to see Annalee waiting next to his limousine in the car parking area of the Stanley.

"Are you okay, Miss Spain?"

"Nice to see you, Mr. Wallace. Enjoy your dinner?" She accepted his handshake.

He pumped her hand. "Not much actually. Just a casual business meeting. I ran into another banker I know. He invited me to talk shop. But I brought all of us—my niece, my brother, my secretary—to join him at the Stanley for dinner. Decent meal, actually. But *you*—you survived a plane crash! Are you okay?"

"Well, Buddy's quite the pilot." She'd give Buddy that at

least. But she didn't want to talk about Buddy. In fact, Buddy—seeing she'd connected with Wallace—had saluted them good-bye and walked away, toward the hotel, glancing back at her only once. What Annalee wanted now was to figure out her next steps. She also needed a place to stay.

"You're not staying here at the Stanley?" She tried to sound casual about it.

"Actually, no. They don't take 'the Jews'—well, not everyone here does. I don't advertise my ancestry or hide it—not as I once did. But people who object find out anyway. But no matter. I have my own place on the other side of town. It's quite nice."

She nodded.

Then she waited. Then she wondered if he'd see her dilemma and his ability to grant merciful help. She cocked her head. He finally seemed to notice.

"Oh! What about you? You probably need a place to stay. Come home with us tonight. It's just family—which reminds me. Any progress on that sad trouble with Jeffrey? . . . What did you say?"

His private secretary—the silent Lilian Gray—was inter-rupting him with a whisper. Standing inches from his elbow, she'd followed his conversation with Annalee with intense atten-tion. Now Miss Gray seemed to be raising an objection with her boss. Annalee wasn't sure exactly what the serious woman was saying, but she insisted the banker listen to her.

"Miss Gray, it's my *home*," Wallace rebuffed her. "And it's not a problem. When we get there, you'll make sure Miss Spain is comfortable and treated well. Put her in the Elk View Room."

Lilian Gray pressed her mouth. "Of course, sir."

Annalee gave her a nod, trying to acknowledge her concern for the woman's boss, whatever it was. *Try to stay on her good side,* she thought. *I don't need any more enemies.* Then she turned back to Wallace.

"Did you say Rebecca and her father are with you?"

"Here they come now." Wallace waved them over but wasn't smiling—perhaps because Rebecca and Uri weren't smiling either. "We ran into each other at the air show. To my surprise, I talked them into coming to Estes with me for a few days. Take a break after Rebecca's hard loss. I never imagined we'd also run into you."

"A surprise to me, too. Interesting coincidence."

"Perhaps." Wallace winced. "But coincidence is fate—as my late mother used to say. So I'm glad you're here." He called to Rebecca. "Here's your friend! It's Miss Spain."

Rebecca's face went pale. "Annalee! I heard what happened! Are you okay?"

"Not totally. I'm still feeling shaky and confused." *Who set the cops on me?* "But what about you?"

"I'm confused, too. How'd you end up on an airplane—?"

"It's getting late, sir," Miss Gray interrupted. "Should we leave?"

The efficient Lilian Gray was directing them all into Wallace's big car and then climbed into the front seat next to the driver.

"Do you need anything else, sir?" Miss Gray asked Simon Wallace, speaking from a small phone device up front.

"We're fine." Wallace shook his head, then said to no one in particular, "Now let's go home. We'll have a nice, comfortable evening."

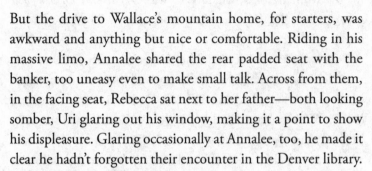

But the drive to Wallace's mountain home, for starters, was awkward and anything but nice or comfortable. Riding in his massive limo, Annalee shared the rear padded seat with the banker, too uneasy even to make small talk. Across from them, in the facing seat, Rebecca sat next to her father—both looking somber, Uri glaring out his window, making it a point to show his displeasure. Glaring occasionally at Annalee, too, he made it clear he hadn't forgotten their encounter in the Denver library.

"You got me up here, Simon," he finally hissed at his brother. "But only for Rebecca. I'm not staying long."

"Don't be in such a hurry. You and I have been working around the clock our entire lives. Maybe as a family, it's time we all slowed down. Together."

"I like the sound of that, Uncle Simon." Rebecca smiled at her father's brother. "For Jeffrey." She looked somber again. "If only we knew what happened." Then speaking almost to herself: "Do you think we'll ever find out?"

Her question hovered over the rest of the ride, following them into the house when they arrived at Bighorn Manor. A sign with that name carved into its wooden surface sat near the road leading to the impressive log home.

Wallace's driver, the same young man who'd driven Annalee to the Rialto movie theater, rushed to open the car doors—helping his boss out first, then Annalee, then Rebecca. Uri had scrambled on his own out the other side, slamming the car door. Annalee flinched. The man lived under a stormy cloud that never broke.

Miss Gray had rushed ahead, letting herself inside, not ringing the bell, speaking to a housekeeper—or maybe it was a maid—standing behind the door. Suddenly lights began to turn on throughout the home.

"Come inside, everyone." Wallace pointed toward his house. "Make yourselves at home."

Annalee sighed gratefully, so ready to sink into whatever warmth and indulgent comforts Wallace's gorgeous home would provide.

But her breath caught. *Something doesn't feel right.* She held back.

Her experience with this family, so far, had offered nothing but trouble.

Stay clear. That's what Mrs. Stallworth would've said. Her other friends—Mrs. Cunningham, Mr. Cunningham, Eddie, and even Mrs. Mason, too.

But where else could she go? She couldn't sleep outdoors. Even more, any danger lurking in Wallace's house might explain the one critical answer Annalee was seeking. For a reason she couldn't explain, she felt sure of it.

"Can we talk later?" Annalee whispered to Rebecca. They were a few steps from Simon Wallace's front door.

"I'll come to your room." Rebecca spoke behind her hand. "I'll be across the hall. Uncle Simon will gather us first in the great room. Then after lights out, I'll tap."

Annalee gave her a nod. "I'll listen for you."

The effectual Lilian Gray, meantime, stood guard at the front door—directing the driver to bring in the family's luggage, relieving Simon Wallace of his briefcase, pointing guests to their assigned bedrooms, all of it spoken in her secretarial, discreet voice.

"And you, Mr. Uri—"

"I know! Back of the house. Ponderosa Room. Silly blasted names!" Uri pushed past Miss Gray, stomping into a large foyer. Yanking off a worn hat, he threw it down on a pine-log table, turned left, and marched toward a long, wide hallway to what must've ended in the back of the house, where the hallway angled right. At the turn, he disappeared but still could be heard—grumbling, huffing, even cursing.

Ignoring him, Miss Gray pointed Rebecca upstairs. "Columbine Room again, Miss Rebecca. I hope that will suit you."

"Of course. You always take care of us." Rebecca took to the stairs, looking back over her shoulder at Annalee, giving her a subtle look, suggesting they would meet later.

"Elk View Room?" Annalee didn't wait for Miss Gray's announcement.

Lilian Gray hiked a brow ever so slightly. "That's right." She pointed to the stairs. "But we weren't expecting you, Miss Spain. So Mr. Wallace's housekeeper may still be in the room, finishing your preparations. Would you like to wait down here by the fire?" She frowned. "I see you're not wearing a coat."

Annalee returned the look. Was that a crime?

"I'd like to freshen up first," Annalee said, "if it's okay. I'll head on up."

"Last door on the left. Across from the Columbine Room." Miss Gray looked at her watch. "In fifteen minutes, Mr. Wallace would like everyone to gather in the great room. We'll enjoy a light repast before retiring for the night. At nine o'clock."

Miss Gray frowned slightly again, looking at Annalee's slim arm. No wristwatch. "You'll find a small clock on your nightstand with the correct time."

Annalee held her tongue. This little back-and-forth with

Miss Gray was making her feel like a charity case—instead of Mr. Wallace's houseguest. And for what?

"I'm grateful, Miss Gray." She'd simply speak truth. "Without Mr. Wallace's kind hospitality, I could be sleeping outdoors tonight. So I'll watch the time, and while I'm here, I'll keep my head down." She gave Lilian Gray a smile. "Rest assured, I won't cause his household any trouble."

Miss Gray squinted. "No, Mr. Wallace doesn't like trouble." She met Annalee's gaze. "So thank you, no. I'm sure you won't cause that."

But there it was again. Trouble. Annalee opened the door to the Elk View bedroom and could've stopped breathing. Wearing a maid's uniform and making up the bed was the young colored woman who'd attended her speech at the bank—pushing, after the applause, a note into Annalee's hands. *"May we meet? About Jeffrey Mann?"*

Seeing Annalee now, the woman dropped the pillow she was fluffing.

"Oh, Miss Spain!" She collapsed on the bed and burst out crying.

Annalee shut the door and locked the latch, grateful for the privacy—especially with yet another young woman connected to Jeffrey Mann crying her eyes out.

Annalee stepped to the bed and sat down on it, put her hands on the young woman's trembling shoulders, trying to comfort, and let her cry.

"It's not your fault." Annalee tried to sound calm. "Murder is so wrong." Only thing worse was not knowing who did it. But this young lady? Annalee didn't want to think her guilty. Her crying sounded more like despair. But who knew? Jack had surprised her last night. Would this crying maid shock her, too?

The woman kept sobbing. "Will God send me to hell? I deserve it!"

"What are you talking about?"

"I've sinned!"

"And who hasn't? Please stop crying. Wipe your face."

Annalee had said the same to Rebecca. As for going to hell, what would Jack, indeed, say? *"God's not sending people to hell. He's trying to keep them out!"* She offered that assurance. "This is a bad business—Jeffrey's murder. Every piece of it. But how did you get involved? And sinning?" Annalee grimaced. "Who are you? You look younger than me."

The young woman sat up, wiped her face with her shaking hands. From a pocket of her uniform, she retrieved a weary handkerchief, wiped her eyes, and blew her nose.

"I'm . . . from Telluride."

Annalee's heart skipped. "What are you saying?"

"Why do you sound angry? I needed a job. I couldn't stay there. I ended up in Denver—"

"From Telluride? That's your home? That's really true?"

"Why would I lie?"

Annalee couldn't answer. This case made her doubt everybody. "So you left Telluride?"

"I had to leave. No future for me there. So I came to Denver, ran into mean ol' Uri, the miner. He has a place near Telluride. Everybody there knows him. He helped me get this job with his brother, Simon. That's how I met Jeffrey and then—"

"What is your name?" Annalee almost wanted to shake her. The young woman was babbling in circles about everything—or nothing—all at once, none of it making a lick of sense.

Annalee stood. "Your *name*, please. Can we start there—?"

But a tap on the door interrupted her.

"Della? Are you bothering Miss Spain?" It was Lilian Gray.

"That's your name? Della?"

The young woman rushed toward the locked door. "I can't talk now," she whispered to Annalee. "Can I come talk to you later? Or maybe tomorrow?"

Annalee slipped behind her to the door. "Do you know who killed Jeffrey?" Her voice too was a whisper and deadly serious.

Della leaned in close. "You mean like your speech at the bank? You said if we know about a murder, we should tell you?"

"So you know who killed Jeffrey?"

Della blinked hard.

"Della?"

She blinked again. "Crazy thing is, I think I do."

A second tap on the door was harder. Annalee released the lock as silently as she could and opened the door.

"Della is a great help. Thank you, Miss Gray."

Lilian Gray looked behind her, frowning at Della. "Mr. Wallace will be waiting in the great room, Miss Spain. Five minutes."

"I'm on my way . . . in just a moment." Annalee stepped aside to let Della through the door, smiled at Miss Gray—who didn't return her smile—and closed the door behind them.

She let herself exhale.

"Mercy, Lord." She suddenly felt *this close* to breaking open a

key door of this case. She could feel it. What did Simon Wallace say? *"Coincidence is fate"*?

Because waiting in this fancy bedroom for her was this Della—from Telluride, of all places—who thought she knew who killed Jeffrey Mann? If that was a fate of coincidence, she'd accept it for all it was worth.

Annalee leaned against the door, letting her eyes take in this unlikely guest room. She was due downstairs, but this was something to see. The suite was all done up in mountain-blue plaid—four-poster bed and wall of tall windows dressed to the nines, the whole space overlooking a mountainside, offering apartment-size comfort, complete with its own bathroom.

On a porcelain counter there, a valet kit awaited. So after a quick freshening up, Annalee brushed down her wool dress—hem to collar—praying she didn't smell of lavender, whiskey, and tequila, too.

In a bathroom drawer, she found a hairbrush and comb, toothbrush and dental supplies, and—*look at that*—three pretty headscarves, each a different design in pleasing shades of blue, accented with a luscious yellow. All silk. Whose were those? For female guests? Brushing back her thick black curls, she twirled a few wisps around her face, folded the pale-blue scarf into a narrow band, and tied it around her head, securing it at the back with a small knot.

"Watch your back," she whispered to herself, looking at her reflection in the fancy bathroom mirror. She started toward the bedroom door. But halfway there, she stopped, stood still, closed her eyes, took in a deep breath, and did what Jack Blake would've done. She looked up.

Lord, for this lodging, I'm grateful. A little prayer. Nothing fancy or holy-sounding. But she finished it. *Now help me while I'm here.*

Because as she already knew, in this house, with these people, she was going to need it.

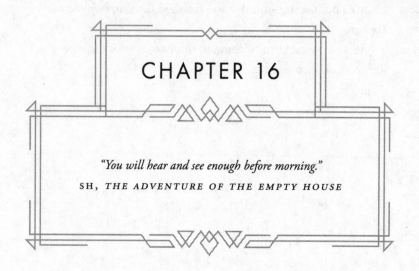

CHAPTER 16

"You will hear and see enough before morning."

SH, *THE ADVENTURE OF THE EMPTY HOUSE*

"RIGHT ON TIME, EVERYONE!" Simon Wallace, the wealthy banker, greeted his poor-as-church-mice guests. Wearing simple wool slacks and a fresh white shirt, he stood near the head of a long buffet table between two floor-to-ceiling French doors at the rear of his massive, great-looking great room. An after-dinner spread of dried fruit, cheeses, nuts, tarts, small sandwiches, and a silver tea service lay atop a pristine white table runner. A comforting wood fire snapped and popped in a nearby fireplace, taking the chill off the vast room.

"Are you expecting other guests, Uncle Simon?" Rebecca walked across to the fire, hugging herself a moment, then moved toward the table, looking hesitant to pick up a napkin and plate.

"Just us." Simon pointed her to a stack of plates. "Help yourself." He gestured to Annalee. "You, too, Miss Spain. It's been a long day. Let's relax and—"

His voice caught. He was looking at the pale-blue scarf on Annalee's head.

She raised her hand to her hair, felt the scarf. *Wrong choice,* she told herself.

"I found this in my room. It was so pretty . . . I thought it was for guests to use and—" *Stop talking.* Clearly she'd made a wrong move. She should've asked permission.

Simon Wallace looked pained, indeed, to see it.

"I'll take it off." She started to untie the knot.

"No!" Simon Wallace cut her off. "It's lovely on you. Please continue to wear it."

"The scarf was Marie's." Rebecca was looking at it, too. "My cousin Marie's—"

"Ah, his only daughter, Marie." Uri Wallace entered the room—late and making a point of it. He sauntered to the plates, picked one up, started piling on food.

"Please, Uri . . ." Simon turned to him.

"*Please?* You're saying please to *me?*" Uri cut his eyes at his older brother, still loading his plate with food. He pressed his jaw.

"If nothing else, since we've mentioned Marie, in her memory, can we spend one evening together without arguing?"

"I didn't ask to come up here—"

"Please, we just lost Jeffrey—"

"*We?* You're claiming Jeffrey, too?"

"Papa!" Rebecca slammed her plate down on a coffee table.

"What? You too, Rebecca?" Uri rolled his eyes. "See what we

invited you into, Miss Spain?" He glared. "That's your name, right?" Uri tossed his questions to Annalee but didn't seem to expect an answer.

She ignored him—because she had her own question. *Why is this family a tinderbox? "Double, double, toil and trouble." Right, Shakespeare?* His alert warned the murdering king, Macbeth. But in this family, what birthed their tension? Did it sweep away Jeffrey, leaving him victim to their undercurrent of anger, resentment, and maybe a hateful revenge?

Annalee pulled a chair over, offered a matching one to Rebecca. They both sat silent. Simon did, too—easing onto a large leather sofa, closing his sad eyes for a moment.

Uri still stood, grabbing at his food. He wiped his mouth with the back of his hand, glared at everyone, chomping loud, his mouth open.

Looking at him, Annalee had an odd thought. "I always wanted a brother," she said in a reference, she supposed, to Uri.

Her confession seemed to catch him off guard. He stopped chomping for a moment, gave her an irritated look. "What's that supposed to mean?"

She didn't answer him. *I won't tussle with you.* He was sour and unpleasant.

Simon, meantime, gave her a concerned frown. "You're an only child?"

"As far as I know." Annalee winced. She didn't mean to tell this family her personal business. Yet here she was, spilling the beans of her most sensitive territory to this curious little house party. "My mother . . . ," she said, feeling her chest tighten. "She abandoned me at birth." She glanced at Uri. "Near Telluride."

"What's that got to do with us?" Uri spat out his question.

Again, she refused to answer. Uri's rudeness didn't deserve a reply. He might have had good reason to be so insulting with his family. Perhaps even a murder motive? But she hadn't herself caused Uri any harm. So she wouldn't suffer his ire. Not tonight. Not after the day she'd had.

"Do you know," she said to Simon, "of Esau and Jacob—the biblical brothers?"

"Sadly, yes."

"Why 'sadly'?" Uri sneered.

"Who were Esau and Jacob?" Rebecca pulled her chair closer.

"Twin brothers." Annalee reflected.

"Double the trouble," Rebecca offered.

"What makes you think of them?" Simon shifted in his chair. "Or do I already know?"

"Why? Did one steal the rug out from under the other?" Uri scoffed.

"You know this story?" Annalee asked.

"Is it about a thief? A brother who steals?" Uri cut his eyes at Simon and then plopped down on the floor, crossed his legs.

"It's getting late." Simon pulled out a watch on a chain. He stood.

Watching him, Uri said, "Oh, so you're done talking, Simon? Getting too hot under the collar?"

"I have an early meeting tomorrow, everyone." Simon turned from Uri, set down the teacup he was holding.

As if on cue, Lilian Gray entered the room, walked over to Simon, leaned to his ear, and spoke too low for anyone else to hear.

"Yes, I was just saying I had to turn in. Let's call it a night."

Lilian turned with a satisfied smile. "Stay and finish your desserts if you'd like."

Uri cocked his head at her, showing clearly what Annalee herself seemed to be thinking—that Lilian had chosen, for some reason, to suddenly sound like Simon's wife, the mistress of the manor.

"But not too late, please," Simon corrected her—to show Lilian her place? "Della has to do the cleanup." He handed Lilian his table napkin. "Do you mind helping her tonight? It's already awfully late."

If looks could kill, Lilian's pained glare would've slayed every person in the room—starting with Simon. He didn't seem to notice, but the atmosphere had turned colder and more awkward.

Everyone stood, Uri included.

"Thanks for the grub, Brother." He stomped out.

"So glad you enjoyed it. Good night, all." Simon slipped out, not turning back.

Sighing, Rebecca set down her napkin, gave Annalee an embarrassed smile. "Guess I'll head up, too."

"Maybe Miss Gray would like my help?" Annalee made her offer, not wanting to seem too important to assist but not expecting Lilian to accept the help.

Lilian Gray didn't. Instead, she snatched up the dirty plates and stacked them atop heavy serving platters, placing all on a single massive tray and soldiering across the room—ignoring Annalee—just as Della came in to start the cleanup.

"Need my help?" Annalee asked, still trying to show gratitude for her lodging.

Della told her no.

"Well, good night." Annalee turned to leave. Della gave her a nod, her eyes searching Annalee's, seeming to show she hoped they could meet—tonight? In the morning? Sometime tomorrow?

Rebecca gave Annalee the same look, one that said, *"Can I come to your room soon? To talk?"*

Lilian Gray, however, had reverted to the person Annalee had first met. Stone silent. As Rebecca and Annalee walked together from the great room to the staircase, Lilian didn't open her mouth.

"Okay, sleep well," Rebecca said.

But Annalee doubted a single soul in this conflicted household would find a way to do that.

In her room, Annalee closed the door, locked it tight, and let out a long sigh. Untying Marie's blue silk scarf, she laid it atop the oversize countertop sink, taking care to smooth the silk fabric and fold it with honor. *I shouldn't have worn it.* Simon Wallace had shown deep grace by encouraging her to leave his dead daughter's scarf on her head.

Ah, Marie.

Simon's dead child was just one matter of business that had rattled his composure during his late-night "family" gathering. But Wallace family business wasn't Annalee's concern tonight. If anything, she should pirate into Simon Wallace's office, probably downstairs on the first floor, to see what banking secrets she might discover. Maybe even something involving Jeffrey.

But Annalee felt plumb exhausted. She hoped Rebecca was worn-out, too. *We can rendezvous tomorrow.*

Tap-tap-tap.

She groaned silently. That would be Rebecca. Annalee turned off the lamp on her nightstand, ruffled her curls to look ready for bed, preparing to ask Rebecca if they could meet in the morning. A dark room would let her know it truly was bedtime. For both of them. *So go back to your room, Rebecca.*

Or Della, the young housemaid? But it was time for Della to get some shut-eye, too.

So Annalee unlocked the door and swung it wide-open. Her jaw dropped.

"I'm sorry to bother you."

It was Buddy Mann. His green eyes shone in the dim hallway light. His hair was wet. He'd had a shower.

"You still up?" he asked.

Speechless wasn't a word Annalee often used. She could see Buddy standing before her, plain as day, whispering in the dark and eyeing her. But she couldn't find words to say how much she couldn't believe it was Buddy standing there whispering. Except it *was* Buddy.

She cocked her head. *What on earth?* "How'd you get in here?" she whispered hard. "What do you want—?"

"I'm a smuggler," Buddy whispered back. "Breaking and entering isn't that different—"

"You're a burglar, too?"

"Uri Wallace—you can't trust him."

Annalee shook her head. "You broke into a locked house at half past bedtime to tell me that?" She set her jaw. "And how'd you know this was my room?"

"Simon always puts favorite guests here. Other folks get the first floor, back of the house. No view! Believe me, I know." He stepped closer.

"Leave now! Or I'm screaming. Loud!"

"This is a dangerous family, Annalee. After you drove off with these people, I knew I had to come over to warn you. Really warn you. A murderer's one of this crowd. I don't know who it is—but I strongly suspect Uri."

Annalee narrowed her eyes at Buddy. "Wait, why Uri?" She couldn't fathom. "Never mind! This is crazy. *Leave.*"

She glanced across the wide pinewood hallway at Rebecca's bedroom door and then down the long hall toward the stairs, praying that neither Rebecca nor anybody else would pick this ridiculous moment to come along. She hated to think what anybody would guess or say if they saw Buddy Mann, of all people, hovering in the doorway of her bedroom.

She gave Buddy a glare, but he didn't budge. "I'm calling the cops!"

"Come to the airfield tomorrow. I'm going to teach you to fly a plane. It's a good thing to know."

"Not on your life. Besides, I already learned—*today.* Now, *please go.*" She stepped back inside her bedroom, anxious to lock the door—tight.

But Buddy grabbed the door and held it. "Somebody killed my twin brother. I wasn't the best brother. But if it was Uri Wallace who killed him—"

"Uri? Jeffrey was his own son-in-law!"

"But Uri doesn't half think straight. That's why he's such a menace—"

"Is this about smuggling?" She frowned. "Wait, don't say another word. You need to go!"

"Smuggling, cheating, lying. Who knows why Jeffrey was killed? But if it was Uri, I need your help to nab him—before he hurts somebody else. He's a loose cannon. A crook, too."

"How would you know?"

"Don't ask. For now, I need you to stay alive."

"I'm trying!" Annalee glared at Buddy—trying not to recall how Jack said those same words to her on her last case. *I need you to stay alive.* She frowned at Buddy. "Now *go*. Good night!"

Buddy stepped back, glanced down the hallway, then back at her. He reached for her, almost as if to push a curl off her forehead—as Jack would. She stepped quickly out of reach. "Please leave!"

"Just be careful." He searched her eyes one more quick time. "Watch your back."

Those words. She'd heard that enough, too.

"Leave!"

"Come find me tomorrow." He melted into the hallway. He was gone.

Annalee stood in the doorway another minute, still peeved at Buddy's brash nerve to break into this house, creep up the steps, and sneak to her room. So she surely looked dumbfounded when the door to Rebecca's room slowly opened and Rebecca peeked out.

"You still up?" Rebecca whispered across the hall.

Annalee rolled her eyes. "I'm going to bed. This day is done."

"Okay." But Rebecca slipped across the hall anyway. "I've been thinking—"

"Can we talk about this tomorrow?" Annalee stifled a long, genuine yawn.

"Just one question. About Esau—"

"Who?"

"The brother in the Bible."

"It's late, Rebecca. I'll tell you the whole story tomorrow."

"Okay, but what did he steal? From his brother?"

"All wrong. Jacob stole from Esau. Jacob was the cheat." She yawned again.

"But what did Jacob steal from Esau?"

"You want to know tonight? Rebecca, it's late."

"Just tell me."

"He stole his blessing."

"That sounds bad." Rebecca looked dismayed.

"Actually it was." Annalee gave Rebecca a weary smile. "Now go to bed."

"You, too. Here's some clean pajamas. A dress for tomorrow, too—if you don't mind wearing one of mine." Rebecca handed over the clothes. "Oh, and here's an extra lipstick." She glanced away. "Also, I'm sorry."

Annalee nodded. "For getting me involved? It's not your fault."

"But you ended up in an airplane! How'd that happen?"

"I had to hide. Somebody set the cops on me. I don't know who. But we'll figure it out." Annalee thanked her for the night-clothes and dress. "Now go to bed. Sleep well."

"Because we have work to do. Don't we, Annalee?"

"To crack a case? That's what detectives do."

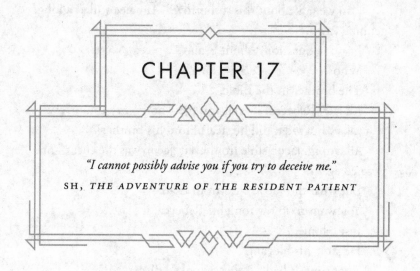

CHAPTER 17

"I cannot possibly advise you if you try to deceive me."
SH, *THE ADVENTURE OF THE RESIDENT PATIENT*

THE CLOCK ON ANNALEE'S NIGHTSTAND said 6:30 a.m. After a deep, dreamless sleep on the guest bed in Simon Wallace's Elk View guest room, Annalee had bathed quickly, brushed her teeth, smoothed her hair, and wiggled into Rebecca's clean but worn dress—an oddly festive yellow-floral shirtwaist better suited for a summer garden party.

But it nicely matched Marie's blue silk scarf. So Annalee tied the scarf on again—not sure why, but thinking it might speak, in some way, to Simon Wallace's secretive soul. The man needed to come clean over *something*—especially if he'd stolen from his brother.

Perhaps the pretty scarf—a visible memory of his daughter—would help.

For now, however, Annalee wanted to get out of this house, breathe in fresh air, take an early morning walk, and clear her head. She had questions needing answers and she could think better walking around. The ancients had a description for it. *Solvitur ambulando.* To solve a problem, walk around. *So here I go.*

She needed a coat, and inside a tall pine armoire, she found several outdoor jackets and coats and whatnot—all for men, but one small coat thin enough for a petite woman to wear. Slipping it on, she stepped quietly through the bedroom door, tiptoed down the hallway, and descended the stairs.

The big house was silent except for the ticking of the hallway clock, its soft bells announcing the time. Seven o'clock. *I'll be back before anybody misses me.*

Opening the heavy front door, Annalee slipped out of the house, closed the door behind her, and let her eyes take in the sky. Yesterday's sunshine was gone. A cloudy sky hovered overhead. But no matter. She'd walk in a downpour just to get alone and think about two things. Who killed Jeffrey Mann? And how soon before Klan cops tracked her down in Estes and threw her in jail?

But first her walk alone. Except somebody was following? She jerked around and her heart leaped.

Uri Wallace stood nose to nose, right in her face. He breathed out cigarette smoke and tossed down a butt onto the gravel path.

"That's my coat." He glared. "And my daughter's dress."

"Thank you." Annalee buttoned the coat, securing it tightly at the neck. "I'll take good care of it. The dress, too." She stepped to the side.

"What do you want from us?" He glared. "Why are you here?"

She sighed. In a family with wealth, maybe suspicion of others was common.

"I'm your brother's houseguest. *He* invited me here. If you have a question about me being here, ask him. Now excuse me. I'm going for a walk. Nothing strange or suspicious about it."

Uri scowled but stepped aside. "Why were you talking about those Bible brothers?"

"That was last night."

She turned, ready to cut him off—eager to get on with her walk—but she stopped herself, listening to his question. She pressed her mouth. "You really want to know? About Esau and Jacob?"

"I asked you, didn't I?"

Annalee ignored that, but she knew his seemingly innocent question was how a case could start to turn. She needed to know who had killed poor Jeffrey, Buddy's twin. Now, here stood the dead man's father-in-law asking her to lead him back centuries to two warring brothers. Because the case really started there?

Thus, her Sherlock Holmes was right. He'd said that "the grand thing" in solving a tough puzzle was "to be able to reason backwards." Most detectives didn't practice that perspective much when looking at a life quandary, Holmes said.

But "reasoning backward" or, what he called reasoning "analytically"—and being unafraid to look hard at the past—led to the answers one was seeking in the present.

"You'll have to walk with me," Annalee told Uri. She headed down the gravel path, grateful to hear him step beside her. Up ahead, a road from the house turned left toward town. So she turned the other direction, not eager on a Sunday morning to run into folks wondering who she was and why she was walking and talking so intimately with a white man.

"This way." She pointed east. The air was crisp, the mountain breeze frigid. She turned up the collar on the borrowed coat, its thin hood hardly worth the trouble. Uri threw up his collar, too. Digging her hands into the coat pockets, she considered how to start.

"It's a story of deceit." She glanced at Uri, saw he was listening. "Family deceit. Understand?"

"So this Jacob tricked Esau?"

"Yep, but it started with the mother." Annalee tightened her collar. "No, with the father—well, actually—"

Uri groaned. "Oh, swell. One of those *he begat* stories." He took out a cigarette, stopped to light it. "If you're gonna *begat* me the Bible all day, forget it."

"No *begats*? But isn't that the point? All my best students—"

"This ain't school!"

"It shouldn't be, but neither should life. That's why this family kept stumbling at it. They didn't learn their obvious lessons!"

"Why not?"

"Impatience." She gave Uri a look, headed toward a mountain path, let Uri follow. "Look, it's a Bible story, so there's God in it and then—" Annalee stopped herself. *Sherlock wouldn't tell the story like this. Watson either.*

"Listen, Uri, you're right. Forget the *begats*. The story starts when Esau and Jacob are born. Twin boys. Born to a couple named Isaac and Rebekah."

"Got it. And then?"

"Good question. *Then* things go off the rails. The father, Isaac, favors Esau, the eldest twin."

"So what happens to Jacob?" Uri scratched his chin. "No, wait. I know. The *mother* must favor Jacob."

"And you must know this story." Annalee glanced at Uri. "Or maybe you've lived it?" She paused her walking, turned to Uri. "Is that why you're so angry at your brother, Simon?"

"That's none of your business."

Annalee stifled a sigh but didn't retort. She walked toward a downed oversize log, kicked through dead leaves, brushed off snow to sit on it.

Uri walked that way, too, standing over her, but he didn't sit. Instead, he asked a question. "What did Jacob steal? Steal from Esau?"

"You really want to know?"

"I asked, didn't I?"

"Forget it." Annalee stood to start back. "Why are you always so rude?"

"If you had half an inkling, young lady, what my family— my brother worst of all—has taken from me—"

"His blessing. That's what Jacob stole from Esau. His blessing."

"What the devil is that?"

"Everything really. Their father's blessing for a good life— which, rightfully, should've been Esau's, as the eldest son. But the worst part is *how* he stole it—"

"Deceit—"

"Family lies."

"Of course."

"The mother cooked up the plan. 'Trick your father. Pretend

you're your brother. Fix the stew he loves. Wear the clothes your brother wears.' It was a pretty elaborate scheme, and it worked."

Uri had grown quiet. He was listening to her, or he appeared to be listening. For sure, he'd stopped arguing. Thus, she too held her tongue and started walking back to the path.

"Wait," Uri called after her.

Annalee turned, waited for him, seeing he had a question—making herself willing to hear it.

"Are you saying," Uri asked, narrowing his eyes at her, "that the *mother* was in on it?"

Important question. Especially coming from Uri. But why? Annalee searched Uri's eyes, looking for the meaning behind his asking. His usual angry man's swagger had dropped a notch. Several notches, in fact. His face looked almost like that of a child asking such a question. The *mother*? The true schemer?

"That's it, yes." Annalee spoke softly. "The mother. She planned the whole thing."

Uri ran a hand through his graying, wild-looking, unkempt hair. He shook his head. "What kind of mother would do such a thing?" He spat on the ground. "And why?"

Annalee turned and started walking again. Uri came up beside her, looked hard at her, waited for her answer, but she stayed silent.

He spat on the ground again. *"Why?"*

"I can't help you." Annalee pulled the coat tighter. "When it comes to mothers, I don't have one blasted clue. Not a single one. I just know they're not perfect." She kicked at a small rock on the path, watched it veer away. "Not by a long shot."

Uri kicked a rock, too, looking confused. "And what was her name again? The mother?"

Annalee glanced at him, still seeing a child asking the question, not the embittered man. "The mother? Her name was Rebekah."

Uri winced, sighing. "I wish she had a different name."

Was that your mother's name? Rebekah?

Annalee wanted to ask that in the worst way. It would make sense because Uri's daughter shared the name, too. But Annalee knew this wasn't the time to ask about the Wallace family tree. For now, she was grateful that Uri had toned down his ire. *So don't mess things up with too many questions,* she told herself. Such as: *Uri, did you kill Jeffrey?*

But then Uri asked an odd question himself: "Did Esau kill him? His brother?" He shrugged. "You know—to get back at him."

"Absolutely not. They were *brothers*, Uri. In fact, they mended their fences eventually. That's what the best brothers do. At least I think that's what happens."

Uri glanced at her. "So you're not sure yourself, are you?"

"Not totally. The first murder in the Bible is between brothers."

"Cain and Abel?"

"You know that story?"

"Who knows what I know anymore?" Annalee heard his question, understood its implication for herself—and for her own mother, whoever in the devil she was. Could she ever forgive her? She thought too of Jack. Could she forgive him? Wherever in the world he was? And for whatever reason he'd left? She pressed her mouth, thinking indeed of Jack, knowing what he would say, so she said it.

"But nothing's too hard for God."

Uri heard her and huffed.

So she left it at that, turned toward the path back to Simon's house, glad for now that Uri was still walking with her and not stomping around. She wanted to ask him about Della. How did they know each other from Telluride?

How did Della know Jeffrey? And what else about Telluride did he know? Had he known *her* mother?

But they'd done enough talking for now. She could tell by the look on his face. She changed the subject.

"Are you coming in for breakfast?"

Uri glanced up at Simon's big log manor. He sniffed and waved away the question.

Turning to the path toward town, he kept walking.

"See you later—" Annalee started to say.

But for now, anyway, Uri was gone.

Inside Simon's place, the household was awake and moving about but not really hurrying—and for that Annalee was glad. Taking in a breath, she could smell fresh-brewed coffee. And cinnamon rolls? Gracious, she hoped so. The aroma was divine.

Upstairs in the Elk View Room, someone had opened the draperies to a stunning mountain view. Della probably. The guest bed was made up, too. Bathroom cleaned. New towels hung. And one more thing.

A penciled note. A tiny little scrap.

But it had been left under a fresh bar of hard-milled scented soap on the bathroom sink. So it could've been overlooked— and maybe discovered by someone who didn't need to see it.

Instead, the handwritten message—scrawled on a tiny piece of heavy, torn stationery—caught Annalee's eye. She gave it a look, praying somebody wasn't trying to lead her astray. *With a secret note?* She rolled her eyes. *Hidden in a fancy bathroom?*

She gave the paper a gentle tug, pulling the message from beneath the sweet-smelling soap, shocked to see who had written it.

Agent Ames. *Mercy.*

Her hand shook as she held the scrap of paper. Ames? How on earth did he know she was at Simon's house and then find his way into *this* bathroom?

But there was his name printed atop the torn piece of paper. Beneath it, a Denver phone number was scribbled in pencil, with two words. *Call me.*

Annalee folded the note over twice but then unwrapped it to reread the number—Main 7876. Easy enough to remember. So she tore the note into tiny pieces, dropping the shreds into the small fire still burning in a grate servicing the bedroom.

Hanging up the coat she'd worn, she changed into her own blue dress. Fancy but more comfortable. It also had been brushed and a stain on the shoulder expertly cleaned. By Della?

Time to huddle with her, too, Annalee told herself. Time also for breakfast.

Most of all, however, time to stay alert. With Agent Ames in play, her time was running out. He must be under pressure to nail Jeffrey's killer—or else she'd get the frame. All with thanks to her fancy-dancy handkerchief. *Thanks, Jack. For nothing.* But she shed that thought. Whatever she felt now about Jack just left confusion.

Straightening her dress, she opened the bedroom door,

stepped into the hallway, and took in a deep breath. She needed to find a telephone to call Ames. But despite everything, she was hungry and ready to eat. A sweet roll and a cup of coffee didn't seem too much to indulge in first.

She glanced at herself in a hallway mirror. Not too much?

Unless breakfast with Simon Wallace came with its own problems, too.

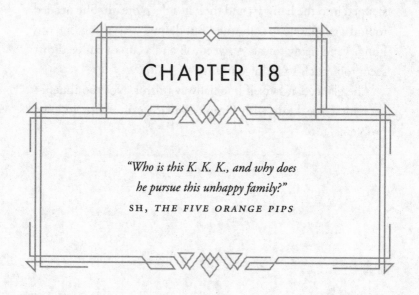

CHAPTER 18

*"Who is this K. K. K., and why does
he pursue this unhappy family?"*
SH, *THE FIVE ORANGE PIPS*

IT DID, OF COURSE. Problems hovered over this family like a dripping gray faucet. Annalee could see it as she followed the alluring aroma of coffee, ending up in a sunny morning room in the east end of the sprawling house. *Yep, breakfast is served.*

But Simon presided over it with a look of pure menace.

He'd heard bad news apparently, and Annalee could see who'd brought it. Seated across from Simon was a person Annalee didn't expect. But *why not?*

It was the tall, thin man she'd seen at the maps table at the Denver Public Library—Hugh Smith. The new gentleman friend of the librarian, Mrs. Flora Quinlan.

Trying not to stare, she simply nodded at the man—and also at Simon—finally whispering a quiet hello.

"Help yourself to breakfast," Simon mumbled to Annalee, gesturing to his buffet setup, giving her a smile, but distracted.

He looked down the table at Lilian Gray. She was thumbing through a neat pile of papers stacked next to her breakfast plate. On cue, she looked up at her boss. "Did you need anything, sir?"

"Is the food still warm? What about more eggs? Could you—?"

"I'll take care of it, sir." Miss Gray pushed back her papers, placed them all in a rectangular leather case, lowered that box into a rolling cart, and locked it all up. The key was on a long, thin chain circling her neck and dropping past her bodice almost to her waist.

Annalee watched this, thinking right away: *I want that key.* Then also wondering: *What else does it lock?*

Trying to look disinterested, however, she stepped to the buffet spread and selected a plate, served herself dainty enough portions of melon slices, cinnamon rolls, scrambled eggs—not worrying if the eggs were cold—and trying to melt into the business of the meal, knowing it was highly unusual for a young Negro woman to be filling her plate to eat at a banker's breakfast table, in his handsome vacation home.

Pulling out a chair midway along the table, she could see Simon preparing to introduce her to Hugh Smith. But the man beat him to it.

"Miss Spain? Is that you?"

"It's nice to see you. Mr. Smith, right?" She gave him a smile. "Good morning."

Simon frowned. "You two know each other?"

The tall man looked suddenly uncomfortable. "We patronize the same library—near Five Points." He gave Annalee a curt nod.

Lilian Gray turned back, watching the exchange with what Annalee would call an odd intensity. Simon was watching, too. Because Lilian lingered a moment too long?

"The eggs?" Simon gave Lilian a look.

"Of course, sir." Lilian walked toward the door but glanced back just as Hugh Smith spoke.

"Miss Spain and I are both friends of the librarian."

Lilian Gray seemed almost to stumble. But watching her boss watch her, she composed herself and finally left to check on the eggs.

"Friends, you say?" Simon's voice sounded casual, but his eyes betrayed a clear concern. He picked up his coffee cup, his hand slightly shaking.

Annalee noticed this, and Mr. Smith appeared to notice, too.

The tall Mr. Smith toned down his chatting, returning to his food. But Annalee figured she now knew his role: he was Simon's new ghost employee, the one running his Phantom Trust.

Clearly a discreet man, he'd helped Simon sell airport bonds for the City of Denver without its Klan politicians knowing Simon, the Jewish banker, owned his firm. Now this discreet man was revealing an unexpected friendship with a Denver librarian—who'd befriended Annalee, too?

Annalee picked at her food, watching this curveball zing around the room, knowing Simon must be trying to weigh every single possible implication of all these connections. He'd shown kindness to Annalee, hoping she might shine a light—as a young detective—on the murder of his niece Rebecca's husband.

But now it turned out she and his ghost employee each shared a close friendship—with a Denver city employee.

If I could melt through this chair, right into the floor, Annalee thought, *I'd do it now.*

She held herself still. *Or?*

Or she could push this envelope and see where it took her, especially regarding every question she still had about her curious case—this puzzle involving Jeffrey, Uri, Rebecca, Della, Buddy, and maybe even Jack. How did in the world did it all fit together?

Lilian Gray returned with the eggs, also carrying a massive silver tray loaded with a fresh pot of coffee and fancy serving platters laden with food. It seemed a weighty load, and Lilian was carrying it like a faithful beast of burden—though not looking pleased about it.

Simon, seeming not to notice, remained silent.

Annalee cleared her throat. "Our friend's a wonderful librarian . . ."

Lilian turned, listening, her eyes narrowed.

". . . and her branch is the city's first," Annalee added. "Up-to-date resources—maps and records and things. Wouldn't you agree, Mr. Smith?"

Annalee looked down the table at the tall man, waiting for him to affirm what she was saying, but she saw him shift in his chair, averting his eyes especially from both Lilian and Simon.

Then he stood up. "Thanks for the breakfast, sir. But I'm running late. I need to get back to . . . to town." He turned to Lilian. "I'll see myself out."

Simon handed him a folder. "Yes, you have a lot to do. Call me when you have an update."

The man headed out, then turned back. "Call you here, sir?"

"Yes, on my Denver line. I'll be here one more day." Simon resumed eating.

One day? Annalee had to work fast.

"More eggs?" Lilian approached Annalee with a platter.

Annalee declined, gave her a smile, let her eyes linger on the secretary a moment, weighing everything. But she then spoke only to Simon.

"I understand what just happened, sir."

Simon put down his fork. "What do you mean?"

"I interrupted your breakfast meeting with your employee. Someone who works for you . . . privately, I assume."

"More coffee?" Again, Lilian.

Annalee declined again. She was trying to talk to Simon, but Lilian always seemed to direct his traffic, blocking the way. In fact, without Lilian present, Simon never seemed to meet with people. How did he ever have a candid conversation with anybody with Lilian always at his elbow?

Or maybe that was his tactic. Lilian was his buffer. To keep hard topics and difficult people—with all their thorny problems and questions and demands—away from him. Thus, as his private secretary, Lilian was cream of the crop.

That might work for his business. But for murder? For digging out its motives and suspects and schemes? Annalee needed to get Simon alone.

"You were saying?" Simon asked.

"Oh, it's nothing." Annalee gave him a smile. *It can wait, except it can't.* She pushed her chair back, stepped to the buffet to replenish her plate.

Rebecca entered then, making a fuss about being late.

"I fell asleep again." She gave her uncle a hug, then yawned. "Thanks for waiting for me."

"A restless night?" Simon looked concerned. "Was your room cold?"

"My room was fine." Rebecca piled food high on her plate. "This looks delicious." She pulled out a chair. "I slept like a log—I took a small sleeping draft last night. But I heard a car gunning its motor out front early this morning. And somebody knocking? Or was I dreaming?"

"You heard right." Simon looked over at Lilian. "More coffee for me, please?" He turned back to Rebecca. "Some fella from the Bureau of Investigations—"

Annalee's throat tightened, but she didn't flinch.

"What's that? Annalee, have you ever heard of that? Some bureau?" Annalee didn't reply, but Rebecca didn't seem to notice. "What did he want, Uncle Simon?"

"Not much. Just said a spree of break-ins have been reported this side of the mountain in private homes. He came by to warn us." Simon shrugged. "Then he asked to use a restroom—"

"You let him in the house, sir?" Lilian's voice stayed polite, but her concern was evident.

"Just a couple of minutes. Afterward, he thanked me and left."

Annalee, still quiet, weighed the information, knowing she had questions. *What did the man look like?* But she already knew. It was Ames. Seeing her blue dress hanging on the closet door in her room, he figured where to leave his penciled note. But why was Lilian so concerned about the man's visit? Rebecca, too?

"What did he look like, Uncle? A *spy*?" Rebecca giggled, making light.

Simon half smiled at her. "Look like? Ordinary man. Tall and broad. Heavy voice. He left me his card."

His card? Annalee didn't look up from her eggs and bun. She was waiting, waiting, waiting for Simon to say more or even pass around the card.

But Simon did neither. Instead, he pushed back from the table. "I'm going for a walk. Would anybody like to join me?"

"A solo walk is better, sir." Lilian offered this. "Give you time to think."

"Solvitur ambulando." Annalee finally spoke, her voice soft, drawing everyone's attention.

"What's that?" Rebecca looked intrigued.

"Ancient wisdom. 'To solve a problem, walk around.'"

"Excellent advice." Simon glanced at Lilian. "In that case, get your coat. You can come with me. I've got business to sort, and I need your help."

Lilian looked conflicted but showed she wouldn't protest. "Right away, sir." She followed Simon from the morning room, their footsteps fading as they departed the east side of the house.

Rebecca stood to leave, too. But Annalee interrupted.

"Actually, Rebecca . . ." Annalee's whisper was urgent.

Rebecca turned, sat back down. "We should talk now?"

Annalee pulled her chair closer. "Actually—you know that more than me."

Finished with their coffee, Annalee and Rebecca headed to the great room to huddle near the fire, but it hadn't been set. The room felt chilled and gloomy. But Annalee had worse worries. Her face showed that.

Seated beside her, Rebecca started with a question. "Did you know that man, Annalee?" Rebecca pulled a blanket off the sofa, pulled it around her shoulders. "The spy?"

Annalee gave her a look. "Honestly, yes. I know him."

"A spy? In my uncle's house?"

"He's not a spy." Annalee yanked up a blanket, too. "He's the law. A federal agent."

"So what did he want? Is he looking for Jeffrey's killer? Or for something else? Am I in trouble?"

"You're not in trouble, because you didn't kill Jeffrey. You know that. You're in trouble because of your family."

"My family?"

"Don't sound so shocked. Your family seems to hold secrets—and I need to find out what they are." Annalee cocked her head. "And I need you to help me."

"But how? And why?"

"To keep me off the prison gallows!"

"Oh . . . your handkerchief." Rebecca wrapped the throw tighter around her shoulders.

"Don't get comfortable, Rebecca. I need us to think. No, for you to think. What is the hidden secret—?"

"I don't know!"

"But look at your dad. He *hates* your uncle Simon! What happened between them? You grew up in this family. You haven't heard any talk? Or overheard something?" Annalee paused. "Or found something?" She gestured at the room. "Like old family photos?" She wrinkled her brow. "But nothing here says 'family.'

Same thing in Simon's office in his bank in Denver. Just fancy art. Same thing here. It's like a museum in here."

"You've been in Simon's bank? In his office?"

"Don't change the subject. In fact, let's start there. Where is the 'family' in this family? Or is Simon trying to hide it?"

Rebecca groaned. "Actually that's the problem."

"What do you mean?"

"I've been asking the same questions since I was a little girl." Rebecca pulled the blanket even tighter. "My mother died when I was young. But I've always been told how beautiful she was. 'A blue-eyed beauty.' I've heard that a thousand times. But I've never seen her. No pictures of her seem to exist."

"Strange. Were they lost? Stolen? Burned? Destroyed?"

"That's what I've always thought. So one day, when I was up here in Estes—and Uncle Simon had gone to town and the house was empty—I started snooping." Rebecca looked sheepish. "Which was wrong."

"Snooping where?" Annalee narrowed her eyes. "In Simon's office?"

"In his bedroom."

Annalee listened. "What'd you find?"

"Nothing. It was just a bedroom. Well, lots of locked doors. His closet. His chest of drawers. Even the bathroom door. Everything locked—"

This didn't surprise Annalee. A locked desk and a curious key had played a pivotal role in her last big case. Folks hiding secrets tended to lock them up.

"But what did the bedroom look like? What was in there?" Annalee threw off the blanket and stood. "I'm going to see it."

"Now? See Uncle Simon's bedroom?"

"We don't have much time. Simon'll be back soon with Lilian." Annalee headed across the room. "Let's go!"

"But what if they—?"

"Hurry!"

"I don't like this!" Rebecca groaned again. "What if we're caught red-handed?"

"You can stand guard. As soon as you hear Simon and Lilian unlock the front door, I'll hightail it out of there."

Rebecca didn't move. But Annalee turned back to the sofa, stood over Rebecca for a moment, then reached down and pulled her to her feet. "Simon's been hiding something for years and Uri's hopping mad about it. Does it involve your mother? Their mother? And Jeffrey? I'm not sure what it means, but I'm willing to bet it means something."

"I should've never told you about this!"

"You told me because it matters."

"But about what?"

"That's what we're going upstairs to find out."

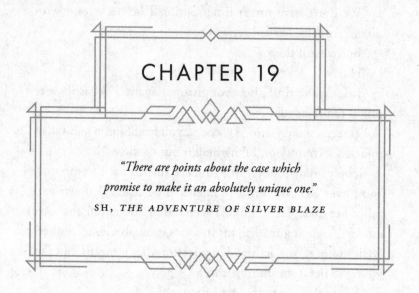

CHAPTER 19

"There are points about the case which
promise to make it an absolutely unique one."
SH, *THE ADVENTURE OF SILVER BLAZE*

THE DOOR TO SIMON'S BEDROOM WASN'T LOCKED.

Annalee took a breath, turned the handle. "I'm going in." She gave Rebecca a look. "Keep your ears peeled. Soon as you hear—"

"Oh, I know! Just hurry!"

They were just off the top of the central staircase. Simon's bedroom was on the right, taking up most of that side of the second floor. Standing there, Annalee pursed her lips. On her last case, she'd rummaged through a fancy bedroom, looking for evidence—and here she was again, preparing to do the same thing. *You need a different approach,* she told herself. *Or different suspects.* Or did all people with secrets hide their most private valuables in their bedchambers?

Annalee didn't have a clue, in fact, what she was looking for in Simon's impressive bedroom, but things out of place tended to announce themselves. So did things that weren't out of place—but should've been. She could think of half a dozen Sherlock stories with that twist. Thus, the curious incident of the dog in the night got solved because the dog didn't bark. It knew the culprit. Case solved.

It was one of the most popular Holmes stories. But right now it was reminding Annalee not to overlook anything ordinary and obvious in Simon Wallace's lavish room. *So pay attention.*

"Mercy, what are you thinking on, Annalee!" Rebecca's whisper sounded stressed.

"Stop worrying!" Annalee opened the door wider and slipped inside, letting her eyes take in the massive space. A banker's bedroom. Way off-limits for someone like her. *Breaking and entering.* The thought rattled around in her head. *Well, you're entering—even if not breaking in.* Either way, she shouldn't be here. But it might be a room that held not just secrets and lies but also truth and answers.

If she couldn't yet see them, she felt them in the shadows. The curtains, for example, hadn't been pulled back, although the bed had been made. This was the owner's suite, after all. So it had been cleaned, dusted, carpets swept, mirrors wiped, pillows fluffed.

Yet like other rooms in the house, not one personal thing was displayed. No framed family mementos. No hair tendrils preserved in glass shadow boxes. No family knickknacks. No beloved heirlooms.

In Simon's bedroom, instead, his big bed sat under an

impressive canopy covered in a smart, modern fabric that matched the room's drapes.

Every wall, meantime, sported what looked to Annalee like museum-quality paintings. She stepped from painting to painting, taking in the exquisite watercolor drawings and oil landscapes. She'd never seen such pieces close enough to touch. Art museums in Chicago didn't admit colored people, and Denver's museum, also segregated, refused colored visitors, too. She didn't recognize every artist's signature, but some—Degas, Monet, Goya, even a Vermeer—were by world-class painters. She couldn't imagine what Simon had paid for such treasures. Or why.

He'd ridiculed such showy luxuries when they'd spoken in his bank office in Denver. So why—in his private bedroom at his mountain home—would he install such a notable art display?

She ran her hand over one gold filigree picture frame. Gorgeous workmanship. Simon sure knew how to pick them. A second piece was even showier. Next to it, a third piece—framing a small but lovely seascape—looked less important, but Annalee couldn't take her eyes off it. She stared at it a full, long minute.

Then touching the frame, she let out a small sigh when the filigree responded to her touch with a soft click. She leaned closer. The picture frame was hinged. Opening it, she stood face-to-face with a wall safe.

She stepped back, took a fast breath, thinking, *Don't touch it.* She could hear Mrs. Stallworth—and mean ol' Mrs. Mason *and* Mr. Mason, plus Mr. Cunningham, Mrs. Cunningham, and everybody else who cared even a bean about her well-being— now warning her away.

But she also wanted to put her fingers on the dial and turn it—even though she knew not one thing about cracking a safe. Yet she longed to try. Her brain, meantime, was screaming, *Get out of here.* How, indeed, would she explain herself to Simon— or worse, the oppressive and protective Lilian Gray—if they caught her now?

Eyeing the safe, however, Annalee could see the one thing that seemed even more out of place in the room.

A plain black telephone. Not fancy, like the room's decor. More for business than a banker's boudoir?

It sat on a small table directly under the seascape. The table drawer was locked, but the telephone sat there, begging her to pick it up.

Annalee ran to the bedroom door, yanked it open, whispered, "Still clear?"

"What's taking so long?" Rebecca paced near the stairs. "They'll be back any second!"

"I'm almost done."

"Find anything?"

"Nothing yet. I'm almost done!"

She closed the door quickly, slipped back to the hinged painting, closed it, and picked up the telephone handset— waiting for the operator and praying it was the Denver line.

"Operator. Number please—"

"Main 7876." Annalee spoke clearly but quickly.

Clicks and blips. Then finally a male voice. "Talk to me."

"Agent Ames—"

"You've got till midnight—"

"But how'd you know I'm in Estes? I found your—"

"Stop talking. You're running out of time." Ames sounded

angry. "I can't hold off these Denver cops much longer. They're hot on your trail. The chief issued an order: Make an arrest."

"But this is the strangest case. I'm following half a dozen threads, all feeling unrelated, but I bet anything they're connected—"

"Of course they're connected. Crime is always connected. But you need to figure out just one thing. Who killed Jeffrey Mann?"

"I'm trying. But can you help me? Or Officer Luther?"

"Gone. He quit the force."

"Luther? But there's still you."

"Those Klan cops would get my number, see right through me. Meantime, they're set on bringing you down."

"You can't secretly help me?"

"I already did. At the air show."

"How'd you—?"

"I went early. I figured you'd be there—looking for clues about Jeffrey. When I got wind that cops were scrambling for you, I started hunting you down, too. I saw you go in the hangar, so I pointed a herd of cops the other way. Then I prayed you'd hide, maybe in a plane, out of sight and harm's way. But next thing I knew, a plane was taking off with you apparently in it."

"You prayed?"

"Annalee!" Rebecca yanked open Simon's door. "They're coming!" She frowned. "You're on the telephone?"

"Almost finished!" Annalee waved her away. She whispered in the phone, "Did you find Jack Blake?"

"I'm not looking for him. I'm trying to take the heat off you."

She sighed.

"Think of your dead father, Annalee—"

"Not a day goes by—"

"Then you know desperate people do evil things. Klan thugs know you're in Estes now. You stick out like a sore thumb. Somebody saw you at the Stanley Hotel walking through the kitchen."

"Lord, have mercy."

"Then climbing into a big limo. I can only hold off these rogue cops today."

"I need tomorrow."

"Why?"

"I'm worried for Jack. He may be in danger. One more day? Please?"

"I can't promise. Well, okay, blast it. One more—"

"Annalee!" Rebecca pleaded.

"I have to go—"

"Find that killer!"

Annalee raced to close the door to Simon's bedroom, then grabbed Rebecca by the shoulders, turning her so they faced eye to eye, giving her a piercing look.

"We've done nothing wrong!" She mouthed the words. *"So say nothing."*

Rebecca nodded. They'd pull it off.

But the door opened to Lilian's room, just across from Simon's.

"Della?" Annalee whispered, shocked to see the young

colored maid looking just as stunned to see her and Rebecca huddled outside Simon's door.

Della was carrying something—a piece of paper, jewelry, money, or something. She jammed it into the pocket of her uniform. Caught red-handed?

But the same question, of Annalee and Rebecca, appeared on Della's face. Caught red-handed?

The three sent signals of alarm to each other with their eyes.

Mercy, how would they recover? Annalee took the lead. "I'll come to find you later, Della. Thanks so much for helping." Her voice sounded natural, she hoped.

"No problem, Miss Annalee." Natural voice in return. Della walked toward the stairs and descended with total calm.

Lilian's voice rose from the foyer. "You're still doing rooms?" She sounded more curious than annoyed.

"Finished now, ma'am." Della was sharp as a tack, Annalee realized. No elaborate lie. No long story that could be questioned. Her short answer was enough. Then she made herself scarce.

Taking that cue, Annalee and Rebecca descended the stairs, nattering about nothing.

"Well, it's a pretty color on you, Annalee . . . Uncle Simon! How was your walk? Did you *solvitur* . . . whatever it's called?"

"Not totally. But I got some fresh air."

"What about this afternoon? Any plans?"

"Maybe a drive. Into the national park? Would you like that? How about you, Miss Spain?"

Annalee gave him a slight smile, seeing his attempt to divert her attention from the curious dramas of his family.

"Sounds nice," she said, knowing she had far more urgent

tasks in order to figure out who killed Jeffrey. She needed to sit people down in this household, one by one, and question them. But she also needed to talk to Buddy Mann—about whatever in the world he wanted.

All of it made her head swim.

Or?

She could look for the common thread.

"I'll get my coat."

"Wonderful." Simon turned to Lilian. "Ask Della to pack a lunch. For the five of us."

"Five?" Lilian looked confused.

"Five?" Rebecca asked, too. "Is Papa coming?"

"We saw Uri when we were out. He's on his way back. If I convince him to join us, we'll have enough for a picnic."

Annalee stifled a laugh. A picnic? What was Simon up to? He made it sound like a happy family outing. Nothing with this household could be called "happy."

The hallway clock sounded eleven soft bells.

"We'll leave at eleven thirty." Simon looked at his watch. "Lilian, you can drive. No need to bother the driver on his Sunday off."

Lilian gave him an odd look but whispered yes and left the room.

"Sunday . . . ," Annalee said, almost to herself. The Sabbath day? For her? She hadn't set foot in a church today. Still, she reminded herself: *Keep it holy.*

Perhaps that's why she noticed Rebecca—who was shaking her head, holding her hands to her stomach. Nobody else seemed to notice, but Annalee asked anyway.

"Rebecca, are you okay?"

"The altitude? Maybe I'll stay here." She turned toward the stairs. "I'll go lie down for a minute."

"I'll help you upstairs." Annalee reached for Rebecca's elbow.

Simon noticed her leaving. "You need to lie down? Feel better soon, sweetheart," he said. "The drive will do you good."

But upstairs, Rebecca looked too sick to even stand. In her room, she dropped to the bed, holding her stomach, moaning.

Annalee watched this, not understanding, but she wanted the reason. Closing the door for privacy, she stepped to the bed and sat down on the edge, leaned toward Rebecca. "Talk to me."

"I can't go back there." Rebecca grabbed a pillow, hugged it to her chest.

"Where? To the national park? What happened there? Tell me, Rebecca."

"*Oh, God—*"

"God actually already knows. Just tell me."

"But why?"

"So I can help you—and help your family." *And help myself, to be honest.* "Something happened to everybody, but whatever it was, Rebecca, you're not to blame. But tell me. What happened?"

"I killed Marie."

"No, you didn't!"

"But I did." Rebecca jerked away the pillow, turned on her back. "Why won't you believe me?"

"What are you saying? She died in the mountains?"

"On a Sunday hike! After a picnic. Like today."

"You all went together? You and your dad?"

"The four of us, yes—me and Papa with Uncle Simon and Marie."

"Not your mother?"

"Mama had died years before."

"You and Marie must've been close."

"Always together." Rebecca glanced down. "We looked like twins."

"Why am I not surprised?"

"Everybody said so. Less than a year apart. Me, the older. But we looked so alike."

"What was wrong with that?"

"It's our fathers—they look so different. My dad and Uncle Simon are brothers, but they don't look anything alike. Dad's ruddy and stocky. Uncle Simon is short, thin, and light."

"Like you."

"And like Marie. When she was born, with all the fuss of her looking like me, something changed in Papa. That's what people eventually told me. That Papa was already bitter, but he turned hard."

"Hard enough to kill?" Annalee frowned at her own hard question, not surprised at Rebecca's whispered answer.

"Yes, to kill."

"To kill Jeffrey?"

"Not Jeffrey. But I hold my breath every day, hoping he won't strike a fatal blow to Uncle Simon. He hates him that much."

Annalee winced. "So what happened to Marie?"

"She fell from a mountain—above Estes."

"*Mercy*, Rebecca, I'm so sorry."

"We were hiking." Rebecca bit her lip. "Uncle Simon wanted 'his beautiful girls'—that's what he called Marie and me—to see the view from one of his favorite trails. But it was narrow and rocky. So Uncle Simon and my dad were arguing."

"About the danger?"

"No, about who would be in charge. Uncle Simon was leading and wouldn't yield to Papa—'I know these hills!' But Papa yelled, 'I'm a miner!' He kept thundering about how to hike a mountain. Then in the middle of their bickering, Papa stepped on a rock that almost gave away. He hollered, 'Watch it, Rebecca!' I yelled, 'What?' Marie turned to look at me, I guess, since Papa called my name—not hers."

"So she kept walking?"

"Just one step—but that whole side of the trail gave way. It just collapsed under her feet, tumbling down the mountainside into a chasm below, taking her with it." Rebecca gave Annalee a pained look.

"Marie screamed my name, *Rebecca*. Because I could've saved her. I was old enough—already thirteen. She was twelve." Rebecca grimaced. "She was right *there* in front of me." Rebecca touched Annalee's arm. "As close as you are to me. Then the next second, she vanished."

"What a horrible accident—for both of you. No child should die like that, and no child should have to watch it happen." Annalee searched Rebecca's eyes. "But you didn't kill her."

"But she's dead."

"A tragic accident, Rebecca—and it haunts you." Annalee stood. "I can't even imagine how it must feel to you. So I agree—you shouldn't go to the 'picnic' today." She paused. "But there's something else?"

"People around me die. Marie and now Jeffrey and—"

"Somebody else?"

"A taxi driver in Denver. A colored man."

"The mugging? The cabbie? He was beaten for—"

"Picking up a young white woman." Rebecca searched Annalee's face. "That woman was me."

"You called a Negro taxi company?"

"No, I was downtown—just window-shopping. No money to buy, but I splurged to take a taxi home. The driver refused to pick me up, but I insisted. Made a fancy speech to him about supporting his right to drive anybody." She looked pained. "Next thing I know, his picture was in the papers—saying he was mugged and beaten for driving a white woman to her house on Franklin Street."

"Is that what you were trying to tell me after we left the library? 'I think I killed somebody'?"

"I meant the taxi driver. But then we found Jeffrey dead, too." Her voice broke. "Now Simon wants me to go the mountains—where Marie died. He wants me to be strong. To 'face my lies'—to stop blaming myself for her death. He's always saying that. But what about his?"

"Simon's lies?" Annalee cocked her head. "What are they?"

"I wish I knew. He's hiding *something*. But going to the mountains won't help, surely not me."

"Well, you're not going." Annalee set her jaw. "I'm not going either. I'll tell Simon—"

"I just wish you could help us. So much in our family feels hidden. We're Jewish, but not enough to matter except to the Klan. Simon spends all his time scheming against them, getting back." Rebecca shuddered. "Makes me wonder if that's why Jeffrey was killed. Some Klan person wanted to get back at Simon? Sometimes I just wish we could start over. Erase everything."

"But you don't know everything—or even know what to

erase." Annalee yanked open the door. "I'm going to talk to Simon."

"What are you going to say?"

"I don't know. But nothing will get right here—not to mention me getting off the hook with the police—until somebody in this household comes clean."

"It has to be him." Rebecca looked resolute.

"But will you agree to do more?"

"Like what?" Rebecca looked wary.

"I don't know. But if finding out the truth means taking risks you haven't taken before, will you take them with me? For Jeffrey?"

"And for Marie? She was the sweetest thing." Rebecca's childlike voice was a whisper. "I will. Just tell me what to do."

Annalee didn't blink. "First, you rest. I'll get us a plan to unravel answers."

"But how?"

"Truly, I don't know. But I promise you this: I will find a way."

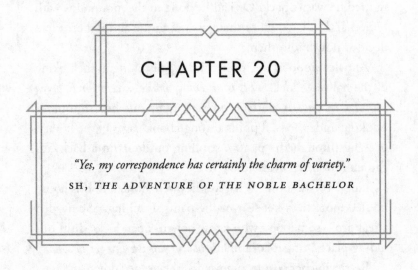

CHAPTER 20

"Yes, my correspondence has certainly the charm of variety."
SH, *THE ADVENTURE OF THE NOBLE BACHELOR*

DOWNSTAIRS IT WAS QUIET AS A MOUSE. Silly phrase. Annalee tiptoed from room to room. Still, it was oddly quiet. Not a soul stirring. Nobody talking or moving.

"Della?" She called out for the young maid. But Della didn't answer. In the kitchen—a bright room with nary a pot nor pan dirty or out of place—a clock ticked on a wall. But no human soul graced the space.

"Lilian?" Annalee called for Simon's private secretary, then checked the first-floor rooms—great room, morning room, dining room, a small library, Simon's probable office (its door locked), Lilian's office (unlocked but every possible thing in it put away and secured). But Lilian wasn't to be found.

Not hearing Uri stomping around and complaining, she

figured he wasn't back. Or had he gone to the mountains with Simon and Lilian—all of them assuming she and Rebecca had decided not to join them?

Annalee stood in the foyer, thinking, listening to the ticking of the hallway clock. *This is an empty house, except for Rebecca upstairs resting.* A perfect time to ramp up her snooping? Looking under beds, flipping through book pages in the library, peeking through the pantry, strolling outdoors in a backyard garden for buried evidence.

Nope, too random. Whatever lies were hidden in this house needed more than her seat-of-the-pants searching. She needed a real pro—somebody who knew how to open locks, sniff out hiding places, finger combinations. *So you need to get to town.*

Retrieving her coat from upstairs, she headed down and outside, whispering a genuine thanks to see Simon's big car coming around from the rear of the house.

It stopped. Simon's driver stepped out, wearing casual clothes. He touched his cap. "Like a ride somewhere, miss? I can drive you."

"I hate to bother you." She gave him an urgent smile.

"I'm going to town anyway. Just need to pick up something before heading back to Denver. Mr. Simon gave me the rest of the day off. Oh, and—"

"Yes?"

"There's some mail here for you. I was going to leave it in the front hall when I came back from my errand. Let me help you into the car and I'll hand it to you."

"Mail?" Annalee took a breath. *For me?* Who besides Ames knew she was staying at Simon's place? She cocked her head. Well, Hugh Smith knew. But he had seemed surprised to see her and left right after breakfast. She blinked. Mrs. Quinlan? Had Hugh Smith told her? But the librarian wasn't a gossip. Who would she tell anyway?

The driver opened the passenger door and Annalee climbed into the back. The car had been cleaned and polished to a fare-thee-well, inside and out. Annalee scooted onto the big leather seat, smelling the pleasing aroma of leather soap, wishing it meant her situation was as pleasing and clean and pliable. But she wasn't in Estes Park on vacation. She was hiding out at Simon's because she had a target on her back. Delivered mail meant somebody knew precisely where to find her.

Reaching over the seat, the driver handed her an envelope—and her mouth went dry. The slim envelope was identical to the one that held the poison-pen letter she'd received at Mrs. Cunningham's place in Five Points.

Same fine stationery. Same typeface from the same European typewriter, its erudite look one she now recognized, making her hand tremble.

Slowly she tore open the seal. Silently she read the typed words.

You're annoying me.

Annalee swallowed. She'd expected an ugly threat. But something about these words felt nastier. More menacing.

Leave Estes.

No signature, of course.

"Good news today?" Simon's driver tried to sound friendly. But his voice belied tension. He was driving a young Negro woman, alone, in his boss's fancy car—as his boss would've required. But if anybody saw him, he'd have to answer to the Klan.

Thinking about that made Annalee wonder other things. Why didn't Simon have the car himself? He'd said Lilian would drive them into the mountains. Did Simon have a second vehicle? What time did he leave? Was Uri with him? What time would he and Lilian be returning? Or was this a trap?

She checked the window but saw nothing suspicious. The driver was headed into downtown Estes. Making no strange turns. She breathed deep. This case was taking its toll. It was perplexing and frustrating and she had one day left. Or jail?

But there was something else, and she knew precisely what it was.

She was frightened—especially without Jack. If he were here, he'd assure and help her, convince her the police wouldn't possibly charge her for Jeffrey Mann's murder. Just because of a handkerchief? And without a motive or means? Indeed, Jack would scoff at the possibility, comfort her, and hold her close. *"Don't you worry."* Then he would kiss away her fear.

But Jack *was* missing. And without him here, she feared for his life. *He's in danger,* she worried. But she hadn't figured out where or how.

"Where can I drop you off, miss?" Simon's driver spoke through the gadget in his front seat. "Any particular place?"

Annalee looked out of her spotless window. The driver was proceeding down the main drag in Estes Park. Quaint supply stores and little shops lined both sides of the street. But it was Sunday, and all but a few looked closed.

"Right here is fine."

"Not much open today."

"I'll just walk—and window-shop."

"Weather's changing. You shouldn't stay out long."

The car came to a stop.

"No need to help me out." Annalee rushed to depart the limo. If anybody was looking—and she was sure one or two folks surely were peeking from behind the curtains in their parlors—she didn't want to stir any gossip that a white man in a fancy car dropped off "a colored gal" on the main street. *"Holding the door for her. Can you believe it?"*

Annalee thanked the driver, exited the car on her own, and quickly crossed the street, trying to look like a service person— maybe a cook or laundry worker from the Stanley Hotel. Or a maid from one of the houses above town on the mountainside.

If she just sauntered along, anybody looking from inside a window would close their curtains and stop their looking. Sure enough, after a while, she felt fairly invisible. Not even the sundry Klan member would be interested—she hoped—as she took her time along the street, ignored by the few people out taking their Sunday afternoon walks.

In truth, she was searching—under cover of feigned indifference—for Mrs. Mason, with Mr. Mason behind the wheel of Jack's car. Eddie perhaps with them. Seeing her, Eddie would dash from the car and hug her like crazy.

Her eyes tingled. *My friends.* They meant the world. But as she walked and window-shopped or whatever she was doing, they were nowhere to be seen.

So at the end of town, Annalee turned west and let herself head toward the Stanley Hotel.

She kept her eyes peeled, knowing who she was looking for but wanting still to keep a low profile. She let fancy cars drive past her without her turning to look, just kept strolling casually beside the drive leading to the main hotel building.

Handsome people—dressed smartly—came and went, out for their Sunday promenades. Not one person acknowledged her, of course. Occasionally a young white mother—seeing Annalee— would draw her child close, pulling away, an insult Annalee knew all too well, as if she wanted to assault or kidnap someone's child.

I'm fighting to save myself.

So don't get distracted. Reaching the hotel grounds proper, she took a side path toward the outbuildings—aiming, in particular, for the small airplane hangar.

In the daytime, she could see it was a modest but fairly new building, set up for the hotel's new airplane entertainment— provided a few days a week by barnstormer Buddy Mann. Flyers posted in the hotel probably showed off his handsome smile, drawing pretty young guests, giving no clue what their young pilot did most of the time—fly smuggled goods in and out of the country.

A flat-out lawbreaker. That's what Buddy Mann was. And now Professor Annalee Spain was sneaking alongside the Stanley Hotel hangar, hoping to convince the light-fingered Buddy to do a bit of underhanded work for her.

The hangar's two big doors were both pushed wide-open. Buddy's damaged plane and a second, larger biplane were parked inside. A third, even larger plane was parked in the field.

Annalee peeked around one door, saw two men—one of them Buddy. They were peering up at one of the damaged wings on Buddy's plane, probably cracked or splintered during their hard landing. She jerked back.

"Hey!" Buddy's voice. "What d'ya want?" He said something to the other man, adding, "Hotel worker, probably. I'll scare him off."

Annalee stepped back toward the far side of the hangar.

Buddy rushed toward her, sounding extra angry. "What do you want?" But he gestured her behind the hangar. "Can't talk!" he whispered. "Find out anything on Uri?"

"Forget Uri!"

"What?"

"Well, I'm still looking."

"But what if—?"

"Listen, can you pick a lock?" She cocked her head, seeing Buddy hesitate. "Well? Can you?"

"Where is it?"

"In Simon Wallace's bedroom."

"Good grief." Buddy frowned. "What is it—a safe?"

"Wall safe. Behind a pretty picture."

"When?"

"Tonight. After everybody's asleep."

"In his bedroom?"

"I have an idea, so he'll be sleeping soundly—"

"Sounds crazy!"

"Not when I could get framed."

"Buddy!" the other man called from the hangar.

"Coming!" Buddy gestured toward the path by the hotel,

pointing Annalee in that direction. "What time?" he whispered. "And what's in the safe?"

"A photo? Family documents maybe?"

"Something about Jeffrey?"

"No, the Wallace family." She squinted. "Well, I'm not sure. But wait until midnight."

"Or till I get my head examined." Buddy backed away.

"We're going to crack this thing." She gave him a smile.

He stepped back. "You have a dimple."

She twisted her mouth. "Only when I show it." Then she frowned. "Buddy, I can't go to jail." She sighed. "Or worse."

He looked her over and reached down. "Does this snap work?" He buttoned the top hook of her coat. The gesture surprised her, but she didn't push him away. In fact, she felt grateful for it—somebody showing that she mattered. Even if it was the smuggler Buddy—especially since Jack wasn't around. *Where is he?*

"That coat's not heavy enough." Buddy glanced at the hills. "It's starting to snow. Pull up the hood."

She fussed with it, pushing her curls inside.

He grinned a crooked smile, waved her toward the path by the hotel. "You better get moving. Look for me tonight."

"You have a watch? To meet me?"

His green eyes flashed. "I won't need one."

Walking back, trying to ignore the cold, Annalee kept the same indifferent pace—to blend in, but her heart was racing. She was keeping a low profile, hood pulled up, but also keeping an eye out for the Masons, Eddie, too. She'd begged for them to come. Now she hoped they wouldn't. Or maybe they came but missed seeing her.

There was nobody to ask. Every storefront looked closed. Even if one were open, if she went inside and asked questions, she risked being told on to the Larimer County Klan. Well organized, they'd run roughshod over Catholics, Mexicans, Blacks, and Jews across northern Colorado, causing farmers and families to go bankrupt. Businesses, too. So what they would do to a nosy, snooping "colored gal," she didn't want to imagine.

Besides, she wanted to get back to Simon's house—and try to talk to Uri, Della, and certainly to Simon. Already the temperature was dropping. Annalee wanted to get to Simon's before a fast-moving blizzard dumped its frigid danger right atop her head. She wasn't dressed for weather. Simon, meantime, would have every fireplace crackling in his manor and she'd appreciate the late-day warmth, especially if she could catch him alone for a talk.

But Simon wasn't there.

"He's in the mountains—searching for Uri." This was Della's nervous announcement just as Annalee came through the front door of Bighorn Manor. Della was pulling off an oversize beaver-skin coat, its fur matted with snowflakes.

"Searching?" Annalee sounded confused. "Why's he searching?"

"Who's searching?" Rebecca walked down the stairs.

Della shook out the big coat, hung it in the foyer's closet. "Mr. Simon. He's looking for—"

"Never mind, Della. I'll explain. Please see about supper." Lilian pointed Della toward the back of the house, probably seeing the hidden look of annoyance on Della's face but ignoring it.

"Who's missing?" Rebecca's face showed panic.

"Now, don't get alarmed—"

"What are you saying, Miss Gray?" Annalee stepped closer.

"Well, we were in the park having our picnic, and it started snowing—"

"Lilian!" Rebecca grabbed her uncle's private secretary by the shoulders. "Who's missing?"

"Your father. He left the campsite and—"

"Papa's missing?"

"Yes, but—"

Rebecca's knees must have given way. Her whole body slid toward the floor.

"Rebecca, here. Sit on the steps." Annalee helped her. "Until we find out what's going on." She turned to Lilian. "Can you explain?"

"Well, when you and Rebecca didn't come down—"

"Uri! Where is he?"

"Della had packed a picnic and—"

"And Uri!" Annalee felt like screaming. Why wasn't Lilian explaining?

Rebecca, meantime, moaned, "Papa! Annalee, I can't lose Papa, too!"

"He's not lost, Miss Rebecca," Lilian insisted. "He'd left the picnic site, heading up a trail he wanted to investigate." Lilian rolled her eyes. "Della packed enough food for an army. So when you and Miss Spain didn't come down for our drive, and Uri came in to get lunch, Simon invited him to join us for the picnic. He invited Della, too." Lilian pulled at her dress sleeves.

"We ate our lunch, enjoying the scenery and wildlife. We saw bighorn sheep—"

"And Uri?" Annalee stood inches from Lilian's face.

"After half an hour or so, he hadn't come back. It was starting to snow. Big flakes. Spring snow. You know what that's like. Fast-moving. Wet and heavy." Lilian looked at Annalee. "In minutes, we could barely see our hands in front of our faces—or even see the ground to get back to the car."

Annalee listened, knowing exactly what Lilian was describing. Spring snow in the Rockies could be deadly. A lost person could freeze to death in less than an hour depending on conditions, like if they fell into icy water or got soaked by freezing snow and couldn't switch to dry clothes to get warm.

"Was he wearing a coat?" Annalee wanted assurance. The light coat Uri had worn this morning wouldn't cut it.

"He carried the beaver skin with us," Lilian said, "but he wasn't wearing it. Della grabbed it and put it on when it started snowing and—"

"So where are they?" Rebecca stood. "Where's my papa and Uncle Simon?" She gestured vaguely toward a window. "Look! A blizzard!"

"I understand, Miss Rebecca." Lilian gave her a smile but sounded patronizing. "They'll be fine. Mr. Simon drove us home—in the Model T—and then headed out again after he called the forest rangers. They're meeting up so he can show them where Uri was last seen—"

"Oh, God, please . . ." Rebecca looked panicked.

"Your dad knows the mountains." Annalee tried calming Rebecca. "If anybody knows how to survive in these conditions, it's him."

"But why'd he go off by himself?" Rebecca turned to a windowpane, scraped at frost. "I should've gone on the ridiculous picnic."

"Let's get dinner first. Is it ready, Miss Gray?" Annalee put the question to Lilian but didn't wait for an answer. "Do you mind if I ask Della? For Rebecca's sake? The kitchen's this way?"

Again, not waiting for a reply, Annalee stepped from the foyer, swung around, and marched toward the back of the house, moving quickly—to talk to Della before Lilian waylaid her.

"Please, don't—" Lilian called after her.

But Annalee was on a mission to get some answers. Lilian Gray would be the last person to stop her.

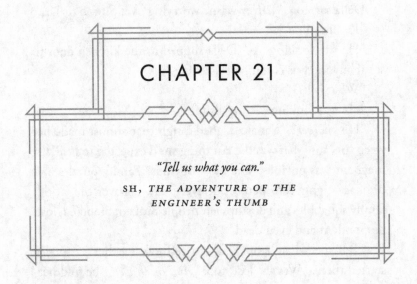

CHAPTER 21

"Tell us what you can."

SH, *THE ADVENTURE OF THE
ENGINEER'S THUMB*

DELLA WAS CARVING COLD CHICKEN, arranging it on a platter. She looked up. "Is he back?" She spoke in a whisper. "Mr. Simon?"

Annalee shook her head. She grabbed a kettle, put it on to boil, opened a cabinet, and took down plates and whatnot. She turned to Della. "Were they arguing? Uri and Simon?"

"Of course." Della rolled her eyes. "What else? That's all those two do."

"But about what? Today at the picnic?"

"Some 'picnic.' It was bickering, start to finish. Who killed Jeffrey! Each blaming the other." Della put down the knife. "But they've got it all wrong, Miss Annalee."

"Tell me." Annalee took a chair.

Della sat, too. "Jeffrey wasn't worrying over Simon or Uri."

"I'm listening."

"He was looking . . ." Della slipped to the kitchen door to see if anyone was coming or listening.

"What is it?"

"He was looking . . . for his mother."

"His *mother*?" Annalee sighed a sigh that almost made her weep. Because that was the last thing she'd expected to hear. Or maybe it was obvious. The most obvious? Family puzzles and dramas might seem petty. But every day, all over the world, family squabbles and dustups left people broken, bloodied, lost, despondent and even dead.

"Tell me what happened—to Jeffrey's mother." Annalee started there. "Was she lost, too?" *And listen well,* she told herself. Jeffrey deserved justice but solving his case was also her ticket home free.

"I hate to talk about it—"

"Della."

"She abandoned him. But she was just a young girl when she gave birth to Jeffrey and his twin, Buddy. Do you know Buddy?"

"Well, I do." Annalee shifted in the chair, not fully sure why. "But just go on. Where was this?"

"In Telluride—"

"Your hometown, too."

"Right. Their mother's name is Belinda. My mama was her little friend. They were in the one-room school together. Then when they were older, Belinda fell for some sweet-talking, good-looking miner, got pregnant out of wedlock, and had to give up the boys. They got moved around to different folks, finally ended up with a family in Denver named Mann. The babies' first names were changed to Buddy and Jeffrey. Half-poor people themselves, they had their hands in one kitty or another."

"That's how the boys learned to steal and carry on?"

"Both of them, right. But before she died, Jeffrey's adoptive mother tried to come clean on things, as much as she could. She told him about Belinda. He told Buddy. But the trail to Belinda was stone-cold. Years went by. Then last year, my mama passed away . . ."

"I'm so sorry." Annalee swallowed, suddenly feeling con-flicted and confused. Della was talking about Telluride and mothers, family and loss, and Annalee had hard questions of such things—even in the middle of a murder investigation.

Who exactly, indeed, was Della's mother? Was Della her only child? Did she know another colored woman who'd given birth near Telluride? But this was no time for such questions. Annalee let out a hard breath. *Stay on track.*

"So Belinda?"

"She left town. Her babies both gone. Their daddy was . . . well, he disappeared."

"What'd Belinda do then?"

"For a while, she was helping other unwed girls—"

"Helping how?" Annalee's voice was a whisper.

"Listening. Letting them cry their eyes out on her shoulder. Setting some up in old mining cabins—ghost towns now."

Annalee let out a breath.

"It wasn't bad. They'd have a place to stay at least. But the pressure took its toll. Finally she cut her ties to Telluride."

"And you were helping Jeffrey find her? Why now?"

Della sighed. "He wanted to help her if she was still poor, but help better than Buddy would. To outdo Buddy—doing whatever it took."

"Even stealing?

"I guess."

Della glanced away, pulled up her chair next to Annalee. She had something hard to say. "See, I was stealing, too."

Annalee withheld judgment. *Just listen.* "Stealing what?"

"From Simon. I was working at his fancy Denver house. Uri helped me get a job there. Uri knew my mom from Telluride. But I took advantage of his help, ended up taking things."

"But everything's locked up."

"Not then. Simon left pocket change laying around. Cuff links, too. Watches. I'd take the stuff and pawn it." Della shifted in her seat. "Jeffrey figured it was me. He found two shiny fountain pens in my apron pocket. He promised not to tell if I stopped my stealing and did him a favor—secretly help him find his mother. 'You're from Telluride,' he said. 'Help me.'"

"And the pawnshop?"

"It was our signal. If I had information, I'd come in and buy a jasper necklace—using a little money Jeffrey gave me. When I passed on information, he'd pay me a bit more. He'd used the system before for other little deals he was working—with some of the pilots, I think. He was no choirboy himself."

"Almost nobody is." Annalee thought of Buddy. "Did one of those pilots kill Jeffrey?"

"Della!" Footsteps sounded. It was Lilian Gray.

Della stood, did things to look busy—taking food from the picnic basket, looking in the icebox. Following her lead, Annalee slipped to the stove and started fussing with the teakettle, grabbing a pot holder off a hook to move it onto the fire.

"Any news?" Annalee asked the question, but Lilian didn't answer.

Instead, she snapped at Della, "What's taking you so long?" She scowled at the platter. "Cold chicken won't do—"

"Yes, miss—"

"We'll need something for warmth. A good hot soup. And a vegetable and hot bread. Pull something together, but don't take all night."

"Yes, miss—"

"Della's doing her best." Annalee set down the teakettle. "I'm sure it will be delicious."

Lilian reacted. "You're not expected to help here, Miss Spain."

"But we have an unusual situation with Mr. Uri." Annalee didn't move to leave. "I'll just help Della with the tea and supper things." She went on. "Is there any news?"

"We're waiting for a call from the forest rangers. A team went out with Mr. Simon. We should hear something soon." Lilian pointed toward the doorway. "Please come to the great room and wait for our meal."

"When I'm finished here." Annalee didn't budge.

Della didn't speak.

Lilian glared but finally turned and left.

"Will they find Uri?" Della sat down again, looking distressed. "If he's not found, I can't stay here."

"Why not? What do you know, Della?"

"That everybody who helps me in this family ends up dead—or now is missing."

"On the day Jeffrey was killed, why didn't you go to the pawnshop that morning?"

"A brunch at Mr. Simon's. I had to help Lilian serve. I don't know if the necklace is still there."

Annalee held her tongue.

"So who killed Jeffrey? Do you know?"

"I thought I did. But sometimes it seems like anybody could've had a hand. Maybe somebody from Telluride—"

"A name? Something to steer me right?"

"But it's really more than a name. Because so much is at stake."

"So who's behind it all?" Annalee searched Della's face. "Is it Simon?"

"You didn't hear it from me."

"You're right. I didn't. That's because I don't know what *it* is." She chewed her lip. "Or maybe I better ask myself a smarter question."

"What's that?"

"Who in this case has the most to lose?"

Dinner was late and tasteless. But Annalee wasn't hungry. She picked at her food, swirled her sad soup, waiting for the hall-way clock to sound the time. But the clock was moving like Grandma's slow molasses. Finally it was eight o'clock. Then eight fifteen. Then eight thirty. Then finally the clock struck nine.

"Where are they?" Rebecca paced to the dining room window, walked through the doorway toward the front of the house.

Lilian, after keeping her composure all evening, had finally given in to fretting, too. "I can't understand why he hasn't called."

She kept leaving the dining room to stare at a hall telephone sitting on a small table just opposite the kitchen, tapping her foot, sounding impatient.

"It's not like him to stay out of contact." Lilian looked in a small mirror above the telephone, smoothed her hair, pinned back side tendrils that had come undone. Peering closer, she pinched her cheeks. Sighing, she licked her lips, then paced by the telephone table again.

Watching her, Annalee cocked her head.

Lilian wasn't acting or sounding like Simon's secretary. Or like the woman of the manor. She was acting—and sounding—like the woman he loved.

Like Annalee would act when waiting for Jack. *Where is he?*

Annalee dropped her eyes, not wanting Lilian to see she was being watched—certainly not in this manner—or to change her behavior because it warranted such a conclusion. But Annalee was suddenly aware and sure of it. *Lilian loves Simon. Loves him like a woman loves a man. Even if he doesn't love her in return.*

Annalee pondered. *Or does he? Could Simon love her with such passion and abandon, pacing the floor if she came home late?*

Annalee took in a long, silent breath. Thoughts of Jack then rushed at her, and she closed her eyes, running the fingers of her right hand alongside her neck, feeling the place where Jack liked to linger with kisses, but now seeing herself in Lilian. Had those kisses mattered to Jack? Did she?

She jerked down her hand.

Stop it, detective. She set her jaw. *Stop it right now.* She had a murder to solve. Idle thoughts were dangerous. Poor Jeffrey Mann had met a hard fate. He needed her attention and concern, but her next thought made her heart jump again.

Buddy Mann.

She moved her mouth, silently saying his name—making her almost groan. Why in the world was she thinking about him? But she already knew why.

Buddy had shown his hand. *"Why aren't you married?"* What man asks such a question—unless he seriously wants to know? Then he fussed over her clothes. *"That coat's not heavy enough."* Mercy, he'd even noticed her dimple. Worse, she hadn't minded.

Jack had disappeared, maybe with the lavender-scented Dora. Now, would she let Buddy take his place? Lie to herself and call it justified? Murder solved or not?

Annalee pressed a trembling hand to her forehead, pushed away a curl, turned her eyes finally from Lilian.

Mercy, this mixed-up world. She needed to solve this case fast. It was dangerous in far too many ways.

Picking up her soupspoon, Annalee sipped deliberately at Della's barely edible chicken soup. Lilian hadn't complained about it, probably because she was too distracted herself to eat it. That's what Annalee figured, and that kind of figuring seemed to change everything.

I'll just be nicer to Lilian, Annalee told herself. *Nicer, indeed, to everyone in this contentious household?* Maybe that would help solve Jeffrey's murder?

Uri, meantime, needed to be found, hopefully alive. *God, please. Let that grumpy, confused, bitter, angry malcontent be found in one piece.*

"Annalee!" Rebecca hollered from the front of the house. "Here they come!"

Lilian rushed past the telephone table, almost knocking it over.

Annalee dropped her soupspoon. "Della!"

Della rushed out from the kitchen. Running behind Lilian, all four crowded into the foyer, letting Lilian throw back the dead bolt and open the heavy front door.

"Mr. Simon?" Lilian's voice was expectant, excited. She ran out into the snow.

"Papa?" Rebecca followed her, squinting into glaring car lights.

Della started to follow, but Annalee pulled her back, pushed her behind the door.

Something wasn't right.

"Wait," Annalee called to Lilian.

The cars were all wrong. Not forest ranger buggies, these were big Model Ts. Three of them. With three or four men in each.

"Give me your cap." Annalee yanked Della's maid's cap off her head. "Your apron, too." She pointed her upstairs. "Where can you hide?"

"Down here. Library." Della untied her white apron, let Annalee pull it over her head and wriggle into it. Della rushed then past the front hall clock, ducked through a hallway, and disappeared. Annalee pulled Della's maid's cap onto her head, pushed her curls underneath, and secured the apron over her blue dress—hiding as much of it as possible.

"State your business!" Lilian was yelling through falling snow at the men approaching.

"Where's my papa!" Rebecca hollered at one of them.

"Simon Wallace!" one of the men barked. "Get him out here."

"State your business!" Lilian barked louder.

"Where's the colored gal?"

"Klan!" Rebecca suddenly screamed. "Get off our property!" She ran forward, pushed hard at the man. "You killed the cabbie!"

He pushed her back. "Shut up!"

"Don't you touch me!"

Annalee stepped outside. This was getting bad. The men were bullies, raring for trouble. It wouldn't take much to set them off. They'd burn the blasted house down. She moved into the car lights.

"That her?" The man motioned toward the door.

Lilian turned, glanced at Annalee wearing Della's white cap and apron. Annalee held her breath, felt unsure suddenly of Lilian. Would Simon's secretary give her up to these goons? Lilian almost looked tempted.

"Answer me!" the man yelled again at Lilian. "Is that Spain?"

Lilian finally hiked a brow. "Idiot! That's our maid!"

"Where's Wallace?"

"This is private property!" Lilian turned to Annalee. "Call the police!"

The man laughed. "We *are* the police—"

"In Estes Park?"

"Wherever we need to be!"

"What'd you want, mister?" Annalee had to stop this.

"You that Spain woman?"

"I'm from Telluride," Annalee yelled out, acting confused. She hated more lying, but that at least was almost the truth.

The man turned back to Lilian. "Where's the Spain gal?"

"Search the house!" another man yelled from a car. He kicked open the door, climbed out.

Annalee flinched. It was the Grand Dragon himself. She gripped the heavy door.

"Private property!" Lilian glared at the cars and the scowling Klan leader. "There is no 'Spain gal' here." She stood her ground, taking Simon's position on this. He'd protect Annalee. "That's our maid! Now please leave."

"Tell Wallace we'll be back!" The head man swung to his car. "He can't have coloreds living on this mountain." He spat in the snow. "You Jews aren't welcome here anyway."

Rebecca reared back, opened her mouth.

Lilian waved her back, waved at the snow, waved at the horrible moment, waved at the horrible men. "Take your leave! All of you!"

She grabbed Rebecca, pulled her toward the house—both of them stumbling and sliding in the drifting snow.

They all helped each other inside, Annalee noticing they were avoiding each other's eyes, not wanting to acknowledge, it seemed, the insult and danger they'd all just experienced, even if they weren't to blame.

"Let's get warm." Annalee brushed snow off Della's apron and pulled it off. The maid's cap, too.

"The fireplace is lit." Lilian smoothed back her wet hair.

In the great room, they pulled chairs up to the fire, staring at the flames.

Then Rebecca looked at the others. "I think I'm mad at my papa."

"Let's trust he'll be okay. But for now, he may not be our worst problem." Annalee stood and grabbed a stoker lying near the fireplace, poked at the fire.

"You're actually right, Miss Spain. He's not." Lilian pushed back her chair, left for the kitchen, calling for tea from Della.

"Well, who is?" Rebecca's face showed confusion.

"I'm not sure yet." Annalee moved white-hot embers onto a smoldering log. The log ignited, flames glowing. "But this could be the night I find out."

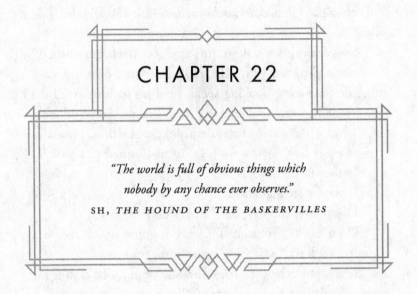

CHAPTER 22

*"The world is full of obvious things which
nobody by any chance ever observes."*

SH, *THE HOUND OF THE BASKERVILLES*

IT WAS NEARLY ELEVEN when Simon pulled into the drive in a forest ranger buggy. Rebecca ran out to meet him, but Lilian stayed inside. He got out of the car alone, Uri not with him, and dragged himself into the house.

"Fix a brandy, please." Lilian pointed Della to a drinks cart. Della barely nodded.

"Car got stuck." Simon shrugged out of a big shearling coat, handed it to Lilian, who held it tight for a moment. Simon reached for Rebecca. He gave her a hug. All eyes searched his face.

"There's no news." Simon hugged Rebecca again, both leading each other into the great room. Lilian followed, Annalee aside her—both seeming to resist the urge to ask a million questions.

"No sign?" Rebecca looked inconsolable. "You didn't find him?"

"Snow's already too deep. Any tracks or traces are covered."

Simon dropped to a sofa, pulled off iced-over galoshes, tugged at his damp-looking socks, held his hands toward the fire—looking as miserable as any miserable person could look. But why? That was Annalee's unspoken question. How did Simon really feel? Sorrow for his missing brother?

Simon rubbed his eyes.

Or was he feeling relief?

"I'll get your slippers, sir." Lilian stood.

"Don't bother yourself, Lilian. I'm going up to bed in a minute. We'll start searching again in the morning."

He accepted a large snifter of brandy from Della, closing his eyes as he sipped. Della offered smaller glasses to everyone else, but only Lilian accepted, looking grateful as she took a generous swallow—followed by several others.

Finishing his glass, Simon offered a rambling description of the search.

A wild trail covered in snow. Drifts blocking the path. Delays to rescue a ranger who fell almost headfirst into a crevasse.

"Four of us were looking for Uri—me and three rangers."

"But why did he go off by himself?" Rebecca kept stating her confusion.

Simon insisted he didn't know, never confessing—as Della had said she witnessed—the blistering argument between the two men, nasty accusations flying, with ugly threats and words, leading to Uri doing what he did with almost everyone and especially Simon. He stomped away seething. But this time, he blundered into a blizzard in the hills.

Simon wasn't telling the truth about it.

Annalee stiffened at his lying.

Lilian, too, had lied. *"He's not lost, Miss Rebecca."* He left the picnic *"heading up a trail he wanted to investigate."* Lie after lie. *"We ate our lunch, enjoying the scenery and wildlife. We saw bighorn sheep . . ."*

A total fabrication. Hiding what? Something worth Uri losing his life?

The clock in the front hallway chimed the half hour. Eleven thirty. Annalee shifted in her seat. At midnight? Buddy Mann. Would he still dig here through drifts of swirling snow to help her find secrets? She'd planned to ask Rebecca for a sleeping draft to help put Simon under for the night, but there wasn't time.

Annalee thought now about yawning—making a show of it—to subtly suggest to everyone that surely they all must be weary, too.

But Simon beat her to it, yawned deeply, stretching and wiping at his eyes, not hiding his exhaustion. He stood, turned to Rebecca. "I'm so sorry, sweetheart." He yawned again. "I'll do everything I can in the morning to find Uri. I know it looks impossible, but if anybody can survive in these hills—"

"I know—it's Papa." Rebecca finished Simon's thought. "But what about the Klan?"

"What Klan?" Simon tensed. "Did they come around here?"

"Let's not bother your uncle now." Annalee stood, let loose that yawn. "Are you fine with that, Miss Gray?"

"We can talk in the morning, yes."

Lilian and Simon agreed on a 7:30 a.m. coffee meeting, called Della in to let her know.

Leaving the great room, the four said their good nights—to each other and also to the young maid. Annalee glanced back once to see Della turning off table lamps. Then Della stood before the fireplace, watching the remaining logs burn, probably thinking on things that Annalee realized she had no way of knowing or understanding—since Annalee's own private thoughts were so often confusing, too.

Annalee took the stairs behind Rebecca, walked down the long hall with her, said good night, opened the door to her bedroom, closed it and set the lock, turned on the small lamp on her nightstand, and almost stopped breathing.

Buddy Mann was already waiting for her.

He was sitting in a large armchair on the opposite side of the guest bed, still wearing his coat, boots crusted with snow. Annalee sighed forever and a day, walked to the matching chair across the room, and sat herself down. She curled her knees up under her blue dress, let out another sigh. In the low bedroom light, they looked at each other—far too long, Annalee thought. Finally she spoke—her voice low.

"The Klan were here tonight."

"Idiots." He glared toward the window, also spoke low.

"They will *kill* you." She cocked her head.

"I haven't done anything."

"You're playing with fire."

"What do you mean?" He scoffed.

"Buddy!" she whispered. "You can't do this!" She shook her head. "*We* can't do this." She gestured at the two of them.

He stood up, started walking toward her.

"No! *Stay there.* Listen to me!" She waved him back. He needed to hear her. "*I'm* saying no!"

"Why? Why can't we?" He sat down, gestured at both of them, too.

She pressed her mouth. She'd been right about Buddy's feelings. But what about her own? She felt confused but also determined.

"Why? Because, for one, I'm working a case. A tough case. Trying to puzzle out this Wallace family so I can figure out who killed *your brother*. But now Uri's missing, too. I know it's connected."

"Uri? Missing? And poor Jeffrey's dead. We never were close, but he'll always be my brother. So what happened to him?"

"That's what I'm trying to figure out." She searched his eyes, pleading. "And I'm out of time. If I can't find the killer, I go to jail." She winced. "Or I hang."

"Over my dead body."

"Don't even say that." She unfolded her legs, straightened her dress. "I don't know how I seem to you—"

"You seem like somebody I want to know—and I don't give a hill of beans what anybody thinks, even if I can't just walk down the street with you."

"But you and me? That makes no sense. Sure, we almost died together in a plane crash. Maybe you feel we survived it together for some crazy reason. But—"

"It's more than that—even if I can't explain it yet, not even to myself. You're like nobody I've ever met before—like somebody I shouldn't lose." He took in a breath. "That's my choice. Nobody's business but mine. That's why I'm here helping you, waiting until

Simon Wallace falls asleep and starts snoring his head off so I can break into his room." He glanced at his watch. "All so I can crack the lock on his safe and get the information *you* need."

He studied her eyes. "Don't you understand? You're the somebody I want to be with!"

"That's not possible."

"Why not?"

"Because."

"Because what?"

"Because of *everything*. Rules. Laws. Buddy, good grief, the Klan—"

"They're idiots!" He glared. "They don't even know you—"

"*You* don't know me. I don't even know myself half the time." She searched for words. "All I know is I'm already . . . in love." Annalee glanced away. "In love with another man."

Buddy scoffed. "*Who?* That guy who won't marry you?"

"Stop saying that! Why are you even asking me that? And good grief, why are you putting him down?"

"Because I was flying my machine on a beautiful Colorado day—minding my own business—and who but you dropped out of the sky, landing in my life."

"That wasn't my fault—"

"Then after we *crash-landed*, you came back. Crawling in and out—"

"I needed shelter!" She glared. "Why are you blaming me, too?"

"Who else can I blame? Where's that man you're so in love with? What kind of man lets his woman—?" He stood, started walking toward her.

"Stop it!"

"Lets her run all over town, no coat in the dead of winter—"

"You're wrong!"

"Wearing that blasted dress—"

Annalee sprang from the chair. "Stop it!"

"I'd at least buy you a decent coat! Keep you warm! What's he ever bought for you?"

"Stop saying that!" She leaped across the room at Buddy, fists balled up. *"Stop talking about him!"* She pounded on his chest, her heart pounding harder.

He grabbed her hands, pulled her to him. She struggled back. He was going to kiss her, in some crazy and irretrievable way, and she knew it—and he acted as if he knew it, too.

"Don't do it, Buddy!"

"Why not?" He pulled her closer, leaning closer—way too close, Annalee thought.

How can I stop this?

"Because I love him!"

"Then where the heck is he?" Buddy huffed, gripping her shoulders.

"I don't know!" A tear fell. Then she couldn't hold it any longer. Her floodgates opened, letting her tears fall, her water-works flowing. She slumped onto Buddy's chest. "Somebody took him!" She sobbed, leaned closer, gripped Buddy's coat to muffle her cries. "Or maybe he left on his own. I don't know! And every day, it seems, people are trying to kill me, too. Kill my spirit. Kill my heart."

She looked up at Buddy. "I didn't make this stupid world, so half the time I don't understand it. But I know I love the man that I love." She placed a hand on his face but dropped it away. "Please let me do that."

Buddy released his harsh hold of her, exchanging it with a sudden, close embrace. He held her. She let him.

"Why'd you come into my life?" he breathed into her ear.

"Coincidence? That's what I thought at first. But all I've been doing since Jeffrey was killed is puzzle through lies." She stepped back. "If it's not Uri or Simon, it's the Klan. That's their stock in trade—lying against people, keeping 'their' nation 'pure,' whatever that's supposed to mean. Seeding lies with more lies, about who to hate and why. Then to counter it, the people they hurt learn to lie, maybe better. If you were with me, Buddy, you'd end up lying every livelong day."

"But where does this leave people like me?" He searched her eyes. "Or *you* and me?"

"Fighting for the truth. Enough truth to turn things around. For you, for Jeffrey. To help find my truth, too." She gestured at the door. "If whatever's in Simon's safe, and whatever he's hiding, can help solve Jeffrey's murder, it may free you of other things, too. Maybe all of us. But only if you help me. So will you?"

Buddy ran a hand through his hair.

"You make a man crazy." He shook his head. "But here I go, into Simon's bedroom—while he's *sleeping*—to break into his safe."

"Will the safe take long?"

"Who knows? Even if you're helping me. Holding my flashlight."

"Oh, my goodness."

"You think I'm going in there by myself?"

Annalee slipped to the door, opened it. "What time is it?" The hallway clock downstairs, in answer, sounded its chorus of soft bells—as if everything in this household, and in the world, would be perfectly fine because it was twelve midnight. Giving Buddy a resigned look, she took a deep breath and then tiptoed down the hall, put her ear to Simon's door. No sound but snoring. Not loud. But steady.

Across the hall to Lilian's door, same thing. Hardly a sound. Lilian was snoring softly, too.

Annalee rushed back to her door. Buddy was already slipping out, not wearing his coat now. Boots off, too, in stocking feet.

"They're asleep," she whispered.

"You sure?"

"No, but I hope so."

"Stick close to me." Buddy grabbed her hand, looked back at her, raised her palm to his mouth as if planning to kiss her right there, bold as you please, making her flinch and maybe swoon a little, too—which she hated, because what about Jack?

She could resist, but she didn't pull away, not wanting to tussle while Buddy was, good grief, breaking and entering.

He gave her a long gaze, released her hand, and turned the handle on Simon's door.

It wasn't locked.

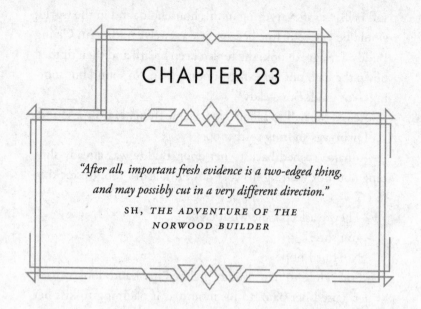

CHAPTER 23

"After all, important fresh evidence is a two-edged thing,
and may possibly cut in a very different direction."

SH, *THE ADVENTURE OF THE*
NORWOOD BUILDER

BUDDY GESTURED THEM INSIDE Simon's bedroom, put a finger to his lips to say, *"Stay quiet."* Annalee nodded. They stepped inside. Buddy closed the door. They stood in the dark, waiting for their eyes to adjust but still looking across the big room toward the prone form of Simon Wallace—curled on his bed under his thick covers, his snoring steady but light.

The sound of him this way, dead to the world in sleep and vulnerable, while they prepared to rob him of possible secrets, made Annalee's heart skip. So did being here with Buddy.

This *was* insane. So was the world they were trying to live in and find their way around. But together? She refused to even think of it.

Annalee was ready to turn tail and clear out. Besides, the

room was dark but not pitch-black. Through the curtains the white, glistening snow outside reflected its light into the room. If Simon woke up and discovered the two of them in his bedroom, he'd know immediately what they were up to. No good. She'd never explain it or live it down.

But Buddy didn't seem bothered. He tiptoed them across the room, past Simon's bed, straight to the pretty seascape hanging on the far wall—as if he knew exactly where to look to find the safe. Because he'd sneaked in this room before? Annalee shook off the thought.

Stop second-guessing. Simon's hiding something big. More than just his ghost company. That's how it felt anyway. *So help Buddy. Not to mention Jeffrey.*

Buddy opened the pretty picture on its hinge. Standing behind him, Annalee looked closer at the painting. It was a peaceful harbor filled with three bobbing boats, nestled beside a picturesque village—in the Mediterranean? An odd choice, she would say, to display in a mountain manor in the snowy Rocky Mountains.

"Hold this for me," Buddy whispered, handing her a metal flashlight.

He moved aside, making room for her to scoot over. He was twirling the dial around and around to the right. Then at some click or signal or sound she couldn't hear, he twirled the dial to the left.

He tried the handle, but it wouldn't give. So back to the twirling, clicking, listening—just as Simon's steady breathing turned to a light cough.

Buddy froze. He pointed to the flashlight. Annalee clicked it off. Her hand shook on the metal switch.

Simon coughed again, half sat up, but turned in his covers, settled back down.

Don't breathe. Annalee told herself the obvious, figured Buddy was doing the same. He put a hand on her back. *Steady.* She nodded at him in the dark but wished he wouldn't touch her like that.

Simon coughed once again, then one more time, then seemed to burrow again under his covers, his breath a light snore. He was back asleep.

Annalee let out a silent sigh. After a moment, Buddy moved away his hand.

"My light!" Barely whispering.

She clicked it on. For too many more minutes, Buddy twirled the dial and listened to the clicks and stops. Finally he took in a deep breath, yanked down the handle.

It opened. He hiked a brow at her—making her smile in spite of herself—pulled at the handle, and opened the safe door ever so slowly. Together, they peered in, blinking, not believing.

The safe was empty. Bare as a baby's bottom.

Buddy shook his head at her. *"What's this?"*

Her eyes answered. *"I don't know."*

Simon coughed again. Then coughed harder, his bedclothes rustling.

Not waiting, Buddy closed the safe, twirled the dial, closed the picture hinge. Grabbing Annalee's hand, he clicked off the flashlight, rushed them across the room, past Simon's bed, opened the bedroom door in flash, pushed them out to the hallway, and closed the door.

Annalee stifled a moan.

They weren't alone.

Standing in the hallway was Della, and she wasn't by herself. Next to her stood Rebecca.

"There's nothing in there," Della whispered, pointing to Simon's bedroom.

"All his files and things," Rebecca whispered back, "are in there." She pointed to Lilian's bedroom, then turned to Buddy. "You know Annalee?"

He turned to Annalee. "What is this?"

Annalee bit her lip, steered them all to the staircase. "Great room. Now."

On the way down, Buddy pulled her back. "I can't work with a crowd of people. Not my style."

She nodded. "Let me sort it out."

In the great room, they all stood by the fireplace, its warmth dying, a few logs still burning but barely.

"Talk to me!" Annalee pleaded in a whisper, looking at Della, who was still wearing her maid's dress. The cap back on, too.

"I met with Miss Rebecca just now." Della wrung her hands. "She deserved to know."

"Know what?" Buddy glared.

"Simon has secrets," Rebecca whispered.

"But they're not in his safe." Della straightened her cap. "I already looked."

Buddy glared at Annalee.

She turned to the young maid. "How'd you know about his safe, Della?"

"The safe in Simon's room?"

"In *any* room. There's more than one safe in this house?"

"Well, I was doing my investigation—"

"She was trying to help Jeffrey," Rebecca cut in.

"Help him with what?" Buddy looked confused.

"Well, Jeffrey was—"

"Wait a minute!" Annalee interrupted. They were moving in dangerous, parallel directions. Buddy didn't know one thing about Jeffrey's search for their mother. But would he want to know? Especially right now? While he was putting himself at risk, trying to help Annalee with her own curious case?

"Can you wait on that, Della? Just tell us about the safe?"

Buddy frowned. "And how'd she know about any safe?"

Della glanced away. "I was trying to steal." She shrugged. "Okay?"

Buddy held his tongue but looked angry and annoyed.

"She needed extra money to send to her mother." Rebecca gave Della an understanding look. "Before her mother passed away."

"And the safe?" Annalee needed to know now.

"I was never able to get it open—"

Buddy gave Annalee a look.

"Then I realized his papers weren't in there—because all Mr. Simon's records and files are in Miss Lilian's room—in a portable safe. She keeps it locked up tight with a key. Takes the box back and forth to Denver."

Annalee nodded. She'd seen that portable box—and Lilian with her key—in the morning room. "Did you break into it?"

Della rolled her eyes. "Okay, I tried. Never got it open. Then one day I overheard Simon tell Lilian to order an extra key. For backup. A locksmith delivered it to his Denver house last week."

"And that's what you were looking for when Rebecca and I saw you yesterday?"

Della pulled a crumpled handkerchief from her pocket, unwrapped it. Inside was a long, shiny key.

Buddy turned to Annalee. "I don't like this."

Annalee understood but couldn't drop the matter now. "What's in the box, Della?"

"I was planning to look now—after everybody went to sleep."

"But what if they woke up?"

Della shook her head. "They won't wake up until morning. I spiked the brandy."

"She used my sleeping medicine." Rebecca gave Della an approving smile.

Buddy stepped back, looked at Annalee. "Now *this* is playing with fire." He turned on Della. "Sleep medicine? How much? What if they never wake up?"

The hallway clock sounded one o'clock. All four looked exhausted and unsure.

Annalee grabbed Buddy's hand. "I want you to leave."

"And leave you here? Not on your life." Buddy's face showed worry.

Della and Rebecca, hearing him, looked confused.

Annalee sat down on a sofa. "Listen to me, please, everybody." She looked up at them. "Enough breaking and entering. It's dangerous. There's too many of us and somebody's bound to make a mistake." She frowned. "I need Simon's files maybe more than anybody. But I'll have to find another way."

"Doing what?" Rebecca sat down next to her.

"I'm not sure. But let's call this a night—right, Buddy?"

"Are you sure?"

"Can you go now?" He didn't answer. "I'll get your coat in my room."

"I'll go up and get it." He headed toward the stairs.

"Then you're leaving?" she called after him.

He shook his head. "Yeah. I'm already gone."

Annalee stood, turned to Della. "Lilian's extra key. I need you to return it to her room. Please."

Della looked uncertain.

"I guess it's for the best," Rebecca assured her.

"But most of what we need is in there—especially you, Miss Annalee."

"I can't force you." Annalee turned toward the stairs. "But returning that key is my strongest advice." She gave them a weary salute. "I'm going to bed. Good night."

Upstairs at her door, she stood a minute, praying Buddy had grabbed his coat and boots and flashlight and was gone. *Please, Lord, let him be gone.*

She turned her door handle, let herself in, closed the door, set the lock, held her breath, turned to look.

Nobody there.

The small lamp was still on.

She sat down in the chair where Buddy had waited for her, surprising her. Then she took a forever-and-a-day deep breath, still breathing in his outdoor, cold-air smell—and not put off by it. So she felt unsure what she thought about him or if she even should. Buddy Mann? Compared to Jack Blake? No two people on earth could be more different. Jack the pastor, a colored war hero. Buddy the thief, who was white.

You must have lost your mind.

She let out a long breath. Playing with fire. Making a match with Buddy? While promising herself to Jack? She'd get burned for sure, and she couldn't bear to think about how, when, or where. Besides, she loved Jack. *No question in my mind that I love Jack.* Well, didn't she? *Right, Mrs. Mason? Right, Eddie?* She swallowed. *Right, Mrs. Stallworth?* Then: *Please, Lord? Isn't my heart for Jack?*

So why in the world was she confounding over Buddy?

She slipped from the chair, fell to her knees, trying to find a prayer, seeking the right words, thinking of Jack and begging God to find him—while stewing still over Simon and Uri, who was somewhere out in the cold, with her knowing Jeffrey's murderer was still walking around free, leaving her to ask a question she couldn't answer.

Lord, how can I sort it all out?

And by tomorrow?

———◆———

A warm bath helped calm Annalee, let her crawl into bed and finally slip into a deep sleep. The priceless gift of rest. On another day, she might've snuggled under the covers for hours. But at daybreak, she couldn't linger. She threw back the spread, freshened up, made the bed. Then she dressed quickly. *Thank you, little blue dress.* No matter what Buddy or anybody else said about it.

Downstairs, she found Della in the kitchen.

They barely exchanged more than a few words. But Della was cooking a decent breakfast. Annalee thanked her, fixed herself a plate, and headed to the morning room, expecting to wait for Simon.

But he was already there, seated not at the dining table but at a small, round tea table by the far window, sipping black coffee from an oversize cup.

She'd expected him to look tousled and disoriented after drinking Della's spiked brandy—and even worse, after failing to find Uri, his only brother, lost in a Colorado blizzard.

Instead, he looked decently rested, freshly shaved, warmly dressed, but worried. And somber. And sad. His face but especially his eyes.

"Cold as the devil today." He pointed at the window, glanced outside.

"Deceptive indeed." Annalee walked to his table. "Dangerous, too."

"Odd, isn't it?" Simon looked at the window. "Storm's over, sunshine is out, skies are blue. But the cold can kill you."

"So it's not like the warmth of Spain." Annalee gestured to the window. "Is it?" She thought of the comely watercolor painting in Simon's bedroom—sun-drenched and peaceful, a million miles away from the icy Rocky Mountains.

Simon looked up at her, pointed her to the chair directly opposite him. "Have a seat." He set down his cup. "What do you want to know about me, Miss Spain?"

"So much—like what went wrong? Between you and Uri. Or with your family?"

Simon turned to gaze out of the window. "We learned to lie." He moved his cup. "To stay alive. We've been doing it for centuries. Since the expulsion. Most folks here don't even know about it."

"The Spanish Expulsion? Of the Jews?" She'd studied that

horror in college, even wrote a paper on it. "But the expulsion was centuries ago. Way back in—what, 1492?—of all things."

"But it changed everything. My family was never the same."

"It was an inquisition. Jews were hunted down, drummed out, tossed by the hundreds from fleeing ships to drown."

"Or you become something else. That's what my family did. To save ourselves, we said we weren't Jews—said whatever we were forced to say—to hold on to life in Spain and not be banished." He squinted harder at the glaring snow. "Then we just kept doing it, changing as needed. We cut out Ladino—"

"That's your accent?"

"A Spanish-Hebrew mix. We stopped speaking it. We even changed our name. We were called Vaz. That's our family name. When I moved to America with Uri, I changed it to Wallace. It always seemed easier. After a while, you just write your own story. At least I did." He folded his arms.

Then bitterly he laughed. "My paintings in my bank? All fake. Here on every wall, in my bedroom, too. You should see them."

Annalee held her tongue. Finally she spoke. "Forgeries?"

"Nope, just fake. Their frames are fabulous. But the paintings. Fake. Painted by very good no-name artists."

"But why?"

"It's my secret joke. They remind me of my family—and how we got the best of our oppressors in Spain. They deserved it. They told their wretched lies about us—so many, for so long, they started to believe them."

"So the paintings are your lies in turn? Double the lies."

"You're judging?"

"I wouldn't dare."

"Perhaps. Besides, my paintings are beautiful enough, and I'll never resell them. My will forbids it, too. If I die, they'll be destroyed. I just enjoy looking at them." He smiled then.

Annalee listened but couldn't smile back—even if she understood his logic.

"Did you lie to the city, sir?" she asked. "About the airport bonds?

Simon turned away for a long minute. "Word has gotten out. That's what my new employee warned me."

"So that's what worries you? Not cheating the city of Denver?"

"Those Klan thugs? They're cheating all of us." He pushed away his cup. "I didn't start this war."

She understood. She'd seen the leaflets plastered all over downtown Denver: *"Doing business with JEWS is BAD BUSINESS."* Then came the threat: *"And we're watching you!"*

"But how do we end it?"

"You're asking the wrong person. Like I said, I didn't start it. They'll have to kill me to end it with me. It's too late for me to change. But how would you understand? Your track record is probably clean. I doubt you've ever lived with a lie, Miss Spain."

She grimaced.

He cocked his head, narrowing his eyes at her. "Or have you?"

She didn't answer. She was thinking about the mother who abandoned her. Then about Buddy Mann. And Jack. And Buddy again—lying to herself right then that she hadn't let him get under her skin, hadn't prioritized him over Jack. *I confess.* Even if she hadn't said it out loud.

But Simon? What on earth was he also hiding? Annalee was desperate to ask.

She put the ball in his court.

"You know you don't have to tell me—about your family lies."

"In fact, I do."

"Why?"

"Because my brother—" His voice broke. "My brother is out there, lost. It will be a miracle if we find him alive. And it didn't have to end this way. If I'd just told him the truth." He looked away. "For both our sakes."

Annalee understood. Simon needed to talk—or at least he seemed ready. She needed to listen. *Tell me, Simon.* She was thinking, in fact, about something that her father's old friend Mr. Cunningham had told her. *"You want information? Act like you couldn't care less."*

She picked up her fork, worked on her eggs, toast, jam, not tasting the food at first—but then deciding to sit there and receive the nourishment. She needed it. Even more, she was confounded by her search. Running all over—just as Buddy Mann, of all people, had said. Fighting to pick up little shreds of information, breaking into folks' bedrooms, when the truth was probably staring her right in the face. Besides, as Mr. Cunningham said, *"If you know about people, you can figure out most things before you hear it."*

Annalee put her fork down, touched her mouth with a napkin. "May I ask you something?" She paused. "What was your mother's first name?"

Simon gave her a sad look. "It was Rebekah."

"Same as Rebekah in the Bible?"

"The very same." Simon looked away. "And yes, Professor, I know the story."

"So was that story like your own mother's? She had a favorite son?"

Simon held her gaze. "Her favorite was me."

"But why, sir?" She shook her head. "Why not Uri? Did she even love him?"

"On any other day, I'd tell you to stay out of my business. To stick to your murder investigation—to dig out who killed young Jeffrey." He sighed. "But this isn't any other day."

"Please tell me."

Simon pushed back his chair. Sorrow, anger, despair pierced his face. "I was her favorite because Uri was not my mother's son."

Annalee listened silently but didn't want to hear this. "Who is he, then?"

"It's a hard family story." Simon's eyes watered. "When I see him, if we find him, I'll tell him the story myself."

"Because he deserves to know!" Her voice pleaded. "No matter how hard or hurtful the truth?"

"No matter how hard or hurtful. That is correct. But now I'm leaving to go and *find him*—"

As he spoke, in fact, Lilian Gray hurried into the room.

"The rangers are here, sir."

Simon looked weary but stood. "Tell them I'm coming."

Lilian turned to leave, but Simon called her back. She looked confused. "Sir?"

"Lilian . . ."

"Yes, sir?"

"You've been faithful to me, Lilian. You've always been loyal to only me."

Annalee stood, turned to leave. If Simon was ready to speak intimately to Lilian—something he might never have done and something she probably desired more than anything after years of service—Annalee felt she needed to leave.

But Simon stopped her. "No need to go, Annalee. I'd like you to hear this, too."

Annalee didn't protest, but she saw disappointment on Lilian's conflicted face. If Simon was going to thank Lilian in a special way, she'd hardly want another woman standing within hearing distance.

Annalee tried to make herself invisible, not moving.

"I'm grateful to you, Lilian," Simon stumbled on. "I don't say that enough. I'm not embarrassed to say it in front of other people." He gestured to Annalee. "You—"

Annalee could've screamed. Simon wasn't declaring love. His words sounded more like a business memo—because Simon didn't know how to love? Or tell a woman she mattered? Mercy, both Jack Blake *and* Buddy Mann could give Simon a lesson or two on that—and neither one of them was anywhere near perfect, because they both were so maddening.

Lilian stopped Simon's rambling. "Thank you, sir," she barely whispered, but disappointment was written plain as day on her middle-aging face. "You can count on me." She blinked her sad eyes. "More than you know."

Annalee wanted, in her heart, to sympathize. But she wasn't sure how she felt about Lilian. One minute Lilian was almost actually kind and to someone other than Simon. But in a second, she could turn cold as ice.

She's carrying a lot, Annalee figured—watching Lilian

lugging Simon's oversize shearling coat. Lilian helped him into it—looking, in fact, like a wife but the farthest thing from it.

"Gloves are in your pocket, sir, and here's a scarf and hat. They're searching by airplane and—"

"Airplane?" Simon looked surprised. "Where'd they find airplane pilots?"

Annalee didn't speak.

"At the Stanley Hotel." Lilian went on, mentioning a "couple of barnstormers who work at the Stanley, flying tourists around. Both flew in the war."

"Must be good flyers." Simon tugged on his gloves.

"I hope so, sir."

"You don't have to sugarcoat it. In these conditions, in the mountains, flying will be treacherous."

Lilian bit her lip, reached up, started to help Simon with his scarf, but he pushed her hand away, looking irritated.

"Please be safe." Lilian set her jaw. "I'm going with you to the hangar. To see you off."

Simon didn't respond. He rushed from the room. Lilian followed, looking confused. Or was it simply hurt?

Annalee acted like she didn't see any of that. Maybe because she was thinking of something else. Buddy might be piloting one of those flying machines today.

But why did she even care?

Except for the life of her, she did.

CHAPTER 24

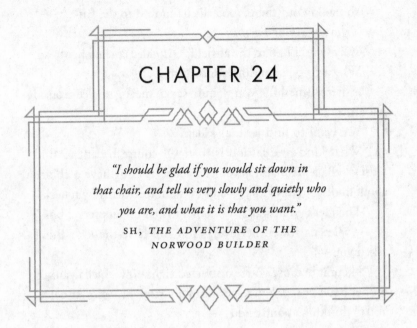

*"I should be glad if you would sit down in
that chair, and tell us very slowly and quietly who
you are, and what it is that you want."*

SH, *THE ADVENTURE OF THE
NORWOOD BUILDER*

ANNALEE STEPPED INTO THE KITCHEN with her plate. "Thank
you for breakfast, Della."

"Everybody gone?"

"Just Simon." Annalee cleaned off her plate at the sink.
"Well, Lilian, too."

"In this weather?"

"They're searching by airplane."

Della put down a dish towel. "Whose airplane? Mr. Buddy's
airplane?"

Annalee heard the question, but she didn't trust herself
enough to respond or know how she felt about it. Because she
shouldn't feel anything, not about Buddy. Not while still looking for his brother's killer.

"You going out there, too?" Della moved to the sink.

Why is she asking me this?

"Why would I go to the airfield?" Annalee cocked her head.

"Why are you sounding angry at me?"

"Is there something you want to say to me?" Annalee crossed her arms.

"You want to find Jeffrey's killer?"

"What kind of question is that? Of course I want to find Jeffrey's killer." Annalee gave her a look. "I don't have a choice about finding Jeffrey's killer—not if I want to save my own neck."

"Then let's go upstairs and look in Miss Lilian's secret box."

Annalee narrowed her eyes. "You still have the key? But I asked you—"

"I kept it because you're distracted right now." Della yanked off her maid's cap. "You're not thinking straight, Miss Annalee. You're thinking about Buddy—"

"Wait just a minute—"

"I saw how he was looking at you."

"Now that's enough!"

"God puts people in funny places sometimes."

"God?"

"Somebody has to talk to you. The Lord doesn't blame you, and I don't either."

"I don't believe this!" Annalee turned to leave.

"What, you think you're too good to be told the truth?"

Annalee swung around. She'd give young Della of Telluride a good piece of her mind.

But Della was pouring herself a fresh cup of coffee. She grabbed another cup and poured one for Annalee, too.

Annalee shook her head. "I'm not having a heart-to-heart with you about Buddy or anybody else."

"Are you in love with him?"

"Why are you saying that to me?"

"Because." Della dropped to a chair. "Because I fell in love with Jeffrey."

"Don't say that." Jeffrey's murder surely was about more than a romantic crush.

Annalee sat down across from Della. "You weren't in love with Jeffrey. You were captivated by Jeffrey."

"You're right." Della allowed a real smile. "For a lot of reasons." She hugged herself. "I loved meeting with him, but his heart was Rebecca's. I'd already figured out who Jeffrey's mother was, almost right away. But I kept dragging it out, just to keep meeting with him—"

"His mother? You know who she is?"

"You know her, too."

"What are you saying?"

"Doesn't matter. I'm not telling you yet anyway—not before Buddy gets told. He deserves to know first. She's his mother, too."

"But what if you have it wrong? We can ruin lives with bad information."

"That's why I kept this." Della reached into her pocket, pulled out Lilian's key. "This will help you get it all right. Because somebody killed poor Jeffrey. If you don't find out who it is, his killer keeps walking free." She pushed back her chair. "You coming?"

Annalee stood. "I will." She touched her heart. "For Jeffrey."

But she knew why she was doing it most. For Jack? For Rebecca? *For me.*

Upstairs, the house was quiet. Rebecca was still sleeping apparently—after their late-night breaking-and-entering foray. *Now, here I am again—the praying detective, aka thief.* Annalee faced Lilian's door, hating to touch the handle with her trembling fingers.

In fact, she was wearing gloves. Della was, too. Church gloves, of all things. Della had an extra pair.

Lilian's door wasn't locked. Della turned the handle and they stepped inside.

The bed was made but not well. It looked rumpled. Closet doors hung open. A dress on a hanger was flung over one door. The well-organized Lilian must've had a rough, spiked-brandy sleep—which, to be honest, Annalee regretted. She'd never been drugged, but she'd never wish a head-zinging loss of consciousness on anybody. It didn't surprise her Lilian had apparently awakened confused, then dressed in a rush to look after Simon's departure to the airfield.

Annalee wasn't worried that Lilian would be back soon. In this snow, it could take her an hour or more to make it back home—even if someone was driving her.

Annalee let her eyes roam the room. "Where's Lilian's box?"

"It's usually over here." Della stepped to a small corner desk.

"*Usually?* How many times have you sneaked your way in here?"

"Once or twice. Don't make it sound so bad."

But stealing *was* bad. Especially stealing not just material things—Annalee pondered now—but robbing a person's spirit of their hopes and dreams. Was that what they'd find in Lilian's private box? Her hopes and dreams? If they could ever find it and get it opened?

Prowling around the room, they certainly found plenty of other curious items. The stoic Lilian loved French perfumes and colognes, apparently, stamped with fancy labels. *La rose eau de parfum.* Odd, since Annalee had never once detected even a scintilla of perfumed scent wafting around Lilian as she moved throughout Simon's surroundings. But Lilian's bathroom cabinet was crammed with the fancy bottles. Imported.

Or smuggled? Was Lilian one of Buddy's customers? Stoic, discreet Lilian—selling imported, smuggled perfume on the side? Because Simon wasn't paying her enough? And Buddy was her supplier?

Annalee backed out of the bathroom, suppressing such thoughts. *Leave that be.* Besides, in the bedroom, Della had stumbled on Lilian's private box.

"Found it!"

It was tucked beside an upholstered bench sitting next to an armoire, atop Lilian's rolling cart. Della lifted the case over to the small corner desk. Annalee pushed away a pair of flannel pajamas, stacks of newspapers, and other unrelated items crowded onto the desktop.

"Well, it's intriguing," Annalee said to Della. "I guess I'd better open it." She lifted the purloined key from Della's hand and placed it in the lock. *Please open.*

The lock clicked and released. Together, she and Della opened the lid. Now *here* was organization. In alphabetical order, the box held what appeared to be Simon's most private keepsakes and documentation—items he apparently didn't trust for safekeeping even in the heavily secured vault in his own bank downtown.

Picking her way carefully through the alphabetized hanging folders, Annalee could see why. The box held a historical treasury. Rare family photos. Copies of deeds and wills, some written both in Spanish and English. *Thank goodness.*

"What are you looking for exactly?" Della pulled up a chair and perched on the edge.

"Not sure. I should actually start with *J*."

"For Jeffrey?"

"Right. But let's start first with *R*." Annalee picked up the labeled folder, opened it. Inside at the top of a stack of pictures lay an old, peeling photograph. "This must be Simon's mother. On the back it says, 'Rebekah, 1883.' She's small like him. Light hair." With gloved hands, Annalee handed the photo to Della.

"Such a proper young woman." Della peered at the photo. "Why not keep this stuff in his bank in a vault?"

"Simon? He'd want to see Lilian's box with his own eyes every day, knowing his secrets are as close as his key."

"They're fancy photos."

"Quite the aristocrat," Annalee agreed. "Especially standing here with her husband at their wedding. Not a hair out of place."

"And nary a smile."

"Not back then. Well-bred people didn't smile in photographs." She looked closer. "Except this picture. Look, it's Mr. Simon—as a baby."

"See how she's holding him."

"Like a precious gift. Gracious, she's glowing. Smiling, too."

"Where's Uri as a baby?" Della picked through the photos. *You won't find one.*

Because clearly Uri wasn't Rebekah's child. He looked nothing whatsoever like this proper young woman. Nor like Simon's dark-eyed, small-statured father. Just as Rebecca had said. So where did Uri come from?

Annalee looked through more folders, handing photos and documents to Della.

She went back to *A*, pulled out a large folder. She set it aside.

"Look in *J*—for Jeffrey." Della peered into the box but then slumped. "Nothing. Not even a folder. Why not?"

"He's not blood family. But here's a folder marked *M*— probably about Marie. Simon's daughter."

"Jeffrey told me about her."

"She died in an accident. She was just twelve years old."

They both reached for *M*. Together, they pulled out the folder. Annalee opened it and her breath caught. "Rebecca was right about Marie. The two look like twins." Annalee looked closer. "Wait, here's Marie's mother. Her name is Carmen. What a beauty."

"Well, where's Rebecca's mother?" Della riffled through the *R* folder. "She's not here."

"Of course she is." Annalee reached for Marie's folder. She hiked a brow. "They're the same person."

"What are you saying?"

Annalee held the folder to her chest. "This box isn't getting me any closer to Jeffrey's killer. This is about Simon and *his* family—a family of a thousand fabrications." She picked up the *R* folder again. "And who got the short end of the stick? Uri. Look at this."

It was a letter, tucked underneath all the photos, written to Simon from his mother in 1901. "It's written in English, thank goodness."

"Can I read it?" Della reached for the letter, unfolded it, started reading. "'My wonderful and beloved Simon . . .'"

And away we go, Annalee thought. She could already guess what the letter would say—and she was right—that Simon's mother was writing in English "to keep the letter confidential, in case it is discovered by your father."

She'd kept a "heartbreaking" secret all of Simon's life. But now that she was near the end of her long and tortured days, she wanted him to know the full truth. Annalee sighed. *Why do we humans do this? Bury a secret, sinking for years under the weight of it. Then at the end, when life prepares to release us, we're suddenly ready to shed the burden—leaving it to others to pick it up and glue together the unrepairable pieces.*

Thus, here was Simon's mother with her confession: His father had a child with another woman and asked Rebekah to raise him. That child was Uri, whose mother had died in childbirth. Simon's guilt-ridden father didn't want the child to be a foundling. So he brought him home.

But Rebekah despised him. Never showing him love.

"No wonder Uri's so mean." Della set down the letter. "Imagine growing up with a 'mother' who hates your guts—"

"While fawning over her favored son, her 'wonderful and beloved' Simon." Annalee could already guess the rest of it, but she let Della keep on reading, shaking her head at this and that.

While Della read, Annalee walked herself around Lilian Gray's bedroom, peeking under furniture, taking a glove off to finger the pretty curtains, peering at the museum-quality artwork on the walls—affordable to Simon because, as his mother wrote, *"your father has agreed to give you the bulk of his estate—to start your life in America. That's only fair. Your brother won't know what to do with it."*

Fair? Annalee scoffed. Uri would get a pittance. Cheated by the only mother he'd ever known.

"Does he know this?" Della asked. "You're going to tell him?"

"That's for Simon to tell." Annalee stepped back from a painting and saw it was a seascape. Gloved again, she touched its gold frame, but it didn't click open. No safe behind it. None of the other paintings in Lilian's bedroom were hiding safes either.

"Anything else in the box?" She walked back to Lilian's corner desk.

"Just two marriage certificates." Della held them up. She looked confused. "What does this mean?"

"What now?"

"Uri was married to Carmen. They had a child—Rebecca. But soon after, Carmen leaves Uri, marries Simon, takes Rebecca with her, and has a child with Simon—Marie."

"Both *his* 'beautiful girls.'"

"And Uri's left out in the cold again." Della pressed her mouth. "No wonder he hates his brother. After Carmen died, whenever that was, he must've brought Rebecca home to raise. But so much bitterness! I wouldn't want Simon to help support Rebecca either. Should I store these away?" Della began putting up the folders, asked Annalee for the key, ready to relock the box, but something stopped her.

"Wait, Miss Annalee. What about this *Airport* folder?"

Annalee hadn't forgotten about it. She didn't expect it to shed new light. Still, she opened it up, started picking through the pages. Sure enough, the papers showed Simon's plans to sell airport bonds for the City of Denver through Phantom Trust—as Annalee knew, a ghost company.

All the paperwork was in the folder. Neat as a pin. Papers all typed neatly, probably by Lilian, with her Royal office type-writer, Annalee noticed—seeing words spelled correctly, grammar perfect. Thus, it was just like the memo, tucked underneath all the paperwork, from Simon to Lilian. She'd taken dictation from him. Silently Annalee read it.

"Oh, my goodness." She spoke in a whisper.

"What's wrong?" Della stepped closer to look.

"Did Jeffrey know about the scheme? Simon's ploy to secretly sell bonds for the city?"

"Why? What'd the memo tell you?"

"It told me to ask you if Jeffrey knew about Simon's scheme."

Della stepped back, shrugged. "Sure. It's a juicy plan. Jeffrey thought it was brilliant. He hated the Klan. 'Serves them right. They'll end up paying more.' That's what he told me."

"But how'd he find out?"

Della didn't respond.

Annalee narrowed her eyes. "*You* told him."

"Well—"

"Della, you broke into Lilian's box, read the file, discovered the 'juicy' plan—so brilliant that you had to tell somebody. So you told Jeffrey? Maybe wrote out a copy for him?"

Della bit her lip.

"Did he tell anybody else about it? Show it to anybody?"

"Wait a second. You're blaming Jeffrey? He wasn't cheating the stupid city. Did that memo mention him by name?"

"No, it mentioned Simon—*by name*—saying he'd 'hold responsible' anyone spilling the beans about Phantom Trust." Annalee stepped closer. "So did Jeffrey spill? Did he tell anybody?" She searched Della's face, saw the young woman's pained look—but also her wounded guilt? Yet she had to ask.

"Della, did he sell the information? Or *try* to sell it—this juicy scheme of Simon's to double-cross the city?"

Della glanced away, wrung her hands.

"Tell me!"

"He needed the money! For Belinda, if he found her. Plus, he and Rebecca were stone broke. Barely making ends meet." Della's eyes flashed. "Uri wouldn't let Simon help them—"

"Did he find a buyer?"

Della sat down on the bed. "He had a couple of people on the hook—"

"At the risk of Simon's life? The Klan would murder him!"

"But no buyer had come through yet." Della's voice pleaded. "He just wanted to be like Buddy and—"

Annalee shook her head. "That's a lie."

"It's true, Miss Annalee. Everything Buddy touches works out great. He always gets what he wants. That's what Jeffrey said." She gestured to Annalee. "Buddy's even going after you—"

"This isn't about me! Or Buddy!" Annalee yanked off the gloves. "If I sound angry, I'm not angry at you. If anything, I'm angry at myself." *For getting distracted by Buddy and not finding*

Jeffrey's killer. "But I need you to tell me the truth. Did Jeffrey find a buyer for Simon's plan?"

Della sat quietly, then started to weep. "He didn't have time." She wiped at the trail of her tears. "Somebody killed him first."

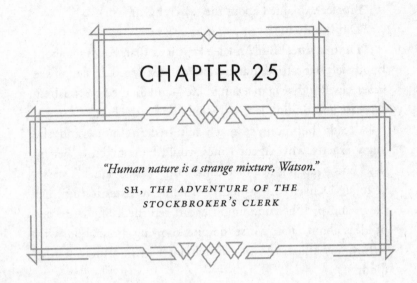

CHAPTER 25

"Human nature is a strange mixture, Watson."

SH, *THE ADVENTURE OF THE
STOCKBROKER'S CLERK*

SIMON DID THIS. Annalee hated the thought. He'd held court over a hornet's nest of family pain, cheating Uri from his share of family wealth, winning away Uri's wife, and robbing Rebecca of having memories of her mother.

But Simon didn't kill Jeffrey. That was top of Annalee's mind as she and Della finally quit Lilian's room and quietly closed the door. Maybe Simon didn't wield the weapon that killed Jeffrey. But he gave somebody good reason to level the fatal blow. Who?

"Let's head back downstairs."

Annalee hoped a call would come in soon about the search for Uri. Indeed, she hoped for Simon's return soon. She needed to sit him down for more serious questioning. Rebecca, pacing in the morning room, showed even greater desperation for news.

Annalee explained about the search by air.

"Did Buddy fly?"

"I'm not sure." But Annalee kept it at that. Any talk about Buddy left her rattled, frankly, and confused, too. In fact, if she never saw Buddy Mann again in life—and focused on finishing this case and finding Jack—it would be for the best.

Already her poor stomach felt tied in knots, and she knew exactly why. Agent Ames would be contacting her by day's end, warning her that "time's up, Miss Spain." A passel of rogue Denver cops would be heading to Estes to hunt her down and pick her up. Simon hadn't returned. She'd run out of ideas about Jack. Worse, despite knowing more about why Jeffrey was killed, she wasn't any closer to figuring out who did it.

Time to stop her stewing about all these things and keep digging.

The hallway clock, affirming that, sounded twelve noon.

"I'm walking down to the airfield."

"It's still storming," Rebecca protested. "Please stay safe."

"I'll be fine. I'll check on Lilian. If she's had any word about Simon's search, I'll give you a call."

Annalee turned to leave, gave Rebecca a sincere smile. But Rebecca didn't look convinced. More than that, she looked downright lost.

Lost in this big house. Lost in her confusing, contentious family. Lost without her missing papa. Lost without her man— who wasn't coming back.

Rebecca had looked like this, Annalee remembered, when she'd first encountered her at the new Denver branch library, crying her eyes out. What had Annalee told her? *"I'll help you."*

But had she helped her? Let alone helped herself?

Annalee pulled out a chair, sat herself down. "I'll stay here with you, Rebecca. No point in going out in the snow and getting hurt or lost, too."

"Who knows if they'll find him." Rebecca peered out a frosted window. "If I lose him, too, I don't think I can stand it."

"I'll call now. See if somebody can find Lilian, put her on the phone."

At the hall telephone, Annalee waited for an operator, asked for the Stanley Hotel, got connected to a proper-sounding voice—probably a nice, on-her-way-up young woman working to get noticed in the hotel telephone room.

"Good afternoon! How may I direct your call, please?"

Annalee wasn't sure what to request. "Is there a telephone line at the hotel airfield? In the hangar area, please?"

"Of course, miss. I'll connect you."

The phone rang. Long time. Ten, fifteen, twenty, umpteen endless rings.

"Dang it!"

"Excuse me!"

"What the—?" the man cursed. "We're running a *search and rescue* here! What in the devil do you—?"

"Buddy Mann." Annalee spoke the name she'd privately sworn she'd never mention again.

"Not here!"

"He's flying?"

"What the—? Who's asking!"

Annalee brushed one wild curl off her forehead. *Mercy, this world and its disagreeable people.* "I'm calling about Uri Wallace—"

"Uri? That idiot!"

"Excuse me!"

"They're bringing him home right now!"

Annalee gestured to Rebecca. "Uri's found!"

"He's safe?" Rebecca ran for the phone.

"Where'd they find him?" Annalee spoke in the receiver, reached for Rebecca, hugged her. "Is he hurt? Where was he found?"

"He wasn't lost."

"Not lost?"

"Lost! Found! Whatever—he's on his way home. Ask Buddy!"

"Buddy's bringing him?" Annalee swallowed. "What about Simon—?"

"Ask Buddy! You're wasting my time!"

The phone was slammed down. The call went silent.

Just as the bell by the front door started clanging like crazy.

"That's him!" Rebecca took off running.

Della rushed from the kitchen. "Uri's back?"

"Right," Annalee mumbled to herself. "And so is Buddy."

Annalee had seen miracles before. That's what she'd called them anyway. Like the winter night when she was eight years old and her daddy came home, exhausted and without money, apologizing for no food, after a second day and night—when the neighbor lady, Sister Nelson, knocked on their door with a soupbone, one baked potato, and two hunks of corn bread. Annalee and her daddy both cried. Or that scorching summer day during her childhood when a raging wildfire, burning through a Colorado mountainside, charring and licking at everything in its tracks, was doused by a sudden July snowstorm, blowing in out of nowhere and stopping it cold.

Watching Uri stomp through Simon's front door, smelling like an outdoor privy, his grizzled face bearing more grizzle, his mouth turned down, his embittered eyes flashing their standard Uri anger—after being lost in a merciless spring blizzard, without shelter or a coat—would go on Annalee's list as a miracle, too.

She couldn't help herself. "Uri!"

Della called to him. "Uri! You're back!"

They both rushed for him, but Rebecca had already thrown herself into her complicated papa's arms.

Uri let himself be loved on for only so long. He shushed her crying. "No bother, baby. I'm back! Hush now!" He grabbed her by the shoulder, wiped away her tears with a filthy hand. "Now stop your bawling."

"But how'd they find you?" Rebecca still clung to him.

"Find? I wasn't even lost."

Buddy had come through the door, glanced at Annalee, but held back, watching Uri have his moment. Buddy was wearing a wool Stetson, brim low, over heavy earmuffs. Wool scarf and gloves, too. The whole kit. He pulled off the headgear and gloves, stood there looking at her, but silent.

"I'll get some coffee." Della headed for the kitchen.

"I'll help you." Annalee turned to follow.

Buddy reached for her. "Can I talk to you?"

Annalee wanted to protest. But what was the point? They were having their good news. Uri was back, safe and halfway sound. Whatever Buddy had to say, she could allow herself to listen.

"In here." She pointed him to the morning room. Sunshine had passed over, so the room felt chilled. She stepped to the corner stove, grabbed a poker, threw in a handful of kindling, and stoked it.

"Come get warm." She reached for a chair, but Buddy stopped her, moved the chair himself, pushed up another one. He pulled off his coat.

"Come here," he said. "Please sit down."

They sat side by side, not looking at each other, their breathing the room's only sound, save for the occasional pop and crackle of burning kindling.

She finally spoke. "What happened?"

"Uri's an idiot."

"It's not all his fault."

"No? Well, he's predictable."

She turned her chair. "What are you saying?"

"From one smuggler to another—"

"So Uri's smuggling, too?"

"Half the world is smuggling. Uri included. That's how I figured where Uri was, and I was right. He and a few other fellas use an old lean-to put up on old Indian ground, to hide stashes."

"What lean-to?"

"Some broken-down wreck above Estes. They're all over these mountains. Fur traders put some up. Old miners, too. They built them years ago, some over old tepee sites. Most are abandoned or torn down. Hard to find unless you know the spot. Uri uses one barely standing."

"How'd he get his stuff up there?"

"On horseback. On mules. Like I did today. When I heard where he was last seen, I knew exactly where he probably was. Like I said. He's predictable. That's why he's lousy at smuggling. He might as well leave a trail of bread crumbs saying, 'Come and get me.'" Buddy scoffed. "He tries to dip his finger in contraband, buy this or that—mostly a lot of perfume, if you can believe it."

"French perfume?"

Buddy gave her a look. "What do you know about that?" He shook his head. "Doesn't matter. That's not why I want to talk to you."

"Buddy—" She put up her hand, saying no. He reached out and grabbed it, held it too long of course, then finally spoke.

"We could live up here in the mountains, far away from everybody. Nobody would bother us."

"Don't—" she started to protest, pulling back her hand, but she searched his face, saw more than she wanted to see, maybe saw part of herself. Because he'd convinced himself that she, Annalee Spain, had fallen into his airplane for some mystical reason—wearing this blasted blue dress that he couldn't seem to stop mooning over. So that meant she was for him? But that couldn't be right.

She relaxed her hand. He released it. "What in the world are you looking for, Buddy? A family? Something of your own?"

"What's wrong with that? I'm getting out of smuggling. I'm sick of it. Sick of being a thief—"

"You robbed from Simon?"

"Whether I did or not, that's all behind me now. Dipping

my hands in this or that. Breaking into places. Looking over my shoulder—"

"Do you know how to type?"

"What are you saying? I'm a pilot. A good pilot. I've got to start over—"

"Like Jeffrey?"

"What about Jeffrey?"

Annalee pushed back her chair. She stood and stepped to the window. "He was looking for your mother."

"*Our* mother?" Buddy's voice dropped. "Belinda?" He stood, walked to her. "Did he find her? Is that why he was killed?"

"Not really. Not directly." Oh, this crazy world. "He was aiming to make a score—get a nest egg together, enough to help Belinda if it turned out she needed a leg up. Provide for Rebecca, too. Get them out of hock. But he set his sights on the wrong man. He was double-crossing Simon. Trying to expose a financial lie that Simon was telling to scam the city."

"Simon scamming? And a murderer? Did he kill Jeffrey? I can't believe that."

"Not Simon. I'm sure it wasn't him. But when he gets back, I want to hear what he knows. I have a lot to ask him."

"But that's the problem." Buddy suddenly looked weary. "Simon's not coming back."

"What do you mean?"

"Annalee, I'm darn sorry. Simon's plane went down. Crashed into a mountain. Search and rescue's been up there all day, but there's no survivors."

"That can't be!"

"But it is. Simon is dead."

Annalee pushed past Buddy. *Please, no, God.*

"Where are you going?"

"To get the police! Or *somebody*." She frowned. "Was it the Klan? Did they tamper with the plane?"

Buddy pressed his mouth. "I wish I could say no, because—" He paused.

"Because what?"

"The Klan wanted Simon gone. They knew he was Jewish—and clever. So he was a target. Top of their list. You probably saw the leaflets all over town? Some even plastered on his bank."

Annalee nodded, showing sadness and anger. "Does Rebecca know about the crash? Does Uri?"

"Search and rescue's sending a minister over—"

"For a family that's Jewish?" She stopped. "But Jeffrey wasn't. And for me, this is all about Jeffrey now." She searched Buddy's face. "And you. I'm doing this for you, Buddy. I'm going to find out who killed your brother if it's the last thing on earth I do before this infernal day ends."

Buddy watched her go. "And then you'll come live with me in the mountains?"

She turned back, looked a long time at his handsome, sad face, in his arresting and hopeful green eyes.

"That's actually one of the most remarkable offers I've received from anybody in my entire life." *Including from Jack.* He'd still never officially proposed to her—despite what Eddie Brown Jr. insisted he longed to do. And Buddy? He wasn't proposing. He was looking for something more.

"I can't be the family you want—even if I understand why you want it, Buddy, because I don't know who my mother is either."

"You don't? Then we'd make quite a pair."

She turned back to him and, despite herself, stepped into his embrace, letting him pull her closer. She looked up at him.

"We can't be that to each other, even if the law allowed it. But there's one thing we can do." She set her jaw. "We can find justice for Jeffrey."

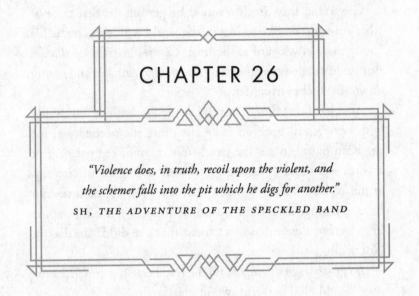

CHAPTER 26

*"Violence does, in truth, recoil upon the violent, and
the schemer falls into the pit which he digs for another."*
SH, *THE ADVENTURE OF THE SPECKLED BAND*

IN THE GREAT ROOM, a self-possessed Methodist pastor was letting Rebecca cry on his shoulder. Two family losses in one week weren't explainable or consolable. So he didn't make it worse by droning on with platitudes.

He held his oversize Bible in one hand—*Property of Sky View Methodist Church, Estes Park*—but he didn't open and read from it.

Seeing Annalee enter the room and sit down with the family, the pastor instead turned to Buddy.

"I'm sorry for your loss, sir."

"Thank you." Annalee gave the reply.

The pastor blinked at her, wrinkled his brow, gave her a hard look.

Observing that, Buddy would be getting his first taste of what it would be like to live in the world with Annalee as his "better half." Awkward at the least. *Can you see it now, Buddy?* But Buddy upped the ante, stepping next to Annalee and sitting down just inches from her.

Annalee didn't flinch, but she wanted *so badly* to tell Buddy with her eyes to back off. The last thing she needed was for the Klan patrol to get the word from a conflicted pastor that a white man and a "colored gal" were acting awful cozy up at the Wallace house. Which wasn't true. But appearances can be everything, and Buddy seemed intent on making some brave, crazy, determined statement that she didn't need now. Not at all.

If I get through this day alive, she told herself, *it will be a miracle.* Would God perform two in one day?

Uri, indeed, stomped into the great room now. He'd had a bath, so he didn't smell. He was wearing fresh clothes, but he was barefoot. He swung a pair of clean-looking socks in his hand.

The pastor looked down at his feet. Uri reacted.

"What? You never saw a man's bare feet before?"

Annalee held her tongue. Uri wasn't her worry. He hadn't killed Jeffrey or anybody. Uri was just bluster and noise, not to mention exhausting and annoying.

She stood to help Della, who'd come in carrying a tray of tea things. The pastor refused a cup, but he convinced Rebecca to take refreshment.

"I doubt you feel like it, but hot tea will do you good."

Rebecca conceded, taking a cup.

Uri, on the other hand, was set on making another ugly scene.

"This all you got? Where's the grub? In case you forgot, I haven't eaten *since yesterday*."

"I'll make you a plate, Mr. Uri," Annalee said. "Come on into the kitchen."

"You're not the maid!"

The pastor looked at Annalee.

"Doesn't matter. I can cook." *Well, good enough.*

Annalee headed toward the kitchen, praying Uri would stop his griping and concede to follow her. For whatever reason, speaking of miracles—*thank you, God*—he did precisely that.

Making it to the kitchen first, she swung around the second he came through the door.

"Uri! You were right."

"Get out of my face. Where's my food?"

"Uri!"

"Why you nagging me? I'm hungry—"

"Uri!"

He finally shut up. *"What?"*

"You were right. About everything. About Simon, about getting cheated, about your mother—Rebekah."

"Watch your mouth."

Annalee pushed a chair at him. "No, *you* sit down!" She took the seat herself, looked up at him, eyes pleading. "Listen to me, *please*. It's *over*, Uri."

"What's over?"

"Your fight, your war, your battle—whatever you want to call it—with your family, with Simon, with everybody, with the whole world. Because you were right." She reached for him. "*You got cheated*—from the day you were born."

"Stop saying that!" He pulled away.

"But it's true. So it's hard to hear. But your family cheated you from your first breath, cheated you from getting your fair start in life." She sighed. "Simon probably cheated you even in death, in his will."

"I don't want Simon's money! Rebecca don't need it either. What are you talking about anyway—I was 'cheated'?"

"It's not my place to tell you. It was Simon's place. I honestly believe he was finally going to tell you. But there is evidence. A letter. I'm going to make sure you get it." Annalee stood, walked to the stove, took eggs from a wire basket, and cracked half a dozen in a bowl.

"I hate eggs!"

"You *don't* hate eggs. Or toast or whatever. You just say you hate everything, and I understand. You've just wanted what we all want—a family who loves us and a fair shake at life. You didn't get either one. Still, some people tried to help you. Lilian bought all that smuggled French perfume from you—"

"You don't know a thing about—"

"Maybe not. But I know you didn't kill Jeffrey, even if you were angry as heck at him, for whatever reason—"

"He was bad-mouthing me. Ruining my game. Telling folks not to do business with me—his own father-in-law. Saying I was a risk." He sat down in a chair. "Heck, maybe I was."

"Is that why you made that scene in the public library?"

"That wasn't a scene. Jeffrey was always 'researching' something. I wanted to find out why. What's he studying on so hard? Making people turn their back on me? Cutting me out?"

"You ransacked the house, too?" Annalee put a plate of scrambled eggs in front of Uri. He dug in.

"Rebecca's house? You crazy? I'd never do that to her. If I ever find out who did—and who killed her man, even if he was bad-mouthing me—they'll be sorry they ever heard of Uri Wallace."

Buddy came in then. "Lilian's here. The Stanley drove her over. She's a mess."

"I'll check on her. She's upstairs? Did the pastor leave?"

"He's gone, but Simon's bank employee's here. He drove up from Denver. Brought a lady friend with him—"

"Mrs. Quinlan?"

"I guess." Buddy nodded toward the great room. "Come back in there with me. I'm not good at making small talk."

"Her name's Mrs. Quinlan." Annalee followed but turned back to Uri. "I'm glad Buddy found you."

"I wasn't lost!"

"Whatever you say." She put a hand on his shoulder, grateful that he let her. "But you still can get found."

Flora Quinlan. Annalee rushed across the great room to her friend, the Denver librarian. Reaching for her, she hugged her, then pulled back, standing stock-still.

"Annalee!" Mrs. Quinlan pulled off her coat. "Let me hug you again. What's wrong?"

"Rough weekend." Annalee stepped back. "One man lost. Simon Wallace killed. I'm just so grateful to see a friendly face." Annalee smiled at her, but she wasn't looking at the librarian's lovely face. She was looking at Flora Quinlan's eyes—because they were green. Green as the day is long. Green as they'd always been green. But more green right now than Annalee believed green eyes could ever be.

Except for Buddy's.

She turned to Della, who turned away in the same instant, acting preoccupied with a teapot. Mrs. Quinlan didn't seem to notice.

"Well, I'm glad I came." Mrs. Quinlan accepted a cup of tea from Della, told her thank you, stirred, and sipped. "As soon as we heard, I told Hugh—"

"Mr. Smith?"

"You remember him? He's been so kind. And look, Annalee!" The librarian held out her wrist, showing a filigree bracelet set with five sparkly blue stones. She rambled on about the gift, a surprise present from Hugh Smith, whom she'd only recently met. "It's truly the nicest gift I've ever been given."

Hugh was seated near Rebecca, consoling her, asking questions about Simon. "Did you know his lawyer? Has he been here?" Rebecca said she didn't know.

Buddy was fussing with the fireplace, adding logs, stoking the flames.

Mrs. Quinlan stepped over to watch him, held out her hands to feel the rise of heat. Smiling at him, she asked Buddy what kind of work he did.

"I'm a pilot." Buddy pulled up a bench near the fire, invited Mrs. Quinlan to join him. He told her he fought in the war and was working now as a barnstormer on weekends, flying tourists around at the Stanley on weekdays, and soon they were having a nice conversation for such a sad, confusing day.

Annalee watched them a moment, stifled a smile at Buddy.

"I'm not good at making small talk." But here he was, talking easily with her librarian friend as if he'd known Flora Quinlan his entire life. She blinked. Because he had?

Annalee turned to Della, who at first refused to return her look. But Annalee was insistent, walking over to help Della clear away the teacups, making Della look her in the eye so the young Telluride maid couldn't ignore Annalee's crazy but urgent question. *Is the librarian actually Belinda—Buddy and Jeffrey's Belinda?*

Surely she couldn't be.

As a young widow, Mrs. Quinlan had befriended Annalee as a child. Helped her find books in the library. Sometimes checked her homework. Came to the colored school in Five Points for story time, gathering the children around her to read from library books. Wearing a name badge. *Flora Quinlan.*

Annalee followed Della into the kitchen.

"Don't ask me," Della whispered as Annalee came through the door.

Annalee sat down. Uri still was at the table but slumped over fast asleep, dead to the world from his ordeal. Annalee watched him a moment, then walked back to the great room and pulled a blanket off a sofa. Back in the kitchen, she plumped the blanket over Uri's shoulders, then turned to Della.

"Buddy deserves to know."

"What if she doesn't want him to know?"

"But if she's his mother?" Annalee squinted. "How'd you find out anyway?"

"Uri bribed somebody in Telluride. They'd heard where Belinda had gone."

"Della, Buddy should be told about her."

"But she's made a new life for herself." Della turned, started to run a sink of soapy water for dishes, changing the subject. "Besides, looks like she has a new boyfriend and everything—"

"That's all you see? You're hopeless—a romantic."

"I don't even know what that means."

"Oh yes, you do. It means being sentimental about every other thing—especially love and men and all they churn up." Annalee gave her a look. "And how do I know so much about it? Maybe because I'm the same way."

Annalee thought then about Buddy, fretted about Jack, thought even more about the killer she still needed to find. She walked to the sink, stood by Della. "Some things in life are bigger than any of us. That's been the whole problem in this family but also with Buddy and Jeffrey. Certain people trying to control other people's truth. Even in my 'family'—whoever my mother is, if she's still alive, she's doing the same thing."

Della searched Annalee's eyes. "You don't know who your mother is?"

"That's right. So I *hate* family lies. Tell one and you have to tell umpteen more." Annalee half dried a teacup, put it on the dish rack, tossed down the towel, turned to Della. "Why'd you leave Telluride?"

"That sorry town? Maybe one day it'll be something. But now, just miners and swindlers and too much snow and, well, whores. 'Working the line.' That's what they called it. Mine companies own everything and everybody. I'm never going back. Maybe I can find a real job. A typing post."

Annalee peered at her. "You know how to type?"

"Not yet. I've never even tried. But maybe I can learn. Anything but going back to Telluride."

Annalee breathed deep. "My mother's from there. Or close by."

Della frowned. "No, she's not. The only colored woman around that town was my mother."

"But that's where I was found—in a mine shaft near Annalee, the ghost town, on the way to Telluride." Annalee felt confused. "This is a crazy question, Della, but did your mother have other children?"

Della cut her eyes. "I'm my mother's only child—and she and Daddy had a hard time having me. They never had other children. Then he died in an avalanche when I was in grade school." Della threw down a towel. "You're smart, Annalee. But you're barking up the wrong tree." She cocked her head. "Unless—"

"Unless what?"

"Unless your mother wasn't a colored woman."

Annalee heard those words. She blinked. "What in the world do you mean?"

"Well, look at us. Both of us. Barely brown. Curls all over our crazy heads. I get that from having a daddy who was white. Maybe you're the same, but it was your mama. She was white."

Annalee opened her mouth. Then she closed it. Never in life had she thought about the possibility, and she didn't know what to say or think of it now. Della didn't seem fazed either way. Annalee grabbed at the table, trying to stop her hands from trembling.

"It's like Buddy and Jeffrey," Della was saying. "Their daddy was colored."

"What?" Annalee gasped an odd whisper. "I don't believe it."

"Don't act so surprised. Folks are complicated."

"Who told you this?"

"A rumor. I heard it in Telluride."

"A *rumor*? That's all you heard?"

"People talk."

"They talk too much—"

"What, you need proof?"

Annalee considered that, struggling now to weigh what it all could mean—for Buddy, for her. *Mercy*, for the two of them? But with Jack still not found, making a life with Buddy—legally?—was the last thing she wanted to think about. She felt her whole body trembling. She grabbed a chair to sit, weighing this information, unsure what to do about it.

She thought about Della's question. Why proof? For who anybody is—white or black or anything else?

"Because without it, lies get ground into weapons. Every person on earth, in fact, gets reduced by it."

"But what if it's true?" Della pulled up a chair, too. "About their dad—Buddy and Jeffrey's?"

"So what?" Annalee blinked hard. "If it's true? Or not true? Honestly, Della, I don't care—not about a rumor. Either way, the world sees them as white. That's how they look. That's what Buddy still believes. I'm not even going to ask him. I've got bigger worries."

Like where was her Jack? And who killed Buddy's actual brother Jeffrey?

"But if Buddy's—"

"Enough, Della. I've got to find a murderer—*today*." She stood from the table.

"Finding out the truth?" Della was saying. "It's—"

"A funny game." Annalee twisted her mouth. "So many people are playing it. Unless—"

"Unless what?"

"Unless you talk to the right person."

Annalee walked to the table and nudged Uri, hating to wake up the grouchy and hurting man. He snuggled deeper into the blanket.

"Maybe just leave him be."

Annalee set her jaw.

Della went back to washing dishes. "At least for now?"

"At least for now." Annalee gave Uri's shoulder a light touch. "He knows Telluride, too. If he'll talk about it."

But she gave him a closer look. Did he look weary of knowing something else? Something murderous? Something wrong? In this household, she suddenly realized who would tell her.

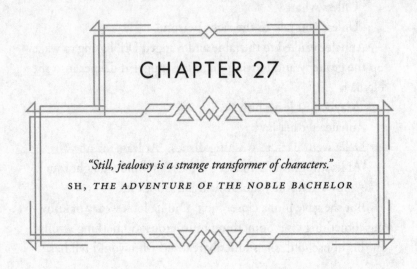

CHAPTER 27

"Still, jealousy is a strange transformer of characters."
SH, *THE ADVENTURE OF THE NOBLE BACHELOR*

BALANCING A TEA TRAY, Annalee headed upstairs to face down Lilian Gray.

She wasn't sure what Lilian would say to her. But if anybody was still holding the last of anyone's secrets, Annalee had the feeling that Lilian was the one. She'd been hiding all manner of sad secrets for Simon for umpteen years. Maybe about Jeffrey too? So what else did she know?

But something more was bothering Annalee about Lilian. She wasn't sure if she could trust her. *Even though I want to trust her.* After hearing the town gossip about Buddy, Annalee simply wanted an easy talk with Lilian, woman to woman, even though she knew nothing to speak of about Lilian's life either. Who, indeed, were her people? Where had she come from? How had she ended up working for Simon, discovering that he wasn't just her boss—but the man she desperately loved?

Maybe more than all—did any of this have to do with poor Jeffrey's murder?

Annalee tapped on Lilian's door, didn't get an answer. But she turned the door handle. Not locked. Annalee stepped inside.

"I don't want to talk." Lilian lay curled under blankets on her bed, facing toward the wall.

"I don't blame you for that." Annalee kept her voice low. "I just brought you some tea, something light to eat—just a little nourishment."

She set down the tea things, poured a steaming cup, replaced the teapot, and carried the tray—including half a chicken sandwich that she'd made with her own hands—to Lilian's nightstand.

The room looked as it had during the morning—closet doors hanging open, that pile of clothes still strewn atop the corner desk. Annalee and Della had left it as they'd found it. Yet even if Lilian had suspected a break-in or worried about one, she wasn't in the mood, at the end of a horrible day, to even notice.

Annalee touched her shoulder. "Simon would want you to eat something—to take care of yourself."

"Simon?" Lilian whispered his name. *"Simon?"* Her voice broke.

Annalee steeled herself to hear hurt, already understanding if Lilian broke down and cried without limits, with no stopping. But Lilian did the opposite.

She cursed.

Annalee tensed. "Excuse me?"

"You never heard a curse word before? Think you're too good to hear a curse word, *Miss Spain*?"

Now what was this?

"Please, one minute. You'd better explain—"

"I don't have to explain one thing to you!"

"Maybe not." The world was filled with things not explained. "But you have no good right to curse me."

"Why not? Simon was *so* taken with you, *so* impressed with you, *so*—"

"Stop it." Annalee yanked back the blanket. She'd heard enough insanity today. "You got a problem with me? You better get out of this bed and explain it."

"I got a problem with a man who took me for granted for *sixteen years.*"

So here it is, Annalee thought.

"You worked sixteen years for Simon?" Annalee couldn't imagine. Sixteen years ago, she was still a child. Eight years old. Skinny, snotty-nosed, half-fed, failing to understand why all she had for help was a drunken father—needing a mother so bad that neighbor women washed her filthy, life-worn clothes, then handed her cold biscuits on her way to school so she wouldn't starve.

"Simon called me pretty. *Once.*" Lilian jerked toward Annalee, her face looking even more bitter than her words. "That first year. 'You're so pretty.' He said that *once.*"

"Then you waited sixteen years for him to say it again?"

"Working every blasted day and night, doing his every bidding. 'Yes, sir. No, sir. In just a minute, sir. Of course, *sir.* I'll carry that, *sir.* It's not heavy, *sir!*'"

"Lilian! Why'd you stay?"

"Where else was I going to go? Back to a dirt farm in the middle of nowhere. Feeding my no-account father and lazy brothers—watching my mother turn from pretty to plain to pathetic." Lilian wiped her mouth with the back of her hand; then she sat up in bed. "And then here *you* come."

"Me? Wait just one minute."

"He couldn't get enough of you. 'Get Miss Spain the car. Give Miss Spain the best room. Miss Spain is so smart. Miss Spain is so clever. Miss Spain is so pretty!'"

"He never said that!"

"*Every word* of that he said—and after everything *I've* done for him. *Everything.*"

Annalee put a hand to her chest, feeling her heart pound, unsure how to appease a woman so obviously distraught, but needing to calm that woman down, if not calm herself.

She'd heard that knee-dropping tattle today about Buddy. Excited, in fact, was how she'd almost felt about it—but that felt disloyal to Jack. Her poor head was swimming, her hands still shaking. To be a target now of Lilian's unfounded ire was simply too much. *Let me calm her.*

"I know this is hard—losing Mr. Simon so sudden." Annalee's hands trembled worse, but she reached for the teacup. "Please have some hot tea, Miss Lilian. It'll make you feel—"

"Get out of my sight!"

Lilian backhanded the cup. It went flying, landed on the bed, the scalding tea quickly staining the bedcovers, soaking into the sheets. Not done, Lilian grabbed the teapot off the nightstand, wildly dumped the whole of it all over the bed.

"You're upset, Miss Lilian." Annalee grabbed at the wet bed-clothes. "You weren't treated well—*for sixteen years*—and that's inexcusable. But that's over now. *Everything's changed.* You can start anew. Mr. Simon's life is over. It ended tragically, but if nothing else, he probably took care of you in his will—"

"I don't want his money!" Lilian finally sobbed then. "I wanted to *mean something* to him. What more did he want me to do?"

The plea hit home.

"Listen, I'm going to help you." Annalee opened dresser drawers, looking for a dry nightgown for Lilian, found one, hung it across the back of a chair. "I have a really good friend— Mr. Castle. He used to be the Denver DA. He knows Mr. Simon. He can help you get a new start—"

"Castle? Sidney Castle?"

"I'll talk to him for you, Miss Lilian."

"You think he'll help me?"

"I'll ask him as soon as I get back to Denver." *If I ever get back.* She pressed her mouth. Annalee helped Lilian move to the chair, pulled wet sheets and blankets from the bed. "Let me get your bed cleaned up. I'll get some sheets. Here, put on a dry gown."

She handed Lilian the nightgown, turned to give her modesty, slipped into the bathroom, half closed the door, looking for a linen closet.

"Nothing like a fresh start, Miss Lilian," Annalee called to her. She glanced at herself in the bathroom mirror. She understood Lilian better now, feeling her confounded dismay, and *I will help her.* Even though every time Annalee said those words to somebody, she ended up being the one who needed help the most.

But at least she could change the sopping wet sheets on the bed.

She opened a closet door in the bathroom, saw a tower of

white towels stacked in a leaning pile and, near the bottom, more piles—clean white sheets—also leaning. So she pulled from the sheet pile, struggling to keep it from falling on itself, but it was already tumbling—a mess of towels and sheets and whatnot that she could only manage by grabbing everything to figure out what she was looking for.

But what she was looking for sat before her, so she couldn't help but see it.

A typewriter. An Olivetti M1 typewriter. A little worn but beautiful and elegant, except for one thing. All over the chassis's right side was dried blood.

Annalee blinked, looked hard at that Olivetti, letting the truth of it sink deep, because maybe she always knew it would be right here. Why? *"Crime is common. Logic is rare,"* said her Sherlock. *So follow the logic*—which had been staring Annalee in the face all the time. Of all the people in this case, along with its wild distractions, only one person knew how to use a blasted typewriter. Lilian Gray.

Now Lilian was jabbering in the other room.

"Can he find me a better position—with a new start—this Mr. Sidney Castle?"

Annalee couldn't answer—because of the blood on the Olivetti. Jeffrey Mann's dried blood. Annalee would bet anything it was Jeffrey's blood. Bet, indeed, that Lilian had gotten wind of Jeffrey's scheme, overhearing talk—maybe from a suspicious Hugh Smith or even from Della.

Then acting in service to Simon Wallace—and doing

everything she possibly could to hold secret Simon's trust scheme against Denver's hateful Klan—Lilian ransacked Rebecca's house, raging room to room, hunting for a stolen copy of Simon's trust, even willing to kill for it.

Then maybe Simon would love her.

Finally maybe he'd see all she really meant to him. How could he not see? Not remember that she was still pretty? Not understand that she'd do anything to protect him and save him from the vile, infernal Klan? Then since she'd do all those self-less and clever and *loving* things, he would open his arms and love her back.

Nothing would stop her, in fact, from seeing this happen. Thus, after thundering her way through Jeffrey's house and not finding what she sought, Lilian was fit to fight when Jeffrey came waltzing home. Discovered his place vandalized. Found Lilian red-handed in his kitchen.

Annalee could imagine the fireworks. The two would go to blows, of course—Jeffrey accusing Lilian of trashing his property, knowing he was guilty of everything Lilian accused him of plotting. Stealing Simon's plans. Flashing them all over town, trying to sell them to the highest bidder.

Yet Jeffrey must've ridiculed her, too. Even used that classic guilty-man's tactic—turning blame back onto her. *Did you do that, handsome Jeffrey? Act not with Buddy's shrewder instincts but your worst? Knowing you're wrong as the day is long but pointing the finger of guilt by association—this time at Lilian Gray?*

"Did you find the sheets?" Lilian called from the bedroom.

"Found them." Annalee kept her voice neutral. "I'm coming." But her heart was pounding. In fact, she could barely breathe.

Because she was imagining Jeffrey mocking and scoffing at

Lilian. Telling her to get out of his house. Turning his back on her, even, to show disdain. Thus, Lilian, to show Jeffrey how wrong he was about everything, picked up the nearest thing she could find—the stylish but hefty and used Olivetti. A second-hand whim of Jeffrey's, it caught his eye, maybe at Fletcher's Pawnshop, where he'd picked it up for a song to type his "business letters" on it.

But Lilian bashed it on the back of Jeffrey's handsome head. One hard, godless, murdering blow. To hurt him, not to kill. To silence Jeffrey's mocking mouth. But Jeffrey wouldn't move. He couldn't. His lips were silent. Jeffrey was dead.

Lilian stood then in his kitchen, looking down at the stillness of him, feeling alarmed and sick at what she'd done but couldn't undo. So for herself, or mostly for Simon, she lifted the heavy typewriter one more time, placing it in her ever-present rolling case, and took off in the dark, deciding it was safe to secretly type a letter on the Olivetti—nobody would ever suspect her—and send that letter to Annalee. As she'd fled in the shadows, she saw Rebecca approaching the house, accompanied by—what's this?—that "colored detective." That smarty gal the papers were always crowing about. *"She's so wonderfully clever."*

So Lilian typed a letter to threaten the clever Annalee.

"Take that Jeffrey Mann case . . . and it will be your last."

Such an ugly threat. But now?

Annalee looked at herself again in the bathroom mirror. *You've got a situation, clever girl.* A killer awaited just steps away. Thus, she heard in her gut what the typewriter man in Denver had warned when she left his shop. *"Watch your back."*

The bathroom door opened.

"Did you find the sheets—?"

Lilian stepped around the half-open door. She was wearing the dry nightgown, white bathrobe, her hair fallen down around her shoulders.

So she *was* once pretty. Annalee could see that. But now, sadly, her pretty was used up and all gone.

Lilian looked down at the pile of sheets, saw the bloodied typewriter.

"What are you doing?" Her voice was a hard whisper. She slammed the bathroom door behind her, loud, and clicked the lock.

Annalee stepped back.

Because she wasn't just looking at Lilian Gray, private secretary. She was standing in a locked bathroom with a killer. So she asked Lilian her first question.

"How'd you know where to deliver the letter?"

"That's the only thing you want to know?" Lilian rolled her eyes.

"You threatened *my friends*."

"They were easy to find. The papers always named them. Mentioned where they all lived." Lilian cocked her head. "Uri delivered the letter for me."

"Did he know what it said?"

"He couldn't care less. He just wanted to get paid. So I bought his fake French perfume, or whatever it is—made him feel like a real smuggler." Lilian rolled her eyes again. "What a desperate family."

"But not so desperate you wouldn't kill for one of them."

"It was Jeffrey's own fault."

Annalee didn't reply, letting Lilian hear in her own words what she'd just said. She'd just confessed to murder.

Lilian sighed.

Annalee sighed longer.

She despaired that Lilian was the killer because, first, she was an ill-treated woman. But more, if Annalee were honest, she hated confirming guilt in anyone. *"For all have sinned."* And yet? *"Thou shalt not kill."*

Lilian had murdered Jeffrey Mann—Buddy's only brother—in cold blood. Now Lilian was looking down at the typewriter, probably thinking about wielding it again. And wouldn't clever Annalee make a lovely victim?

Annalee allowed herself a thought, indeed, about her fearless Sherlock—and the problem of evil. Mercy, the world was full of it. But in the dark of night, said the irrepressible Holmes, evil's powers—exalted as they may be—can be brought down. Holmes even quoted the Bible. *"Sufficient for tomorrow is the evil thereof."* Yet as he told his faithful Watson, *"I hope before the day is past to have the upper hand."*

Annalee hoped for the same. She stepped eye to eye with Lilian. "I don't know what you're thinking, but you're not going to kill me. Not tonight. Especially not in a blasted bathroom."

"I have nothing to lose now. Not a single thing."

"Well, *I* do. I have my whole life ahead of me—just like Jeffrey did. Maybe he wasn't living right, but he didn't deserve to die with his head bashed in by a used typewriter. It's not even yours."

"So what do you intend to do?"

"That's *your* question." Annalee kicked at a towel lying crumpled between them on the bathroom floor. "You hold the cards, but you always did. You could've walked out on Simon years ago—or stayed but let him fight the Klan alone, on his terms. But now here you are, soon to be facing a murder charge. So what are you going to do?"

"I'm not hanging from a prison gallows." Lilian pushed tendrils of hair away from her neck.

"Maybe you should've thought about that when you cracked that Olivetti typewriter on poor Jeffrey's head. Now unlock that door and get out of the way."

"But *Simon* did this." Lilian turned to the door, banged a fist on it.

"Because things were done *to* Simon." Annalee grabbed for Lilian's shoulders, turned her to face her. "Don't you see? Nobody gets through this life unscathed. Good word, right? Scathing gets to everybody sooner or later. Simon got it, too. From his family, from the Klan—"

"But why did he end up using me? And hurting me?"

"I don't know. Lies started it. But telling the truth can finally end it. You can redeem a family, save your soul—not to mention this whole contentious 'Rocky Mountain' whatever we call it state—by finally telling the blasted truth."

"I don't even know what it is."

"You were wronged, Lilian. But doing more wrong didn't fix it. Are you willing to say *that*?"

"I'm not sure I can."

"I'll help you." Annalee moved her aside, unlocked the bathroom door. "Against my better judgment, I will help you—and I can't believe I'm still saying that. But first, I need to find a telephone."

Annalee moved into the bedroom—just as Buddy came through the door. "I've been looking for you—"

"Buddy, I need a phone—" She started to explain, and he looked ready to hear, but the look on his face turned to horror.

"Annalee!"

"What?"

His face spoke his answer. *Watch your back.*

Buddy leaped at her, dragging her down to the floor, rolling them both away from Lilian, who was throwing the Olivetti, aiming to hit Annalee square in the head.

Lilian missed. So Lilian Gray screamed. She screamed bloody murder at Buddy—and also at Annalee. Or maybe she was screaming at all the infernal and evil scathing that humanity wields on one another, because too much of it had come, as well, to scathe her.

Again, she wouldn't escape it.

Agent Ames had just walked through the door.

He nodded at Annalee, pointed at Lilian Gray, her screams now sorrowful moans.

"Is this your killer?"

"What took you so long?" Annalee crawled up to her knees—a perfect position, she suddenly thought, to pray the good, long prayer she should've prayed from the second this case started. Instead, she stood tall, letting Buddy help her, by holding both her hands, because that's what she also needed to do in this household and in the world—take a stand.

"The killer." She pointed Ames to Lilian.

"You know this guy?" Buddy gestured toward Ames. "Are you the cops?"

Buddy's question made Ames stifle a laugh. "Not always," he said. "Just when it counts."

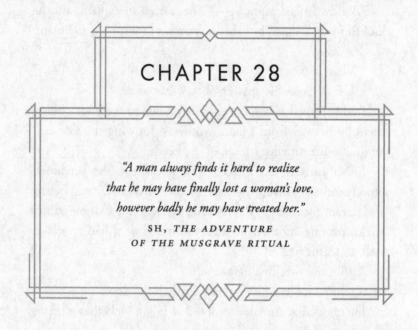

CHAPTER 28

"A man always finds it hard to realize
that he may have finally lost a woman's love,
however badly he may have treated her."

SH, *THE ADVENTURE*
OF THE MUSGRAVE RITUAL

DOWN IN THE KITCHEN AT THE TABLE, Ames explained to her privately what, indeed, had taken him so long.

"I kept waiting for your phone call. When it didn't come, I hit the road and came on up. Beat the goons. They were chomping at the bit."

"Ready to bring me down."

"Not just for murder. Something about you and some pilot? Young white guy?"

Annalee buried her face in her hands. "You don't want to know."

"But you better tell me. Look at me. If you're planning on breaking the law, I can't help you."

"It's nothing like that." She turned to Ames. "I don't even

know how to explain it." Annalee studied his eyes. "His name is Buddy. He's Jeffrey's twin. A pilot. And we survived a crash landing together. He saw it as our 'destiny'—being together. That we'll go live in the mountains, defy the law, and nobody will bother us." She tried to laugh. "Crazy thing is, part of that plan sounds great. Hiding away from the troubles of life. Because I actually like this Buddy, Agent Ames. There's something in his heart that is good. And something in my heart that responds to it. But it doesn't matter unless we were meant for each other—which we're not." She gave a weak grin. "At least I think that's right."

"Well, that's a problem I didn't see coming. Not with this case. But that's what I get for hiring young agents."

"I'm not your agent!"

Ames waved an envelope at her. "So I can keep your pay?"

"I have nary a pocketbook to put it in."

"With this, you can buy yourself one."

"Maybe a new dress, too."

"That reminds me. What about your pastor friend? Where does he stand now?"

"*Jack.* I don't know where he is. But he's everything to me—and also to his church and to so many people all over crazy Denver. But he's disappeared!"

Buddy walked into the kitchen then. "Annalee, I know where he is—"

Annalee stood.

"Uri just told me. Jack's in Telluride—locked up in Uri's broken-down cabin, the place on his property there."

"What are you saying?"

"Lilian paid Uri to get rid of him—to distract you, keep

351

you worried about Jack, so you'd drop the murder case. But Uri's not a killer, so he paid some pilot crony to take down Jack—fly him to Telluride and stash him in Uri's cabin outside of town."

"A kidnapping?" Ames stood.

"How could Uri do such a thing?" Annalee showed her anger.

"Uri doesn't think, just like I told you," Buddy tried to explain. "He just took the money. But he'd never kill anybody, let alone Jack. He doesn't even know him. If anything, he probably helped save his life."

Annalee's heart skipped. "Buddy, I have to go get Jack now!"

"I understand."

"But you don't!"

"You're right, I don't. I wish I did." Buddy stepped back. "But I'm going to take you to him."

They'd leave first thing in the morning, Buddy told her. "I'll fly the biplane. The big one." He didn't explain why, but Annalee understood. If Jack was injured, there would be room in a big plane to fly him out. Annalee hated to think of it.

So she thanked Buddy for making such a stand-up offer.

"I can pay you." To be fair to Buddy. "Or Jack's church can pay you."

"You didn't say that, and I didn't hear it."

They were sitting on a sofa pushed near the fireplace in Simon's great room, talking about the case. She'd asked Buddy to join her. He sat down on one end. She sat on the other.

"I'm just trying to make everything right." Annalee pulled up a blanket. "I stirred up quite a hornet's nest this time."

"You didn't stir anything; you solved it all—your way. All except, that is, with Flora . . . well, with Belinda."

"Did Della tell you?"

"She didn't have to. With some things, I guess you just know. Or you want to believe that you know. Talking to Mrs. Quinlan was so easy, watching her gestures, looking in her eyes—"

"Same color. Not a coincidence?"

"I wasn't sure. But being with her and looking at her, it was like looking at myself in the mirror. All I kept wondering was, is she family? As in *Mother*?"

"But you didn't tell her?"

"I couldn't. I don't know for sure. Besides, she looks so happy . . . with that Hugh fella. I think they'll end up married. He already gave her jewelry."

"Jewelry's not much. Well, not compared to a family. If she is Belinda, think how much happier she'd be to find you."

"But it would be spoiled when she realizes Jeffrey was her other son—and he's dead." Buddy set his shoulders. "One day I'll ask. Maybe sooner than later. But for now, I'm letting it be." He searched her face. "You'll let me keep my secret?"

"It's yours to keep. But don't wait too long. Promise me?"

Buddy tugged on her blanket. "Promise me? Annalee Spain, that's supposed to be my line."

She laughed. Then they went into the kitchen and cleaned up leftover dishes.

Ames's people had taken Lilian away, driving her down to Denver. Ames had evidence now. She was going to jail. Then Ames himself had piled Rebecca, Uri, and Della into his own car—ready to hear more information about the case while driving them all back down the mountain to town.

"I'm grateful for you." Rebecca had reached for Annalee. "The lies can finally end."

"Your dad will need help."

"I will, too."

"Make sure you help each other. You'll have many things to sort through. Your uncle's will. His bank. His trust business." She pursed her lips. "Other family matters."

"Like what?" Rebecca asked.

"Ask Mr. Hugh Smith to go over everything with you. Just take it one thing at a time."

"It sounds so hard."

"It will be. You'll have some hard things to forgive."

"I don't know how to do that—forgive."

"I don't know how either, but it's time I started working on it, too. If I figure it out, I'll let you know."

Rebecca agreed, telling Annalee, "Thank you. You helped me. Maybe for a long time."

The hug they gave each other was hopeful and right, with Annalee saying she had the jasper necklace that had belonged to Rebecca's mother. "I'll make sure you get it."

The Klan crowd, meantime—some parked all afternoon in the snow outside Simon's house—finally turned their cars around and, thankfully, left. Annalee stood at a window and watched them leave. "'The Lord is my shepherd,'" she whispered, as their headlights faded. *Now, woeful people, don't come back.*

Hugh Smith and Flora Quinlan departed, too. But first, the librarian pulled Annalee aside to whisper in her ear. Annalee held her breath. Had she figured it out on her own? Perceived what Buddy now guessed, too?

But Flora Quinlan spoke of another thing. "This nice young man—this Buddy—he's quite taken with you." Mrs. Quinlan kept her voice low. "And I approve."

Annalee put up a hand—but held her tongue.

"I know, Annalee. The laws and rules." Mrs. Quinlan hugged her close. "Maybe one day things will change."

Annalee leaned close. She had so many things to ask of Mrs. Quinlan. First, *was* she Belinda? If so, how'd she end up in Telluride—then in Denver, a young "widow"? But most of all, did she know Annalee's mother? Let her cry a young mother's tears on her shoulder?

But to ask would be to rip the veil off long-buried lies that Flora Quinlan had constructed, apparently, around her past— but also the pasts of others.

Biting her lip, Annalee kept her questions to herself, asking God to show her the right time.

In the empty house, Annalee and Buddy straightened up the rooms, chatting, reflecting, Buddy flirting, Annalee push- ing him away. Two young people without traditional families "playing house" a little bit? Was that what she and Buddy were doing? An unsettling thought. So she pushed it deep into the back of her mind, telling herself to think instead about Jack— and the promise of finally seeing him on the morrow. *So keep me for Jack tonight, Lord,* she silently prayed.

Police would be back sometime soon for more evidence, so she and Buddy didn't throw out trash or wipe away fingerprints. Just cleaned up dishware, swept a couple of floors.

Walking from room to room, their walls covered with

Simon's fake but beautiful art, Annalee felt sad for his family—and for Simon and his sad end. He'd given life the best that he knew how. But in the end, life had written his final chapter, and it wasn't one he would've chosen.

Annalee started turning out lights. Buddy helped her. They stood in the dark in the front hallway.

"I'll stay here with you tonight." Buddy looked out a window, then turned, took a slow step toward her. "You shouldn't be here alone."

"That might not be such a good idea. The two of us."

"I'll sleep downstairs—in the back of the house."

"Promise?"

"I promise." He gave her a look. "But do us a favor."

"What?"

"Lock your door."

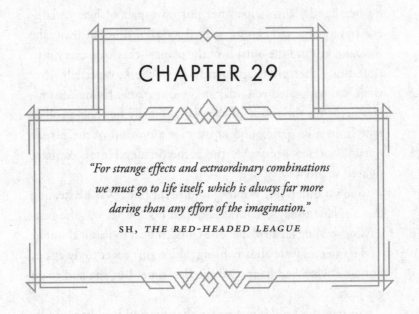

CHAPTER 29

*"For strange effects and extraordinary combinations
we must go to life itself, which is always far more
daring than any effort of the imagination."*

SH, *THE RED-HEADED LEAGUE*

THEY LEFT AT DAYBREAK FOR THE AIRFIELD. Buddy called a friend, who drove them to the hangar, the young man glancing once at Annalee, but he didn't seem put out by her sitting in the back seat of his car. Buddy gave him a ten-dollar bill, thanked him, and his friend waved and drove off, and that was that. She and Buddy had bigger things to do and worry about.

It was freezing cold, but the sun was hot and bright, the sky clear and blue. Not much wind. No gusts.

"Good flying weather." Buddy winked at her.

"You sure?"

"I wouldn't take you up if it wasn't."

He settled her in the seat to the right of the cockpit, covered her in blankets, placed a helmet on her head, thick mittens on her hands, and helped her put on a pair of heavy, darkened eye goggles. Then he walked a dozen times at least, she thought, around the outside of the plane—checking every possible thing that pilots apparently must check, especially after what had happened yesterday to Simon's plane. He made similar checks on the inside of the plane. Finally he took a roll of tape from a knapsack and taped over a portion of the plane's outside surface—probably the name Stanley Hotel. Annalee figured so anyway.

She sat quiet, not wanting to distract him. Was he stealing this airplane today? Mercy, she hoped not. What was the penalty for stealing an airplane? She couldn't bear to think about it.

Her nerves were already firing. She wasn't eager to fly again, not after what had happened the first time. But she had to go get Jack.

So that this could be over. So that she and Buddy could be done with whatever situation they'd found themselves in.

Annalee had telephoned Jack's landlady, Mrs. Mason, late last night to tell her all about it.

Mrs. Mason listened, silent for once. Annalee thought the phone line had gone dead.

"You're not saying anything, Mrs. Mason."

The landlady finally spoke. "Maybe you like danger."

"I'm just trying to help the world—by solving crime and helping people. I don't make the rules—or the laws."

"I'm not talking about crime and laws and whatnot. I'm talking about keeping two men dangling on a string—*one of them white.*"

"Well, it's complicated, Mrs. Mason."

"Life always is."

"That's why I'm going to get Jack and put an end to all that." Annalee's voice caught. "I'm trying to do the right thing. That's why I called you. To finally listen to you. Haven't you ever had a situation where you've been pulled in two directions? Caught between two opposite attractions?"

Mrs. Mason's silence lasted forever. Finally she answered, "Yes."

"Well, *what did you do*?"

"I made a choice. I chose Mason, who I married—thirty-two years ago *next week*. And I never looked back."

"But did you love him? I hate to ask you that, Mrs. Mason, but would you tell me the truth? When you married Mr. Mason, did you love him? Love only him?"

"If you were anybody else, I'd bang this phone down and never speak to you again. But you don't have a mother to talk to, and I hear your confusion. So I'm going to tell you something that I've never told another living soul—"

"Thank you, Mrs. Mason."

"Because life isn't wrapped up nice and neat like a pin."

"I suppose that's why we need God?" Jack could answer that, she thought, swallowing. But what did Mrs. Mason think?

"We need him to keep us from falling off the straight and narrow. Then we don't fall into a pit of miry clay."

"Is that what God did for you?"

"He did that, but I had to climb out of that pit first." She let a minute pass. "I was pregnant, Annalee, when I married Mason—and he knew it. Lennie wasn't his son, and Mason always knew that, too. I was young and starry-eyed, and I got myself in a fix. But I had to make a choice. Not for love but for right. Do you hear me!"

"I'm listening."

"Mason would make a better husband for me—and a better father for my son. So it stopped being about love and roses and taking foolish, selfish risks. Then when I made that choice, something good started to happen."

"You learned to love Mr. Mason."

"Say that again."

"You learned to love Mr. Mason—"

"And I still do."

Annalee gripped the phone receiver. She knew what Mrs. Mason was telling her, even if she didn't quite know what to do with all the information.

"Good night, Mrs. Mason," Annalee whispered into the phone.

"Good night, honey." Mrs. Mason sighed. "Now don't call me again at midnight!"

"I'll try, Mrs. Mason." Annalee hung up the phone. "Believe me, I'll try."

Buddy's takeoff was smooth and steady. Annalee's stomach was in her throat. But she couldn't fret about that now. She was thinking about Jack, praying he wasn't hurt, sick, or worse. Locked up in Uri's broken-down cabin since Saturday? He'd be half-frozen or half-starved or both. And it was all her fault. All because of her case.

"Doing okay?"

Buddy touched her arm. She was cold as ice, but she gave

him a thumbs-up, thought about not touching him back. Then sighing, she did.

He was pointing out the window at mountain ranges, each one newly blanketed and glistening with spring snow. They'd fly through the valleys, he told her. Not over peaks.

"Safer that way."

She wasn't sure what she'd expected airplane travel to be. It had seemed to her, at first, to be frivolous and impractical. But it had turned out to be not daredevil nonsense but breathtaking and amazing and now, for Jack, maybe lifesaving.

Buddy sure adored flying, and she hoped, more than anything, he'd find in flying a way to make an honest living. Maybe work for that new US Air Mail outfit—delivering packages and mail, legally, across the country. With a regular pilot's job like that, he could say goodbye to smuggling and live a right life. She glanced at him. And then he could fall in love with the right girl?

Please, God. That was her prayer for Buddy.

But what about her? And what about Jack? She was counting the minutes.

The flight was long and cold—with stops at places where Buddy could refuel or at least they could warm up a bit. But the first place, a rancher's field in a mountain valley, yielded them only two cups of chuckwagon coffee—and the wary glances of two nearly silent cowboys.

Same with the next stop. A dour-faced woman in a one-room farmhouse allowed Annalee to use an outhouse, despite her husband objecting. Seeing a "white" man with a "colored gal," the man scowled, disapproving. So they hauled back into the plane and took off.

"Just one more stop." Buddy showed Annalee a flight map. "Then we'll head into Montrose, rent a rig, and head up to Uri's place."

That one last stop sounded like blessed relief to Annalee. But as they landed in a field just outside a tiny mountain hamlet, they saw what neither wanted or needed.

"Trouble ahead." Buddy nodded toward a sheriff's car parked by a lean-to, with two sour-faced men—one boxy and short, the other skinny and tall—standing next to it.

"Don't get us arrested," Annalee pleaded. *Not today, please.*

"Stay here." Buddy gave her a thumbs-up. She gave him a hopeful look.

He climbed from the plane, but the two men were already walking over.

"What's your business?" The shorter man gestured at the plane.

Buddy explained. "Fuel. Some coffee. Then I'm on my way."

"Can't serve you here." The shorter man spat from a plug of tobacco. "Not with that gal."

Buddy stepped back, narrowed his eyes. "I just need a refuel. Can't make it to Montrose without it."

"Not my problem."

"But you're making it a problem."

Annalee grimaced. *Please, Buddy.* She wished he'd turn around, look in her eyes, see she'd rather walk herself to Montrose than get in a tussle with two contentious deputies in the middle of Colorado nowhere.

Indeed, some fights aren't worth it. Jack himself would say that to him. Uri might even say that. Simon Wallace, if he could wake from the dead, surely would tell Buddy the same—to let it go. She and Buddy would just have to fly to Montrose—on a wing and a prayer and whatever fumes were still in the fuel tank.

"We'd better go!" she whispered to Buddy from his open plane door.

The afternoon sun was fading. Buddy had a change of heart, maybe hearing the need for it in her voice.

So they flew to Montrose—the plane barely making it, almost stalling once. But Buddy managed to land his stolen-for-the-day machine. Then they rented a rig—pulled by a stoic big mule—and headed up toward Telluride to Uri's cabin. The nearest place? The ghost town Annalee.

No, Annalee Spain wasn't ready for it.

Covered under a quilted tarp with Buddy, she snuggled against him for warmth, watching his vapor breath mingling in the thin air with hers. Annalee had never seen, even in Colorado, snow so pristine, pine trees so sturdy and tall, nor heard such winter silence. The snow was deep, but the mule knew the trail and didn't stop.

"Yeah, fella." Buddy kept coaxing it. "Walk it, fella."

From time to time, Buddy would check on her, turning to glance at her, the look on his face leaving her confused—or breaking her heart.

I was born in these hills. She tried not to think about it because that also meant it was where she was tossed away and abandoned. She'd wanted more than anything to return here, hoping to find answers to her beginnings.

But now that she was climbing this trail—with a man who didn't want her to leave him—she saw her beginnings were far less important than where she was going and who was going with her.

He told her as much when they got to the cabin.

Tying up the mule on a post, he came around to help her down from the rig. She turned toward him but didn't get down, just sat there, letting him face her, wondering what he would say. He pulled her close, searched her eyes.

Finally he spoke, looking more determined than she'd ever seen anyone look. "Will you listen to me?"

She nodded. "I'm listening—"

"I'm crazy for you."

She gave him her smile, dimple probably showing, not understanding really but also not arguing. What would even be the point? So she took off her gloves, warmed her hands, breathing on them, and placed them on his face.

"There'll be somebody else one day. Maybe soon. She'll come along and you'll—"

"Forget you?" He shook his head. "That will never happen. But to make sure, will you help me to remember?"

She knew what he meant.

He wanted to kiss her. And he wanted for her to kiss him back.

Yet as plumb crazy as that would be—with Jack so close she could whisper his name and he probably would hear her— Annalee almost wanted it, too. She wasn't even sure why. But she knew if she said yes, she'd lose something with Jack so precious that it could never be recovered.

"Please help me down," she whispered instead to Buddy.

He nodded, understanding.

It was time for them to rescue Jack.

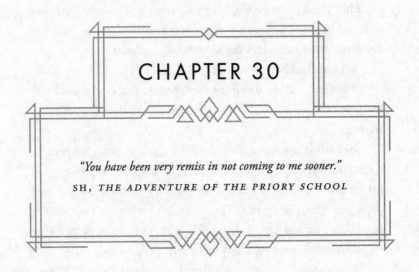

CHAPTER 30

"You have been very remiss in not coming to me sooner."

SH, *THE ADVENTURE OF THE PRIORY SCHOOL*

URI'S CABIN WAS DARK except for a smoky fire burning in a corner stove. Jack lay near it on a kind of pallet, his eyes half-closed, in a way that he'd never want to be seen, in his own filth.

Annalee gasped. *"Lord, have mercy."*

She ran to him, pushing past the kind of junk she'd expect to find in a cabin that belonged to Uri. The place was a pigpen.

"Jack!"

He opened his eyes, tried to look at her. He didn't speak.

"Jack!"

"Annalee?" His voice was a rasp.

She reached for him, saw and smelled that he'd also vomited, looked for something to clean off the mess. Jack moaned.

"Buddy! Help!"

They tried to move him. But as Annalee could see, Jack was chained by one ankle to a thick metal hook bolted to the floor. Both his arms were handcuffed behind his back.

"Mercy, Buddy, can you help—?"

"I got it." Buddy slung off a knapsack, grabbed a penknife from inside a pocket. "Open the door, Annalee. Let in some fresh air."

She pulled open the door, found a chair to prop it open. At a rusted tin sink, she looked for a rag or soap or *something* good for cleaning. But all she could find was a wretched filthy towel, dank and gray with grime. Tears sprang to her eyes. *God, forgive me.* If she ever saw Uri again, she'd give him enough piece of her mind to curl his bitter, confused heart.

"Look in my knapsack." Buddy pointed to it. "There's towels, soap. My canteen."

Every item was ice-cold. Annalee reached across Jack, set the canteen atop the stove, praying the frozen water would soon start to melt.

"Annalee, don't stay in here, not with me like this." Jack searched her face.

"This is my fault." She was crying now. "You told me to drop this case. Too dangerous. *I didn't listen.*"

"Did you solve it?"

"She did." Buddy looked over at Annalee, then knelt at Jack's ankles, maneuvered the chain lock. It sprang, letting Buddy release Jack's chained leg, remove his sock, and check for any injury to his skin. An ulcer near the ankle had started to form. They'd probably arrived just in time to stop it.

"Uri will have to answer for this," Buddy mumbled.

He scooted behind Jack, worked the lock on the handcuffs

with his knife. It sprang, too, letting Jack sit up enough to lean against an old, soiled trunk. Jack rubbed his wrists, shoulders, held his arm against his nose.

"Man, I can't keep on these clothes." Jack kept apologizing.

Buddy touched his shoulder. "We'll get you right." He pointed to his sack. "There's fresh clothes in there, Annalee."

She yanked open the knapsack, pulled out dry, clean clothes—long johns, a pair of jeans, sweaters, clean socks, underclothes, woolen hat and gloves. Underneath the pile, she found a pair of cowboy boots. Then wrapped in clean towels was a razor blade, facecloths, a new toothbrush and paste, a men's manicure kit, even a couple of soap bars from the Stanley Hotel. They were scented like pine. Buddy had thought of everything.

She looked over at him, telling him with her eyes *thank you*. Buddy held her gaze, nodding.

Jack watched their exchange, sat quiet for a moment, finally looked again at Annalee, his eyes urging her to look at him.

"I'm sorry—for what I did." His raspy voice was a whisper.

Annalee searched Jack's face, wanting just to hold him, assure him like crazy, but she couldn't yet. "It's . . . Don't talk now." She reached for Buddy's canteen. "Here—drink some water."

She pulled the canteen off the stove, heard ice still clanging around inside. But enough ice had melted to make pourable water.

Unscrewing the top, she held the canteen to Jack's lips while he drank every possible drop. Then she shook out a shard of melting ice, wrapped a corner of a clean towel around it.

"This will be cold."

"Doesn't matter."

With her hand, she held Jack's face to clean it. He sighed at her touch, turned his face into her palm, nestled it there. Tears formed in both his eyes. She wiped them away. Then she cleared four days of, well, everything that had collected on his face. She couldn't talk to him openly, not with Buddy here. *But we will soon enough,* she told herself.

For now, Buddy asked her to please check on the mule while he helped Jack get cleaned up.

"It's stupid cold out there," Jack protested. "Just turn your eyes."

She moved to the stove, opened the little door, stooped down, and watched the smoky blaze, keeping her eyes on the sight of the flames.

She could hear Buddy help Jack stand. Buddy cut away every inch of Jack's clothes, rolled them in a pile, along with his shoes, and took them outside to burn.

Jack was silent. Annalee, too. She wanted to turn and tell him if they got through this, nothing again ever in life would stand between them. Jack might've been thinking the same.

"Who's your friend?" Jack finally said.

"He's . . . not somebody for you to worry about today."

"Well, should I worry about him any other day?"

She took a moment, not sure how to answer.

"Nothing like that." Annalee sighed. "Jack, no. That's not true." She swallowed. Enough of lies. She'd lied to herself about Buddy, maybe more than she'd lied about anybody or anything. She'd just tell Jack the truth.

"He's somebody who almost made me forget about everything. Even about us. Right up to the moment I walked through the door of this cabin."

"Annalee, he's white."

She stayed silent. Finally she spoke.

"I know how it looks. We can talk about it all later—"

"Later's too late. Hear me right now—"

"But you're standing behind me, half-frozen and—"

"Without a lick of clothes—or a decent excuse. Best time for me to confess. I was wrong." He paused. She held her breath. "Worse, I lied to you."

She listened, watched the earnest fire in the stove, gazed at the smoke and flames, let herself feel the inadequate heat. Finally she spoke. "I know."

Because I lied to myself, too.

Jack let out a sigh, shifted his weight. "It's so easy, lying. Maybe that's why God hates it. I tried to tell myself I didn't care anymore about Katherine. I didn't think I did. Then out of the blue, here comes her twin, Dora—pretty as a picture, looking just like her sister. It was like seeing somebody risen from the dead—from the worst of that blasted war, as if we'd been given a second chance together—" Jack's voice broke.

Annalee didn't move. She could've said something, but she knew she shouldn't, so she stayed silent, asking God with all she knew how to, *please*, keep her mouth shut—for once—so she could just listen.

Jack went on. "There she was, standing up smiling in the Masons' parlor. Katherine again. Resurrected. Then I open my mouth, and what comes out? I start lying—to you." He looked pained. "When you walked away, and I saw what I was doing, I wanted to kick myself and die—"

His voice broke again.

"And I almost did—right here in this blasted cabin. They gave me rotten food, offal and garbage. Annalee, chained me up. Food made me sick as a dog. I *should* be dead." He tried to laugh. "And the crazy thing? I wasn't even taken with Dora, not really. She was nice enough, I guess, just like her sister. But neither one of them is you. I guess that'll always be true. Some women are nice, some good, some even great-looking."

"Others a bit dangerous." Annalee said that thinking maybe of Buddy.

"But after five minutes with somebody else," Jack went on, "all I wanted was to be with you. I lusted with my eyes, and it almost killed me."

Annalee let herself half smile. "That'll make an interesting sermon."

Jack tried to laugh but let out a long sigh instead. "I want to hold you so bad I could cry."

Buddy walked back inside.

"Let me help clean you up first, man."

Annalee helped Buddy heat enough water in a couple of pails on the corner stove for a sponge bath for Jack—who waited, wrapped in a tarp and seated on Uri's old, broken-up trunk.

Annalee answered his questions about her case, including who Uri was and why Uri had his crony abduct him at the train station and what happened to his car.

"Mr. Mason's watching it now?" Jack seemed grateful. "Good man."

Then after a long sigh, Jack asked about his church, wondering what they must be thinking. Annalee said she didn't know, but she felt sure they'd be crazy excited when he returned.

"Not half as much as me."

Then Annalee unwrapped the fancy Stanley Hotel soap, handed Jack a facecloth and towel, turned away again while he dropped the tarp and scrubbed himself, surely head to toe.

"You were in the 369th?" Buddy asked. "I see your tattoo."

Annalee sat quiet. *Jack has a tattoo.* She wondered where but tried not to think about that.

"Yep, out of Harlem."

"The Hellfighters—"

"Yep." Jack kept scrubbing. "Did you serve?"

"Air Service. First Reserve Wing."

"Really? You're a pilot?"

Annalee listened to this, these two men talking—well, exchanging information, out of courtesy, it seemed, since both were here in this cabin only because of her.

She bit her lip, staying silent, not daring to act conversational, especially since she didn't know how she felt about them meeting each other, especially like this. *Mercy, this is complicated, Lord.* She kept her eyes trained on the smoky fire.

Jack kept scrubbing, done with talking, too. Same with Buddy, also now quiet. Then after a sighing rinse, Jack repeated his cleansing—started with a fresh towel and cloth, new soap bar, and scrubbed himself head to toe again, then unsnapped the manicure kit and took a good long time apparently on his fingernails and hands, grumbling.

"Never used this kind of thing, but I'm glad it's here."

He scrubbed all over one last time, rinsing with intent—the cabin finally filling with the fresh, piney scent of the Stanley Hotel's blessed soap. Then with newly cleaned hands, Jack brushed his teeth with the new toothbrush and paste.

"Ready to shave?" Buddy offered him the razor.

"I'll wait, thanks, until I get back home to Denver. I want to look myself in the eye in the mirror while I do it."

"So you'll remember?" Buddy glanced toward Annalee, let his gaze rest there.

Jack watched Buddy's eyes find Annalee, then turned to her himself.

"So I won't forget."

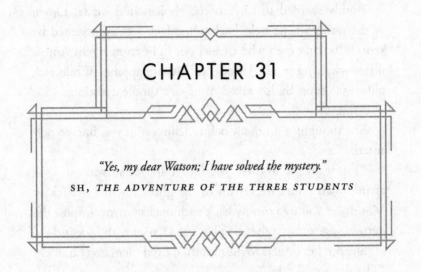

CHAPTER 31

"Yes, my dear Watson; I have solved the mystery."

SH, *THE ADVENTURE OF THE THREE STUDENTS*

THE RIDE BACK DOWN THE MOUNTAIN was dark, cold, and frankly dangerous. The mule was sure-footed enough; despite slipping several times, it never dumped them out over the trail's edge.

Buddy drove the rig. Annalee sat on the narrow wooden bench under blankets and the worn but clean quilted tarp, nestled between him and Jack, feeling their warmth on either side—Buddy smelling like winter snow, Jack smelling sweet as a pine forest.

She took in a long breath.

Maybe I don't deserve either one of these two men. That's how she talked to God. *So thank you for helping me hear my heart and not look back.* Just like Mrs. Mason told her was right.

Buddy seemed to discern the choice she'd made. Down at the trailhead, he held back while Jack was approached by serious-looking men who turned out to be from Agent Ames's office—waiting to ask Jack about his kidnapping. While Jack talked to them, Buddy asked Annalee a simple question.

"You okay?"

She thought a moment before telling him yes, but he persisted.

"You want me to drive you into Telluride so you can look at the town yourself? Or up to the ghost town? Or back to Montrose? You two can fly back with me tomorrow or take the narrow-gage tonight, heading back to Denver with Jack and—"

She put her fingers to his mouth, moved them away quickly. "Thank you, Buddy."

"I hardly did anything—"

"Hardly? The airplane, clothes, mule, rig—"

"I always carry extra clothes in my sack." He reached for something. "Here, look what else I found." He pushed back a pile of blankets to pull out a surprise. Her little secondhand pocketbook.

"My purse?"

"I found it in the hangar this morning."

"From Agent Ames? I bet he found it at the airfield in Denver." She gave him a grin. "This may sound silly, but I missed my faithful little purse."

He laughed, searching her eyes. "I'm going to miss you more than I can stand."

"Until another detective falls into your plane."

"I actually wouldn't mind that. Now here's your purse. There's money in it. And a fancy handkerchief with your initial *A*."

Thank you, Officer Luther.

"In fact, you're loaded," Buddy added.

She laughed. He laughed with her. She was glad for that—and for him. She wanted Buddy to know that.

"I know you won't take it—the money. But if you ever need anything from me—"

"From you? There's only one thing I need from you."

She understood but stepped back. "That will change." *If you let it.* Her smile found his eyes. "But if you need anything ever from Jack—or from me—would you call?"

"Next time I have a case?"

She gave him a look. "Stop teasing. You're not joining the detective game."

"Probably not. But I am thinking of opening a flight school. Classes for everybody. Men, women, kids, white, and, well—"

"Everybody?"

He nodded.

"You'll be a pioneer."

He touched her face. "I already am."

The narrow-gage train that Annalee and Jack took from Montrose to Pueblo, on the way to Denver, stopped in a town called Salida. It meant *exit* in Spanish, a man waiting for the train told them. "When you leave here, you're either going someplace new or leaving something behind."

"We're doing both," Jack told him.

"Godspeed to you then." The man climbed onto his train car.

The depot restaurant had souvenirs and whatnots, so Annalee bought a box of marbles, made from a nearby quarry, to give to Eddie. Then for Mrs. Mason, she bought a matchbox shaped like a butterfly.

She bought a key chain sporting a "gold" nugget for Mr. Cunningham. Then she decided to buy another one just like it for Mr. Mason. She believed he would enjoy it.

She saw "genuine Indian" beaded earrings in a glass case and purchased three pair—red for Mrs. Cunningham, green for Mrs. Stallworth, and blue for herself.

Finally for Jack, she bought a cowboy hat—just to tease, because he never wore that style. But he pulled it low on his head, set the rodeo brim at an angle, and wore it the rest of the trip home.

They weren't allowed to sit in the depot restaurant. The manager apologized.

"Doesn't matter to me one way or another, but it's the times." He handed a menu to Jack. "If you want, I can fix you some sandwiches and things, put some paper napkins in there for you."

Jack didn't argue. It was late. They ate their food on a bench in the snow.

On the train to Denver, Annalee unwrapped her new earrings, admiring them with a shy smile—because they were the first pretty baubles she'd ever purchased for herself, even if she wasn't quite sure she deserved the gift. But she prayed that she did.

With trembling hands, she put them on her earlobes, hoping they looked pretty, perhaps, to Jack—dabbing on a dash of fresh lipstick, from her purse, just to make sure. Then as the train started, while she let herself reflect on being with just him again, she finally fell asleep, lulled by the sway of the car.

When Annalee awoke, Jack was sitting across from her, gazing at her from under the brim of his cowboy hat, his dark eyes searching her face.

"What is it?"

"I don't have a right to ask this, but if it's okay, I'd like to marry you tonight. Soon as we get back to town. I'll call a friend, a preacher."

She returned his gaze for a long time, then finally shook her head. Her earrings jangled softly. "Let's not do that."

"Why not?"

"I've got so much to figure out first."

"About your friend?" He gave her a look.

"No, Jack. About me. What kind of person am I becoming? I've got to figure that out—before my next case."

"You don't trust yourself?"

"Not always."

"What if you had my help?" His dark eyes sparkled.

"What are you saying?"

"Detective work is dangerous. I know that firsthand now—and I learned a few things in the war that you could use. For your sleuthing. If you'll let me help you." He reached for both her hands. She didn't pull away.

"But it's a crazy game—solving crime. Being a detective."

"So let me help you." He hiked a brow. "Then marry me tonight."

"Mrs. Mason wouldn't hear of it. She wants a church."

He squinted. "Mean ol' Mrs. Mason? She's your friend now?"

"A good friend, actually. So I know she wants a church." She gave him a smile. "Same with Mrs. Stallworth." Annalee counted off her friends. "And Mrs. Cunningham. Good grief, Mr. Cunningham. Mr. Mason, too. And Eddie, of course."

"You have too many mothers-in-waiting—and fathers- and sons-in-waiting, too—or whatever the heck they're called."

She laughed softly, moved from her seat to share his. She laid her head on his shoulder. "But the best thing would be finding my mother—or my 'real' father. If they'd come."

"I'll help you find them." He hugged her. "If they don't find you first."

She leaned closer, breathed deep. "If I marry you, Jack—"

"I have to convince you again, don't I?"

"After I convince myself—that I know what I'm doing. And why." She sat up, searched his eyes. "Then when that happens, Jack, I'll marry you." She cocked her head. "Well, at a church." She flicked an earring. "With music and a choir. Flower girls and a summer rose. Maybe even two."

"Oh, and a long white dress?"

"I've become rather partial to blue." She flicked her other earring. "Just as long as it matches this." She opened her purse. Her lacy white handkerchief, the embroidered *A* still a glory, peeked out—spotless again and looking, somehow, better than new.

His eyes grew wide. "I thought my special gift for you was lost." He pulled her close again.

"Maybe we both were lost," she told him. "But we're together again."

"Daring to fight crime!"

"You're really willing to do that? With me?"

"Willing? I thought you'd never ask."

She tugged down his brim, leaned in with a sudden kiss, lingering there.

His sigh sounded breathless. "Looks like you saved that for your new detective."

"That would be you, Dr. Watson."

"This ol' world will never be the same."

She opened her mouth for a slow grin, then moved a curl off her neck, giving him a wink, scooting closer to whisper in his ear.

"Then we'd better get started."

A NOTE FROM
THE AUTHOR

THANK YOU SO MUCH FOR READING the sequel to Annalee Spain's first mystery, *All That Is Secret*. This second story, *Double the Lies*, developed after I read several biographies of famed barnstormer Bessie Coleman, the first female pilot of Black and Native American descent to be licensed to fly. Turned down by every flight school she approached in the US, Coleman took her dream of learning to fly to France, where she earned an international aviation pilot's license in June 1921 from the Fédération Aéronautique Internationale.

A subplot to her inspiring story was her effort to start a flight school in the US, open to all, by earning steady income as a pilot—the same challenge for most American barnstormer pilots, many of whom struggled to find work in aviation after serving with the US Air Service during World War I.

A tempting option was flying smuggled goods and people in and out of the US to earn illegal but bountiful pay. (Coleman was offered a smuggling job once but said she turned it down.) At the Stanley Hotel in Estes Park, pilots found work flying tourists around to experience flight, but the pay was minimal and wasn't steady. The US Air Mail had started in 1918, but it took almost a decade, and dozens of crashes and sixteen fatalities, before the service carried mail coast to coast, becoming a viable employer.

In *Double the Lies*, I'd planned for Bessie Coleman to make an appearance. But when my fictional pilot Buddy Mann emerged and, to my surprise, showed romantic interest in Annalee, I followed that thread, learning more about America's contentious anti-miscegenation laws that defined interracial marriage as a criminal offense.

During the time of *Double the Lies*, all but seven of the then forty-eight states in the US had passed such laws, with thirty of the states—including Colorado—enforcing them. In 1957, however, Colorado's legislature repealed its law as unconstitutional. Ten years later in 1967, the US Supreme Court, in the famed *Loving v. Virginia* decision, overturned unanimously any anti-miscegenation statutes still in effect, at that point, in sixteen states.

As for interracial adoption, formal legislation to protect that right in the US wasn't passed until 1994 with the Multiethnic Placement Act, which aimed to reduce pervasive discrimination against cross-racial adoptions.

Amid such racial and cultural turmoil, my characters in the Annalee Spain Mysteries seek to live out their lives with hope and dignity. Thus, Pastor Jack Blake visited, in this story, the real town of Dearfield—a farming settlement founded in Weld County, Colorado, by Black businessman Oliver Toussaint Jackson for African Americans looking for opportunities denied them elsewhere. A bustling community of some two hundred at its height, Dearfield surpassed all expectations until hit hard by the Depression and Dust Bowl. Now a ghost town, it was listed in 1995 on the National Register of Historic Places.

Dearfield's promise, however, is reflected in the dreams of my young detective Annalee Spain, who found herself aloft in a Ford Tri-Motor airplane—which, as students of vintage aviation will know, didn't arrive until 1925, a year after my story. I pushed that boundary by saying the pilot Buddy Mann was testing a prototype. (Yes, that's literary license.)

A true historical backstory to this mystery, however, was the Spanish expulsion of the Jews in 1492. One of the cruelest inquisitions in recorded history, the mandate of King Ferdinand and Queen Isabella followed Spain's defeat of its longtime conquerors, the Muslim Moors, by expelling from Spanish lands all Sephardic Jews who didn't convert to Christianity. (*Sepharad* is the Hebrew word for the Spanish Iberian Peninsula.)

Impacting anywhere from 100,000 to 800,000 Jews, who had developed one of Europe's most thriving and advanced Jewish communities, the edict gave Jews three months to leave Spain. Forced to sell their houses, vineyards, fields, and cattle for a pittance, they also had to surrender all silver and gold for cloth or skins. Many fled to Portugal but, after six months, faced expulsion and horrific atrocities there as well.

(In 2015, Spain sought to atone for the expulsion by offering citizenship to Sephardic Jews whose families were expelled, an effort met thus far with mixed results.)

I referenced the event in *Double the Lies* as context for what Jews in Colorado experienced when they found themselves targeted by the state's Ku Klux Klan. By the time of this story, in 1924, some one million Jews had immigrated to the US.

Hoping to find a warm welcome, they instead encountered rampant bigotry, including by the Klan.

In Estes Park, Colorado, for example, more than two thousand hooded Klansmen gathered in June 1922 for the initiation of three hundred recruits in a ceremony rife with anti-Jewish, anti-Black, and anti-Catholic rhetoric.

Keeping a close eye on all this activity was the US Bureau of Investigation, precursor to the Federal Bureau of Investigation, renamed as such in 1935. My fictional agent, Robert Ames, "hired" Annalee to help unravel the murder in *Double the Lies*. The FBI's first African American agent, however, was a World War I veteran and explosives expert, James Wormley Jones, hired in November 1919 to work undercover as a special agent under future FBI director J. Edgar Hoover. The bureau's first female agent was Alaska Packard Davidson, hired in October 1922. The first Black female agent was Sylvia Mathis, who received her special agent badge in June 1976 after passing the agency's grueling four-month training program.

America's dynamic social landscape informs my character Annalee's life, dreams, friendships, and even her romantic love. What's next for Denver's newest young detective? Her next mystery, coming soon, will dish up more intriguing adventures and answers.

ACKNOWLEDGMENTS

WRITING HISTORICAL MYSTERY FICTION invites inspiration and help from many corners. I'm grateful first for historical fiction authors who've personally inspired me to work in this remarkable genre, including Sujata Massey, Rhys Bowen, Stephanie Landsem, Jennifer L. Wright, Vaseem Khan, Lynn Austin, Jocelyn Green, Rachel McMillan, and Anna Lee Huber, among many others.

I'm indebted, indeed, to historians and journalists whose insight and research helped inform *Double the Lies*, including researcher Roger Douglas Connor and his eye-opening monograph for the Smithsonian Institution's National Air and Space Museum titled "Boardwalk Empire of the Air: Aerial Bootlegging in Prohibition Era America" and John Dunning's fictionalized account of the Ku Klux Klan in Colorado titled *Denver*.

I'm also grateful for historic newspaper editions of the *Estes Park Trail Talk*, the *Colorado Statesman*, the *Denver Express*, the *Denver Jewish News*, *Intermountain Jewish News*, and the *Rocky*

Mountain American made available through the remarkable Colorado Historic Newspapers Collection.

Deepest thanks also to the outstanding Denver Public Library's extraordinary archive of oral histories, maps, municipal records, and other exceptional and related material available through its truly priceless DPL Digital Collections.

My ongoing thanks to my incomparable team of supporters, advocates, and friends at Tyndale House Publishers, including my one-of-a-kind and invaluable editors Stephanie Broene and Sarah Rische, our amazing publisher Karen Watson, and my remarkably accomplished team of support experts, including Isabella Graunke (publicity), Lindsey Bergsma (designer), Andrea Martin and Wendie Connors (author representatives), Elizabeth Jackson and Laurel Bacote (social media), and Kristi Gravemann (marketing).

My warmest thanks as well to my upstanding and hard-working agent Greg Johnson and my wonderful agent friend Rachelle Gardner.

I'm also grateful for authors, writers, and friends who are supporting and promoting my historical mystery series and my fiction journey, especially Donnell Bell, Denise Materre, Kaitlyn Bouchillon, Amy Boucher Pye, Brian Allain, Judith Briles, Kate Rademacher, Michelle Ule, Sharon Elliott, Ruth and Steve Shepard, Marsha and Collis Johnson, Dr. Brenda Salter McNeil, Larry Sears, Lesa Shackelford Engelthaler, Jennifer Grant, Becky Keife, Carla Foote, Matt and Teresa Weesner, Chris Jager, Damyanti Biswas, Elisa Morgan, Robin W. Pearson, Laura Padgett, Delia C. Pitts, Susie Finkbeiner, Natasha Sistrunk Robinson, Dr. Saundra Dalton-Smith, Toni Shiloh, Janet Singleton, Lisa Kewish, Dr. Jeanne Porter King,

Lamar Keener, Patricia Sargeant, Bethany Turner, Jaime Jo Wright, Don Pape, Cynthia Herron, Robert Justice, Judith Briles; all my new Fiction Readers Summit pals; my pastor Dr. Timothy Tyler; his wife, Dr. Dwinita Mosby Tyler; every beloved member of Shorter Community AME Church; and every single member of the launch teams for the Annalee Spain series.

My grateful thanks also to podcasters and book clubs—and their amazing hosts—including Ryan Warner; Don Payne; Nichelle Downing; Patricia O'Neal; Kathi Lipp; Georgia Tatum; Angie Baughman; Sandra Shreve; Dorina Lazo Gilmore-Young; Carrie Schmidt; Carolyn Arends; Emily Braucher; Courtney Russell Jr., MD; Sheila Arrington; Chautona Havig; KyLee Woodley; Darcy Fornier; Mary Jo Starmer; Christine Tan; Donna Fahrenkrug; Nancy Cummins Bierman; Mary Carver; Amy Julia Becker; Scott Lundeen; Jan Jorgensen; Peggy Ritchey; Maura Schneider; Karen Gonzalez; Kathy Campeau; Sarah Hilkemann; Sandy Graham; Colorado Press Women; and every amazing member of INK: A Creative Collective, Sisters in Crime, Sisters in Crime–Colorado, Mystery Writers of America, Rocky Mountain Mystery Writers of America, Crime Writers of Color, Rocky Mountain Fiction Writers, and Colorado Authors League.

Then there's NBA all-star Stephen Curry. My special thanks to this remarkable leader—on and off the court—for selecting *All That Is Secret* as his March 2022 pick for his Literati Book Club. Special thanks, indeed, to amazing Erika Hardison for introducing me and my mystery series to Stephen Curry and to the Curry teams at SC30 Inc. and Literati.

Speaking of books, I'm sincerely humbled to thank the

library staffs across the Front Range in Colorado for embracing my mystery series with full-out enthusiasm. (My huge thanks also to library staffs nationwide.) My special thanks, as well, to Colorado's Front Range booksellers for their amazing advocacy and support, especially from the phenomenal managers and staffs at metro Denver's Barnes & Noble locations—yes, my grateful thanks to you, amazing managers Janice, Randall, Lauren, Liz, Milinda, and more—and at the Tattered Cover bookstores (thank you, Kwami and Alan); Books Are Awesome; West Side Books; Sudden Fiction Books in Castle Rock; Barnes & Noble in Pueblo, Loveland, Colorado Springs, Fort Collins, Boulder, and more; and the many other amazing and impassioned booksellers, especially in the Parable, IndieBound, and other independent networks across Colorado and beyond. (Yes, Baker Book House, Books-A-Million, Christianbook, Lifeway, Cokesbury, and more, that includes you!)

Finally, to my family, my greatest cheerleaders, I owe particular thanks for your early support of *Double the Lies*—especially for the early reading of my story by my always-supportive husband, Dan Raybon, and my wonderful sister, Dr. Lauretta Lyle. Wonderful thanks, indeed, to everyone in my family, from the youngest to the oldest, for your incomparable support, help, and especially your belief in me by every amazing one of you, including my phenomenal daughters, son-in-law, grandchildren, sister-in-law, brothers-in-law, nephews, nieces, cousins, and every loving kin-circle friend.

For each of you, and for the joy Annalee's story is giving me, I thank my God.

DISCUSSION QUESTIONS

1. Annalee is establishing herself as a detective but still struggles at times to know what to do next or to feel confident in her skills. Describe a time when you've felt in over your head, unsure of your next move or of your abilities. What did you do? What was the outcome?

2. When she stops in a neighborhood church to pray, Annalee wonders, "Why did the church, on an ordinary weekday, feel not fancy but like a good ol' home?" What images does the word *church* bring up for you? What feelings?

3. Annalee thinks several times about the meaning of hospitality, especially when confronted with difficult people like Mrs. Mason. What does she conclude about the nature of hospitality? How would you define what it means to extend hospitality to others?

4. Mrs. Quinlan cautions Annalee about making assumptions based on what library visitors read. How does that end up relating to her case? Is Mrs. Quinlan

right to protect the privacy and confidentiality of her patrons? Later in the story, Annalee concludes that information she has been told about Buddy Mann isn't hers to reveal—even to him. Do you agree, or do you think Annalee should tell him what she learned?

5. Jack tells his congregation, "We're wounded. So some of us might make mistakes in life. Especially when it comes to looking for love." How does this message come to apply to Jack himself? To Annalee? What do they each learn about themselves and their relationship as a result?

6. Speaking to an audience at the First Denver National Bank, Annalee advises, "If you keep talking to the right people and asking the right questions and knocking on the right doors, one will open. Then you'll see the light—which is what we're all looking for in life, right? . . . So don't stop looking. Like a detective, if you want truth in your life, never stop searching for it. Truth *wants* to be found." Do you agree with her perspective on finding the truth? How could this advice be applied in your own life? Where do you turn to find truth?

7. As Annalee tries to solve Jeffrey Mann's murder, she uncovers a tangle of secrets and lies in the Wallace family, some of them going back generations. How do these pieces of the past contribute to Jeffrey's death?

Are there past incidents or patterns in your own family that are still showing consequences even today?

8. One of Annalee's gifts is an ability to look deeply at people and understand the things that have made them who they are. Where in the story do you see her extending this insight and compassion to others? How does it help her solve her case?

9. When Annalee is surprised by Della's suggestion about another character's racial identity, Della challenges her with the question "What, you need proof?" What conclusion does Annalee reach? Why do you think many in our world today still look for labels or categories when it comes to race?

10. Along with everything else she is juggling, Annalee has not given up on the search for her birth mother. Does she come any closer to finding her in this story? Where do you think her search will go from here?

ABOUT THE AUTHOR

PATRICIA RAYBON is an award-winning author and essayist who writes at the daring intersection of faith and race. Her published books include *My First White Friend*, a Christopher Award–winning memoir about racial forgiveness, and *I Told the Mountain to Move*, a prayer memoir that was a *Christianity Today* Book of the Year finalist. Patricia's other books include *The One Year God's Great Blessings Devotional* and *Undivided: A Muslim Daughter, Her Christian Mother, Their Path to Peace*, coauthored with her younger daughter, Alana Raybon.

Patricia's essays on faith, race, and grace have been published in the *New York Times Sunday Magazine*, *Newsweek*, *USA Today*, *USA Weekend*, *Country Living*, *Chicago Tribune*, *Denver Post*, *Guideposts*, *Our Daily Bread*, *In Touch* magazine (In Touch Ministries), *Christianity Today*, *HomeLife* magazine; posted on popular blogs including the *Washington Post's Acts of Faith* and DaySpring's *(in)courage*; and aired on National Public Radio.

A journalist by training, Patricia earned a BA in journalism from the Ohio State University, an MA in journalism from the

University of Colorado Boulder, and formerly was editor of the *Denver Post*'s Sunday Contemporary Magazine and a feature writer at the *Rocky Mountain News*, Colorado's oldest newspaper, which published for 150 years. Midcareer, she joined the journalism faculty at the University of Colorado Boulder, teaching print journalism for fifteen years. She now writes fulltime on matters of faith, also teaching at writing conferences and workshops nationwide.

Patricia lives with her husband, Dan, a retired educator, in her beloved home state of Colorado, where they enjoy movies, popcorn, soapy costume dramas, and Masterpiece mysteries.

They have two amazing daughters, an attentive and smart son-in-law, five glorious grandchildren, and a grand dog Max. *Double the Lies* follows her debut novel, *All That Is Secret.* Visit her online at patriciaraybon.com.

Connect with Patricia online at
PATRICIARAYBON.COM

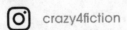
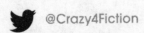

By purchasing this book from Tyndale, you have
helped us meet the spiritual and physical needs of
people all around the world.

Tyndale | Trusted. For Life.